Praise for Anne Shade

Masquerade

"The atmosphere is brilliant. The way Anne Shade describes the places, the clothes, the vocabulary and turns of phrases she uses carried me easily to Harlem in the 1920s...*Masquerade* is an unexpectedly wild ride, in turns thrilling and chilling. There's nothing more exciting than a woman's quest for freedom and self-discovery."—*Jude in the Stars*

"Heartbreakingly beautiful. This story made me happy and at the same time broke my heart! It was filled with passion and drama that made for an exciting story, packed with emotions that take the reader on quite the ride. It was everything I had expected and so much more. The story was dramatic, and I just couldn't put it down. I had no idea how the story was going to go, and at times I was worried it would all end in a dramatic gangster ending, but that just added to the thrill."—*LezBiReviewed*

Femme Tales

"Shade twines together three sensual novellas, each based on a classic fairy tale and centering black lesbian love...The fairy tale connections put a fun, creative spin on these quick outings. Readers looking for sweet and spicy lesbian romance will be pleased."—*Publishers Weekly*

"If you're a sucker for fairy tales, this trio of racy lesbian retellings is for you. Bringing a modern sensibility to classics like 'Beauty and the Beast,' 'Sleeping Beauty,' and 'Cinderella,' Shade puts a sapphic spin on them that manages to feel realistic."—*Rachel Kramer Bussel, BuzzFeed: 20 Super Sexy Novels Full of Taboo, Kink, Toys, and More*

"All three novellas are quick and easy reads with lovely characters, beautiful settings, and some very steamy romances. They are the perfect stories if you want to sit and escape from the real world for a while and enjoy a bit of fairy tale magic with your romance. I thoroughly enjoyed all three stories."—*Rainbow Reflections*

"I sped through this queer book because the stories were so juicy and sweet, with contemporary storylines that place these characters in Chicago. Each story is packed with tension and smouldering desire with adorably sweet endings. If you're looking for some
with B/F dynamic, then these stories
the bedtime stories you loved as a k
about women of colour."—*Minka Guic*

By the Author

Femme Tales

Masquerade

In Our Words:
Queer Stories from Black, Indigenous and People of Color

Stories Selected by Anne Shade
Edited by Victoria Villaseñor

Love and Lotus Blossoms

by

Anne Shade

2021

LOVE AND LOTUS BLOSSOMS

ISBN 13: 978-1-63555-985-9

This Trade Paperback Original Is Published By
Bold Strokes Books, Inc.
P.O. Box 249
Valley Falls, NY 12185

First Edition: September 2021

THIS IS A WORK OF FICTION. NAMES, CHARACTERS, PLACES, AND INCIDENTS ARE THE PRODUCT OF THE AUTHOR'S IMAGINATION OR ARE USED FICTITIOUSLY. ANY RESEMBLANCE TO ACTUAL PERSONS, LIVING OR DEAD, BUSINESS ESTABLISHMENTS, EVENTS, OR LOCALES IS ENTIRELY COINCIDENTAL.

Credits
Editor: Cindy Cresap
Production Design: Stacia Seaman
Cover Design by Tammy Seidick

This book is dedicated to all the women who have struggled, or are currently struggling, with self-love and self-acceptance in a society that tells you focusing on your own happiness is selfish. As long as you draw breath, it's never too late to discover who you truly are and live the life you deserve.

I am fully aware that I am not the image you see in the fashion
    magazines,
Or America's version of a svelte beauty,
But I know that I am strong in mind, body and spirit.

I no longer need
Validation,
Attention,
Approval,
And love
To define who I am.

I accept that I am
Perfect,
Strong,
Beautiful,
And loving
In my own way.

I accept that I am…
And always will be…
ME.

—Anne Shade

Chapter One

1980

This was not how I imagined starting my summer break, sitting miserably in the third-row seat of our family's station wagon traveling thousands of miles from everything I knew and loved. Okay, maybe not thousands but still. My five-year-old little brother, Jacob Jr., J.J. for short, or "the Accident" as my sister and I liked to refer to him, had turned the entire second-row seat into his personal war zone with his G.I. Joes battling his Justice League Heroes for the right to be his favorite action figures of the week. My sister, Jackie, was moping in the front seat next to Mom with her face buried in a book, as she had deemed us unworthy of speaking to since the last rest stop where we embarrassed her by singing along to the Jacksons' "ABC" playing throughout the building.

We were on our way to Montclair, New Jersey, where we were moving to be closer to Mom's family who lived throughout New Jersey and New York. Jackie wasn't too thrilled until she found out we would only be a thirty-minute train ride from New York City and her dream of becoming a Broadway star. My brother was clueless and only saw it as a new adventure. I, on the other hand, hated having to move away from all my friends and having to start high school in a new city with a bunch of strangers. I begged my parents to let me stay in Indianapolis with my father. My mother wasn't happy about the idea of leaving me behind, but she said if Dad was all right with it then she was. Turned out Dad's twenty-something-year-old girlfriend wasn't too keen on having to compete full-time for his affection. Dealing with us visiting every other weekend was one thing, every day was another story. Turned out her tantrum was more effective than my rationale on why I should stay. So here I was, away from everything I'd ever known in my entire fourteen years on this earth. Okay, maybe that was a bit dramatic, but not having a choice in the matter still sucked.

"Hey, gang, we're just one exit away from our new life!" Mom said.

"Yaaaay!" J.J. cheered. He popped up next to me and tapped my shoulder. "Aren't you excited, Ness?"

I tore my gaze from the fascinating view of other speeding cars, looked past my brother's grinning face, and met my mother's eyes pleading with me through the rearview mirror. I looked back at J.J., gave him my best big sister smile, and lied straight to his sweet, innocent face.

"Yes, I am, buddy." I planted a wet, sloppy kiss on his cheek just the way he liked it but pretended was gross.

"Yucky, Ness!" He wiped his cheek in mock disgust, then grabbed Batman to look out the window.

Exit 148
Bloomfield
Montclair
1 mile

One mile for me to just accept my situation and make the best of it. Look at it the way Mom had been trying to tell me to do, as if it was a new adventure in our life's journey. Looking at my brother and sister reminded me that their lives were also changing. Jackie had also left friends behind, including her boyfriend, Gabriel. With her eighteenth birthday just a month away, I asked why she didn't stay in Indy and go to school like he had asked her to do. She said that Mom needed her. Thinking back on how Mom reacted when Dad asked her for a divorce, Jackie was probably right.

Mom called it an episode. The doctors called it a nervous breakdown. Mom had to go away for a month, and Dad had no idea how to run the household since he traveled so much for work. Schedules and routines flew right out the window until Jackie had stepped up and, with Mom's military precision, whipped things right back into shape. When Mom came home, Dad still left, and Jackie once again stepped up and helped get her back to somewhat normal. Mom found a part-time job as a real estate agent, her career before us kids came along, and went to therapy regularly. She wasn't her old self, but she also wasn't the mess she had been when she went away. Jackie became the glue that kept our family together. Personally, that seemed like a lot for a seventeen-year-old to take on. I sure couldn't do it.

Then there was our little brother, the Accident. We started calling him that because he was the result of our parents trying to make up after an argument when things started falling apart between them. Jackie said Mom got pregnant to try to keep Dad, which obviously didn't work seeing as where we were now. Dad adored J.J. and the feeling was mutual so I knew J.J. would miss not having him around. Jackie told me J.J. was the only reason Dad was against us moving, but, like us, he knew that Mom wouldn't be able to stay in Indianapolis with only his family for support. To keep herself from falling apart again she needed to be surrounded by her own people. Our last weekend with Dad was tough for us all, but when he held J.J. for the last time, it was the first time I'd ever seen him cry.

I looked at Mom. She seemed genuinely happy for the first time in a long time. If this move kept her from going to the dark place, then I could force myself to shut up and accept it, whether I liked it or not. Besides, we would be going to visit Dad at the end of the summer. I could see all my friends then.

"We're here!" Mom said.

Jackie decided this was worthy of looking up from her book as we pulled up to a three-story multifamily house.

"This is it?" she said, not hiding her frown of disappointment.

Mom's happy expression fell a bit. "I know it's not what you guys are used to, but it's just until we can get back on our feet once the house in Indiana is sold."

Jackie looked as if she wished she could take back what she said. "I know, Mom. I'm sorry. It looks nice. Really."

"I think it's kinda cute," I said.

The house was surrounded by a wrought iron fence and waist-high hedges and was painted a soft yellow with dark green trim and shutters on the windows. There was a wraparound porch with a few lounge chairs, and a large tree stood in the neatly trimmed front yard with a scattering of rock sculpture bunnies in a flower bed around the base.

Mom gave me a relieved smile. "Your uncle should be here with the moving truck any minute now. Why don't we go in so you guys can look around before we get busy unloading?"

We all climbed out of the car, and I took J.J.'s hand as we followed Mom up the walkway. She had flown here a week ago to sign the lease and pick up the keys, so she was able to let us into the first-floor apartment. As soon as the door was opened, J.J. let go of my hand and took off to explore his new surroundings. There was a large main room with a fireplace that was so neat and clean that it looked as if it hadn't been used for an actual fire in years. Windows were on either side of the fireplace facing out to a backyard that had a garage and more concrete for parking than grass. A big bay window looked out onto the front of the house, and there was an open archway that led to the kitchen. Next to the kitchen was a bedroom and bathroom, and on the other side of the room were two more bedrooms. I walked over to the bathroom, stood in the doorway, and sighed. It wasn't large but it was clean.

"There's only three bedrooms," Jackie whispered as she came up beside me.

"Guess we're back to sharing a room."

It must not have been the answer she wanted to hear because she sucked her teeth and walked away. The sleeping arrangements wouldn't bother me too much, but Jackie had gotten used to having her own space for the last ten years. After Dad got promoted to vice president at the travel public relations agency he worked at, he bought us a house up in the hoity-toity Geist area of Indianapolis and we all got our own rooms. It didn't take long for the excitement of having my own space to wear off. I missed sharing a room with her and our late-night talks. Mom told us during the drive here that until the house in Indianapolis was sold, we had to make some adjustments. Going from a big house that gave us each our own space, more bathrooms than we needed, a pool, and private fenced-in yard to an apartment where we had to share a bedroom and one bathroom was going to be quite an adjustment, especially for Jackie, who had worn our financial status like a security blanket.

I never cared about the fancy clothes or the need to impress the kids of the Geist. My wardrobe consisted of blue jeans, T-shirts, and Converse tennis shoes, which were my obsession. My collection of Converse had taken up an entire wall in my room. I had packed and brought all of them without realizing there might not be enough space for them here. I turned away from the bathroom, walked over to Mom as she stared out the front window, slipped an arm around her waist, and laid my head on her shoulder. She was about five ten, and at fourteen, my height of five eight made me almost as tall as she was.

"I know this is a big change for you guys, but I think it's a change for the better." She sounded so hopeful that it felt wrong for me to even consider this change as something negative.

"A new adventure," I said.

"Exactly. I'm sure you're probably not too thrilled having to share a room with your sister again, but this was the best place your uncle and I could find that's centrally located. You guys can walk to the library and the movie theater, the high school is also a good walking distance, and there's a washer and dryer in the basement. I'm going to give you and Jackie the master bedroom since it's bigger. I don't need that much room."

"Mom, you don't have to sell me on this. I know you're doing the best that you can."

"Thanks, Ness. I really needed to hear that."

A U-Haul truck rumbled up the street and stopped in front of the house.

Mom sighed. "Your uncle is here! Let's get to work!"

J.J. came bouncing happily out of the bedroom he had staked his claim on. "Ness, I have a secret hiding place in my room!"

"That's pretty cool, buddy. Let's go help Mom and Uncle Frank." He took my hand as he bounced down each step from the porch, then took off to throw himself into Uncle Frank's arms.

Jackie stepped up beside me. Her eyes looked red and puffy, as if she'd been crying. I grasped her hand as we walked toward the truck, and she gave it a brief squeeze before releasing it and walking ahead of me. Movement to my left caught my attention, and I turned to find an extremely cute boy sitting on the porch of the house next door watching all the activity. He looked to be about my age, with a golden tanned complexion, and hair styled in a short, curly afro. He wore a blue-and-white striped T-shirt, blue jeans, and a pair of white Vans slip-on tennis shoes. As if he sensed I was watching him, he turned and looked at me with a smile that made my stomach flip. He gave me a wave, and I smiled and waved back.

"Ness!" Mom called. "Stop dawdling and come grab some of this stuff."

"Yes, ma'am," I said, hurrying toward the truck.

I grabbed a box and turned back around, but the boy was gone.

By the time the sun set, with the help of Uncle Frank and several of his friends, we managed to get the kitchen boxes unpacked and our beds set up. We were all relieved that we wouldn't have to spend the night in the sleeping bags Mom bought before we left Indianapolis in case we arrived too late to unpack or Uncle Frank was delayed. After a dinner of takeout pizza, J.J. had already gone to bed, Jackie was in our room moping, and Mom sat in the kitchen with Uncle Frank talking. I could hear the rumble of his deep voice through the open window as I sat in one of the chairs on the porch.

Frank was my mother's older brother. He had his own real estate agency in town and lived just a couple of blocks from us. It was good to see Mom happy again, but I still had doubts about starting high school in a new city. Never really a part of any of the cliques at school back in Indiana, I wasn't sure where I'd fit in. I'd had my small group of friends and that was enough for me. My eyes began to feel heavy and I must have drifted to sleep. A screen door slamming jolted me awake.

"Hey," a voice said.

"Jeez!" Surprise almost had me jumping from my seat. I looked in the direction the voice came from and saw the cute boy from earlier standing in the neighboring yard smiling at me.

"Sorry, I didn't mean to scare you. I just wanted to welcome you to the neighborhood." He held a tin over the waist-high hedge separating the yards.

Trying to calm my racing heart, I walked down to him and accepted the tin.

"They're homemade cookies," he said.

"Thank you."

"I'm Nikki Carter. Spelled like Nikki Giovanni." He gave me a shy grin.

"Thank you, Nikki. I'm Janesse Phillips, but my family and friends call me Ness." I held my free hand out to him.

His hand was soft and warm when he took mine.

"I like Janesse much better than Ness."

My face heated with a blush. "My sister, Jackie, was four years old when I was born and couldn't say my name, so she just called me Ness and it stuck. I don't even think my brother knows my full name."

"Jackie and Janesse. Does your brother's name start with a J also?"

"Yes, Jacob, after my father. We call him J.J. for short. My mother's name is Janet. They thought it would be cute to have a family full of Js." It still surprised me that my parents used to be that sickly sweet in love once.

Nikki looked amused. "Well, it's unique."

"Yeah, I guess."

"At least you don't share a name with one of the most talented

Black female writers of our time. My mothers didn't give me a tough image to live up to at all," he said with sarcastic humor.

I looked at him in confusion. "Your mothers, as in more than one?"

Nikki looked down as he began picking at a leaf on the hedge between us. "Uh, yeah, I have two moms as parents. I usually don't tell people that right away."

Not wanting him to feel embarrassed to have told me something so personal, I shrugged. "Hey, that sounds pretty cool. I have a cousin who's gay, and her and her life partner are thinking of adopting."

Nikki's shoulders relaxed and he gave me a broad smile.

"I was a donor baby, but it's cool because the donor was one of their college friends, so I know who my dad is."

"Wow, so you have three parents?"

"Well, four if you count his wife. They're actually my godparents," Nikki said proudly.

"Wow." This was a lot for my tired brain to take in. Nikki must have picked up on it because he gave me an embarrassed grin.

"Sorry. It's late, you're obviously tired from your busy day and I'm talking your ear off. I'll let you go. Good night." He turned away.

I didn't want him to leave, but I was too tired to focus on a full conversation. "Nikki, wait."

He turned back toward me.

"If you're not busy tomorrow, maybe you can show me around."

"Yeah, I can do that. Come by when you're ready."

"Okay. Thanks again for the cookies."

"You're welcome." Nikki gave a wave as he jogged up his front stairs.

After I watched him disappear into his house, my body finally decided it had had enough for the day. I barely said good night to Mom and Uncle Frank before I entered my bedroom to find Jackie was already asleep with a wadded-up tissue in her hand and dried mucus crusted under her nose. Just for a moment I considered grabbing my camera. It would be the perfect blackmail picture, but then I thought better of it. Jackie was hurting and it wouldn't be right to remind her of that.

Yawning again, I sat on the bed and realized the tin of cookies was still in my hands. Going back to the kitchen wasn't an option so I set it on top of the box with my Converse. Too tired to search for my pajamas, I stripped down to my undies and climbed under the covers.

The last thought on my mind before drifting off to sleep was how soft Nikki's hands were when he passed me the tin of cookies.

The smell of coffee and bacon and my brother singing the Sesame Street song at the top of his lungs were my alarm clock. I sat up with a groan, feeling like every muscle in my body had been through the wringer. Lifting boxes and arranging furniture yesterday was probably the most exercise I had done in months. Jackie's bed was already empty. The added scent of pancakes gave me the energy to get up and grab my suitcase to find something to wear. When I left my room to go take a shower, stepping through the door was like entering another world. The TV, stereo system, and most of the living room furniture was all set up. There were barely any boxes left to unpack.

"G'morning, Ness!" J.J. bounded from the sofa and threw himself at me, wrapping his little arms around my hips.

"G'morning, buddy." I bent over and gave him a kiss atop his head. Satisfied, he ran back to his spot on the sofa to finish watching Grover telling him the word of the day. Accident or not, I absolutely adored the kid.

With my clothes bundled in my arms, I went to the kitchen instead of the bathroom. Jackie and Uncle Frank sat at the kitchen table eating while Mom stood at the stove flipping pancakes.

"Good morning, sleepyhead," Mom said.

"G'morning. When did you have time to do all that?" I pointed toward the living room.

Mom shrugged. "I wasn't tired, and since your uncle was already here, we just finished setting up the living room. I wanted you guys to wake up with the place feeling as much like a home as possible."

"Did you sleep?"

"Yes, a few hours. I'll take a nap later when J.J. takes his. Go get dressed so you can eat breakfast before it gets cold."

I sent a questioning gaze Jackie's way. She surprised me with a smile and mouthed "She's fine." The last time Mom couldn't sleep was when she ended up in the hospital. If Jackie said she was fine then I had to trust that she was, so I turned and continued my original path to the bathroom. After a much-needed shower and clothes that didn't smell like I had run a marathon in them, I went back to the kitchen.

She gave my head a pat as I walked by. "You're going to need your braids redone soon."

I made a face at her back. I hated getting my hair braided. For the first few days it felt like somebody was pulling my scalp off my head until the cornrows loosened up. Unfortunately, I inherited Dad's thick and curly family hair, so it took Mom forever to braid it. I didn't look forward to sitting on the floor on a pillow for hours with her yanking and pulling on my head, but she always did such cool designs that sometimes it was worth it.

"What do you girls have planned today?" Uncle Frank asked.

Mom answered for us. "Before they think about doing anything or going anywhere, they need to finish unpacking their room. I don't want full boxes still in your room at the end of summer."

"Yes, ma'am," Jackie and I responded in unison.

Uncle Frank grinned. "Okay, what do you have planned after my slave-driver sister sets you free?"

Mom swatted him with a dish towel, and he winked at me.

"I have to call Gabriel," Jackie answered.

"Jackie, you are not going to spend this whole beautiful day holed up in your room on the phone with that boy," Mom said.

"Oh my God! Can I just live my life!" Jackie stood and put her dishes in the sink before leaving the kitchen in a huff.

Uncle Frank and I smirked at each other.

"What about you, Ness?" he asked.

Mom picked up her cup of coffee and sat in Jackie's vacated seat.

I took a few bites of bacon before answering. "I met the boy next door, Nikki. He's going to show me around."

"Which house?" Uncle Frank asked.

"The one to the left of us. The all white one."

He and Mom exchanged a curious look.

"Ness, Nikki is a girl," she said.

Both she and Uncle Frank watched me intently as I absorbed this not so surprising information. I had thought about that last night before I went to sleep. It made sense as I remembered the smoothness of her hands and the way her voice sounded just a little too soft for a boy. The brief look I got when I first saw her, exhaustion from the day, and it being too dark for me to really get a good look at her last night, had me assuming that Nikki had been a boy. My stomach still did that little flip, despite now knowing she was a girl. As much as I would like to believe the feeling had to do with her looking so much like a boy, it wasn't new for me to have a crush on a girl, but they were feelings I hadn't told anyone about.

I shrugged. "Oh, okay. I just assumed she was a boy. No big deal."

I could still feel their eyes on me, but I continued eating my breakfast, ignoring them.

"Okay then," Uncle Frank said as he stood and put his dishes in the sink. "I better get home and clean up before I head into the office." He gave Mom a kiss on the cheek and lowered his hand toward me. "Gimme some skin."

I gave his palm a slap and he turned his hand over for another. "Catch ya on the flip side, Ness."

"See ya later, Uncle Frank." I scraped the last of the syrup up on my plate with the last bite of pancakes.

"All done?" Mom asked.

"Yes, ma'am."

Mom stood and picked up my dishes. "You go finish unpacking so you can meet your new friend."

"Thank you, Mom."

I went to my bedroom to find Jackie standing in the middle of the room frowning.

"I don't know where you plan on putting all those stinky tennis shoes, but there's no room in the closet for them and both our clothes." She sounded irritated.

Besides being offended because I barely wore a pair of my Converse long enough for them to get stinky, I was tired of being the punching bag for her emotions lately. It took everything in me to keep myself from throwing one of my shoes at her.

"Look, I don't like this setup any more than you do, but we need to make the best of it for Mom. Besides, nobody told you to come with us. You could have stayed to be near your flaky boyfriend and gone to school in Indy."

Jackie snorted. "What, and leave you to pick up the pieces if Mom falls apart again? I think not."

That was it. We hadn't gotten into a physical fight since we were little, but she was trying my patience. I turned and practically shoved my shoe in her face. "You know what, Jackie? You aren't the only one this has been hard on. At least you got to go through high school with your friends. I not only have to start at a whole new school but try to make all new friends at the worst possible time in a kid's life. Teenagers aren't the nicest people to the new kid. And look at poor J.J. We've had Dad around for our whole lives. He's gotta grow up with a father he only sees during summer breaks and holidays. And lastly, it couldn't have been easy for Mom to make the decision to take us from everything we know and love to start over, which, by the way is what she also has to do." I blew out an angry breath and continued. "Mom hasn't had to work since you were in grade school, and now she's had to start a career in her forties, be a single parent to three kids, and keep a roof over our heads. So, get your head out of your own ass and stop being so damn selfish." I turned my back on her and slammed the shoe back into the box.

At the sound of sniffling, I turned to find Jackie sitting on her bed crying. Aw hell, I broke my sister. I went over and sat beside her on the bed and put my arm around her shoulder.

"I'm sorry, Jackie," I said to comfort her, even though I really wasn't sorry.

Jackie pulled her shirtsleeve over her hand and used it to wipe away her tears. "No, you're right. I've been selfish. I was just so mad at Dad for what he did, and then he couldn't even step up and be a father when we needed him to be after Mom went away. All I could think about was what would happen if Mom couldn't come home. If she never got better and they kept her locked away in some loony bin for the rest of her life. What would happen to us then?" Jackie's voice broke and she took a deep breath. "Nana Lois sure wouldn't take us in. God forbid her grandchildren would have the nerve to sit on her expensive furniture. With the way Dad's travel schedule was, we probably would've ended up out here anyway with Uncle Frank. As much as I love him and the rest of Mom's family, Indy was our home, and I wanted to do whatever needed to be done to make sure we stayed there. I also wanted to make sure that when Mom did come home, she wouldn't have to worry about anything."

I gave Jackie's shoulder a squeeze. "You did a great job. I don't think anybody could've taken better care of us than you did, but Mom did come home, and she's been fine. Moving here is probably the best thing for her, so we have to suck it up and deal with it for her sake."

Jackie chuckled. "Suck it up and deal with it, huh? You couldn't come up with something more inspiring?"

I grinned. "It seemed to fit the situation."

Jackie laid her head on my shoulder. "I'm sorry I've been so mean to you."

"You've been mean? I hardly noticed."

Jackie gave me a playful shove. "Seriously." She took my hands with a look of sisterly concern. "If you need to talk or have a hard time adjusting at school, you can come to me. I know I haven't been there for you like I should, but I am now. I'm your big sister, not your mother, and I need to act more like it."

My eyes began to tear up. I quickly blinked them away. "Thanks."

Jackie nodded then stood and went over to one of the three boxes with my Converse and opened it. "Since this is a rental, we probably can't mount shelves on the wall like Dad did back home, but I'm sure we can find a few inexpensive bookcases to put along the wall by your bed to store them."

Maybe I hadn't broken my sister after all. Maybe she just needed a little adjustment.

The four of us spent the rest of the morning and early afternoon unpacking and organizing. By two o'clock, Jackie and I could see Mom's energy was waning. Other than a few boxes of knickknack items, everything was unpacked, so we insisted she go lie down. J.J. joined her.

"So, what are you gonna do?" Jackie asked.

"The girl next door is going to show me around. You want to come?"

"The one that gave us the cookies?"

I nodded.

"Look at you, making friends already. No, I'm going to call Gabriel and a few of my other friends. You go have fun."

"Okay, see ya later." I went back to the bedroom, grabbed my wallet and keys, then went to the kitchen to get the now empty cookie tin, and hurried out of the house.

Nikki stepped out onto the porch just as I was coming up her walkway. "Hey there, I thought maybe you forgot."

I handed her the tin. "No, we just had a lot to finish unpacking. Thanks again for the cookies. They were really good."

Nikki looked at the tin in surprise. "You finished them all?"

"We had them with our lunch today. A dozen cookies and four people, they didn't stand a chance. My mom wanted me to ask if your mom wouldn't mind giving her the recipe."

Nikki blushed and gave me a sheepish grin. "I made them. I'll be happy to give her the recipe."

"Oh, wow, they were like on a professional level."

Nikki's blush darkened. "Thanks. I want to open up my own bakery someday."

She was cute and made baked goods. There went those flips in my belly again. I tried to ignore them. Seeing Nikki now, up close in the light of day, I could see the soft facial features, the long slender fingers, and the subtle roundness beneath the upper part of her T-shirt. From a distance, she could easily be mistaken for a boy, but up close, you would have to be blind not to know she was a girl.

"Well, if these cookies are on the menu, I'll be one of your best customers."

"Thanks again. Let me put this in the house, then we can go." Nikki opened the screen door to go in, then stopped. "Do you want to come in and meet my mothers?"

"Uh, yeah, sure." I smoothed down my shirt and wiped my hands on my shorts. I hadn't been prepared to meet any parents.

I followed Nikki into her home. The decor and furnishings were warm and comfortable. They also had a fireplace like the one in our apartment, but theirs looked as if they actually used it. There was no television, but a large stereo system took up a portion of the wall near the fireplace. Nikki led me to an office area that also had the same bay window as our apartment looking out onto the front of the house. This must have been what the house we lived in looked like before it was converted to a two-unit house. Two women sat at desks placed at opposite ends of the area. One's fingers were flying over the keys of a typewriter. She had smooth dark brown complexion, her hair was in a full-blown Angela Davis afro, and she wore a white halter top with jeans and sandals. The other woman was looking at architectural plans spread out across her desk and had Nikki's light golden complexion. Her hair lay in long, thick curls down her back. She wore a yellow sundress and was barefoot.

"Mom and Mommy, I want you to meet Janesse, the girl who moved in next door," Nikki said over the click-clacking of the typewriter.

Both women stopped what they were doing, turned in unison, and gave me a friendly smile.

"Janesse, this is my mom, Carol Hart," Nikki said, indicating the woman with the afro. "And this is my mommy, Frieda Carter," Nikki said of the other woman.

"Hello," I said, offering my hand to each. "Nice to meet you, Ms. Hart, Ms. Carter."

"Nice to meet you too, Janesse, and what a pretty name," Ms. Carter said.

"Thank you, ma'am."

"Where are you from?" Ms. Hart asked.

"Indiana, ma'am."

They looked at each other in amusement, which might have been over my use of ma'am, but I could have been wrong, so I chose to ignore it.

"Well, she's definitely a polite young lady," Ms. Hart said. "How old are you, Janesse?"

"Fourteen."

"So, what do you two have planned today?" Ms. Carter asked.

"I was going to show her around, maybe walk up to the high school," Nikki said.

Ms. Hart nodded. "Sounds like a good plan. Grab a ten out of my bag and get some ice cream or something while you're out."

Nikki smiled and gave her a hug. "Thanks, Mom." She gave her other mother a hug and kiss as well. "See you later, Mommy."

"Don't eat too much junk," Ms. Carter said.

"I won't." Nikki grabbed my hand, pulling me out of the room.

"Nice to meet you!" I said over my shoulder.

Nikki held the gate open for me as we left her yard. "Let's go to the library first, then Church Street, then up to the high school, and on our way back down here we can stop at the YWCA."

It made me tired just hearing about all the places she had planned for us to go. "You know we don't have to do all of this in one day. I'm not going anywhere."

Nikki blushed. "Yeah, I guess we can do the high school and the Y on another day."

"That works for me."

We quietly walked up the two blocks to the library before I finally got up the nerve to ask a question that had been on my mind since this morning.

"Can I ask you something?"

"Sure."

"Are you…I mean…Do you like…" I found the words difficult to say.

Nikki smiled and looked at me expectantly. "Well?"

It was probably best to think of it like ripping off a bandage and just go for it. "Are you like your moms?"

Nikki looked at me in confusion. "What are you asking me?"

"Are you gay?"

Nikki looked nervously around, then went over to a nearby bench. I followed and sat beside her.

"You thought I was boy at first, didn't you?"

My heart ached at the disappointment on her face. "At first, but that was because I only saw you for like a minute when you were sitting on your porch. Then when you brought over the cookies it was dark and I was tired, so I honestly wasn't paying that much attention. Can you really blame me?" I indicated her attire.

"Girls can't wear T-shirts, jeans, and sneakers? It's no different than what you're wearing," Nikki said angrily.

"Of course, but most girls wear things that look more like what a girl would wear. Your ears aren't even pierced." As if that made all the sense in the world.

Nikki stood and began walking away. "You're just like everybody else. This was a bad idea."

"Nikki, wait!"

She was already crossing the street heading back toward home before I could catch up to her. When she didn't stop, I grabbed her arm and ran in front of her to cut her off. She looked down at my hand on her arm then up at me like she was going to hit me, so I quickly let go. It wouldn't be a good start to my new adventure by getting into a fight in the middle of the street with our neighbor on the second day here.

"Listen, I went about this all wrong. I'm sorry if I offended you. I was only curious. I've never met a girl like you before. I mean, I've been called a tomboy, but I've never been mistaken for a boy."

Nikki looked down with a shake of her head. "I'm tired of people making guesses about me when I'm still trying to figure out who I am. Why can't I just be me? Why do I have to fit into some label or box that everybody thinks I should be in?"

It felt horrible being one of those people. It was obvious Nikki was a friendly and caring person. It shouldn't matter what she looked like.

"I'm sorry, Nikki. It doesn't matter to me one way or the other. I'd still like to hang out with you if you still want to."

She peeked up at me. "Really?"

"Really." I gave her a big smile to reassure her that I meant it.

She smiled back. "Cool."

We headed back toward the library where she gave me a brief tour, then we headed a block up to Church Street. Nikki took me to a diner where we sat in a corner booth and ordered hot fudge sundaes. We both sat quietly fidgeting in our seats. I had so many questions but knew they would probably upset her, so I was at a loss as to what to talk about. I hadn't had to make new friends in so long I wasn't sure I remembered how.

Nikki folded her hands on the table in front of her. "I dress this way because I feel more comfortable in boy's clothes. Even when I was little, I'd pitch a fit if my mothers put a dress on me. When I was old enough to have a say in how I dressed, and after my mothers had a long, closed-door discussion, they let me choose what I wanted to wear. My ears aren't pierced because that was another decision they allowed me to make, and I said no. This is me, Nikki Carter. I'm not trying to be a boy, but I also don't feel it's necessary to shout to the world that I'm a girl. I'm just a kid trying to figure out who they are."

"That makes sense."

What's that saying? Never a judge a book by its cover. That's exactly what I, and probably a lot of others, had done to Nikki.

"I sincerely am sorry if I offended you."

Nikki gave me a grin. "It's okay. You aren't the first and probably won't be the last."

Our sundaes arrived and we dug in.

"Good, isn't it?" Nikki said knowingly. "They get the ice cream from a place in Upper Montclair that makes it from scratch."

"Wait, there's an Upper Montclair?" I asked.

Nikki chuckled. "Yeah, we're in the unofficial downtown of Montclair. Upper Montclair is up the hill and fancier. If you have a bike, maybe we can ride up there sometime."

"I do have a bike. It sounds like the part of town where we lived in Indianapolis called the Geist. It's a fancy suburb."

"Really? Do you mind me asking how you ended up here?"

"My parents got divorced and my mom moved us here to be closer to her family." It still caused an ache in my heart saying it, but I tried to sound nonchalant about it.

"Oh, wow, sorry to hear that." I could see in Nikki's eyes that she genuinely meant it.

"My father is back in Indianapolis with his homewrecker girlfriend." No, I wasn't still bitter at all.

"Wow. That's not cool. He couldn't even wait until you all left to start going around with someone?" Nikki sounded angry on my behalf. It was kinda cute.

I shrugged. "He's a good-looking successful man. He wouldn't have stayed single for long."

"What do you your parents do?" Nikki asked.

"My mom is a Realtor. My dad helps hotels and resorts with their public relations. What do your mothers do?"

"One is a writer and the other is an architect."

Nikki signaled the waitress and paid our check. "You ready?"

"Yep."

We made our way out of the diner and strolled slowly down Church Street.

"What kind of activities do you like to do? Do you play any sports?" Nikki asked.

"No, but I like to watch football and boxing. I'm into photography."

"What do you like to take pictures of?"

"Whatever catches my eye. I don't have a particular style yet."

"There's styles? I thought all you had to do was just point a camera at something and take a picture."

"Oh yeah, there's like seven main styles. Portrait, still life, photojournalism, editorial, fashion, sports, and architectural, which I've really been into lately, but still life and portrait are my favorites."

Writing was always my creative go-to, but photography had become my passion lately. No one had really taken the time to talk to me about it, and like some dork, I droned on and on for like five minutes about technique and form. As we stopped at a corner, I glanced over at Nikki, who was grinning at me in amusement. My face heated in embarrassment.

"I'm sorry. I tend to get carried away talking about that subject."

Nikki chuckled. "Hey, I'm the same way about baking. My mothers call me Betty Crocker whenever I get the opportunity to talk about it. Maybe you can show me some of your pictures some time?"

"That would be cool."

We stared at each other for a moment, then she turned away as her face darkened with a blush.

"So, uh, this is Hahne's Department Store. It's like the biggest store in town and sort of like New Jersey's own version of Macy's."

"This is probably where Jackie will be spending most of her time, and Mom and Dad's money."

The next part of Nikki's tour took us down Bloomfield Avenue past shops, places to eat, and a movie theater, and ended at a record store called Disco Brown's where the R&B group A Taste of Honey's song "Boogie Oogie Oogie" greeted us as we walked in. My body had a mind of its own when a good dance song came on, so we were barely in the door before I was grooving to the song.

"All right now. Don't hurt yourself," Nikki said with a chuckle.

"I love this song."

Without a care of who was in the store, I continued two-stepping down the narrow aisles like I was on the Soul Train line as we spent a good half hour looking through the albums while snapping our fingers and bobbing our heads to the music Disco played while we were there.

"You really like to dance," Nikki said.

"A little bit."

"A little bit, huh? You didn't stop moving until we left. Even when you were talking to Disco, your foot was tapping, and your hips were moving nonstop."

Nikki was looking at my hips. My face got hot and I grinned so hard my cheeks hurt. What was wrong with me? Nikki was nice and we were having a good time. Why did these weird feelings have to come up and ruin them? The image of shoving the feelings into a box and kicking it into a corner helped to get my mind back into friend mode. Keep it platonic, Ness. Don't mess it up before it even has a chance to start.

"Do you dance?" I asked.

"I got a few moves." Nikki did a little shuffle and spin that reminded me of Michael Jackson.

"Impressive."

Our walk from Disco Brown's was only a couple of blocks, so we were home within minutes. To my surprise, my family were all sitting on the porch.

"Ness!" J.J. shouted, waving frantically at me.

"Your brother is adorable," Nikki said.

"Would you like to meet my family? It's only fair since I met yours." It was the only thing I could think of to prolong our time together. Even if it meant having my family embarrass me, which there was no doubt they probably would.

"Yeah, I'd like that."

We walked up onto the porch where Mom and Jackie were lounging in chairs reading magazines and J.J. was playing with his Matchbox cars.

"Hey, guys," I said in greeting. "Mom, Jackie, J.J., this is Nikki from next door."

"It's a pleasure to meet you, Nikki." Mom offered her hand to Nikki, then Jackie did the same.

"You too, Mrs. Phillips and Jackie," Nikki said, giving them that smile that I wished I could bottle up and save for a rainy day.

"J.J., aren't you going to say hi? Nikki was the one who gave us the cookies we had after lunch."

My brother looked from me to Nikki, then smiled broadly. "Hi. Do you have any more of those cookies?"

Nikki smiled and sat on the floor with J.J. "I might have a few more. Maybe next time your sister comes over she can bring you. Not only can you have more cookies, but I'll let you play with my Matchbox collection."

J.J.'s eyes widened in surprise. "You have Matchbox cars? But aren't those for boys?"

Nikki leaned in close to J.J. "I won't tell if you won't," she said in a conspiratorial tone.

J.J. peeked around her looking at the rest of us suspiciously, then looked back at her with an adorably serious expression on his little face. "Okay," he whispered back.

"Then it's a deal?" Nikki offered him her hand.

J.J. shook it. "It's a deal!"

Nikki ruffled his curly hair and stood. "Well, I better get home. I promised I would make dessert tonight. Mrs. Phillips, I'll bring the recipe for the cookies over tomorrow if that's all right."

Mom smiled but it didn't seem very genuine. "That would be fine. We'll have to have you over for dinner one night soon."

"I'd like that. It was nice meeting you both." She turned back to J.J. "Don't forget our deal."

"I won't!" J.J. said.

"I'll walk you out." For some reason, having my family overhear our good-bye made me nervous.

"Thank you for showing me around," I said.

"You're welcome. I had fun."

"So did I."

"You want to hang out tomorrow? We can ride our bikes to the high school instead of walk."

It took everything I had not to excitedly blurt out yes. "I'd like that."

"Cool. Can you go early? Say around ten in the morning? We can meet here."

"That works for me."

Nikki nodded. "See you tomorrow."

"See you tomorrow." My heart was beating a mile a minute just thinking about seeing her again.

After watching her jog to her gate then up her walkway into her house, I turned back toward my own porch where Mom was watching me curiously and my sister grinned knowingly. Trying to play it cool, I strolled up to the porch and sat in the chair on the other side of Mom.

She went back to flipping through her magazine. "It looks like you two have become fast friends."

"She's cool." It wasn't hard for me to keep my tone casual as I worried how Mom would react if I told her how I really felt about Nikki.

Mom wasn't too keen on the topic of homosexuality. Even Uncle Frank avoided talking to her about his daughter, Denise. Denise was the cousin I had told Nikki about who was considering adoption. She was ten years older than me and lived in San Francisco, so we didn't see her a lot. You could see it hurt Uncle Frank when Mom would look disinterested if he started talking about Denise and her life partner of the past five years. Denise rarely spoke to Mom, if at all, when she was around. She was my only first cousin on Mom's side of the family. Mom's silence regarding Denise's sexuality kept me from talking to her about my feelings.

"Well, I'm glad you've made a friend already. Hopefully, you'll make even more once you start school. It won't hurt to be more social with other kids your age with similar interests."

In "Mom Speak" that meant she wasn't too keen on a friendship with Nikki. I caught Jackie's slight frown at Mom before she went back to reading her magazine.

Wanting to hold on to the small flame of happiness spending the afternoon with Nikki sparked, I joined J.J. on the floor. "Hey, buddy, how about a car race?"

J.J.'s sweet face beamed happily up at me. "Yaaaay!"

CHAPTER TWO

After dinner we all sat in the living room watching TV. Thoughts of Nikki racing through my mind kept me too distracted to pay attention.

"I think I'm just going to hang in my bedroom the rest of the night."

Mom looked at me in concern. "Are you feeling all right?"

"Yes, I think all the unpacking then walking around town tired me out. Besides, Nikki and I want to get an early start tomorrow. I have to make sure my bike is good for a day of riding."

"Okay, well then, good night," she said hesitantly. She looked as if she wanted to say more but changed her mind.

Relieved that she said nothing further, I gave her a kiss on the cheek and went to my room. Jackie came in a short time later as I was going through my camera bag.

"Gonna try and get some pictures while you're out?" she asked.

"Yeah. Nikki told me the high school has some great architecture."

"That's cool. You really like her, huh?"

"Yeah, she's nice." I kept my eyes down and my answer short to keep her from delving further.

"You know, if you like her like I would like a boy, that's okay."

My whole body suddenly felt hot and my mouth went dry. "I don't know what you're talking about," I managed to croak in response.

Jackie came over to sit beside me on my bed. "I see the way you look at her. You don't have to hide anything from me. I don't see anything wrong if you like girls instead of boys."

I set my camera bag aside, shot up from the bed, and walked over to the dresser to get my pajamas. "I don't know what you think you saw, but it's not like that."

"If you won't talk to me about it then you should at least call Denise and talk to her."

Tears burned the back of my eyes. I wanted so much to talk to Jackie about how I'd been feeling for the past year. About how my friend Lisa and I would "practice" kissing whenever we had sleepovers with the excuse that it would get us ready for our first real kiss with a boy. About how the idea of doing such a thing was about as appealing as kissing a rock and how I dreamed of growing up to be as happy as Denise was with Elizabeth.

"Mom would be so upset." Tears slid down my face.

Jackie's arms wrapped around me from behind and the flood gates opened. I turned in her arms and buried my face in her neck. Everything that had been bottled up within me flowed out like a river held back too long. Somehow, she walked us over to my bed and sat me down. I told her everything, and it felt like a weight was being lifted off my chest after not realizing how heavy holding such a secret had been.

"I love you, sis, and I'll support you no matter what, but you should really talk to Denise since she, more than anybody, would understand what you're feeling. Also, probably Uncle Frank as to the best way to tell Mom."

"I can't tell Mom. You see how she is with Denise, and that's her only niece. Imagine how she'd be if it were her daughter? She'd probably disown me."

Jackie chuckled. "And you guys call me a drama queen."

I nudged her with my shoulder.

"She may be upset and probably need some time to accept it, but I seriously doubt she would disown you."

"You heard her earlier. She doesn't even want me to be friends with Nikki."

"She didn't say that."

"I know you heard what she said and what she actually meant."

Jackie couldn't even look at me because she knew it was true.

"Maybe because Nikki is the extreme. Look at Denise and Elizabeth, you can't even tell they're gay. The same with Nikki's mothers. I saw them this afternoon, and I would have never imagined those two beautiful women were gay. You're pretty and a bit tomboyish, but you aren't butch," Jackie said, running her hands over my cornrows.

There it was, the very thing I had pretty much said and done to Nikki, stereotyping sexuality based on someone's looks.

"Wow, I can't believe you just said that."

"What? I gave you a compliment."

"And you basically called Nikki butch."

"You know I didn't mean it that way, but you have to admit that at first glance she could be mistaken for a boy."

Guilt left me with no response.

"You did, didn't you?" Jackie said.

"Yeah. I apologized, but I still feel like a jerk about it."

"Well, it didn't look like it affected your new friendship."

"She said she's used to it, but it still doesn't make it right."

Jackie took my hands in hers. "Ness, I'm sure Nikki knows there are going to be a lot of things said to and about her that aren't right, and if you remain friends with her, they may very well be said about you as well. You have to be able to handle that. I know you're tough but being physically tough and emotionally tough are two different things. You've always been mature for your age, so I know you understand what I'm telling you."

Jackie was right. Nikki grew up here. She was probably well-known, especially by the kids we would be going to school with. If rumors based on her appearance were already discussed, then people more than likely assumed she was gay, which meant I could be labeled gay for hanging out with her. I'd only been here a day so I hadn't met any of her friends, nor had she mentioned any she might have. I wasn't even ready to accept my attraction to girls, so there was no way I was ready to accept being labeled because of my friendship with Nikki.

"I'm sorry if I upset you talking about this, but I thought it was important you not only knew I supported you but also what you may be getting yourself into," Jackie said.

My heart was heavy. "I know. Thanks."

Jackie gave my hand a gentle squeeze. "How about a Popsicle. I know how much they make you feel better when you're down."

My mind was too jumbled with thoughts to do anything but nod in response. After she left the room I stood and went over to the full-length mirror we had put on the closet door earlier that afternoon. Although I recognized the girl who looked back out at me, I felt as if I no longer really knew her. Before me was Dad's cocoa brown complexion, thick black curly hair barely contained by my braids, his dark brown arched eyes with thick lashes, and Mom's round face and full lips. I was told I inherited my grandmother Elaine's slight overbite, broad shoulders, and her full figure. She was Mom's mother and died when I was young. I seriously hoped my boobs didn't get as big as hers were.

My gaze landed on the two generous mounds that attracted far more attention than I liked. I couldn't even wear a tube top like most girls these days for fear of them popping out for all the world to see if I moved the wrong way or, God forbid, needed to run somewhere. No matter what I dressed like, there was no way I could be mistaken for a boy with these things protruding from my chest. Jackie told me once that it was a good thing that I was tall because if I were shorter, with my broad shoulders, big breasts and behind, I would probably be fat. She said my height evenly distributed everything. As I looked at myself in the mirror, I sort of wished I had Nikki's boyish figure. At least I'd be free of the unwanted taunts I got from boys, and sometimes, grown men when I walked down the street.

Thinking about Nikki made me think about other names I could get called walking down the street with her—dyke, lesbo, homo—and I wondered if I could handle that. An image of Nikki's hurt and disappointed face when she thought I wouldn't want to hang out with her because of the assumption I made about her appeared before me in the mirror, and I realized I was doing it again. Assuming something I knew nothing about. That she had no friends and was constantly harassed for what she might or might not be. Besides the obvious crush I had on her, Nikki was nice and fun, that's all that should matter.

Jackie's reflection appeared behind me looking at me curiously. "What are you doing?"

"Just thinking." I turned and took the orange Popsicle she offered.

We both walked over to our individual beds and sat cross-legged facing each other like we used to do when we shared a room years ago.

"So, tell me all about what you and Nikki did today."

We talked about the places Nikki took me, the goings-on back in Indy that Gabriel and her friends told her about, as well as Jackie's thoughts on what I could do to fit in more easily once school started. We talked until Mom knocked on the door to say good night, then we also went to bed. Jackie was lightly snoring moments later, but indecision about Nikki still worried my thoughts and, despite how tired I was from the day, kept me awake for quite a while.

I woke up bright and early the next morning to give myself time to shower, eat breakfast, and find the perfect outfit, which consisted of one of my many pairs of cutoff denim shorts, a pair of white Converse, and instead of my usual T-shirt, a yellow button-down sleeveless blouse with lace trim on the collar and sleeves. Was I trying to go for a more girly look to offset Nikki's boyish appearance if we came across anyone? Maybe. Or maybe I felt particularly girly. Either way, I liked the look and even got a genuine compliment from Jackie, who usually just sighed and shook her head in disappointment whenever she saw what I wore.

As I rolled my bike out of the garage, Nikki came out of her back door.

"Hey!" She gave me a wave as she made her way to her garage as well.

A moment later, she rolled out her bike and I drooled in envy. "Is that a Chopper?"

Nikki smiled proudly. "Yeah. My moms got it for my birthday."

I wheeled my bike over to the fence that separated the yards.

"Wow, you got the whole kit. That must have cost a fortune."

Nikki shrugged. "I guess. It was the only thing I asked for. They told me if I kept my grades up, they would get it for me. My birthday was three months ago, but I had to wait until my final report card before they bought it last month.

"Your bike is pretty cool also. I like the blue. Is that the Schwinn Stingray?" Nikki asked.

Aww, she was trying to be nice. "Yeah, I've had her for a year. She's been good to me. I do need to put some air in the tires though."

"Come on over. I have an air pump."

"Okay."

I rode down the driveway, then over to Nikki's house. She met me at the end of her driveway, and we walked back to her yard. Nikki attached the pump to my front tire and pushed the handle up and down.

"I can do that," I said.

"No, I got it. You just relax."

"So, how long have you lived in this house?"

"Since I was in kindergarten. We lived in Manhattan and my moms wanted me to grow up in a house in an area with a good school system. As soon as I was ready to start school we moved here. It's a good area. A little more accepting of my moms than some of the other towns they had been considering. It's not perfect, but they won't be chasing us out of town with pitchforks and axes," Nikki said with a grin.

"Are there other couples like your moms here?"

Nikki felt my back tire, then switched the tube to that one. "A few that we know of. There could be more, but it's not like they have a special power that tells them if someone they meet is gay."

My face flushed with embarrassment. "I didn't mean—"

"I know. You're just so cute when you blush, I couldn't help it." Nikki winked.

She unhooked the pump. "You're good to go. Let me just put this back and we'll be on our way."

Relief surged through me when she turned away because if she would have noticed how happy saying I was cute made me, then it would have ruined everything. As much as I was crushing on Nikki, I wanted her friendship more than anything. By the time she came back I had managed to school my expression enough to keep her from guessing what was going on in my head.

"What's in the bag?" Nikki asked.

"It's my camera bag." I adjusted the strap so the bag would lay across my back while I rode.

"Wow, that looks professional."

"It was my own Chopper request."

Nikki smiled. "Ah, got it. Let's ride."

Even at this hour of the morning, the weather was warmer than yesterday so the breeze from riding felt good against my face. Especially since it heated every time Nikki looked over at me as she rode beside me.

"Be sure to let me know if you want to stop anywhere and take pictures."

"Okay, thanks."

Could she really be this nice to some girl she just met yesterday or was she that desperate for a friend? How come she hadn't mentioned any friends she did have? These questions, and a few others, buzzed around in my head as we rode along. We had just crossed over another main street when someone called out.

"Hey! Nikki!"

A boy, well, at least I thought it was a boy, I've obviously been wrong before, stood waving from the porch a couple of houses ahead. Nikki slowed her bike, and I did the same as he came jogging toward us. He wore bell-bottom jeans that seemed molded to his thighs and behind, a white tank top with a black power fist on it, and Converse tennis shoes. He was cute if you went for the light-skinned, big afro, pretty boy type.

"Hey, Justin," Nikki said. They gave each other one of the most complicated soul brother handshakes I'd ever seen.

Justin looked over at me and gave me a crooked grin that I guess was supposed to make me go all aflutter. "Who's your friend?"

"Oh, this is Janesse. She just moved into the apartment at Mrs. Walsh's place. Janesse, this is Justin."

Justin held out his hand. "Nice to meet you, Janesse," he said, his voice suddenly going deeper.

The boy must have thought he was a player with the way he was looking me up and down. "Nice to meet you too."

"Where'd you move here from?" he asked, still holding my hand.

"Indiana." Geez, why couldn't I have been a boy to avoid all of this. Or even been like Jackie who loved to be flirted with.

"Well, welcome to Montclair."

He finally, slowly, released my hand, gave my chest one last look, then brought his attention back to Nikki, who looked annoyed, which confused me. Was it because she liked Justin? She never did answer my question about being gay.

"Where are you guys headed?" Justin asked.

"I'm just showing Janesse around. We're on our way to the high school. She'll be starting as a freshman with us."

"Cool, let me get my bike and I'll go with you."

Before Nikki could say anything, Justin had taken off back toward his house.

Nikki sighed. "Do you mind if he comes with us?"

"No, he's your friend. Why would I mind?"

Nikki opened her mouth to say something then shook her head.

Something told me she wasn't too happy with my answer. "Do YOU mind if he comes with us?"

Nikki picked at a loose string on her shorts. "Oh, naw, I was hoping it would be just the two of us hanging out."

That's when I realized that her look of annoyance at Justin flirting with me might not have been because she liked him, but because she liked me. The possibility of that made me both happy and nervous. Happy because I so obviously liked her, but nervous because some weird part of me didn't want her to like me. If she didn't like me the way I liked her, then it would be easier to keep things between us strictly friendly. But now that there was a chance that she felt the same way, I wasn't sure how to handle it. Before we could say anything further, Justin skidded to a halt in front of us on a BMX Motomag, which was a street and race bike. Yeah, Justin was definitely a showoff.

"Ready whenever you are," he said, looking at me.

I looked over at Nikki, who rolled her eyes at Justin then started riding. I quickly followed and rode alongside her and Justin rode up alongside me. Sandwiched between them, I couldn't help but wonder if this was what my life was leading to. Always caught between what I wanted and what I was supposed to want. I was only fourteen, I shouldn't have to worry about these things. Unfortunately, that's another thing Mom said I inherited from Grandma Elaine, spending way too much time in my own head worrying over life. She was always telling me I needed to just enjoy being a kid. I was determined to do that today.

We continued our trek up the street with Justin, who would show off by doing wheelies and tricks on his bike while also still trying to flirt with me. He was starting to get on my nerves. He was Nikki's friend, so I didn't want to insult him. I just ignored him as best I could. When we finally made it to the high school, I blew out a loud breath of relief. Nikki snickered in response. Justin, so full of himself, didn't even notice.

Before us was a park with benches, a brook running through it, and a three-story school building in the distance. It looked nice and very suburban. It wasn't anything fancy but having the park right next to it would be cool for breaks and studying outside sometimes.

"So that's the high school?"

"Well, yes and no. That's the freshman building." Nikki pointed to another, larger building in the next block. "That's the main building."

It looked like some of the college campuses we had visited with Jackie. "You have a whole building just for freshmen?"

Nikki looked amused at my shocked expression. "It's the town's way of making the transition from middle school to high school easier. You'll still probably have to come over to the main building for some classes, but most of them will be in the freshman building."

That bit of news didn't help lessen my nervousness at starting over at a new school. "So, I may not only have to worry about going from one class to the next but also running from one building to the other?"

"My sister said it's even worse during the winter," Justin unhelpfully added.

Nikki punched him in the arm.

"Hey, what was that for? It's true. Just trying to prepare her."

"This is why I thought you might want to look around now to get you used to the idea by the time school starts. C'mon, let's walk around so you can get the lay of the land." Nikki started walking her bike down a path to a bridge that crossed over the brook.

"My sister also said they throw freshmen in the brook as initiation.

They'd have to catch me first. I'm too fast." Justin gave me a cocky grin that made me want to push him in the brook.

"Don't listen to him. That's just rumors the upperclassmen spread to keep the lowerclassmen in check."

I looked back at Justin, who shrugged and jerked his head toward the brook. Great, now I had to worry about being tossed into a brook on my first day of school. When we got around to the front of the freshman building, the main building directly across the street intimidated me even more. It was massive, taking up almost two blocks. They even had an outdoor Roman-style amphitheater. What high school had a Roman amphitheater? Once the awe of everything began to fade, I couldn't help but start seeing what it would all look like through my camera lens.

"Can we go in the amphitheater?"

"Yeah, c'mon."

Nikki led the way across the street. I propped my bike against the rock wall and pulled my camera case around to the front of me.

"Wow, that's some fancy equipment you got there," Justin said as I started pulling out my 35mm Nikon camera, camera stand, and a flash that I probably wouldn't need with all the sun we had.

"How would you guys like to be my models?"

Justin jumped at the chance. Nikki hesitated.

"Are you sure you want pictures of me?" she asked quietly.

"Why wouldn't I?"

Nikki shrugged. "I'm not exactly model material."

I reached over, grasped Nikki's hand, and gave her an encouraging smile. "I think you're perfect."

She blushed and I slowly slid my hand from hers to finish loading film into my camera. Not surprisingly, Justin was checking himself out in his bike mirror and patting his afro in place, so he completely missed the exchange between us. Once I was ready, I did several posed shots with Nikki and Justin in the amphitheater, then walked around and took several more of the building's architectural features. Nikki followed along asking me questions about why I took certain shots. What about it made it so interesting. It was nice having someone show genuine interest in what I was doing.

After almost an hour we were standing in the middle of the circular drive at the front of the school when Justin rode up to us and groaned dramatically.

"This has gotten boring. Can we go now? I need some food."

"You invited yourself. No one asked you to stick around, Justin," Nikki snapped at him.

"What are your panties all in a bunch for? You know what, cool, I'm out." He started to ride off.

"Justin! Wait!" Nikki called to him.

Justin stopped and sat pouting while he waited for us to approach.

"I'm sorry. It's hot and I'm also hungry. Why don't we go to Calabrese. Is that cool with you?" Nikki said, offering Justin her hand.

"Yeah, that's cool." Justin accepted it. After another soul brother handshake, he seemed to be happy again.

I personally didn't think she needed to apologize. After all, she was right. He had invited himself along and could've left at any time. He chose to stick around to race and do wheelies up and down the street. Her making amends with him just proved she was not just nicer than I thought but had a kind heart.

"Why don't I ride ahead and order for us. I'm getting a meatball sub. What do you guys want?"

"It's an Italian joint with pizza, stromboli, and stuff like that," Nikki explained to me. "I'll take two pepperoni slices and a 7UP."

"I'll take two cheese slices and whatever orange pop they have," I said.

Justin and Nikki looked at me in confusion.

"Pop?" Justin said.

I didn't know where the confusion lay since Nikki had just ordered a 7UP. Wasn't that a pop? "Yes, like an Orange Crush or something like that."

Nikki grinned in amusement, but Justin burst out laughing.

"Justin, it's not funny. You know she's not from here."

"Pop." Justin laughed as he took off down the street.

"What did I say that was so funny?"

"We say soda, not pop."

"Oh. I'm glad the way I talk amuses you all." I angrily began shoving my equipment back into my camera bag. Nikki laid a hand over mine. When I looked up at her she looked apologetic.

"We weren't making fun of you, honestly. It was just surprising to hear something we've called one thing being called something else."

"You may not have been making fun of me, but I'm pretty sure Justin was."

"Well, you may be right there. He can be a jerk sometimes, but he's really a nice guy once you look past his conceited exterior."

"Yeah, he is a little full of himself."

"He's the youngest of four kids and the only boy, so he's been spoiled, but he's got a kind heart. I also think he likes you." Nikki had a slight frown.

I didn't have to fake my disinterest. "He's probably just flirting. Besides, I just moved here. The last thing I'm interested in is mooning over some guy."

That seemed to bring back her smile, which made me happy. She helped me put the rest of my equipment away, and we headed up the street to the little pizza place we had passed coming here. We arrived just as Justin was paying for our food.

I reached into my back pocket for my wallet. "How much do I owe you?"

Justin waved dismissively. "It's my treat. Consider it my welcome to Montclair."

Nikki gave me an "I told you so" smirk. I stuck my tongue out at her. She barely held back a snicker then grabbed the pizza box.

"Why don't we eat at the park outside the freshman building," Nikki suggested.

"Cool," Justin said, grabbing the bag his sandwich must have been in.

"Sounds good to me." I grabbed the carrying case with the drinks.

After finding a shady spot under a tree, we sat down to eat our lunch.

"So, Janesse, you have a boyfriend back in Indiana?" Justin asked.

I almost choked on the sip of pop—or should I say soda—I had taken. Nikki slapped my back a few times as I went into a coughing fit.

"Real smooth, Casanova." Nikki laughed.

I loudly cleared my throat to give myself time to come up with a good answer to deter him. "Uh…no…my parents think I'm too young to have a boyfriend."

"Oh." Justin looked disappointed.

"Now that we've gotten that awkward conversation out of the way, can we enjoy our summer and just hang out? I don't understand why turning fourteen suddenly means everybody has to start looking for girlfriends and boyfriends," Nikki said.

"You're just mad because no one is asking you out because you haven't figured out what you like," Justin said.

If looks could kill, Justin's head would have probably exploded from the way Nikki was looking at him. Judging by the way he was avoiding her gaze, he knew he had gone too far. I didn't know how close their friendship was, but I didn't want to be the cause of any problems between them.

"At fourteen do any of us know what we want? Two weeks ago, I swore *Marvin & Tige* was my favorite book of all time. Then last week I read *Roll of Thunder, Hear My Cry* and it changed everything for me," I said with a dramatic sigh.

Both Nikki and Justin looked at me as if I had lost my mind, then burst out laughing.

"You're such a weirdo," Nikki said.

"You know I didn't mean that, right?" Justin said guiltily.

"Hey, it's cool. We both said some rude stuff, everything's copacetic." Nikki gave Justin a playful shove and it was as if they were back to normal.

As we ate our lunch, Nikki and Justin told me about all the sports activities and clubs offered at the high school. Having all this early information on what to expect was helping to curb my anxiety. It also helped that I would already know at least two people.

"I'll be trying out for the track team. Maybe you can come see me compete," Justin said hopefully.

Nikki grinned and shook her head. It was obvious Justin was not going to give up easily.

I smiled and shrugged. "Maybe. I'm more into football."

"We've got a great team," Nikki said.

A couple of boys rode up on their bikes and waved to Justin.

"I'll be right back," he said, leaving his bike with us and running over to his friends.

"Nikki, I know Justin is your friend, and because of that I'm trying to figure out a way to let him know I'm not interested without being rude and hurting his feelings."

Nikki looked over at Justin then back at me with a sympathetic smile. "You're just going to have to tell him straight up that you don't like him that way. He's not used to being told he can't have something so he may mope for a while, but he'll be fine. That's just how Justin is."

"Are you sure? I mean, I'd like to at least stay friends with him."

Nikki pat me on the shoulder. "Don't worry, Justin has been popular with the girls since we were in grade school. He'll have no problem bouncing back in no time."

For some reason I felt an inkling of insult that I would be gotten over so easily. Then had to mentally slap some sense into myself since I didn't want him to like me in the first place. The topic of our conversation ran back over to us.

"The guys are going to Nishuane Park and asked if I wanted to go with them. You all don't mind if I leave, do you?" He seemed to direct the question more toward me than Nikki.

"No, not at all. We wouldn't want to keep you from the fellas," I answered on behalf of Nikki and me.

Justin looked disappointed but quickly recovered. "Okay, then I guess I'll see you around. Later, Nikki," he said as he hopped on his bike and rode back over to his friends.

"I guess that just leaves you and me," Nikki said with a wide grin.

"I guess so. What do you want to do now?"

"Why don't we go and chill at my house. I made a chocolate cake last night that I haven't had a chance to eat and I think we have some ice cream to go with it."

"You had me at chocolate."

Nikki and I were inseparable that whole summer. We would get together right after breakfast until dinnertime. We had even begun having almost weekly sleepovers, usually at her house since she had her own room. We spent most days biking or walking around town, and she patiently waited and watched when I decided I needed to take pictures. Occasionally, Justin would hang out with us, and I would make a point of ignoring or laughing off his flirting. After a few weeks, I think he finally got tired of being subtly rejected and stopped trying, which meant I didn't have to hurt his feelings and he became a pretty cool friend.

One late summer afternoon while Nikki and I were at the park just chilling on the swings, a group of girls walked onto the playground. One broke off from the group and headed toward us wearing a pair of tight yellow shorts and a matching tube top. The yellow looked good against her dark brown skin. Her jet-black hair brushed her bare shoulders and was styled in a feathered flip that I had tried once, and it frizzed out within five minutes of going outside. She was very pretty, her full lips glistened with lip gloss, and as she switched toward us in her flip-flop sandals, all I could hear was the Commodores singing "Brick House" and I wondered why tube tops wouldn't stay up on me like that because her boobs weren't that much smaller than mine. Looking down at my overall shorts, tank top and dust covered tennis shoes, I felt like a frump compared to her.

She stopped directly in front of Nikki's swing, cocked her head to the side, and smiled prettily. "Hey, Nikki."

"Hey, Carrie, what's happening?"

The way she looked at Nikki brought on a sudden bout of jealousy that surprised me.

"I haven't seen you in a while. Where you been hiding?" Carrie asked.

Nikki shrugged. "I've been around, just been hanging with my girl Janesse here. She's my new neighbor, so I thought I'd take her under my wing and show her the ropes. Janesse, this is Carrie."

Nikki directed that wonderful smile at me, and my jealousy for Carrie scattered like a dandelion in the wind. Not surprisingly, my face heated from a blush as I smiled back and quickly looked away to nod at Carrie in greeting.

"Hi," I said.

Carrie gave me a quick glance, popped her gum, and looked right back at Nikki without returning my greeting. Rude.

"You're such a nice person to do that. You've always had a soft spot for strays. Remember that scroungy dog we found over here one day when were like seven and you tried to take it home, but your moms wouldn't let you? I remember you cried for like fifteen minutes until they promised to call the shelter to come pick it up."

I know this girl didn't just compare me to a scroungy dog. My face got hot. With my height and thick frame, I usually wasn't someone many girls my age tried to push into a fight. I also always smiled, which gave the impression that I was too nice and not a fighter. What they didn't know was that I had a bit of a temper when pushed the wrong way, and little miss Black Barbie was about to find out how much like a scroungy dog I could really be. I stood up and Nikki must have seen the look on my face because she stood as well, putting herself between me and Carrie.

"Did you come over here for anything in particular, Carrie?" Nikki asked.

Carrie was clueless that she was about to get her ass whooped. She dismissed me with a look and put her attention back on Nikki. "Yes, I haven't gotten your RSVP to my birthday party next week and just wanted to check and see if you were coming."

"Yeah, sorry, I forgot. No, we're going away for the week, so I won't be here."

Carrie pouted her lips in disappointment. "Oh, okay, well maybe you can make it for our annual Labor Day cookout."

"Sure, I'll let you know," Nikki said.

"I'll call you?" Carrie said, her smile sliding back in place as she touched Nikki's arm.

I saw Nikki's shoulders tense at the touch. "Uh, yeah, do that. See you, Carrie."

Carrie gave me one last glance, or should I say glare, then sashayed back to the group of giggling girls waiting for her. Nikki turned and grinned knowingly at me.

"What?"

"Don't act like you weren't about to stomp her."

"Maybe." After only a couple months as friends she already knew me too well. "Anyway, let's go. I want to get to Hahne's and find a bathing suit."

"You already have one. You've worn it up here to the pool a bunch of times already."

"That's a pool bathing suit. I need something different for the beach."

Nikki shrugged. "Okay," she said, as if that made perfect sense when she knew it didn't.

It was our thing. I hid my discomfort behind silly reasoning, and she accepted it without argument. It worked for us. We jumped on our bikes and made our way down the hill for me to spend my allowance on something I absolutely didn't need because Carrie had me feeling less girly than I've ever felt before.

CHAPTER THREE

Nikki's moms invited me along with them for their annual stay at their vacation house in Martha's Vineyard. I went through two rolls of film within the first couple of hours of our arrival. I was practically snapping pictures of everything, the cottages that looked like life-size gingerbread houses, the views of the ocean and, most surprising to me, all the Black folks there.

Even after Nikki told me about the importance of Martha's Vineyard to the Black community after slavery was abolished when freed slaves took shelter there, I was still shocked to see so many of our people gathered without one White face among them. It was the most beautiful sight I had ever seen and one I would never forget. I promised myself that when I became a rich and famous photographer that I would also buy a home there and just spend my days writing and taking endless pictures of the ocean.

Everybody seemed to know everybody, which made sense when I found out that the homes were pretty much handed down from one generation to the next. Nikki's cottage belonged to her mother Carol's family whose ancestors were part of the original freed slaves that settled in the Vineyards. She was currently working on a fiction novel based on her family's history in Martha's Vineyard. Carol, who insisted I call her by her first name, which I still hadn't gotten used to, knew of my love for anything Black history and was even going to take me with her to the Martha's Vineyard Museum to help her do research for her book during our vacation.

Her other mom, Frieda, who also insisted on being on a first-name basis, was helping me put together a portfolio of my photography, so I spent so much time over at their house it was like I had two homes. Both Nikki's moms worked from home and I could tell my mother wasn't too crazy about it, but other than the times I spent the night over at Nikki's house, I made sure to be home for dinner and not leave before breakfast. Since Mom started working, she put J.J. in day camp and Jackie had gotten a job at Hahne's, which was why I was able to spend so much time at Nikki's during the day. At least Mom wouldn't have to worry where I was or if I was safe being home alone.

I had asked Nikki once if she minded me spending so much time with her mothers, and she told me, "Not at all. I think it's cool that they like you so much."

Other than staying with relatives or at away camp, this was my first time away from home without my parents and siblings, and I didn't mind one bit. When we woke up for our first full day there, I helped Nikki make a breakfast of waffles from scratch with fresh berries, bacon, and fresh-squeezed orange juice.

"Wow, that was delicious. I don't think I'll ever look at an Eggo waffle the same again." I couldn't resist swirling the last bite of my waffle in the remaining syrup on my plate.

"Yes, my compliments to the chef," Carol said.

Nikki beamed happily. "I couldn't have done it without my assistant."

I gave an unladylike snort. "Yeah, cutting up fruit and putting oranges in the juicer was really hard."

"Well, unless there's another claim on them, I will be taking the last two waffles." Frieda jammed her fork into the plate of waffles sitting in the middle of the table. "Speak now or forever hold your peace." She grinned knowingly at me.

Having spent the night at their house, they all knew I could really go to town on some pancakes, waffles, and French toast, but knowing I had to fit into my brand-new swimsuit kept me from eating more than the two I already had.

"I'm good."

Nikki looked at me in surprise. "Are you feeling okay?"

"I'm fine. I just don't want to get a cramp from eating too much when we get in the water."

"Okay," Nikki said doubtfully.

After breakfast, Nikki and I went to change for the beach. Nikki wore the same suit she usually wore when we went to the community pool at home, a two-piece that looked like a white tank top with red-and-navy striped trim and navy bottoms. She looked more like a girl in it than anything I had ever seen her wear as it emphasized her rounded behind and small breasts. Although she'd been with me when I picked my suit, I had been too self-conscious to let her see me in it and was still self-conscious as I stood looking at myself in the bathroom mirror. I had Carrie on my mind when I chose it and now wondered if that had been a good idea. It was a yellow one-piece halter top with a bow closure at my breasts, which looked even bigger in the suit than I remembered when I tried it on.

"You know you're going to have to come out of there at some point," Nikki teased me.

"I'll be out in a minute," I said when all I wanted to do was hide. *Well, here goes nothing.*

I took a deep breath and walked out of the bathroom into the bedroom Nikki and I shared. Her eyes widened and her mouth fell open. I quickly tried to cover myself by crossing my arms.

"Does it look that bad?"

"No, you look…" Nikki just stared.

"I look what? Fat? Like a yellow canary? What?"

"Beautiful."

My face grew hot. That wasn't quite what I had expected to hear. Nice, cute, pretty, but not beautiful. "Uh, thanks."

We stared at each other for a moment longer before Nikki turned away.

"I didn't know if you brought one, so I brought two of my big beach towels for us. My moms are already out there setting up the umbrella. If you're ready, we can head out." She turned back to me, her face dark with a blush. "You ready?"

"Yes." I lowered my head to hide my grin, grabbed my beach bag, and followed her out.

My time in Martha's Vineyard with Nikki's family was the most fun I'd had in a long time. I felt free and comfortable to just be me and not tiptoe around to avoid getting anyone upset. Nikki's mothers were very much open and free-spirited women, and although they rarely showed public displays of affection other than an innocent touch here or there, they didn't hide that they were together if anyone asked. Most people assumed that they were two friends vacationing together and that Nikki and I were their daughters, but some that already knew or had a suspicion that they were more than that kept their distance, whispered behind their hands, or just shook their heads in disgust as they walked by. Carol and Frieda didn't seem to let it bother them. They continued about their business as if those people didn't exist. They reminded me so much of Denise and Elizabeth that it helped me to feel a little more comfortable with seeing myself in that life. That Denise and Elizabeth weren't the rarities and that there were more women like them willing to openly share a life and love with another woman.

During our last day there I sat with Carol in their little yard off the beach while Nikki and Frieda played volleyball with one of their neighbors. They had been so wonderful to me. I almost didn't want to leave.

"I can't thank you enough for inviting me on your vacation. With all the drama in my family over the past year it was nice to escape for a little while," I said.

Smiling, Carol reached over to give my hand a quick squeeze. "It was a pleasure having you here. This is the most fun I've seen Nikki have since we started these vacations. We have you to thank for that. It's not easy for her to make new friends because people are so quick to judge her by her outward appearance."

"I'm afraid I started out as one of those people when I originally thought she was a boy. She forgave me for it, but I still feel bad about it."

"It's understandable. Believe it or not, the decision to allow her to present herself more like a boy was not an easy one for Frieda and me, but I thought it was important for Nikki to be able to express herself any way she chose. Frieda thought Nikki was too young to know what she wanted and was afraid she would be bullied and labeled. As a matter of fact, it was one of our biggest arguments since we'd been together."

That surprised me since they seemed so comfortable with the way Nikki chose to look. "Really? What made Frieda come around?"

"Nikki did. Even at that young age, she was determined to be who she wanted to be. She's also just as stubborn as her mother," Carol said with a grin.

I watched Nikki make a dive to save the ball from hitting the ground, not caring that she would end up with a face full of sand or maybe even some bruises and scratches from sliding across it. All she cared about was saving the point. That was Nikki, stubborn and willing to put herself on the line for you when you ended up in a bind. She was the sweetest and kindest girl I had ever met, and I couldn't imagine not having her as a friend.

"You really like her, don't you?" Carol said.

I looked over to find her watching me with knowing but kind eyes.

"She's been a great friend. I don't know how I would have been able to deal with moving here without her." That's all I was willing to admit despite her probably knowing otherwise.

"Janesse, you're both young women coming of age in a time that is far more accepting than when I was your age. It was already tough being Black and a woman but add the fact that I was also attracted to other women, it did not make it any easier for me and my Methodist parents. They had even sent me to some camp that they thought would straighten me out, but all that did was make me rebel even more. When I told them about Frieda and that I was going to be living openly with her as my life partner, they refused to speak to me for years." Carol gazed wistfully out at Frieda and Nikki. "It wasn't until my brother was killed in Vietnam that we finally came together again as a family. They still wouldn't acknowledge Frieda and me as a couple, but at least we were speaking, and they were getting to know Nikki before they passed a few years ago."

My heart ached for the regret in Carol's voice. "I'm sorry for your loss."

She turned back to me again. "Thank you. Now, I'm saying all this so that you'll understand that although Frieda and I act as if the sneers and snide comments don't bother us, it's not easy living this life. You're young and have plenty of time to figure out who you are and what you want, so don't feel the need to rush into something you may not be ready for. Just keep that in mind as your and Nikki's friendship grows."

Carol's expression was kind and understanding, but I didn't miss the warning in her words. "Yes, ma'am."

She patted my cheek affectionately. "Well, let me get in the kitchen and start lunch. I'm sure those two are going to be starving when they get back."

"Would you like some help?"

"No, honey, it's your last day here. You just relax," Carol said over her shoulder as she walked into the house.

As I continued watching Nikki play volleyball, I thought about what Carol said and my confidence in accepting my attraction to girls waned once again. Would my parents react the same way as Carol's? They weren't religious fanatics or anything, but I knew Mom, at least, believed homosexuality was a sin, which was why it was so hard for her to accept Denise's lifestyle. Would she send me to one of those camps Carol's parents sent her to? Did they still have such camps in this day and age?

What were my other choices in life? Grow up, go to college, start a career, get married, quit my job to raise my kids, and possibly have my husband cheat on me with a twenty-something, miniskirt-wearing hoochie? Just the thought of that made me want to throw up, but it was what was probably expected of me as a woman. I looked at Nikki and had a feeling she would be paving her own way without a care of what was expected of her. I could only hope that as an adult I would have half the self-awareness she had at fourteen.

After dinner, Nikki and I sat on the beach, sharing a blanket, watching the tide come in. It was our last night, and I wanted to get just a few more shots of the sunset to add to my already growing collection.

"I wish I could just live out here forever," Nikki said with a sigh.

Closing my eyes, I took in a lungful of salty sea air. "Yeah, it's so nice. I think I've taken more pictures in the past week than I have in a year. Thanks for letting me tag along."

"Thanks for coming with us. Having you here was awesome."

Nikki's hand rested next to mine on the blanket, and the urge to touch her came over me so strong that I slid my hand over until our pinkies touched. I held my breath waiting to see what Nikki would do and released a slow steady breath as she laid her hand on top of mine. Our fingers entwined, and we sat quietly like that for a moment with my heart beating a mile a minute.

"I'm going to miss you when you go visit your father," Nikki said.

J.J. and I would be leaving in a little over a week to stay with Dad until Labor Day weekend. "I sort of wish I didn't have to go."

Still holding my hand, Nikki shifted to face me, and I did the same. We sat cross-legged from each other, still holding hands and our knees touching.

"Can I tell you something?" she asked.

"You can tell me anything."

I could barely see the expression on her face in the dark, but I could feel her hand trembling slightly in mine.

"I like you," she said.

My heart skipped a beat. "I like you too."

"I mean, I really like you. Like, more than a friend."

I felt a warm glow go through me. "I knew what you meant. I like you too."

"Really?" Nikki whispered.

"Really," I whispered back.

"Cool," she said.

Working up the courage to do something I'd wanted to do for weeks, I slowly leaned in toward Nikki, and, to my relief, she met me halfway. Our lips touched and hers were soft, warm, and tasted like the mint chocolate ice cream we had for dessert. Our kiss was tentative at first, then, as if it had a mind of its own, the tip of my tongue traced the outline of her lips and eased its way between them. I thought I might have gone too far when I felt Nikki stiffen, but it was only for a few seconds and she was following my lead. The sound of a screen door slamming shut broke the spell. Our kiss was less than a minute, but it felt like forever as we broke apart and looked guiltily back toward the house. Music was playing, and we could see Carol and Frieda through the picture window dancing around the living room. We turned and looked at each other with goofy grins.

"You've done that before, haven't you?" Nikki asked.

I shrugged, not wanting to talk about nights spent at sleepovers with my friend Lisa in Indiana just kissing and holding each other for hours.

Nikki looked down at our clasped hands and fidgeted with my fingers. "That was my first kiss."

What? Did I hear her right? "Ever?"

She looked back up at me, and I wished I could see her face more clearly. "Ever. I don't have anything to compare it to, but you're a good kisser."

I saw her teeth shining in the dark. "Wow…uh…thanks."

"Girls! Come on in and get packing. We're leaving early in the morning," Frieda called from the house.

"Okay, Mommy," Nikki called back. "We better go in."

"I guess so."

But we sat there for another moment, hands clasped, gazing at each other in the dark. Nikki was the first to break contact, and I felt a sense of loss as her warm hand left mine. We gathered our things and headed up to the house.

We said our good nights to Nikki's mothers and headed to our shared bedroom. Neither of us said anything as we packed our things then each took time in the bathroom to shower and get ready for bed. We said good night to each other as if our admissions and the kiss never happened, turned out the lights, and climbed into our own beds. I lay staring at the ceiling wondering if I had possibly dreamt it all, then I heard shuffling, and a moment later Nikki was standing beside my bed.

"Can I…do you mind if I…"

I scooted over to make room for her.

Nikki climbed in and we curled up facing each other. "I don't want to do anything. I just want be next to you. Is that okay?" she said.

"Yes," I said. I wouldn't know what to do anyway since all I'd ever done before was kiss a girl.

"Well, maybe a good night kiss."

"I think that's a fair request."

This time when our lips touched it felt as if I had waited my whole life for this moment as we took our time, and a little longer than a minute, to kiss each other good night. Afterward, Nikki turned her back to me and I wrapped my arms and curled my body around her as we fell asleep.

The day before my trip to Indianapolis, I had a farewell lunch with Nikki and her mothers. As we were finishing lunch, Mom came by, not looking too thrilled with me.

"I'm sorry to interrupt, but Ness needs to get home and start packing for her trip."

"Of course. I hope we haven't gotten her into too much trouble. We just wanted to say good-bye to her," Frieda said.

"Of course. I appreciate everything you all have done for her." Her words didn't match the strained look on her face. "Ness, let's go."

I looked around at the people who had become my second family since we had moved here and tried to convey my apology for my mother's rudeness with my eyes.

"Thank you for lunch, Ms. Carter and Ms. Hart." I knew better than to call them by their first names in front of my mother.

They must have understood because both Carol and Frieda gave me a smile and a slight nod. When I turned and looked at Nikki, her eyes had taken on that shine that happens right before someone is going to cry. I wanted to walk over and pull her into my arms, but I knew if I did, then we'd both be bawling like babies, so I smiled and gave her a little wave.

"See ya in a couple of weeks," I said and quickly turned back toward Mom, who was watching us like a hawk scoping its prey.

As soon as we got to our house, she rounded on me so fast that I almost fell backward.

"How dare you disobey me!" she said, glaring at me angrily.

"I didn't disobey you. You said to be home before you got off work. I didn't know you were going to be home early."

For the first time in my life, I thought my mother was going to do what she had threatened to do on numerous occasions when she thought we were getting smart with her, slap the taste out of my mouth. Don't get me wrong, she dealt some serious spankings when I was a little kid acting up, but she never slapped me. I had seen that look on her face only once, and that was after Dad announced he had just bought a condo with his girlfriend with plenty of room for when we visited. Mom's cool demeanor turned into dark anger, and I think if all us kids hadn't been there, she would have beaten him to a bloody pulp. I think that's why he waited until then to tell her. Because he probably knew Mom wouldn't kill him in front of us.

"Go to your room and start packing," Mom said through clenched teeth.

I knew not to argue and practically ran to my room. Jackie stood just inside the door, so I knew she heard everything. She closed the door behind me.

I flopped angrily onto my bed. "What did I do? We were finishing up lunch and I was planning to leave in like five minutes when she barged into Nikki's being all rude with her moms and looking at me like I stole something."

Jackie sat beside me. "It's not you so much as her fear of what hanging out with Nikki and her family may do to you."

Tears pricked at the back of my eyes. "I knew it. I told you she wouldn't be cool with my friendship with Nikki."

"It's practically been the whole summer. I thought she would have come around by now." Jackie sounded disappointed.

"If she would just take the time to talk to Nikki's moms. To get to know them, she'd see they have more in common than she could imagine. Frieda was married before she even met Carol. Her husband cheated on her and left her for another woman. It took her a long time to get over it, then she met Carol. First, they were friends, then they fell in love."

Jackie looked at me in surprise. "They told you all of this?"

"Of course not. Nikki did. You think they're going to tell a fourteen-year-old neighbor kid their business? Anyway, Frieda is also originally from Brooklyn like Mom."

"Wow, I had no idea."

"Of course you didn't, because Mom always make excuses as to why the whole family can't accept their invitations to dinner. Whenever I suggest inviting them over here to make her feel more comfortable, she claims we don't have the space for it right now."

My mother might as well have worn a T-shirt that said "I'm a Homophobe" on it with how obvious she was being about it. I'm surprised Carol and Frieda even bothered anymore, but they insisted that as long as Nikki and I were friends it was important for the families to meet at least once just to get to know each other better. I wasn't sure how much longer Nikki would want to be my friend, or anything else, with my mother always turning her nose up at her mothers.

Jackie sighed. "Look, maybe some time away might be good to give Mom time to just relax and not have you and Nikki's friendship in front of her daily. It could also give me time to talk to her, and maybe even include Uncle Frank, if you're okay with that."

"Jackie, you can't tell Uncle Frank about me and Nikki! He'll tell Mom for sure!" I whispered vehemently, looking toward the door in a panic that Mom would walk in any minute.

"Hey, hey, calm down. I won't give him any details about you and Nikki, just how Mom is reacting to your friendship with her."

"Okay." I agreed hesitantly but still felt a sense of panic that he would guess the truth.

If I wanted to be able to keep seeing Nikki without resorting to sneaking around, then I would need all the help I could get to get Mom to loosen her own panic. I didn't want to be the reason she lost it again and ended back up in a mental hospital.

"You go ahead and starting packing and I'll check on Mom," Jackie said.

With a nod, I watched her leave. As soon as she closed the door behind her, the tears fell. All I wanted was for Nikki and me to be able to be ourselves without having to worry about what everybody was thinking. Nikki told me that her moms had asked about our friendship and if it was turning into something more and she had lied. She said she didn't see any reason for her mothers to object to us becoming more than just friends, but she was worried about them telling my mother. Wiping away my tears, I got up to start packing. I didn't want to give Mom any other reason to be mad at me. She walked in just as I was closing my second suitcase.

"You're only going to be gone for two weeks, Ness. Do you really need two suitcases full of clothes?"

I eyed her warily. Like someone who'd just been told that the bear they were facing was friendly, but as soon as you eased your hand over to pet it, the animal went crazy and bit your fingers off, and now you're too afraid to move because it might attack again.

"The second one is for my shoes."

Mom smirked and sat on my bed next to the suitcase. "Can we talk?"

"I don't know, can we?" was what I wanted to say but chose "Sure," to keep me from getting the taste slapped out of my mouth.

I placed my suitcase on the floor and sat beside her. There seemed to be a lot of conversations happening on my bed lately.

Mom looked down at her hands clasped in her lap. "I'm sorry for snapping at you earlier. You were right, I did tell you to be home before I got home and then took off early without letting you guys know. I just wanted to surprise you since I won't see you for a couple of weeks and was a bit thrown when I found out you were next door, again."

"Mom, why don't you like Nikki?"

Mom's brow furrowed. "What makes you think I don't like Nikki?"

"You barely talk to her when she comes over here and you never go over there whenever her mothers invite us over for dinner. Other than a wave in passing, you never even have a conversation with them." As much as I tried, I couldn't keep the hurt from my voice.

Mom was quiet for a moment. When she began to talk, she wouldn't look at me. If there was one thing I could trust, it was that Mom was always honest and straightforward with me, talking to me like I was an adult for as long as I could remember. When she wouldn't look at me, I knew something was wrong.

"Nikki seems like a nice enough girl and her mothers seem to be very friendly. I appreciate how they've let you spend so much time at their house, but I really think you should have been out making more than just one friend the whole summer, not limiting yourself. Once school starts you don't want people to define you by your one and only friendship."

"I've met plenty of kids through Nikki. Who better to introduce me to new people than someone who grew up here? As a matter of fact, if it weren't for my friendship with Nikki, I would probably have spent the summer in the house because I barely knew anything about this town or anyone in it. Nikki is not only well-known but also well-liked. She's been going to school with a lot of these kids since kindergarten, so if I'm defined by my friendship with her then I'm going to be pretty popular."

Mom looked annoyed by my response. "Ness, Nikki's household is not the type of household I want you exposed to on a daily basis."

Ignoring every warning signal going off in my head not to, I questioned my mother. "Why? She has two loving parents, both of whom have great jobs, they vacation on Martha's Vineyard, and she's an honor roll student. Change Martha's Vineyard to Disney World and you've got Lisa's family."

Mom finally turned to look at me, but it was with an angry glare. "You know damn well what I'm talking about. Lisa didn't have two mothers for parents. I wouldn't call being a writer a very stable job, and Lisa wasn't purposely walking around looking like a boy."

There it was. What I needed her to say but was so afraid to hear. Behind the anger in her eyes was a panic I had only seen once before, when she had her breakdown. My friendship with Nikki could very well be breaking my mother. My heart was breaking, but I couldn't see sacrificing my mother's sanity for a few stolen moments that might lead to a decision that would affect my entire family.

"I understand. If we're done, I need to go down to the basement and wash some things."

Mom suddenly looked sad. "Okay, I'm going to pick up J.J. then stop at the store to get a few things for dinner. Do you want that ice cream you like so much?"

A lump had gathered in my throat and kept me from speaking so I just nodded. Mom got up to leave but hesitated at the door and turned back around.

"Ness, you know I love you and only want what's best for you, don't you?"

I simply nodded. Words were failing me because all I wanted to do was scream and yell at her that she couldn't possibly know what was best for me. That would require asking me what I wanted and how I was feeling. I was a kid, which meant I had to follow along with whatever the grown-ups wanted, even if it meant breaking my own heart. Without another word, Mom left, and all the happiness I had managed to extract this summer after the disaster of the past year floated right out with her.

❖

"What's wrong, kiddo?" Dad asked as he stepped out onto the patio.

J.J. and I had been back in Indianapolis for three days, and I already wanted to go home. Funny, after only a couple of months I was calling Montclair home, and it was all because of Nikki, who I missed so much. We had only spoken once since I had left and that was when I called to tell her I had arrived. I purposely kept the conversation short because I couldn't bear talking to her knowing that things wouldn't be the same when I got back.

"Just tired I guess."

We had spent the whole day at the Children's Museum, so it was a legitimate excuse for my funky mood. It had been J.J.'s favorite place to go, so Dad made sure that it was one of the places we visited during our stay. Dad's girlfriend practically whined the whole time about all the walking we did, but no one told her homewrecking behind to wear high heels. Who wore high heels to a museum? Dad even got tired of her about halfway through and suggested she have a seat in the lobby and wait for us. She had pouted thinking that would make Dad want to leave, but it hadn't worked. She sucked her teeth, sent an evil glare J.J.'s and my way, then stomped off. When we got back to the townhouse, she complained of a headache and went to their room. Dad didn't seem to mind. He ordered pizzas and we had a picnic on the patio. J.J. was already in bed, and I lay out on one of the lounge chairs staring out at nothing.

"C'mon, kiddo, I know you better than that. You've been pretty quiet since you got here."

Until J.J. got old enough to walk and take places, Dad had treated me like his son, and I didn't mind. He taught me how to play football, everything there was to know about boxing, was the main supplier of my Converse, and listened when I couldn't talk to Mom about stuff. Then his long-awaited son had come, his new pride and joy. We still watched football and boxing together and he still bought me my Converse, but he determined that since I was a girl, I would probably want to start doing girl things, so J.J. took my place. I resented it at first, but then the kid grew on me and when Dad started traveling more, J.J. became my little sidekick and I started teaching him all the things Dad had taught me.

"It's Mom. She doesn't like my new friend, and now I'm probably going to have to stop hanging out with her when I get back." Those damn tears were back pricking my eyes.

"I can't imagine your mom keeping you from being friends with someone unless she had a really good reason."

"Yeah, she's a homophobe."

"Whoa, okay, is your friend gay?"

"I don't know for sure, but she has two mothers who are, and she dresses more like a boy than a girl, so Mom has decided they're a bad influence on me." It wasn't really a lie since Nikki hadn't really said if she was gay or not. After all, I was the first person, let alone girl she had ever kissed.

"I see." Dad sat in the chair next to me. "You and I have always been straight with each other, right?"

Uh-oh, where was this going? "Yes, I guess."

"I'm going to ask you something, and I hope you feel you can trust me enough to answer honestly."

My heart started beating a mile a minute. "Okay."

"Do you like this girl as more than just a friend and that's why your mom may be overreacting?"

Jackie had been the only person I had opened up to about my feelings for Nikki. I wasn't sure if I was ready to talk to anyone else.

"Nessy, whatever your answer is, I'll love you no matter what." He used the nickname he'd given me after we'd watched a PBS show about the Loch Ness monster.

Closing my eyes, I took a deep breath, let it out slowly, and decided I needed to talk to a real grown-up about all of this. No offense to my sister, but she hadn't really lived life yet enough to advise me on such a major life twist.

"Probably."

"Have you talked to your mother about your feelings?"

"No, she never gave me a chance. She just freaked out on me and told me I need to make some new friends because Nikki and her family are a bad influence."

"Has Nikki's family given her any reason to worry?"

"No. As a matter of fact they've been nothing but nice toward us. Always inviting the family to dinner and trying to have conversations with Mom, but she brushes them off. She won't even give them a chance. And before you ask, they aren't trying to make me a lesbian."

Dad laughed out loud. "Well, that's good to know."

I even had to smirk at that dramatic statement.

"In all seriousness, do you think you might be a lesbian?"

I hadn't expected him to just come right out and ask me. "I

honestly don't know. I mean, I haven't liked any boys since third grade. Ever since then I've had crushes on girls. Nikki's the first one I've really liked as more than a friend."

"What about your friend Lisa?" Dad asked.

I whipped my head around so quickly to look at him that my neck popped. "Lisa?"

Dad gave me a look that I knew all too well whenever I tried to get away with cheating at a game with him. It said he was always watching and that nothing could get past him.

Instead of admitting to anything I switched tactics. "What do you know about Lisa?"

"I walked past your room one night when she slept over and heard whispering. It was after midnight and I was going to tell you to go to bed, but when I opened the door the two of you were sitting on the floor kissing. I closed the door and walked away. When I tried to talk to your mom about it, she wouldn't hear it. Accused me of seeing things, so I let it drop. Then things got crazy with your mom and me, so I never had a chance to talk to you about it. Is that why you guys stopped hanging out shortly after?"

I knew what night he was talking about. It was the last time Lisa had spent the night. It had been one of many nights we had "practiced" kissing after we knew everyone had gone to bed, but this time Lisa wanted to do more than kissing. She pushed me back on the bed, lay on top of me and started grinding her privates against mine through our nightgowns. I didn't know what to do at first, but then when she started making little squeaking noises, and when I started getting a little tingling feeling down there, I pushed her off and climbed up into the top bunk of my bunkbeds. A few minutes later, she climbed out of her bed and stood next to my bunk whispering my name. I acted like I was asleep and ignored her. The next morning, we barely said a word to each other, and she left before Mom even made breakfast.

After that night, whenever she called, I would make excuses why I couldn't hang out or talk on the phone for long. After a while, she just stopped calling. We had been best friends since grade school, and in one night I had freaked out and instead of talking to her I treated her like the plague. Not long after that was when my family fell apart, and my confusing feelings for my best friend were shoved to the back of my mind.

"Yeah, sort of," I answered Dad's question.

Dad reached over and wiped a tear from my cheek I didn't realize had fallen and wrapped an arm around my shoulder to pull me into a hug. "I'm sorry you've had to go through all of this by yourself. Your mom and I have been so wrapped up in our own issues we haven't given you guys the attention you deserve. I promise, from now on, you, your sister, and brother come first in my life."

"Thanks, Dad," I said.

"Now, as far as how to deal with your mom, the best person to talk to about that would be your uncle Frank."

"That's what Jackie said."

"So, she knows as well?"

"Yes, she kind of guessed it from watching Nikki and me together. I guess if she did then Mom probably did, and it's probably why she's freaking out."

Dad nodded. "Probably. She took your cousin Denise's coming out pretty hard. After Denise's mom died your mom stepped in to help Uncle Frank out as much as she could, which is why Denise was here every summer. Your mom treated her as if she were her own daughter, so it was a shock when Frank told your mom Denise was gay. She believed it was just a phase, which is what she told Denise. They had a big fight, and their relationship has never recovered from it."

"If she's that upset about Denise being gay, what would she do if I was?"

"Denise isn't her daughter."

"Exactly, which means she would be even more upset with me. You didn't see her face, Dad. When we talked about Nikki, she had the same look in her eyes as when she was sent away. I don't want to do anything that could hurt Mom. She's finally happy and doing well. This would break her again."

"What happened with your mom was something that had been building up over time and she refused to get help for it. Even if we had stayed together, something else would have caused her breakdown. She took her mother's death extremely hard, and instead of letting the feelings out she held them in and then added our issues on top of it. Like a kettle left on a stove too long, the steam built up to the point of explosion."

Dad's explanation made me realize that Jackie and I had been unfairly blaming him for Mom's breakdown all this time and it wasn't even his fault. But that didn't stop me from worrying about how Mom would take me admitting to liking girls. Who knows what else she'd been packing in her kettle this past year and what would happen if I added that to it?

"Can I make a suggestion?" Dad asked.

"Sure, it couldn't hurt."

"Don't cut yourself off with Nikki. From what I can tell, she seems to have become an important part of your new life in Jersey. Maybe, slow down on anything happening that's more than friendship. Not just for your mom's state of mind but also to give you time to figure out who you are. You're only fourteen, Nessy. Even when you were little you always thought you had to have everything figured out, but you don't. No one at your age does. This is the time of your life where you should be just enjoying being young. Don't be in such a hurry to rush to adult activities because they only lead to adult problems."

It was good advice, but was it possible to slow things down with Nikki? Physically, all we had done was kiss. I was really into her. Like goofy, giggly schoolgirl into her. My choices were either take Dad's advice or completely cut Nikki off like I did Lisa. Or I could be honest with Nikki about everything and see if we could take it slow. At least then we could still be friends.

"I guess that could work," I admitted reluctantly.

"One more thing that you probably won't like to hear. I do agree with your mom about making more friends outside your friendship with Nikki. Not only will it show your mom that there's nothing to worry about, but it will also keep you from becoming the weird new kid with no friends." Dad gave me a wink.

"Are you coming up anytime soon?" a whining voice interrupted.

Dad closed his eyes and sighed before turning around toward his girlfriend standing in the patio doorway dressed in her usual long satiny gown with a matching robe. I thought it was sort of funny that I had more boobs at fourteen then she did at twenty-six. Except for her adolescent boobs, she reminded me of Carrie back in Jersey with her small waist and big hips and behind.

"I'll be up in a few, Yolanda." I didn't miss the irritation in his voice. Obviously, Yolanda must not have heard it because she smiled cluelessly.

"All right, I'll be waiting." She kissed Dad's cheek and rolled her eyes at me.

I wanted to slap her. Like, really, lady? You seriously think this is a competition? He helped to create me. He only sleeps with you. We both watched until we heard the creak of the stairs as she walked up.

"Sorry, kiddo. Where were we?"

"We were done. I'll think about your suggestions." I figured I'd let him off the hook. Surprisingly, he looked disappointed about ending our conversation.

"Okay, well, I'm here if you need me." He leaned over and kissed my forehead. "Good night."

"Good night, Dad."

I sat on the patio for a while longer, thinking about what Dad said. He was probably right. Nikki and I had barely been friends and we were already going in a direction that there might be no coming back from without someone getting hurt. I looked down at my watch. It was nine thirty at night, fortunately the same time as Jersey.

"Dad! Do you mind if I make a call!" I shouted up the stairs.

"No, but don't stay on too late. We're leaving early for King's Island."

"Yes, sir!"

I hurried to the den for privacy and dialed Nikki's number. She had her own phone line, so I wasn't worried about waking her moms.

Nikki picked up on the second ring. "Hello?"

"Hey, Nikki, it's Janesse. Did I wake you?"

"Janesse! No, I was hoping it was you. Wait, hold on." I heard muffled voices on the other end. "Okay, I'm back. Mom was wondering who was calling me so late. She said to tell you hi and not stay on too late."

"Tell them both I said hi."

"Will do. How's it going?"

"It's okay. Dad is being good about making sure we're having a good time and spending as much time with us as he can. The only downer is—"

"The homewrecker," Nikki finished for me with a chuckle.

I grinned. "Yeah, she's a real pain. Complaining if we're taking too long some place, about the food no matter where we go, that J.J. and I are messing up the brand-new furniture with our snacks. Her whining is even getting on J.J.'s nerves. He asked her the other day why she was so unhappy, and she nearly had a conniption fit. She called J.J. a rude little boy and stomped out of the room. I don't understand what Dad sees in her."

"Wow, she definitely doesn't sound like someone worth wrecking a home for. Well, you only have a little over a week left and you'll be home."

I could hear the smile in Nikki's voice and my heart ached. "Yeah."

"You don't sound happy about it. What's wrong?"

"Mom and I had an argument the night before I left, and we were barely speaking the next morning."

"Have you spoken to her since then?"

"Just to say hello and give the phone to J.J."

"Was the argument about us being friends?"

"How'd you guess?"

"I could tell she wasn't too happy with you when she came to the house."

"Look, Nikki—"

"I told my moms about us," Nikki blurted out.

I was too shocked to respond for a minute.

"You still there?"

"Uh, yeah. What exactly did you tell them?"

"Everything. They came right out and asked me, and I couldn't lie to them anymore."

"Wow, you could have at least warned me. What if they talk to my mother?" Panic started to set in, and I stood up and began pacing back and forth for the length of the telephone cord.

"They would never do that. Don't be mad at me, Janesse." I could hear sadness in Nikki's voice.

"I'm not mad. I told my dad."

"Really? What did he say?"

"He was surprisingly cool about it."

"What about your mom?"

I flopped dejectedly back into Dad's chair. "I didn't tell her, but I think she guessed and isn't happy about it. She doesn't want us hanging out so much together. Thinks I need to find more friends."

"Oh. What do you want to do?"

"I don't want to stop seeing you, but maybe we should slow it down a little just until my mom is more comfortable. At least that's what my dad suggested. He thinks we might be taking things too fast too soon."

"My moms said the same thing."

"Oh."

We were both quiet for a moment then Nikki sighed. "Maybe

they're right. I like you, I really do, but we're both only fourteen. Who knows, once school starts, you'll meet some boy you like and figure out maybe you don't like girls so much."

"The same could happen to you."

Nikki snorted. "Not likely. I definitely like girls. You helped me figure that out."

"I did?" I couldn't help but feel a little smug.

"Yeah, you did, but don't get all conceited about it," Nikki said knowingly.

"So, you're okay with us just being friends?" The idea didn't bother me as much as I thought it would.

"Yeah. I mean, I wish it could be more, but I'd rather have you as a friend than lose you because your mom can't handle it or because you figure out maybe you like something else."

Our summer romance had fizzled out in one phone call.

"Well, I guess that's it. I better go. We're going to an amusement park in Ohio in the morning, so I should get to bed."

"Okay. Good night."

"Good night."

"Oh, and Janesse?"

"Yeah."

"This was the best summer I ever had, and I don't regret a thing about it."

"Me either. Can I call you tomorrow after we get back?"

"You better."

We said good night once more and hung up. That was probably the most grown-up conversation Nikki and I had since we met. As much as I wish we hadn't had to make that decision, it was probably the best thing for us. Not for my mother's or other people's ignorance, but for Nikki and me.

CHAPTER FOUR

1984

"Will you keep still?" Jackie said for the fifth time.

"How long is this going to take? I didn't want to wear makeup in the first place." The urge to rub my eye was killing me as she started lining my eyelid with a mascara pencil.

"It's your prom, Ness. You have to wear makeup."

"I hadn't heard that rule. Can we at least skip the eye stuff? I don't mind blush, lipstick, and even some eyeshadow, but if you don't want me looking like a raccoon halfway through the night then this stuff needs to go."

Jackie sighed. "Fine."

After an excruciating several minutes of her trying to carefully clean off the mascara and eyeliner while I tried not to blink, she stepped back and surveyed her handiwork.

"Why do you look so shocked? Is it that bad?"

Jackie pulled me up off my bed to walk me over to our full-length mirror. "See for yourself," she said, stepping away.

My dress had been custom-made from a picture I had seen in *Essence* magazine. It was a burgundy satin gown belted at the waist with a flowy cap sleeve top that had a modestly cut V-neckline in the front and back, and a full-length A-line skirt that was just long enough to get a peek of my metallic gold leather strappy heels and burgundy polished toenails. With the very feminine clothes, makeup, my hair relaxed and bump curled into submission to fall in soft curls just past my shoulders, I didn't recognize the grown-ass woman that looked back at me with shock from the mirror.

It's amazing what can happen to a person in four years. When we first moved to Montclair, I was just a hick, awkward tomboy from the Midwest calling soda, pop and sneakers, tennis shoes, intimidated by the fast-paced talk and lifestyle of Easterners, and trying to find a way to fit in while not looking like the new geek in town. I still had a bit of that tomboy left, but she had been hidden under a cheerleader's uniform for most of the past three years, her Converse still made an appearance but had been set aside for cute flats and, to Jackie's delight, platform heels. The no-name cutoff beat-up jeans and kitschy T-shirts went the way of designer jeans and soft, pretty blouses and sweaters. Fortunately, I only got a couple of inches taller, and despite all the physical activity from cheerleading slimming my waistline and tightening my curves, I was still considered "thick."

"You look fantastic," Jackie said proudly, as if she had created this version of me. Which, in a way, she had since she was the one to help me put this look together.

"I do look sort of good." I didn't want to sound too conceited.

Jackie wrapped her arms around my waist and laid her chin on my shoulder, which she had to stand on tiptoe to do. "One day you'll see yourself as the beauty you are," she said, placing a light kiss on my cheek.

"Thanks, Jackie."

Our eyes locked in understanding for a moment before she gave my waist a quick squeeze and stepped away. With one last look in the mirror, I took a deep breath and turned away.

"Wow, Ness, you look so pretty!" J.J. said.

He, Mom, and Uncle Frank were waiting in the living room for my appearance. At nine years old, J.J. had lost the adorably rounded baby face and was turning into the spitting image of Dad. Like me, he had gotten our parents' height, already standing a little over five feet. It seemed Jackie was the only one who inherited the short gene from Dad's mother, Nana Lois.

"You do look beautiful, honey," Mom said.

Uncle Frank grinned broadly. "I may have to hang around and beat the boys off with a stick after I drop you off."

"I think I'll be fine, Uncle Frank."

"We have to get pictures," Mom said, holding up her small camera.

I posed in front of the fireplace for a few shots alone, then Uncle Frank insisted I get some with Mom, Jackie, and J.J. After another five minutes, I put a stop to all the photos.

"Okay, enough. I have to go grab Nikki before we go."

Mom handed me a wrap and clutch purse she was letting me borrow.

"I'll wait in the car," Uncle Frank said as I headed next door.

Carol answered the door and clapped in delight.

"Janesse, you look absolutely stunning! Nikki is almost ready. We had to do a quick alteration to her tux. Come on in."

"Thank you, Carol."

"Is that our girl, Janesse?" Frieda walked into the foyer.

"Yes, and doesn't she look stunning?" Carol said.

"Wow, I always knew you were a knockout, but who knew all that woman was hiding under there." Frieda gave me a teasing wink. Then she turned and yelled up the stairs, "Nikki, c'mon, Janesse is waiting!"

"I'm coming, I'm coming," Nikki said as she hurried down the stairs straightening her bowtie.

When she reached the last landing, our eyes widened in surprise as we caught sight of each other. "Wow," we said in unison.

Nikki wore a black tuxedo tailored to fit her now muscular frame, a burgundy bow tie and cummerbund that matched my dress, and a pair of black patent leather Stacy Adam shoes. She had bulked up and filled out since we first met after she joined the track team doing discus and shot put. She had also gotten more attractive over time. Her face had lost the feminine softness that had held on until a couple of years ago when she started weightlifting. It was more angular, her nose spread a little wider, and her lips were fuller but not pouty or anything like that, and she wore her hair in a low, neatly cropped afro. Her breasts had not grown much, and what was there was barely noticeable under the men's clothing she wore. I still saw the Nikki I met four years ago, but if I were just meeting her now, there would be no wondering if she were a girl or guy because she could definitely pass as a guy if she chose to. The only feminine concession she'd made over the years was getting her ears pierced, which I had proudly talked her into doing on her sixteenth birthday. They were currently filled with two large diamond stud earrings.

"You clean up nice," I teased her.

Nikki grinned. "Yeah, so do you. You look amazing. Dante is going to regret breaking up with you."

I wrinkled my nose in disgust. "I don't regret a thing. Sherry can have him. We should get going. We still have to swing by and pick up Justin."

"Wait! We have to get pictures!" Carol said, running into the other room.

Frieda herded Nikki and me to their fireplace and Carol came out of the office with a camera. "You two look fantastic together."

"Moooom," Nikki groaned.

Carol laughed. "Okay, okay. C'mon, give me a smile."

We took pictures for several minutes, and I made sure to get behind the camera to get some with Nikki and her moms before they let us leave. They followed us out of the house and my family was also waiting on our porch. Nikki and I waved to both houses as we got into Uncle Frank's white Cadillac.

"You look quite dapper there, Nikki," Uncle Frank said.

Nikki cheesed proudly. "Thanks, Uncle Frank."

"Off to the next stop?" he asked.

"Yes, to pick up Justin, then we can head over to Mayfair Farms."

"Got it. Sit back and relax. Uncle Frank is on it." The car pulled away from the curb, and Nikki and I settled back into the plush leather seats.

"Are you going to be all right seeing Dante and Sherry together?" Nikki asked.

"I'm fine. I was about to break up with him anyway. He just gave me a legitimate way out other than he was starting to get on my nerves."

Dante Campbell had started out as an experiment for me. He was a running back on the football team when I started on the cheer squad my sophomore year. He was tall, dark, and handsome, and I enjoyed watching him play. At that point Nikki and I had counted that first summer together as the jumping off point for our self-discovery. She had discovered there was no doubt of her attraction to girls, and I had discovered I was more confused than ever because once school started, just as Nikki predicted, I started noticing boys. Not just any boys, though. Boys who were athletic and not looking for a serious girlfriend. It hadn't stopped me from still being attracted to girls, but it was enough to have me exploring what exactly I wanted. I wasn't allowed to go on any actual dates until junior year, and Dante just happened to be the one guy I was interested in at the time.

He asked me out, I said yes, and before I knew it, we ended up becoming the stereotypical high school football star and the cheerleader couple you saw in all those high school angst movies. It was nice at first. The attention, the little gifts, and kindnesses, how cool he was with my friendship with Nikki, his respect toward my mom and not minding J.J. tagging along on some of our dates when Mom had to work late. Then it all changed after the first time we had sex. Dante knew I was a virgin so tried to make our first time together special. His parents were out of town, something I conveniently left out when I had asked Mom if I could go over there one night to watch movies. When I got to his house, he had set up a candlelit dinner of pizza and sundaes and had even cleaned his room and made the bed.

It was very romantic, and I was all into it until the actual deed had to be done. I had insisted he wear a condom. He had insisted it wouldn't feel "real." I told him then we weren't having sex, and he miraculously found a box of condoms in his dresser drawer. After that battle was won, the next battle was getting him to slow down and take his time. I don't know if I had read one too many of Jackie's Harlequin romances or if it was just my inexperience, but I didn't want to rush this. Prior to that, I'd had a small number of make-out sessions with boys, as well as a few of my fellow cheerleaders who were just as in the closet as I was, but this was different. I felt like this was what would be the overwhelming factor to help me figure out who I was and what I wanted. Would I become a closeted lesbian old maid sneaking kisses with women behind closed doors, or would I become a loving wife popping out 2.5 kids and taking care of our white picket fence dream home?

When I managed to get Dante to slow down and enjoy the moment, it turned out to be nice. I mean, it wasn't all fireworks and opera singers, but it wasn't horrible, and it got better over time once Dante let me show him what I liked. Then he started becoming possessive. I could barely go to class without him hovering nearby between classes to check on me. If I wanted to hang out with my friends or some of the girls from the squad, he would question me about where we went, what we did, and who was there. During away games while he was on the sideline, he'd be watching me instead of what was happening on the field. Asking me what I was laughing at, why was I talking to the bass drummer from the marching band, why was I late getting to the bus.

I was relieved when SATs came around because I was able to use the excuse of needing to study to avoid seeing Dante so much. Once those were finished, I had the yearbook and my part-time job at the movie theater to keep me busy. For the past two years, I had been on the yearbook committee as a photographer, and since this was my senior year, I had also thrown myself in as a writer. With the yearbook, cheerleader competitions, and my job, we barely saw each other. When we did it wasn't the same. I was barely interested, and he seemed equally distracted. I found out why when I had asked to borrow his algebra book a few weeks ago and found a letter from one of my fellow cheerleaders, Sherry Rodriguez. She and I never really hung out or barely said two words to each other unless it had to do with the squad, but I had seen how she looked at Dante, so I wasn't surprised when she conveniently stepped into my vacated spot. Dante didn't even try to explain it, and I simply walked away. We hadn't officially broken up, but we both knew it was over, so I figured why bother with formalities.

Now, he was going to prom with Sherry, and I was going to prom with my best friends, Nikki and Justin. All of us were conveniently single, me by circumstance, Nikki by a lack of girls she was interested in, and Justin by choice because he said he just wanted to enjoy prom without having to be handcuffed to some date all night. We arrived at Justin's house, and once again had to go through more picture taking. Justin had filled out physically as well over the years but was not bulky like Nikki. His long slim frame had just gotten more muscular and tighter. He wore the same style tuxedo as Nikki since we had decided to match as a group.

"Don't you all make a good-looking trio," Justin's mother said.

His father grinned at him and gave him a slap on the arm. "Don't go doing anything I wouldn't do, son," he said with a wink toward me.

Justin rolled his eyes. "Okay, we're leaving now."

Uncle Frank held the door open as we all piled into the back seat together. He had insisted we treat him as if he were our limo driver.

"Uncle Frank, when are you going to let me drive this baby?" Justin asked, running his hand along the leather.

Uncle Frank snorted. "When you are man enough to handle it, youngun."

Nikki and I snickered, and Justin gave us the finger.

"Have you heard from NYU?" Justin asked me.

"Not yet. Jackie said she'll see what she can find out when she goes to school on Monday."

"I can't believe that's the only school you're focusing on," Nikki said.

New York University was where Jackie ended up going for a bachelor's degree in performance studies after she took a year off when we moved here. She loved it, told me about their photography program, and took me for a visit. I applied shortly after.

"It's a great program, close to home so I can commute. I can also participate in the creative writing program. How's that any different than you only applying to the Culinary Institute of America?"

Nikki snorted loudly. "Because I didn't get a full academic scholarship offer from Spelman."

Justin looked at me in surprise. "You turned down a full scholarship from Spelman?"

"Can we not talk about this now? I thought we were supposed to be enjoying tonight and not focusing on school for once."

Both Nikki and Justin looked as if they were going to argue then thought better of it.

"You're right," Nikki said. "Let's party! Hey, Uncle Frank, can you turn on some dancing music to get us in the mood?"

"I got ya." Uncle Frank slipped a tape into the cassette player and all discussion about my college choice was quickly forgotten as the three of us practically rocked the car with our seated dance moves.

We arrived at the venue and Uncle Frank pulled in along the line of limos dropping kids off. Despite our busy academic and extracurricular schedules, all three of us managed to hold part-time jobs during the school year, but we had decided it was a waste of money to get a limo. Uncle Frank offered to drive us in his Caddy and we immediately accepted. One reason was because it was fly, the other was because we wanted to save our money for our week at the shore after graduation. Our parents had reluctantly agreed to let us spend our graduation week down at Seaside Heights together without parental supervision. Nikki's moms even paid for a rental for us so we wouldn't have to stay at a cheap hotel. Nikki said it was so they knew where they could find us. I didn't care because either way, it was a chance for us to get away and relax.

Uncle Frank, dressed in a black suit and Kangol hat, pulled up, got out of the car, pimped around it to the passenger's side, and opened the door for us. Justin got out first, offered me his hand, and after I took it and got out, I offered Nikki my hand. When she exited the car, I put my arms through theirs and we walked into the venue like we were celebrities. The photographers taking pictures as people arrived made us feel like we really were walking the red carpet.

"I think we got some tongues wagging," Nikki said.

"Let them wag. They're just jealous they don't have the bomb friendship we do," Justin said.

"Let's get them talking some more." I led us toward the photo backdrop everyone stopped at for the obligatory prom photo.

We did a few poses making sure they were as far from the traditional prom poses as we could get. The first was with both of them on either side of me giving me a kiss on the cheek. The next was with me striking my best queen of Egypt pose with them kneeling at my feet, and the last was them holding me in their arms like they were carrying a surfboard. It was awesome. Nikki and Justin were the best friends I could ever have, and I wouldn't trade them, or that moment, for the world. It was a great start to an awesome evening.

Uncle Frank picked us up at the allotted time and dropped us off at Nikki's house, as we had decided to spend the night there.

I wrapped my arms around Uncle Frank's neck from the back seat and plopped a kiss on his cheek. "Thanks, Uncle Frank."

He reached up and patted my cheek. "Anything for you, honey. You know you can talk to me anytime you need a shoulder to lean on."

"I know. Good night."

"G'night, Ness."

He waited until we were all in the house and I gave him a wave before he drove off. We tried to be as quiet as possible, but it turned out Nikki's mother Carol was still up.

"Hey, guys, did you have a good time?" she asked.

"It was the best night."

"It was so cool."

"We had a blast."

We all said in unison.

"Well, that answered my question. We left you some pizza and a little bit of mimosa in the fridge to celebrate your big night. Not enough to get you drunk or in trouble with your parents, but just a taste." She gave us a conspiratorial wink.

Nikki's mothers were cool like that. They made it a point to remind us that they were still parents and not our friends but were a little more lenient than Justin's or my parents. We wished her a good night then went to enjoy our late-night feast. Although all three of us had been to house parties where alcohol found its way into our underaged hands, I had sworn off it due to my getting falling down drunk after some spiked punch at one of those parties. Mom was not happy when she had to come pick me up, and I was banned from any activities that were not school or work-related for a month. I looked warily at the large glass of mimosa Nikki poured me.

"If you get drunk again, I promise not to tell. Besides, you're staying here tonight, remember?" Nikki said in understanding.

She was right and it did look harmless. I took a sip and was glad to taste more juice than champagne.

"So, what do you all want to do now?" Justin asked.

Nikki untied her bow tie. "I don't know about you, but I need to get out of this monkey suit."

"Why don't we grab the pitcher of mimosa and go up to your room and chill," I suggested.

Nikki and Justin nodded in agreement and we headed up to her room, which was about the size of my living room. For Nikki's sixteenth birthday her mothers had knocked down a wall between her room and one of the two guest rooms to give Nikki a bigger space as well as her own bathroom. She had two queen-size beds separated by a nightstand, so she and I lounged on hers and Justin took the other one, which I normally slept in during sleepovers. I had seen Justin partially clothed plenty of times when we went swimming, but for some reason tonight, dressed in a pair of plaid pajama pants that rode low on his hips and no shirt, he looked a little sexy to me. I gazed down at the glass in my hand. Maybe there was more alcohol in this than I thought. I looked back up and caught him grinning at me like he knew what I was thinking and raised his glass in a salute.

With Justin joining us, I hadn't even thought about changing the type of pajamas I normally wore when I slept over at Nikki's. Now my skimpy little pajama shorts and tank top with no bra suddenly made me self-conscious. Justin grinned even more at my attempt to try to adjust my top over my huge breasts spilling out of the low neckline. I quickly glanced over at Nikki, who had a knowing smirk on her face that made me want to pop her.

"So, the rental my moms got us is about a block from the beach. It's two levels, has four bedrooms, one bathroom, a full eat-in kitchen, a living room, and an enclosed backyard," Nikki said.

I was thankful for the distraction. "Wow, that's a lot for just the three of us."

"It's about the same layout as our Martha's Vineyard cottage but with a second floor."

"Oh, okay. I guess we get our own rooms then," I said.

"That's cool with me. If I meet a cute little honey that I want to get to know a little better, then I won't disturb you guys." Justin winked at me.

The sudden rise of jealousy in me was surprising. "I guess the same goes if either one of us meets somebody."

Nikki laughed. "Y'all go ahead and do you. I just want some time to chill and not worry about school, parents, or trying to impress some chick." She yawned loudly. "I don't know about you two, but I'm beat. My moms had me up at six in the morning to get me to the barber and the tailor before it got crazy."

I looked over at the clock and was surprised to find it was already two in the morning. I made one more trip to the bathroom, and when I came out Justin was leaning against the doorframe with his arms crossed, wearing a cocky smile.

"Did I tell you how good you looked tonight?" he asked.

My face heated in a blush. What the hell was going on? Okay, there had to be more alcohol in that drink than Carol claimed.

"Uh, yes, you did. Thanks." I moved to walk past him, but he partially blocked my way.

"And you look really good right now," he said, giving me what I could only describe as bedroom eyes.

I faked a yawn and squeezed past him, causing my barely covered breasts to glide across his bare chest. My nipples reacted immediately. Aw, hell no, I told my body. I know it had been a while but, damn, anybody but Justin.

"G'night, Justin."

"G'night, Ness."

The bathroom door closed, and I quickly jumped into bed with Nikki, who popped an eye open and looked at me.

"What was that?" she whispered.

I looked back toward the bathroom. "I have no idea. Maybe I'm drunk."

Nikki snorted. "Girl, there was barely enough alcohol in that stuff to get a bee drunk. Maybe you're feeling a little something, something."

I gave her a shove. "It's Justin."

"And…"

"And he's our friend. It's not like that between us."

"Feelings can change, Janesse. You two were looking quite cozy dancing to that Shalamar song."

I knew exactly what Nikki was talking about. "There It Is" by Shalamar was one of my favorite slow jams, and when the DJ played it, Nikki left Justin and me alone on the dance floor. Justin twirled me in a little spin and pulled me in close. His hands rested on my hips and mine on his shoulders as we did a slow and easy two-step. The three of us partied together plenty of times, but this was the first slow dance I'd had with Justin. For some reason, the way he looked down at me and the feel of his hands resting on my hips had changed the dynamic between us.

He was no longer Justin the cute, skinny, annoyingly cocky boy. Somewhere between sophomore and senior year he turned into a handsome, still somewhat annoying but charming man.

"This can't be happening," I groaned, covering my face.

"Why fight it? He's a good guy."

"Because he's Justin," I said dramatically.

"Aaand…"

"Would you stop that? I thought you were tired. Go to sleep."

Nikki gave me a smirk. "You know it's possible to like both men and women."

"Nikki, I swear if you say one more thing."

She turned over but not before needing to get one last word in. "I'm just saying."

I couldn't respond because Justin chose that moment to come out of the bathroom. I quickly closed my eyes trying to play sleep but peeked to watch his tall muscular figure walk toward the bed in the partial light coming through the windows. He lay down on top of the covers and faced our way.

"Like what you see?" I could hear the laughter in his tone.

I sucked my teeth and turned my back to him, embarrassed at having been caught watching him. I tried to lull myself to sleep repeating over and over in my head, "Not him, not him." But every "Not him" was followed by a "Why not?" and left me tossing and turning most of what little was left of the night.

After a restless night of sleep, I was the first to wake up. I took advantage of it and ran to the bathroom to be able to take my time to shower and dress. When I finished, Nikki and Justin were still fast asleep. I walked over and stood over Justin, who was lying spread-eagle on his back. After last night I could no longer picture him as just Justin my friend. All I could see now, with his six foot four, bronze muscled body and the good looks of some mythic geek god (yes, I said geek because he was still a bit geeky at times), was that he was a grown-ass man that I was becoming more attracted to by the minute. How was that possible? How could we be best buds one day and be hot for each other the next? Well, I was hot and bothered, I didn't know about him. I knew Justin had been crushing on me when we first met, but I figured he'd gotten over that long ago with the trail of girls he'd gone through in the past four years. No, this was simply the effects of all the fun we had last night. These feelings would be gone by tomorrow. I tried to convince myself despite the way my stomach flipped when I gazed down and noticed how dangerously low his pajama pants had traveled and that what lay beneath appeared to be quite impressive.

"STOP IT!" I mentally reprimanded myself. I marched out of the bedroom before I did something foolish or he woke up and caught me staring at him drooling like some starved woman looking at a plate of food.

As I made my way downstairs, the smell of waffles and coffee drifted up toward me. Frieda was manning the stove while Carol was setting the dining room table.

"Good morning, Janesse. The early bird as usual, I see," Carol said.

"Good morning. Yeah, I guess. I didn't sleep very well."

Carol felt my forehead. "You are looking a little flushed. Are you feeling okay?"

"Nothing that a good strong cup of tea won't cure." Liar. You mean a good strong cup of Justin, said that annoying little voice in my head.

"Well, you don't have a fever. We've got your favorite, chai tea. The coffee is for your partners in crime." Carol walked back to finish what she was doing.

Since this was basically my second home I walked over and grabbed a mug out of the cabinet, the milk from the fridge, the container of chai tea bags they kept just for me, and Frieda handed me the tea kettle she had already heated on the stove. We moved around each other as if we had been doing it all my life and not just four years.

"We're going to miss you guys and mornings like this," Frieda said, rubbing circles on my back as I made my tea.

"Please, they're not going anywhere," Carol said as she sat on one of the stools by the counter. "They're only going to be in New York and they'll both be right back home on weekends and summer breaks."

"You sure you want to turn down that scholarship for Spelman? The chance to go to a historically Black college with a full academic scholarship is a dream of a Black girl's lifetime," Frieda said.

I sat on a stool next to Carol. "I'm positive. Spelman is a great school, it's my mother's alma mater, but I think it's best if I stay close to home."

Carol turned fully in her seat toward me. "Janesse, now you know we love you like you're our very own, which is why we know we can be honest with you and tell you that you're making a big mistake. Spelman's arts programs include photography, and it's just as good as NYU's. You can choose photography as your major and writing as your minor and cover two birds with one stone." Carol raised her hand to stop me from interrupting her with the same lame excuses I gave to everyone for why I chose NYU.

"I know what you're going to say, but the truth is you're afraid of leaving your mother and J.J., aren't you?"

I looked at Carol and decided that I needed to talk to someone before I ended up doing something I might regret later. Someone who wasn't close to my mother and the situation we were in. Carol was close, but she was still outside of the situation enough to be impartial.

With a sigh of relief, I admitted the truth. "Yes."

"That's what we thought." Frieda leaned on the counter to include herself in the conversation.

"Look, we know your mother has been through some difficulties, but you can't spend your life protecting her from herself. Your sister is still just a train ride away if your mom or brother need something, your uncle is literally around the corner and, if necessary, we're right next door, so there is no need for you to turn down this opportunity," Frieda said.

Carol took my hand. "At least think about it some more before officially making a decision."

I looked at both of these strong, extraordinary women who obviously cared about me, and I wanted to cry. I had always come to them when I needed some motherly advice that I felt my own mother would not be able to handle. After all, my mother still thought I was a virgin. Carol had been hesitant to talk to me about something so important in a young woman's life, but when I tried to bring up the subject with Mom, she would put off the conversation until later. I didn't want to burden Jackie with it because she was busy with school and auditions. Nikki suggested I talk to Carol. As uncomfortable as she was talking about sex with someone else's daughter, she felt it was better I talked to someone than no one at all. I'd come to lean on them more and more over the years when Mom didn't seem to want to face the fact that I was practically a grown woman. For them to encourage me this way meant the world to me because Mom looked almost relieved when I told her I was going to turn Spelman down and stay close to home.

She had come to depend on me a little too much when it came to J.J. Despite my busy schedule I still managed to spend more time with him than she did, and I felt bad for the kid. It wasn't his fault that his arrival didn't save our parents' marriage like Mom hoped. Well, that was the reason I believe she had slowly distanced herself from him since we moved here. Frieda and Carol were right. I had to take this opportunity to break out on my own before I got stuck here raising my little brother in my mother's place.

"I can see the wheels spinning in her head," Frieda said knowingly.

I smiled. "I'll think about what you said before responding to Spelman's offer."

"That's all we ask. Now, let's get you guys fed."

As I helped Frieda and Carol set up the feast they had prepared for us, noise from above told us Nikki and Justin were up and about. One problem solved, another to deal with.

CHAPTER FIVE

After breakfast, Justin sat back and patted his belly that barely had a bulge even after the four waffles, half a plate of scrambled eggs, and almost a dozen pieces of bacon.

"Your moms are not only the coolest, but they can throw down."

"They're all right," Nikki said. "What do you guys have planned for the day?"

"I have a flag football game this afternoon with my boys and a crew from South Orange. Y'all should come through. We're playing at Woodman around two." Justin grabbed the last piece of bacon and stuffed it in his mouth.

Nikki threw her napkin at him. "I have to work tonight, but I may do that since I'm free all afternoon."

"My mom has an open house today so I'm hanging with J.J." Another Saturday off spent babysitting.

"Let's take him to the game. He might like it," Nikki suggested.

It was a good idea that would get us both out of the house and still let me hang with my friends. "Sounds like a plan."

Justin stood and stretched, and I watched as his T-shirt lifted and revealed his abs and that fine line of hair pointing the way down into his pants. Nikki kicked me under the table, which was good because I could've sworn that I felt myself about to drool.

"Cool. I wish I could stay and help with the cleanup, but I gotta get home and take care of some chores before the game," he said.

"What? You ate most of this. You should be doing all the cleanup," Nikki said.

"Y'all got me, right? I'll owe you." Justin winked and gave us a thumb-up as he backed out of the room. "Catch you guys later."

"Whatever," Nikki said, waving him away.

"Later, Ness," Justin said, blowing me a kiss. A few minutes later, we heard the front door close.

After clearing the table, we worked together to load the dishwasher and were finished with the cleanup quickly. Nikki leaned on the counter looking at me curiously.

"So, seriously, what's up with you and Justin?"

I blew out a frustrated breath. "I honestly don't know. I feel like I've been pulled in two different directions for years now and still don't know what to do about it. I'm so confused."

"You're talking about your sexuality."

I nodded. "All my dreams, all my fantasies, are women. When I'm fooling around with Callie and Dana from the cheer squad, I feel like yeah, this is what I want. This is what feels natural. But then, the few times I've made out with a guy and then sex with Dante, I think maybe I'm not into girls and I get confused all over again. What's happening with Justin isn't helping."

"Let me ask you something. When you were with Dante, how did it feel? Did you enjoy it? I mean REALLY enjoy it, like you can see yourself being with a guy for the rest of your life?"

I had to think about that. Nikki and I never really discussed that part of my relationship with Dante in depth. I mean, we could have. She offered to talk about it after I told her it happened, but it felt weird. I don't know why. After all, she was my best friend.

"It was nice. I honestly couldn't get off unless he went down on me first, but it was good."

"Damn, simply good? I hope you didn't tell him that."

I threw a dishtowel at her and she managed to catch it before it hit her. "Since I don't have anything to compare it to, that's the only way that I can describe it."

"Okay, the reason I asked is because you said the feeling you got from just making out with Callie and Dana felt natural and that you felt like being with them, essentially being with another woman, is what you could see in your life. Seems to me there's your answer right there. Like I said last night, you can be attracted to both. It's possible you're bisexual but your attraction leans more toward women. You used to always talk about how you wanted a relationship like your cousin Denise's or like my moms, which tells me you see yourself in a long-term with a woman, not marrying some man and being a happy little homemaker."

I knew Nikki was right, but I still couldn't equate all of that to my attraction to Justin. "But what I'm starting to feel for Justin is different than Dante. Dante was just a good-looking distraction and made my mother happy to see that spending so much time here hadn't rubbed off on me. Justin is getting me all hot and bothered and it's annoying."

"Hey, I'm as gay as they come, and even I think Justin has grown into a hot man. That doesn't mean I want to sleep with him."

I frowned. "That's the problem. I do."

"Oh. Well, maybe you should. See if it's something more than that."

"Are you crazy? Sleep with Justin? No, not happening." I walked out of the kitchen and headed upstairs to get my things.

I heard Nikki following close behind. "Just a suggestion. I know I can't really understand what you're going through with the dual attraction, but I can understand your confusion about your sexuality. You know what I've been through."

I stopped halfway up the stairs and turned toward Nikki. "I know you're trying to help, but I think I just need to figure this one out on my own." I pulled her into a hug. "Thanks for trying though."

"You're my girl. You know I'll do anything for you."

"Ride or die?" I said.

"Ride or die," Nikki answered.

Mom was packing her briefcase as I walked into the house. "Hey, Mom."

"Hey, Ness. Did you have a good time last night?"

"Yes, it was a lot fun."

"I'm glad. Sorry to leave you with J.J. again. I should be home by four at the latest. Maybe the three of us can go to Pizza Hut or something for dinner."

"No worries, you gotta sell those houses."

"Thanks, Ness. I genuinely appreciate you. J.J., I'm leaving."

"Bye, Mom!" J.J. yelled from his room.

Mom gave me a quick wave and hurried out the door. I walked to J.J.'s room, leaned against the doorway, and watched him sitting at his desk drawing something in the sketchbook I got him for Christmas. When he was little, we always thought his scribbles were good because we could actually tell what they were, but when he started taking art classes in school his talent really showed through. His favorite subject was animals, so he and I spent many a day at Turtle Back Zoo. Him with his sketch pad and me with my camera. His attention to detail was amazing for a kid his age.

"What are you drawing, buddy?"

"A blue jay I saw in the yard this morning."

I walked over and looked over his shoulder. He had managed to catch the bird midflight, and it was so realistic it looked as if it were about to fly off the page.

"Wow, that looks awesome."

"Thanks. So how late will Mom be tonight?" I could hear the sadness and frustration in his voice.

"She said she'll be back in time for dinner. She's thinking we could go to Pizza Hut. Would you like that?"

J.J. shrugged. "I guess. There," he said, putting the finishing touches on his masterpiece and closing the book. He turned and smiled up at me. "So, what's the plan for today?"

I grabbed a small plastic football off the floor and sat down on his bed. "Well, Justin has a flag football game today, and Nikki and I thought you might like to go with us." I tossed him the football and he caught it smoothly.

"That'll be cool. Can we get ice cream after?" He tossed the ball back, and I faked almost fumbling it before I caught it and quickly threw it back at him.

"Of course. Right now, I need to finish an essay for school. You think you can entertain yourself for about an hour then I'll fix you some lunch?"

"Yeah, I have to finish reading *The Adventures of Tom Sawyer* for a book report. I'm halfway through."

"Really, what do you think of it so far?"

J.J. frowned. "I don't like it. How did they get away with writing such racist stuff and still make kids like us read it?"

I couldn't help but beam with pride at the kid's thinking. "I don't know, buddy, but I don't see them changing that anytime soon."

I stood and ruffled the curly bush on top of his head. I was going to have to take him to the barber soon. "I'll be in my room if you need me."

I sat on my bed and instead of working on my essay I thought about all the responsibilities I had. It weighed heavily on me. Trying to lessen as much burden on Mom as possible, taking care of J.J., trying to maintain my straight A average, hold a part-time job, and school activities. The last three didn't bother me as much as the first two. I loved my mother and completely adored my little brother, but I couldn't keep going like this. I wanted to be able to enjoy the college experience, not look at it as another chore or the only way to escape from home every day. The only way anything was going to change was for me to change it. I turned to an empty page in my notebook and started writing the letter that I had put off long enough.

"So, I wrote the letter to Spelman accepting the scholarship. I just have to type it up and send it," I told Nikki. We sat on a blanket watching Justin's game with J.J. cheering excitedly beside me.

Nikki gave me a little shove with her shoulder. "That's great! What changed your mind?"

I looked at her and grinned. "Your mothers."

She didn't look surprised. "Yeah, they have a way of making you see the bigger picture."

"Did you put them up to talking to me?"

Nikki raised her hands. "Nope, that was all them. When are you going to tell your mom?"

"Tonight. We're supposed to be going out to dinner. I figured that would be the best time. You know she hates to make a scene in public."

"Good luck. I'm going to miss you like hell, but I'm so excited for you."

I wrapped my arm around Nikki's shoulder and pulled her in for a half hug. "I'm going to miss you too."

"You're so lucky. A school full of beautiful Black women. I'd be like a kid in a candy store," Nikki said.

"Yeah, you'd probably spend more time looking at the women than your books."

Nikki nodded. "I'm not going to lie. You're right."

We watched the remainder of the game cheering along with J.J. When it was over, Justin came over to us and gave Nikki their usual soul brother handshake and tried to hug up on me. I quickly dodged his sweaty arms. "Nope, you're not getting all your sweat and body funk on me."

Justin laughed. "If your brother wasn't here, I'd have a good comeback to that, but I don't want to corrupt the little man."

Justin turned to J.J. "Hey, man, thanks for coming to the game. You wanna toss the ball around with me for a little bit?"

J.J. nodded excitedly then looked up at me. "Can I, Ness?"

"Of course, buddy."

I appreciated the way Justin had stepped in over the past few years and became sort of a big brother to J.J. He would hang out with us sometimes knowing it kept me from getting too worn out with my brother. Justin really was a sweet guy, and as I watched the way the sun glistened on his sweat covered biceps and muscular legs, being sweet wasn't the only thing that came to mind. I shook my head and looked away to find Nikki looking knowingly at me.

"You need to just sleep with the boy and get it out your system."

"Shut up."

Nikki, J.J., and I stopped for ice cream. As we sat enjoying our treats, J.J., who normally talked a mile a minute, was unusually quiet and picked at his melting ice cream.

"What's up, buddy? I thought you liked strawberry."

"I do," he said, taking a small spoonful and eating it before continuing to pick at it.

"Do you have a stomachache?"

He shook his head and I worried because I had never seen him so serious while eating ice cream. I reached across the table and took his hand.

"What's going on? You know you can talk to me, right?"

He nodded and laid his spoon down. "Do you think Mom would let me go live with Dad?"

I was too shocked at first to do anything but stare at him, then Nikki poked me in the side. I realized he was waiting for an answer. "Why do you want to go live with Dad?"

He looked dejectedly down at his bowl. "Because Mom doesn't want me."

My heart clenched at the sadness in his voice. "Oh, J.J., that's not true. Mom loves you."

He looked at me, and I could see he knew more than the adults in his life thought he did. "She may love me, but she doesn't want me. She's never home with me and when she is, she barely talks to me. She's always making you stay home with me or dropping me at Uncle Frank's when you're busy."

The sad thing was that I couldn't argue his point. He was right. Mom barely paid attention to him unless she had to. It had gotten worse as he went from the adorable kindergartner to the growing young boy that he was now.

"Have you talked to Dad about this?" I asked.

J.J. nodded. "He said it would be fine with him, but it was up to Mom."

I moved to sit beside him and, wrapping my sad little brother in my arms, my heart broke as he started to cry. I looked over at Nikki at a loss as to what to say or do next. She looked just as heartbroken as I felt.

"It's okay, buddy. Why don't we talk to Mom about it tonight? I'll be right there to help you, okay?"

J.J. nodded. "Thanks, Ness."

"So, what did you guys do today?" Mom asked as we had dinner.

"After we both did some homework, we went to watch Justin play football with his friends, then stopped for ice cream," I answered for both of us.

"Sounds like you had a productive day."

"I also wrote my letter accepting the scholarship from Spelman," I hesitantly announced.

The forkful of food Mom was about to eat halted halfway to her mouth, and she stared at me open-mouthed for a moment before she lowered the fork to her plate and set her hands in her lap.

"When did you make this decision? I thought you were going to NYU like your sister?" Mom asked calmly but the look on her face told me she was anything but calm.

My throat suddenly felt too dry to speak, so I took a quick sip of my iced tea before answering. "I haven't heard back from NYU yet, and after thinking on it a little more, turning down a scholarship like Spelman is offering wouldn't make sense. I don't want to burden you and Dad with trying to pay my tuition or end up graduating with debt from student loans that could possibly hurt me in the end." I hoped that sounded reasonable enough. Better than saying I couldn't take being home anymore and this would be my chance to escape.

"But what about wanting to stay close to home?"

"Mom, that was what you wanted. I applied to Spelman because it was your alma mater. You always talked about how great the experience was to not only get a chance to study away from home but also to be amongst other strong Black women with goals to be successful pillars of their communities. I thought you would want the same thing for me.

The only reason I didn't discuss it further was because the tuition was more than what I thought was doable. So, I also applied close to home to be less of a burden on the family's finances."

"So, you're saying you want to leave home? That you don't want to be with your family?" I could hear the anger in her voice, and it wasn't what I had expected. I expected her to maybe be sad about the decision, but not angry.

"Mom, why are you angry about this? I thought you'd be happy. I've got a full ride for a great school. What's the problem?"

Mom looked around the restaurant, caught our waitress's attention, and asked for the check. "We'll discuss this at home. I'd prefer not to make a scene here."

I was the one angry now. "Why would there need to be a scene made? Why can't we sit here and calmly enjoy our dinner and celebrate the fact that this is a good thing? That this is what I want?"

"Not another word until we get home, Janesse." Mom using my full name with a look that brooked no argument ended the conversation.

We silently boxed up the rest of our food and left. It was a quiet ride home. Even J.J. sat silently gazing out the window with that same serious expression he'd had earlier that afternoon. That's when I realized we never got a chance to talk about his wanting live with Dad and I worried how agreeable Mom would be to that after our college conversation. Would she be relieved to let him leave? Would it help to make my leaving easier? Well, only one way to find out. Mom had a tendency to put off uncomfortable conversations until it was either forgotten or resolved itself, but that wasn't happening tonight. I was determined to have this out with her for J.J.'s sake and mine. We had all spent the past four years tiptoeing around her, trying to make sure we didn't upset her too much to the point we sacrificed our own wants to make sure she was good. It was past time to stop coddling her, and as much as I wished I had Jackie or Uncle Frank to soften the blow, there was no time to bring either in on it, so I was on my own.

We got home, and as soon as we walked through the door Mom was already on the defense. "We'll talk about this in the morning. I have a headache and need a clear head for this discussion."

"No, you said when we get home. We're home and we need to talk about it now."

"Ness, please," she practically begged as she walked to the kitchen.

I followed her, determined to talk this out. I wasn't letting one of her "headaches" stop another conversation from happening because she didn't want to deal with it.

"Mom, I need to do this. It's an opportunity of a lifetime that I'd be foolish to turn down."

She took some aspirin and turned an angry glare on me. "Why are you doing this to me? Why are you so determined to leave? Has life here been that bad for you? I've kept a roof over your head, clothes on your back, food in your mouth, and this is how you repay me? Leaving when I need you here?"

"What am I doing to you, Mom? How is me accepting a full scholarship at a school you attended hurting you?"

"Because it's in Georgia. I need you here, close to home, not in Georgia."

"But why? You've got Uncle Frank around the corner, and Jackie is a train ride away. Why do you need me here?"

She gazed nervously past me and quickly back. "I can't do this alone, Ness," she whispered.

I turned around and saw J.J. sitting on the sofa watching TV, then looked back at her with a shake of my head. "You can, you just choose not to. Mom, I'm seventeen years old and I've practically raised J.J. for the past few years. He's your son and I'm your daughter. You're supposed to be the one taking care of us, yet we've all been taking care of you since we moved here."

My mother's face turned a mottled red. "How dare you!"

"How dare I what? Tell you the truth? When was the last time you went somewhere alone with J.J.? Spent longer than five minutes in a conversation with him? Told him you loved him?" I tried to keep my voice down, but I was so upset with Mom at that moment that it was difficult. "I've spent the past three years being more mother to him than you have."

The slap that came across my face was so fast I don't even remember seeing her hand move. "You ungrateful child. Your father left us to fend for ourselves and I've managed to make a good life for us here and all you can think of is yourself."

I held back the tears that threatened to fall because I was determined to stay strong as I said everything that should have been said years ago. "Dad has been there for us as best as he could under the circumstances. Yes, what he did was wrong, and he knows that, but he has not left us to fend for ourselves. I see the checks he sends you every month, I know he's the one that pays for us to fly to and from

Indianapolis every summer, and he makes sure to call and talk to each of us at least once a week. That doesn't count the many times when he's available to take our calls no matter what he has going on. Yes, you can blame Dad for leaving, but you can't blame him for us moving out here and you having to take care of your children alone." My mother's eyes were as round as saucers and her mouth opened and closed like a fish out of water. If it weren't so sad it would've been funny.

"Is that how you really feel? You think this is all my fault?"

I flopped down in a chair in frustration. I hadn't realized how self-absorbed my mother was until that moment. "Mom, I didn't say anything was your fault. You're always telling us that we have to take responsibility for the decisions we make. You made the decision to leave Indianapolis without even asking us what we wanted. We're the kids so we just accepted it. I've never once in the past four years complained about the move or the fact that while Jackie gets to live her life, I have to be responsible for not only my life and schoolwork but also J.J.'s. Did you know that he got into a fight last week with one of his classmates because they were calling him a bastard because he has no father? Did you know that he won a prize for his artwork at school and that it's been submitted to a national art contest? Do you even know what his favorite flavor of ice cream is?"

"It's strawberry and Ness even knows that sometimes, when I'm sad, I like to have it with rainbow sprinkles," J.J. said from behind me.

I turned and looked at him. He looked so sad. I probably should have sent him to his room to have this conversation, but the apartment wasn't that big; he would've heard it all anyway. He walked over and stood beside me. Mom looked guiltily at him but made no move to physically comfort him so, out of habit, I took his hand.

"J.J., you know I love you, right?" she asked. I wasn't sure if she was trying to convince him or herself.

"I want to go live with Dad. He said I could, but it was up to you." I had to give it to the kid. He didn't pull any punches.

Mom flinched as if she had been slapped this time. I guess this was probably all too much. Me wanting to go away to college and now J.J. wanting to leave.

"Did you two plan this little coup? To gang up on me like this?" Mom said angrily.

"Mom, we are not ganging up on you. We're trying to be honest and tell you what we want. Why are you making this seem like we're out to hurt you?" I said.

"Because you're both just like your father. Thinking about only yourselves. You know what, fine, leave, both of you. I'm done. I gave up my life, my dreams to be with that man and raise you kids, and this is what I get in return. Treated as if I'm the one that's wrong. Well, it's time for me to live my life, and with all of you out living yours, I can do that." She walked out of the kitchen and went to her room, slamming the door on any further conversation.

"Well, that went well," I said sarcastically.

"Can I call Dad?" J.J. said, tears in his eyes.

I gave him a tight hug. "Sure, buddy. You can call from my room. That way it'll be a private conversation."

I watched him run to my room and picked up the phone in the kitchen. Jackie and I had gotten our own separate line in our room that first year so that Jackie could call and talk to her friends for hours without holding up the one phone line in the house. I called Uncle Frank, told him everything that happened, and suggested that he may want to come by tomorrow to talk to Mom. I wasn't sure if she meant it about J.J. being able to live with Dad, but for J.J.'s sake I hoped she did because I couldn't bear the thought of leaving him here alone with her. Uncle Frank would be the best person to find that out. I thought any further conversation between us would just be another pointless one like tonight's. I then called Jackie and gave her a heads up in case Mom called her and she got any of the backlash. Once that was done, I did the only thing that would normally make me feel better after a day like today. I had an orange Popsicle.

After some time, J.J. came into the kitchen in a much better mood.

"Hey, how was your talk with Dad?"

"Good. He wants to talk to you."

"Okay, go get ready for bed. I'll come tuck you in after. Don't forget to brush your teeth."

"Okay." He headed toward his room, stopping for a moment in front of Mom's door, then changed his mind and went to his room without telling her good night.

"Hey, Dad."

"Hey, how's my girl doing? Did you enjoy your prom?"

"I'm okay. Yes, it was a great night. We had a blast."

"I'm glad to hear it. So J.J. told me you guys are having a tough night with your mom but wouldn't give me details. You want to clue me in? Anything I need to be aware of?"

For the third time in the past half hour, I explained the drama of the evening. Afterward, Dad sighed heavily, sounding about as tired as I felt. A late night, my emotions all over the place about my sexuality, and then Mom, I felt as if I could just curl up and sleep for days.

"First, congrats on Spelman. I'm so proud of you for managing to keep up your grades on top of everything else you handle out there. You and your sister, when all this started happening, took on far more than you should have, and that's your mother's and my fault. From this point on I want you to focus on enjoying your final days in high school and your summer. When I come down for your graduation, I plan to bring J.J. back home with me for good," Dad said.

I felt relieved and nervous at the same time. I didn't want my big day turned into a family battle. "What about Mom? What if she was just talking out of anger and doesn't want J.J. to leave?"

"I'll talk to your mom, and I'm sure with Frank's help we can figure something out. You've been wonderful for your brother, but it's no longer your responsibility, okay?"

"Yes," I said hesitantly. As much as I no longer wanted the responsibility, it was weird knowing I would no longer have it.

"Good. I love you, Nessy. We'll talk again soon."

"I love you too, Dad."

We hung up and I headed to J.J.'s room to check on him. He was sitting up in bed reading one of his comic books.

"Hey, buddy. How're you doing?"

"I'm good, I guess. Dad tell you I'm going back with him after your graduation?"

"Yep, how do you feel about that?"

"Is it bad that I'm happy about it? I mean, I love Mom, but I think it would be better if I lived with Dad." I hated that he sounded guilty for wanting to be happy.

"No, it's not bad. I'm happy for you and I think you're right."

"I'm happy for you too. I could tell you really didn't want to go NYU."

I looked at him in surprise. "How could you tell that?"

"When you talk about it you don't look happy, but when you told Nikki and Mom about Spelman, I could tell you were happy."

"When did you get to be so smart?"

He shrugged and smiled bashfully. I pulled him into a hug then covered his face in sloppy kisses. After a few cries of uncle, I stopped.

"G'night, buddy."

"G'night, Ness, I love you."

"I love you too."

With one final hug, I tucked him in, even though we both knew he was probably too old for me to do that every night, and went back to my room to tuck myself in. I looked toward Mom's room considering whether I should check on her or say good night but, like J.J., thought better of it.

By the time I got up in the morning Mom was gone. Probably for another open house. J.J. was already at the table eating a bowl of cereal.

I made myself one and joined him. "Well, buddy, it looks like it's just you and me again. What would you like to do today?" I said.

"Can we go to Turtle Back Zoo? I want to get a few sketches from the reptile house."

"Sure thing. I'll bring my camera and get some pictures for you to work from."

"Thanks, Ness. Maybe go to McDonald's after?" he asked hopefully.

I chuckled. "Maybe."

It was our tradition whenever we went to the zoo to spend hours walking around looking at the same animals that we saw every time, then go across the street to McDonald's. It took us two buses to get there even though it was just one town over, but it was worth it to make my brother happy. Just as we were finishing our breakfast, the doorbell rang. Before I could get up, I heard the door open.

"Anybody home?" Uncle Frank called.

"In the kitchen," I called back.

He walked in with a Dunkin' Donuts bag in hand. "Aw, man, you already had breakfast. I guess I'll just have to take these back home and eat them all myself."

J.J. was out of his seat in a flash. "No, we can still eat them, can't we, Ness?"

I couldn't resist his happy smile. "Yes, we can."

"Where's your mom?" Uncle Frank asked as J.J. relieved him of the bags.

"She wasn't here when we got up. I thought she was at the office or something."

Uncle Frank's realty office was attached to his home, so he would know if Mom was there. "No, I was there before I left a little while ago."

"Oh, well, we don't know where she is."

Uncle Frank frowned. "Hey, champ, you mind giving your sis and I a minute to talk grown-up stuff?" he asked J.J., who already had a mouthful of donut and one in each hand.

"Can I eat them in my room?" J.J. asked me.

"Yes, but take a plate and be sure to sweep up after. You don't want ants all over your room like last time." J.J. nodded, placed his donuts on a plate, grabbed the broom and dustpan, and headed for his room.

Uncle Frank waited for him to close his door before he sat down. "Your father called me last night. After hearing from you about what happened and speaking with him, I think it probably would be best if J.J. went back to Indy with him." He sounded sad.

"Is she heading for another breakdown?"

Uncle Frank shrugged. "I don't know about that, but what I do know is that you will if you stay here and keep going the way you are. It's time for you to live your life. As much as I love my sister, she's wrong for having put so much of a burden on you these past few years."

It felt good hearing that from him. He had tried to help when he could, picking up J.J. from school when I had activities or taking him on weekends that I worked, but his schedule was pretty much the same as Mom's, if not busier since it was his real estate agency she worked at.

"Thanks, Uncle Frank."

"Why don't I take J.J. for the day and you go do whatever it is you teenagers do these days."

"Are you sure? We were going to Turtle Back."

"I'm positive. Besides, I haven't been there in ages. It'll be fun."

I got up and gave Uncle Frank a kiss on his balding head. "Thanks."

"I'll go let him know. Tonight, I'll talk to your mom," he said and headed out the kitchen but turned back. "Oh, and Ness?"

"Yes?"

"If I haven't told you lately, I'm proud of you."

"Thanks. That means a lot coming from you."

"Well, it's the truth. You're a wonderful young lady. Don't let anyone have you believing otherwise."

The lump in my throat kept me from saying anything further, so I just nodded and cleaned up the remnants of our breakfast. Afterward I went to my room to figure out what to do with myself. Nikki was working today. I was too chicken to call Justin to hang out after the other night, and really didn't feel like working on my essay. I decided a trip to the mall to get some clothes for our graduation getaway was in order.

Chapter Six

About an hour later, I stood in front of a three-way mirror in the juniors department of Macy's trying to figure out if I was brave enough to wear a scandalously low-cut swimsuit I had dared to try on. Another girl walked out of a nearby dressing room wearing the same suit. We looked at each other and laughed.

"Great minds think alike," she said.

"I guess so. Although, it looks much better on you than me. I think I have a little too much up top to pull it off without flashing someone," I said.

It didn't just look better, it looked sexy as hell on her. She was about a head shorter than me with just enough curves not to be slim but also not to be thick like me. Her breasts lay perfectly perky beneath the top, unlike mine that threatened to fall out if I moved the wrong way, and her perfectly round behind was covered just enough to give a peek of butt cheek while mine was starting to look like a G-string the longer I stood there twisting and turning to see the right angle. Her skin was the color of coffee with just a touch of cream, her eyes were a hypnotic hazel, her lips were full and spread into a wide, dimpled smile that revealed beautiful teeth but with one flaw, a small gap between the top two. Suddenly, a hand waving in front of my face made me realize I had been staring.

My face heated with embarrassment. "I'm sorry. Did you say something?"

The girl grinned knowingly. "I said are you buying the suit for anything special?"

"Oh, yeah. My friends and I are going to the shore for a week after graduation and I thought I'd get something new for the occasion, but I'm thinking this might be a bit much."

She chuckled, a deep, husky sound that sent a bolt of pleasure throughout my body. "I was thinking the same thing." She moved to stand next to me and twisted and turned in the mirror.

"I think you could pull off. You look great," I said.

"You really think so?"

"Yeah, you should get it. I think I'll just stick with one I already have."

"No, it's a special occasion. You should definitely get something new. I'll help you. By the way, my name is Maya."

"I'm Janesse."

She nodded. "Cool. Well, Janesse, how about we go find you a swimsuit?"

I was so thrown I simply said, "Okay," and followed her back toward our dressing rooms, which happened to be next to each other.

"So, what school do you go to?" Maya asked.

"Montclair High. What about you?"

"West Orange. That means we could've run into each other at a football game or something and didn't know it. You sort of look familiar. That's why I approached you."

"Maybe. I'm a cheerleader."

"Wow, really? That's probably where I recognize you. I thought I wanted to be a cheerleader, but I never got up the nerve to try out. Are you almost ready?"

I heard her dressing room door open and close. "Uh, yeah, I'll be out in a sec."

"Okay. I'll go scout it out and see what I can find."

I waited to hear the chime that notified you if someone came in or out of the dressing room and took a deep breath. I looked at myself in the mirror and wondered what had just happened and if I was reading too much into the situation. Yes, Maya was gorgeous, even the gap in her teeth was adorable, and she did approach me, but that didn't mean it was like THAT. Like she approached me because she liked what she saw as much as I did when she walked out of that dressing room wearing that swimsuit like it was made for her. I needed to get a grip. I didn't know what was happening to me, if my hormones were doing some weird thing, but lately my body had become a roller coaster of sexual confusion. Well, not just my body. My mind was just as confused about what and how to feel for who.

"She's only offering to help you pick a swimsuit, not asking you out on a date. Geez, get it together," I said to my reflection.

I took another deep breath, grabbed the suit I had tried on, and headed out of the dressing room just as Maya was returning.

She held out an armful of bathing suits. "Sorry, I probably should have waited for you to see what you liked, but I saw these and thought they could work. Especially the white one."

I took the suits from her. "How do you know what size I am?"

Maya shrugged and took the other suit from me. "I took a guess based on how this one fit you."

Damn, she was looking at me that closely? "Thanks."

"So, what are you buying a new suit for?" I asked as I sorted through the ones Maya picked out. I had to admit, I liked the styles. They were all sexy without trying too hard like the last one. I particularly liked the white one she thought would look best and figured I'd try that one on first.

"A friend's pool party Memorial Day weekend," Maya said.

"Oh, okay. Well, you'll definitely show up and show out with that suit," I said.

"Thanks." I heard the smile in her tone, and I secretly hoped I had made her blush. That would mean she liked me.

STOP IT! I reprimanded myself and turned to look in the mirror. The suit was sexy. There was a mesh panel that ran along the sides that showed skin from underarm to hips but still managed to be modest enough not to show anything important. The straps were wide, and the bra cups held my breasts up nicely. The rounded neckline hit just at the top of my breasts and had a triangle of crisscrossing string that closed the material between them. If I tied it right it gave me a nice peekaboo of cleavage. I normally didn't wear all white, but the suit fit me like a glove, smoothing out and cupping my behind nicely. Everything was in its place and there was no threat of flashing anyone. I stepped out of the dressing room and Maya whistled in appreciation.

"Wow, now that suit was made for you," she said.

I grinned, trying not to blush. "You think so?"

"Look for yourself." She pointed toward the three-way mirror.

"Damn, and your ass looks great," she said.

I couldn't stop the blush at that compliment. "Thanks."

I stood in front of the mirror, turning this way and that, and knew I was getting the suit. "I like it."

"I'm glad. I asked the saleslady about the wet T-shirt effect and she said you should be fine. The under bra will keep that from happening."

"The wet T-shirt effect, what's that?"

"You know how when you wear a T-shirt, and it gets all wet and becomes practically see-through? You wouldn't want that to happen when you come out of the water at the beach."

My eyes widened in horror at the thought. "How do we know for sure that won't happen?"

"Well, I could get a cup of water and pour it over you," she said with a smirk.

I shook my head. "I'll take the saleslady's word for it."

Maya shrugged. "Okay, but the offer still stands if you change your mind."

Wait, was she flirting with me? "I'll keep that in mind. In the meantime, I'll just get the suit. Thanks for your help."

"You're welcome."

We stood smiling at each other for a moment. I was the first to break eye contact as Maya's eyes were like two hypnotic pools pulling me into something I wasn't sure I was ready for.

"Well, um, have a good time at your pool party," I said as I walked back to the dressing room.

"Thanks."

I shut the dressing room door and leaned back against it trying to calm my racing heart waiting to hear the chime letting me know Maya left.

"Hey, Janesse?"

"Yes?"

"I was going to grab something to eat at the food court. Would you like to join me?"

"Yeah, sure."

"Cool. I'll go pay for my swimsuit and wait for you by the register."

"Okay."

I stayed where I was until the bell chimed, then grinned stupidly at my reflection in the mirror. I changed as quickly as I could and practically ran out of the dressing area afraid that I had imagined the whole thing and that Maya really wasn't there, but there she stood, giving me that gap-toothed dimpled smile. After I made my purchase, we took our time making our way across the mall to the food court, window shopping, even stopping at more shops to buy a few more cute outfits and accessories for my beach getaway. I was normally very thrifty with my money, but I wanted to spend as much time as possible with Maya. It also didn't hurt that she was great at picking out what looked good on me.

"I'm really into fashion," she explained when we finally made it to the food court and were sitting down to eat. "I want to be a wardrobe stylist or dress models for fashion shoots someday."

"That sounds like a pretty cool career. Imagine all the free clothes you'll get."

"Yeah, that's one perk I look forward to. What about you? What do you wanna do?"

"Photography. I don't know which one yet, I'd like to be able to explore a few fields, journalism, artistic, fashion."

"Hey, maybe we'll get to work together one day. I'll dress the models and you'll take their pictures for whatever fashion spread we're both working on."

"That would be pretty cool. Do you know where you're going to school yet?"

"Clark College in Atlanta. What about you?"

I looked at her wide-eyed. "Spelman."

"For real?"

"Yeah."

"We'll be neighbors. Maybe we could hang out occasionally," Maya said excitedly.

I was just as excited but decided to play it cool. After all, what were the chances we were even going to see each other after today since we currently went to different schools in different towns. "Yeah, maybe."

Maya looked down at her pizza slice and picked at the cheese. "Maybe we can hang out before then. You know. Go shopping again, maybe a movie or something."

I could hear the hopefulness in her voice. "I'd like that."

Maya looked up and gave me a shy smile. "Cool."

We quietly finished our pizza, and I wondered if she felt the same way I did. That we didn't want the afternoon to end.

"Well, I've gotta go. My mom's probably waiting outside. You have a pen?" she asked.

I quickly dug my pen and phonebook out of my purse and handed both to Maya. She wrote down her phone number and address.

"It's my own line, so feel free to call anytime," she said, sliding the notebook and pen back over to me.

"You want mine?" I asked.

She cocked her head. "No, I'll let you make the first move," she said with a wink, then stood and left with a quick wave.

I watched her retreating figure and wondered how she knew. Was having gaydar a real thing? Was mine all screwy because I was so confused? It didn't matter at that moment as I watched her cute little bottom switch through the door.

Maya was on my mind for the rest of the afternoon. I was so distracted by thoughts of her I barely noticed a car slowing down and following beside me as I walked home from the bus stop loaded down with shopping bags. I figured it was some guy trying to push up on me, which happened often when I walked alone.

A horn honked and I heard, "Hey! Janesse!"

I turned to find Nikki grinning at me from Frieda's car. "Oh, hey, I didn't see you."

"Yeah, I can see that. Want a ride?"

"Yes, please."

Nikki leaned over to open the passenger side door. I tossed my bags in the back seat and climbed in.

"Wow, did you buy out the mall? That's the first time I've ever seen you come home with more than one bag."

My face heated. "Yeah, I think I went a little crazy."

"I guess so. We haven't talked since yesterday afternoon. How'd it go with your mom? I'm sure she was floored by both your and J.J.'s announcements."

"Floored doesn't describe it." I told her about the start of the conversation at dinner and how it ultimately ended once we got home. I also told her about my conversation with Dad and Uncle Frank.

"I'm sorry to hear that. You know if you need a place to crash for a couple of nights, you're more than welcome to come to us."

"I know and I appreciate that, but hiding from the situation isn't going to make it any better. Hopefully, Uncle Frank can calm her down and get her to see we aren't doing any of this to hurt her."

We were home within about five minutes since the bus stop wasn't that far.

"Call me later if you need to talk," Nikki said.

"Thanks."

With a quick wave, she backed out and was in her driveway before I even got up my front steps.

"Anybody home?" I asked as I walked into the foyer.

"Hey, sis, we're in the kitchen."

Jackie and Uncle Frank were sitting at the kitchen table and J.J. was planted in front of the TV. I dropped my bags by the sofa, gave J.J. a quick kiss on the head, and went in the kitchen.

"Hey, I didn't expect you to be back so soon," I said to Jackie as she got up to give me a hug.

"Well, I couldn't go without congratulating you in person, Ms. Spelman," she said proudly. "I was hoping you would change your mind."

"Yeah, that seems to be the consensus with everyone except Mom. Hey, Uncle Frank. Did you guys have a good time?"

Uncle Frank stood and gave me one of his bear hugs. "Yes, we did. That boy is as smart as they come, just like his sisters."

I grabbed a glass of water and leaned against the counter facing them. "Do I need to guess what you guys were talking about?"

Jackie frowned. "That's the other reason I'm here. I spoke to Dad, and he and I agreed that it would probably be best if we were all here to talk to her."

"You know she's going to say we're ganging up on her."

"Think of it more like an intervention," Uncle Frank said.

"I don't think J.J. should be here. I could ask Nikki if he could hang out over there," I said.

Uncle Frank shook his head. "No, he wants to be here. We had a long talk today and he wants her to hear from him why he wants to leave."

"That's a lot to put on a nine-year-old," Jackie said worriedly.

"If it becomes too much, we'll let Ness take him next door," Uncle Frank said.

"Has anyone heard from her? Do you know where she is?"

Uncle Frank sighed. "No. I called the few friends she has, and they haven't heard from her. If she's not home or doesn't call within the next few hours, then I'm going to reach out to my friends at the police station and see what we can do to find her."

As if she knew we were talking about her, we heard Mom pull into the driveway.

"Well, here we go," Jackie said.

I wondered if she even cared that she had left all day without telling anyone where she was going.

"Can somebody help me with these groceries?" Mom shouted from the foyer.

Jackie and I looked at each other hoping the other would go.

Uncle Frank chuckled. "I'll go."

He came back followed by Mom.

"Oh, hey, I didn't expect you here tonight, Jackie. Is everything okay?"

Jackie and I looked worriedly at each other and back at her.

"Everything is fine with me. Everything good with you?" Jackie asked.

Mom looked at her as if she had no idea what she was talking about. "I'm fine. Why wouldn't I be?"

I couldn't believe she was going to act like last night didn't happen.

"Where have you been all day, Mom? You left this morning without telling anyone where you were going." I tried to keep my voice even.

"I had some errands to run. I didn't realize the time, which is why I stopped to pick up dinner." Mom refused to even look my way. Just unloaded the groceries like today was just a regular old day.

"Janet, stop and sit down. We need to talk," Uncle Frank said.

That's when Mom finally looked at me and I could practically feel the anger rolling off her. "I knew you couldn't leave well enough alone. You had to get them involved?" she said, pointing to Jackie and Uncle Frank.

I saw J.J. slowly walk in and stand next to Uncle Frank, watching Mom warily.

"Mom, you refused to listen to what J.J. and I were trying to say. I thought maybe Uncle Frank could help you understand," I said.

"Understand what? That my children are ungrateful? That they hate me so much they want to leave me here alone? What's there to understand, Janesse?"

She was using my full name, which meant she was past angry or reasonable.

Jackie walked over to her and took her hand. "Mom, that's not what they're doing."

She turned her anger on Jackie, snatching her hand away. "How would you know? You left too. You pop in every now and then when it's convenient for you."

"Wow, is that how you really feel?" Jackie looked hurt and disappointed.

"Does it matter how I feel? Obviously not. You all are scheming and making plans behind my back like I'm not your mother. Like I have no say in the matter. After everything I've done for you all, sacrificed for you all, you treat me like I'm the bad guy and your father like he's a saint. Well, he's not. He's a selfish, cheating bastard, and he's obviously passed that selfish gene right on down to you all." Mom was practically shouting at this point, and J.J. scooted behind Uncle Frank in fear.

"Janet, stop it," Uncle Frank said in a commanding tone I hadn't heard before.

Mom turned on him. "How could you, Frank? How could you side with them…with him?" she said, her voice breaking on a sob.

Uncle Frank walked up to her, towering over Mom even with her height. "Janet, these are your kids, not Jacob. They're trying to talk to you. To let you know how they feel and what they want, and you're making them pay for their father's mistakes. You need to look at what holding on to that pain has wrought. Jackie had to step up to be mother not only to her sister and brother but also to you, J.J. doesn't think you want him, and Ness has not only had to step up to care for him and herself but was willing to give up an opportunity of a lifetime to stay here and continue to do so. Do you think that's fair? Don't you see what you're doing to them?"

Mom looked at the three of us. J.J. had made his way over to me and the three of us were holding hands looking at her as if we didn't know who this woman in front of us was. It brought back memories of when she had been taken away. J.J. was too young to remember, but Jackie and I remembered all too well. I'm sure she was thinking the same thing. She looked as if she didn't know what to do with us. It felt like a knife in my heart. I think I wanted what each of us wanted, for her to just acknowledge us as her children and not some people she got stuck taking care of.

"Mom, I'll go to NYU. I'll stay here—"

"No, Ness, you're going to Spelman." Uncle Frank looked angrily at Mom. "And J.J. is going to live with Jacob in Indianapolis."

Mom started to argue, but Frank raised his hand to stop her. "No, I won't stand by as you make these kids suffer for something they had nothing to do with. You're going to let them go live their lives while you get the help you need. I thought I could help you. Thought being here would be good for you, but obviously it's only made the situation worse."

"How dare you! These are MY kids!" Mom said.

"Dammit, then act like it!" Uncle Frank yelled, making all three of us stare at him in surprise.

Uncle Frank was always so cool and laid-back. For as long as I'd known him, he had never raised his voice unless it was cheering for his favorite sports teams. Mom even looked surprised at him.

"Now, sit down and listen to what they have to say," he said, pointing to the closest chair.

With a pout that rivaled J.J.'s when he didn't get his way, Mom did as she was told, looking at us just as warily as we were probably looking at her. Then, with a tired sigh she reached out to J.J.

"Come here, J.J."

J.J. looked up at me for reassurance and I nodded. It was as if her own son needed his sister to tell him it was okay to talk to her. I noticed Mom watched the interaction with sadness in her eyes. J.J. slowly walked over to her without taking her offered hand. She lowered it and gave him a sad smile.

"Would you really rather live with your dad than here?" Mom asked him.

J.J., bless his heart, straightened his back, and looked our mother straight in the eye, and answered her without hesitation. "Yes."

"Are you not happy here? Do you feel like you're not wanted?"

"Yes, but I only feel that way from Ness, Jackie, and Uncle Frank. You act like you don't even like me most of the time." Once again, he answered without hesitation and honestly.

Mom suddenly looked tired. "I'm sorry I've made you feel that way. I do love you."

"I love you too, Mom, but I think it would be better if I lived with Dad for a little while. I miss him."

Mom took a shuddering breath then nodded. "I'm sure you do. I'll call Dad tonight to talk about it, okay?"

"Okay," J.J. said.

With some hesitation, he walked up to her and wrapped his arms around her neck for a brief hug before stepping back to take my hand.

Mom looked at our clasped hands and up at me. "Have I put too much on you?"

"Maybe a little," I said.

"Did I make you feel as if you couldn't talk to me?"

"Do you really want to hear my answer?"

"Yes."

I hesitated, waiting to see any shift in her gaze that would tell me to keep my mouth shut, but all I saw was sadness. "Yes. Every time

I've tried to talk to you about anything serious going on with me, you always put the conversation off for later and later never came. There were so many times I needed you…" A lump in my throat kept me from continuing and tears I had been holding back began to fall.

"Oh, Ness." For a moment, Mom started to reach out toward me but seemed to change her mind. "I'm sorry I made you feel that way."

I would have been happy with a hug, a touch of her hand, anything to show she really cared, but she continued to just sit there looking as if she didn't know what else to say or do.

"And you, Jackie. Taking care of me and everyone else when you should have been enjoying your final year of high school. I'm sorry."

Jackie gave my hand a comforting squeeze in place of Mom's lack of affection. "It's okay, Mom. I did what I had to do. I don't regret it."

Mom took a deep breath and stood before us with her hands clasped tightly before her. As if she were afraid of touching us. "I'm going to try and do better by all of you, if you let me."

We all gave her a smile and nodded.

"Good." She looked at me. "Ness, if you wouldn't mind, I'd like to see the letter you wrote to Spelman. Maybe we can work together on making sure they're aware you'll be a legacy student. It may help you get a few little perks the other freshmen won't have," she said with a small smile.

"I'd like that."

She turned to Uncle Frank. "I promise I'll go back to therapy, but I may need to lean on you once in a while for support."

"I got you, sis," Uncle Frank said.

"I'm just a train ride away," Jackie said.

Mom nodded and gave us a tentative smile. I seriously hoped things would be different now and that, eventually, I would be able to talk to her about what was going on in my life, but I wouldn't hold my breath.

With all the family drama, I was in no state of mind to call Maya like I had planned to that night, so I waited until the next evening. I wasn't sure what the rules were since I usually got asked for my phone number first instead of the other way around. Even then, I gave it out to only a few guys who had asked for it and they called me that same day. I always felt like they could've at least waited until the next day since they had just talked to me, but guys seemed different that way. Ready to jump in without taking time to consider the moment and let a person miss you for a minute.

All day long I thought about what I would say to Maya and how I would say it. I had been so distracted with it during lunch that Nikki and Justin got frustrated having to repeat themselves because I wasn't paying attention to them.

"What's going on in that head of yours? You said things at home were better. You still worried?" Nikki asked as we walked home from school.

"They are better. Mom's even going to pick J.J. up from school every day this week, so I'm going to be working extra days at the theater."

"That's cool. A little extra padding in the paycheck doesn't hurt. Especially after your shopping trip yesterday," Nikki teased. "So, what's up?"

I didn't know why I was so hesitant to tell Nikki about meeting Maya. She'd been the only real female friend I'd had these past four years. For some reason, the thought of Maya becoming a friend, possibly more, seemed like a betrayal to Nikki's friendship.

"You know nothing you could tell me would make me not want to be friends with you. Even if it's about finally giving it up to Justin." She knew me entirely too well.

"Shut up." I playfully shoved her off the sidewalk.

Nikki took my hand. "Talk to me, Janesse."

I looked down at the sidewalk as we walked. "I met someone at the mall yesterday. I think she likes me."

Nikki stopped walking. Since she had my hand, I stopped a step ahead of her but didn't turn around. "She?"

I nodded.

She tugged my hand. "Janesse, look at me."

I slowly turned around and met her intense gaze. Nikki had always been able to read me like a book, and I could practically feel her turning the pages of my mind and heart to see what I wasn't telling her.

"And you like her." It was a statement rather than a question.

I nodded.

"Not the kind of like you had for your cheer buddies but a serious like."

I nodded again.

"Wow." We started walking again. "Why didn't you tell me yesterday?"

"I honestly don't know. It happened so fast I wasn't even sure if I had imagined the flirting and was reading too much into how well we got along or if it was genuine. She gave me her number and told me she'd let me make the first move."

Nikki grinned. "Nice play."

"Nikki," I said with exasperation.

"Sorry. Tell me everything that happened."

I told her about meeting in the dressing room, walking through the mall, and our lunch together. "It felt so easy to talk to her. Like when you and I first met, but different."

"Wish I had been a fly on that dressing room wall. Two sexy women trying on swimsuits and flirting. Sounds like the start of a lesbian porn."

"Nikki!" I shoved her off the sidewalk again.

She held up her hands in surrender. "Okay, okay. Let me stop before you shove me in front of a car next time. What's this mystery chick's name?"

"Maya Lawson. She lives in West Orange."

Nikki's brow furrowed in thought for a moment, then she snapped her fingers. "The name sounded familiar and I had to think about it. I met her at a party earlier this year."

My heart dropped. "You didn't try and push up on her, did you?"

Nikki chuckled. "No, don't worry. She's not my type. You know I like them thick. She's got a cute little figure, but I need at least two handfuls to hold on to." She acted like she was grabbing wide hips and started pumping her own as we walked.

I shook my head at her antics. "You're a fool. Did you talk to her? What did you think of her?"

"Yeah, we talked for a bit. She seemed to be cool people. She wasn't the type to just talk to anybody. She came to the party with a guy friend of hers but ended up leaving alone. I saw quite a few players trying to talk to her, but I don't think they were her type. After what you told me, I see why. She obviously likes them thick and femme also." Nikki gave me a hip bump. "When are you going to call her?"

"Tonight. I didn't want to seem too desperate by calling her the same day."

Nikki nodded in approval. "Good idea. Give her time to think about you. So, uh, what about Justin?"

"What about him? We're friends and that's all we're going to be. I think the night and the mimosas had me feeling some kinda way and it's over. I honestly haven't even thought about it since I met Maya."

"Okay, well, from what I saw, that boy is still as into you now as he was that first summer."

"Nothing has happened between us and I've deterred him as much as I can. I can't help how he feels about me when I haven't given him any reason to think I feel the same way."

"Look, I know you're right and maybe you two were just caught up in the moment, but whether you want to admit it or not, something sparked that night and Justin is going to be looking to fan the flames."

I knew Nikki was right. I hated when Nikki was right. "I'll face that road when I get to it."

"There's one more thing you need to know about Maya," Nikki said.

"What's that?"

"She's out and proud. Are you sure you're ready for that? No offense, my friend, but you've barely got the closet door open."

"It's just a phone call, Nikki."

Nikki shrugged. "I'm just saying, keep it in mind. If what I know about Maya is true, she's approaching this like a potential dating thing. Your only experience in the lesbian dating pool is a few make-out sessions with other closeted girls. Dating a woman is a whole other universe and can get intense. I don't want to see you get caught up in something you aren't ready for. Gotta look out for my girl."

"I know and I appreciate it."

I tried to look confident about the whole situation, but hearing what Nikki said about Maya had me a little worried.

I picked up and hung up the phone three times before I dialed Maya's number. My heart was beating a mile a minute as I waited for her to answer. By the fourth ring I was about to hang up when a breathless "Hello," came on the other line.

"Uh, hello, may I speak to Maya?"

"This is Maya."

"Oh, uh, hey, Maya, it's Janesse. Janesse Phillips. We met at the mall this weekend."

"Hey, Janesse, I remember."

"Is this a good time? You sound like you were busy."

"Oh, no, it's fine. I was downstairs and had to run up to get the phone. So how did the rest of your weekend go?"

"It was good. A little family drama, but everything is fine now." I slapped my head, why the hell would I tell her that?

"Yeah, we all have family drama every now and then. So, what made you call me?"

"You gave me your number."

Maya laughed. "I know that, silly. What made you decide to dial it?"

"I thought you were nice, and I had a good time with you."

"I did too. I usually hate going to the mall alone, but all my friends were busy. You made the afternoon much better."

My face heated with a blush. I was so glad we were talking on the phone and she couldn't see it. "Same here."

"So, what do you like to do for fun?"

"Photography, obviously, writing, hanging with my friends. Nothing spectacular. What about you?" I fluffed my pillows against my headboard and got comfortable.

"Shopping, obviously. Sketching, painting, and hanging out with my friends as well."

"Oh, you're an artist?"

"I wouldn't call myself an artist, but I think I'm all right."

"Modest, huh."

She chuckled and the sound made me all warm and tingly.

"I'll let you be the judge of that."

"I'm curious, why did you approach me in the dressing room? I mean, I know we ended up in the same swimsuit, but I get the feeling it was more than that."

"Honestly, I saw you when you first got to the mall. My mom was dropping me off and you were walking from the bus stop. I recognized you from some of the West Orange-Montclair football games. When I saw you in the dressing room, I figured I'd speak."

"Oh, okay." Maybe I was wrong, read too much into our interaction.

"I also thought you were cute," Maya said.

My shoulders drooped with relief.

"Does that bother you? I just assumed when I was flirting with you that you were flirting back. Was I wrong?"

"Oh, no, not at all. I-I was flirting. I just wasn't sure if I was reading too much into what was happening."

"You weren't."

"That's good to know. I haven't done this before, at least not with a girl." Remembering what Nikki said, I hoped my admission wouldn't turn her off.

"I figured."

"That doesn't bother you?"

"No. Does it bother you?"

"No."

"Good. So, when can I see you again?"

"Oh, wow, uh…" I had expected us to talk about hanging out again, but for some reason the way she said it made me feel like she was asking me on a date.

"Janesse, I'm just asking when we can hang out. Maybe spend some time getting to know each other as friends and see where it goes. I've been in your shoes. I'm not going to push you into something you're not ready for."

I felt like such a coward. "Thanks."

"Are you free this Friday or Saturday?" Maya asked.

"I work at the Wellmont Theater and since it's the holiday weekend I'll be working and probably won't get off until about ten or eleven o'clock at night," I said dejectedly.

"Are you busy Memorial Day? You can test out your new swimsuit at my friend's pool party."

If I didn't have plans with anyone else except my family, I would've canceled them just for the chance to see Maya in that bathing suit again. "It's my birthday. My family is throwing me a party."

"Oh, happy early birthday."

"Thanks."

"Well, maybe we can plan for the following weekend. In the meantime, how do you plan to spend your summer?" Maya asked.

We talked for another two hours, and it was the longest and best phone conversation I'd ever had.

Chapter Seven

Maya and I talked almost every night that week about school, our friends and families, music, the news, any and everything there was to talk about, we covered it. By the end of the week, I was trying to figure out how we could work out seeing each other. I had even suggested breakfast since I didn't need to be at work until the afternoon, but she helped with a community art class on Saturday and had church on Sunday. I considered asking her to blow off her pool party and come to my party, but then I felt self-conscious about my family reading too much into our friendship.

Sitting at lunch with Nikki and Justin, once again thoughts of Maya occupied my mind.

"What are you grinning about?" Justin asked.

Nikki chuckled. "I think our Janesse is falling hard."

I slapped Nikki's arm. "Shut up."

Justin looked between the two of us. "Falling hard for who?"

Nikki cocked an eyebrow at me, and I stuck my tongue out at her, but neither of us said anything further.

"Oh, so it's like that now? Y'all can't include a brother in your love lives anymore?" Justin said with an exaggerated pout.

I looked down at my lunch and swirled a leftover tomato in the remainders of salad dressing. "I met someone last weekend and we've been talking for a week now."

"Oh."

I looked up just in time to see the flash of disappointment on Justin's face before it was quickly replaced with his carefree cocky grin.

"So, who is the guy? Do I need to check him out to give him my best friend stamp of approval?"

I hesitated in answering. Justin knew of my attraction to girls, but there had never been anyone serious worth mentioning to him. Maybe telling him would put a stop to whatever he was feeling for me beyond friendship. "It's a girl."

His eyes widened in surprise. "Oh, uh, do I know her?"

"No, she's from another school."

He recovered from his surprise and nodded. "Cool. That's cool. Uh, I have to stop by the library before my next class. I'll see you guys later."

"Justin," I called, starting to rise and follow him, but Nikki placed a hand on my arm to stop me.

"Give him some time to deal with it. He'll be all right," she said.

I wasn't so sure, and I felt a little guilty about it. I know I did nothing to encourage him, but I think he was seriously holding on to some hope that I would come around. There was a time I wished I could. Justin was a sweet guy, but a guy wasn't what I wanted.

"You really are into Maya," Nikki said.

"I think so. We've been talking every day. We just can't seem to find a way to see each other. As much as it will be nice to have the extra money for our getaway, I'm wishing I hadn't asked for more hours at work."

"What about your birthday party?"

"I thought of inviting her, but I'm not ready for the family, particularly my mother, finding out I may be dating a girl."

Nikki nodded. "I understand that. Maybe you can see each other after the party."

I slapped my palm to my forehead. "I didn't even think of that. But where are we going to go? Everything will be closed."

"Since you were planning to spend the night, hang at my house. Unless you want to be alone with her," Nikki said.

"No, I think, at least for now, we should be around other people. I don't want to blow this by listening to my body instead of my head. Maya said she wouldn't rush me into anything I'm not ready for and I promised myself, after Dante, that sex is going to be put on the back burner in any new relationships until I'm ready for something long-term. Right now, I'm not ready for that."

"Good for you. I just hope you can stick with it," she said.

I frowned. "So do I."

❖

That night I finished work at eleven and was so tired I dreaded the few blocks I had to walk home. My feet were killing me, I reeked of buttered popcorn, and I was starving because I didn't get a chance to eat anything but a candy bar for dinner. I walked out of the theater and saw Maya spotlighted by a streetlight, leaning against a bright yellow Volkswagen Beetle on the other side of the street.

"Maya?" I was confused and excited at the same time.

"Hey." Maya's dimples and gapped teeth were on full display when she greeted me.

I couldn't believe she was there. I walked slowly toward her. "Hey."

"I hope you don't mind. I couldn't wait another week without seeing you," she said.

I forgot how hypnotic her eyes were. "No, I don't mind at all."

Frowning, Maya reached up to run a thumb across my cheek. "You look tired."

I suddenly didn't feel as tired as I did when I walked out the theater. "A little."

"Would you like a ride home?"

She knew from our extensive conversations that I only lived a few blocks away, but I thought it was sweet she was offering. "Yes."

"You're not much for conversation tonight."

"Just trying to get over the shock of seeing you here. All day I was trying to figure out how to make this happen and here you are."

"Maybe we're psychically connected because I was doing the same thing, which is why I'm here."

We gazed at each other for a moment, and I was so tempted to kiss her that I had to physically step back to stop myself from doing it. She gave me a sexy look that told me she was thinking the same thing, then turned and opened the passenger door of her car.

"Cute car," I said after she got in.

"Thanks. It was passed along to me by my mother."

"It looks like you take really good care of it."

"I try. My father and I work on it together to keep it running smoothly."

"You didn't tell me you knew how to work on cars."

"Oh, I didn't? I'm a bit of a grease monkey. You already know my father loves classic cars, and I'm a daddy's girl, so I figured the only way I could spend as much time as possible with him is if I asked him to let me help with his cars. We've completely restored two together so far. Well, three if you count this one, but I did most of the work since it was going to be mine."

"That is so sexy," I said out loud before I could stop myself. I had less of a filter when I was tired.

"You think so?" she asked.

Well, the words were out there. I might as well claim them. "Yes."

We arrived at my house far too soon for my taste. "You can just pull up in the driveway."

Maya did as I suggested then turned off the engine and lights. We spent hours on the phone talking yet it seemed as if we suddenly had nothing to say as we sat silently in the car. After a few minutes she turned toward me.

"Janesse."

I turned toward her. "Yes."

"I really like you."

"I like you too."

"I mean REALLY like you."

I looked at her for a moment. Even in the dark I could see the brightness of her eyes and felt as if I could've sat there staring into them all night. I reached up and moved her bangs aside so that I could see them even better.

"I REALLY like you too." There, I said it out loud. The world didn't come crashing down, the ground didn't open beneath us to suck the car down into the fires of hell, and it felt wonderful.

"Are you sure? I told you I wouldn't rush you, but I also thought it would be better to be up front so that we can either walk away now before we get all caught up in feelings or just keep going and see where it leads us."

It was strange to hear the doubt in Maya's voice. When we talked, she always sounded so confident and sure of herself, and it bothered me that I was the reason for that doubt. I didn't want her to doubt herself. She was beautiful, talented, intelligent, had a great sense of humor, and any girl would be lucky to have her attention. For some strange reason, she picked closeted, confused, possibly bisexual, insecure me to be that girl.

"Yes, I'm sure."

"Good," she said before leaning across the console and pressing her lips to mine.

For a moment, I allowed myself to get lost in that kiss. In the feel of her soft lips, so much softer than any lips I had kissed before. Lost in the physical pleasure that warmed and tingled throughout my body. Lost in the feel of her soft body up against mine as our arms wrapped around each other. So lost that I forgot we were sitting in a car in front of my house where my mother could walk out any minute because she always waited up for me to come home when I worked late. I abruptly ended our heated kiss and pulled away breathing heavily. Trying to will my body to calm down.

"I'm sorry, that was definitely too soon," Maya said, looking flustered.

"No, it's just that…" I sort of pointed toward the house.

Maya looked toward the house and nodded. "Yeah, I guess making out in the car in your driveway wouldn't be the best way to come out to your mother."

I chuckled. "No, it wouldn't."

"You better go. I wouldn't want your mom worrying about where you are," Maya said sweetly.

I took her hand and brought it to my lips, placing a kiss on her knuckles. "Thank you for the ride home."

"You're very welcome. Call me tomorrow when you get off work. I don't care how late it is."

"Okay." I got out the car.

"Hey, Janesse."

I turned and leaned in the window. "Yeah."

"I'll always think of our first kiss whenever I smell buttered popcorn," she said with a grin.

I couldn't help but laugh. "Thanks."

I watched her pull off and gave a final wave before I made my way into the house. Mom was asleep on the sofa. I walked over, turned the TV off, and gave her a gentle shake.

"Mom."

She blinked sleepily up at me. "Ness, you're home." She looked up at the clock on the VCR. It was just past eleven thirty. It usually only took me five minutes to walk home. "You're late. Was everything all right?"

"Yeah, just a busy night. I'm going to take a shower and go to bed."

She stood up with a stretch and yawn. "Okay. J.J. and I were talking about going out to breakfast in the morning. You want to come with us?"

"No, you two have a good time."

Mom reached over and took my hand. "You know, you were right. He's a pretty special kid, and I wish I could take credit for it, but he's the way he is because he had you. Thank you for being such a wonderful big sister."

"That means a lot, but there's no need to thank me. I love the little guy."

Mom nodded then wrinkled her nose. "Go shower. You're making me want popcorn."

The morning of my birthday party, Nikki and I stood in front of my closet trying to decide what I should wear. Normally Jackie oversaw my special occasion wardrobe, but she was at Uncle Frank's with Mom and J.J. helping to set up. We were having the party at his house because he had a huge backyard and a whole outdoor kitchen set up.

"Who's all going to be there?" Nikki asked.

"Mom invited the entire clan, her and Uncle Frank's coworkers, Denise and Elizabeth flew in last night, most of the cheer squad and some of the players from the football team, the crew from the yearbook committee, and, of course, you and Justin. That's if he shows. He's been avoiding me all week."

"He'll be there. Either way, you definitely have to show up looking good."

"I guess," I said, not really into making a spectacle of myself.

"Janesse, c'mon, it's your eighteenth birthday, we're graduating high school in a few weeks, and you got a free ride to Spelman. It's time to celebrate. Heeeyy!" Nikki did a little dance move.

"I know, but you also know I don't like being the center of attention."

Nikki looked at me skeptically. "This coming from the girl who is the star of the cheer squad."

"That's different. I'm one of many, not the only one being gawked at and fawned over."

"I know what it is. You're pouting because your new girlfriend can't be there."

"Am not." I playfully pouted like a spoiled child.

"Okay, how about this. You pick something you think she'd like to see you wearing, then you'll feel like she's there."

"You're silly," I said.

My phone rang.

"Hello."

"Happy birthday, pretty lady."

I smiled so broadly my cheeks hurt. "Thank you, Maya."

Nikki started making kissing noises behind me, and I threw one of my stuffed animals from my bed at her.

"I won't keep you. I just wanted to wish you a happy birthday and to tell you I'll do my best to see you tonight."

"Okay. We should be back at Nikki's by ten at the latest."

"Okay. Tell her thank you for me."

"I will. Enjoy the pool party. Don't hurt anybody with that swimsuit."

Maya laughed and, as usual, it made me feel all tingly. "I'll try not to. Have a wonderful time at your party. I wish I could be there to celebrate with you."

"So do I. Bye."

"Bye."

I hung up the phone and turned back toward Nikki, who was grinning like the Cheshire cat.

"Shut up," I said, unable to stop smiling.

"You know, it's nice seeing you this way. All soft and glowing with love."

"Nobody said anything about love."

Nikki shrugged. "It's only a matter of time. Now, let's get you ready to party."

We decided on an outfit created by different colorful items Maya had picked out the day we met. Blue jeans; a pink, yellow, and blue striped off the shoulder blouse; a yellow belt; and a pair of pink ballet style flats. I finished the look off with mismatched yellow and blue acrylic hoop earrings for fun and pulled my recently braided hair back into a ponytail, tied up with a pink scarf. It was bright, fun, and comfortable.

"You look like birthday confetti," Nikki said.

I did a quick turn in the mirror. "Exactly what I was going for."

I looked at the clock. "We better head out."

"Wait, one more thing before we go. I wanted to give you my gift in private." Nikki took a small gift-wrapped box from her pocket and handed it to me.

"I told you not to get me anything."

Nikki snorted. "You tell me that every year, and when do I ever listen?"

"Never." I took the box and gently unwrapped it to reveal a small jewelry box that held a gold sculpted lotus flower pendant on a gold chain.

It wasn't fancy but it was the perfect gift. Nikki and her mothers practiced Buddhism. I had recently expressed an interest in it, even trying meditation for a few minutes each morning. Of all the symbols within the faith, the lotus flower was my favorite. I loved how the flower grew from mud to rise above the surface of the water into a beautiful blossom. The meaning of the three stages of the lotus flower also connected with me—a closed bud symbolized the beginning of a journey, a partly open flower symbolized the path, and a fully bloomed flower symbolized the end of the journey, the enlightenment. I felt like I was in the muck and mire of my journey right now, waiting for something to happen to give me the strength to break through and fully bloom. I had told Nikki all this recently.

Tears clouded my vision. "You remembered."

Nikki gave me a crooked grin, her eyes sparkling with unshed tears as well. "Of course." She took the box, removed the necklace, and walked behind me to put it on. "Janesse, since the first day I saw you something clicked in me." She turned me around to face her and took my hands. "And I don't mean romantically, I mean spiritually. I think it happened to you also. I didn't realize it at the time, I think we were both too young and too confused about our sexuality to even know what it was, so we just mistook it for a different kind of attraction. But then, when we decided our friendship was more important than the physical feelings we had, it felt like everything kinda fell into place. Over the past four years you have brought a love, understanding, and acceptance that none of my other friends have been able to do. You've become my friend, my sister, and most of all, my spiritual soul mate." Nikki's voice broke and she took a deep breath before continuing.

"If we had ever acted on what we were feeling back then I don't think we would have remained friends, and a piece of me would have always been missing in my life. You love me without boundaries, you accept me without question, and you've helped me with my own journey to finding the true me. I know you're struggling with finding your own path, but I hope that if I can't guide you, I can at least be there to hold your hand through your own journey. You deserve to be given everything you've given to me during our friendship. I hope this lotus flower will remind you not to give up because, like the lotus, you're stronger and more beautiful than you think."

"Wow," was all I could manage to get past the lump in my throat.

Simultaneously, we reached up to wipe away each other's tears and then started laughing.

"I see why you wanted to give me this in private." I laid my hand over the necklace. "Thank you, Nikki. For the necklace, for your friendship, for accepting me with all my drama and confusion, and for loving me like no one else has. I'm also glad we didn't act on what we were feeling and remained friends because I don't know how I would have gotten through some of the things I have without you to lean on. You are forever my sister-friend, and nothing will ever change that."

Nikki nodded and we embraced. "You're welcome. Now," she separated us, "let's go celebrate your big day."

When we arrived at Uncle Frank's house, they were pretty much finished with setting up. He was showing J.J. how to clean the grill and Mom, Jackie, my cousin Denise, and her partner, Elizabeth, were in the kitchen prepping the food.

"There's the birthday girl!" Denise said, coming around the counter with open arms.

I met her halfway for a big hug. "Hey, Denise."

She stepped back and held me at arm's length. "Look at you." She turned to Elizabeth who joined us. "Look at her, Liz. Doesn't she get more beautiful every time we see her?"

Liz and I hugged. "She sure does. So, how does it feel to be eighteen today?"

"The same as it did to be seventeen yesterday."

"Good. Always remember that. Age is just a number and you're as old as you feel," Liz said.

They both turned toward Nikki and greeted her with hugs as well. "Tell me your fabulous mothers will be here," Denise said.

"Yes. They were getting ready when we left, so they should be here soon."

"I just read Carol's latest book. It was wonderful," Liz said.

"I'm sure she'll be thrilled to hear that," Nikki said.

Denise took my hand. "If you all don't mind, I'm going to steal the birthday girl for a chat. Nikki, why don't you take my place helping Liz with the macaroni salad."

Denise led me to her old bedroom, which was now a guest room. The *Right On!* magazine celebrity posters that covered the wall were replaced by tasteful wallpaper and framed family photos. The frilly lace-and-pink-canopied bed was replaced by a king-size four-poster with Egyptian cotton sheets, a matching comforter, and various throw pillows. We sat on the bench at the end of the bed.

"Okay, Miss Ness, talk to me," Denise said.

"Now?"

"No better time than the present. Besides, it's going to be crazy in a couple of hours and there will be no place for privacy to talk."

I had called Denise and told her I'd like to talk while she was in town. I didn't think she would want to do it this soon. I touched the lotus necklace from Nikki, took a deep breath, and told Denise everything. From the time I first realized I liked girls in Indianapolis, to when I realized I was also attracted to boys and finished with what was happening with Maya. I even told her about how my friendship with Nikki started.

"Wow, you've had a lot going on and you've been dealing with it alone?" she asked.

"Not completely alone. I've had Nikki to lean on."

"It seems, from what you just told me, that you've both been going through an identity crisis. Nikki just found herself a lot quicker than you did. Why haven't you tried to talk to me about this sooner?"

I shrugged. "I guess I wasn't ready to talk about it with anyone besides Nikki."

"But now this girl Maya has you wanting to open up?"

I nodded. "She and Nikki are so open and unashamed of who they are. Then there's you, Liz, and Nikki's mothers. I want to be able to be like that. To decide who I am and stick with it so there isn't all this confusion."

"Oh, honey, just because we're all out and proud doesn't mean we aren't going through our own identity crisis. Do you know for the first three years after Liz and I moved in together as a couple her parents thought we were just roommates? When they came to visit, I had to sleep on the pullout sofa because they had to use what they thought was my room, but it was really the guest room. She kept promising me she was going to tell them, she just had to find the right time. Then her father had a heart attack, and although he recovered, she used that as an excuse for why she couldn't tell them. I finally couldn't take it anymore. I told her that until she could be open enough to come out to her parents then we couldn't be together. I wasn't trying to force her to choose between us, I was only tired of always having to be put back in the closet every time we were with her family. I had struggled long enough to come out and shut that door behind me for good, and nothing was making me go back in there. Not even the love I had for Liz."

"I take it she came around since you're still together."

Denise gazed down at her hands. "It took her a few months after I left to do it. Her parents barely spoke to her for the longest time. Her family is one of those old rich White Southern families that doesn't believe in mixing races and that homosexuality is a choice or mental illness. Me being her roommate was fine but finding out I was her lover and blaming me for corrupting their lily-white daughter wasn't. They no longer come to the house when they visit. They stay at a hotel and Liz has to go there to see them. I'm also no longer invited to any of their family functions. In the beginning, Liz wouldn't go either if I weren't welcome, but I told her I didn't want to be the one to keep her from her family.

I shook my head in disbelief. "Wow, I'm so sorry, Denise. I had no idea."

"I'm sure Nikki's mothers have their own stories to tell as well. Liz and I would love to get married, have our own kids, be confident that we could take care of each other in our old age, but we know none of that may ever be possible. Having kids, yeah, with a donor and both of us being inseminated at some point, but I'm sure you've probably seen how difficult it is for Nikki and her mothers with the bias, the looks, and the whispers. That's something Liz and I aren't sure we want to put a child through. Forget getting legally married, and if either of us ends up seriously ill or in the hospital, we wouldn't even be able to see each other."

This conversation was not making me feel confident about continuing to see Maya. "Then why do it? Why live a life like that?"

Denise patted my leg. "I know all of this sounds miserable, but when you love someone like I love Liz, it's all background noise. A love like ours goes deeper because it has to overcome so much adversity to last. If I had to choose to be gay I probably wouldn't, but I didn't have a choice. I was born this way. I've known since I was a little girl that I was different. That I didn't dream of a Prince Charming riding in on a white horse to sweep me off my feet like all my other female friends. I pictured an afro wearing, gun toting, wisecracking Foxy Brown blasting in the room and carrying me off into the sunset," she said with a smirk.

I couldn't help but laugh at that image. "She is hot. I'm sure there were a lot of straight women who would give it up for Foxy."

Denise chuckled. "Maybe. But they would be able to claim curiosity and continue with their lives. People like us can't always do that. Sure, there are a lot of gay people living normal hetero lives on the outside and creeping out of the closet on the downlow, but I can't imagine they're happy. I considered it when I saw how disappointed the family was when I came out, but the person I thought would be the most disappointed turned out to be the most accepting."

"Uncle Frank," I said.

"Yep. It had been just him and me for so long after Mommy died that all he wanted was for me to be happy. He's not worried about missing the opportunity to walk me down the aisle and hand me off to some wonderful man who will love and take care of his daughter like he did. Although he would love to have dozens of grandchildren and great-grandchildren to bounce on his knee, it won't be the end of the world if he doesn't get it."

I looked toward the door with a frown. "After finding out how my mom reacted toward you, I don't see her being as understanding as Uncle Frank."

Denise's brow furrowed. "Yeah, I'm not going to lie, Auntie's reaction hurt far more than I let on. It still hurts. She's been courteous to Liz, but that's about it. She only speaks to her when she has to, and she looks away if Liz and I publicly display the slightest bit of affection for each other. I almost told Liz not to come, but she insisted that if I can deal with her family being the bigots that they are then she can deal with Auntie."

"I wanted to invite Maya to the party, but I don't think I could act like she's just another one of my friends. Especially after Nikki told me I get all moon-eyed when I talk about her."

Denise's mouth quirked with amusement. "Moon-eyed, huh. So, you really do like this girl."

"Yeah, I do. This is different than with Dante. It was nice but it never really felt right to be with him. Like something was missing and that I always had to put on a show. With Maya I feel like I can be my regular, goofy, awkward self and she accepts it. It feels normal to be with her. It's kind of like my friendship with Nikki but more…" I couldn't think of the right words.

"On a more intimate level."

"Yeah, that's it. From the first day we met it was like we had known each other already."

"Some folks would call that soul mates."

I touched my lotus pendant. "Nikki said we were soul mates this morning."

Denise's brow quirked. "I thought you two were just friends."

I waved dismissively. "Oh, we are. We haven't thought about each other that way since that first summer. She believes friends can be soul mates. You think it's possible to have more than one soul mate?"

Denise shrugged. "I have no idea about any of that new age stuff, but I do believe it's possible to have a deep connection with more than one person on different levels. There's still an intimacy with a friendship that can almost surpass that of a lover or partner just without the physical aspect of the relationship. Your friendship with Nikki is obviously something special because it's born of acceptance. You accepted her for who she was from the beginning. Many gay women like Nikki have a difficult time finding relationships with family, friends, or otherwise that are so accepting because they can't accept themselves for who they are. They don't know how to be comfortable in their own skin because society is telling them that they're one way while their heart and mind tells them they're another. Your acceptance helped Nikki find her own in a time in her life when most young women like her get so frustrated trying to be what society thinks they should be that they spend their lives lost and unhappy, or worse, can't handle it and think maybe the world would be better off without them."

I hadn't thought of that in all these years of friendship with Nikki. I knew it bothered her sometimes when she got looks of outright disgust when people found out she was a girl. Especially when we were out, and she had to go to the restroom only to be embarrassed when she was told she couldn't be in there because it was the woman's restroom. She'd always been just Nikki to me, so I had no idea to what extent she might have been hurting from those incidents. It was something I would make sure to ask her about later.

Denise brought me back to our conversation. "Ness, let me ask you something. With Maya being out and you still figuring things out, do you really think it's the best thing for you to get into this relationship? Are you ready to deal with the rest of the family finding out, particularly your mom?"

I had avoided thinking about that problem since I started talking to Maya. "I don't know. I just know I like her and want to see where it goes."

"Okay, I'm going to suggest you find a gay and lesbian youth group that offers some type of counseling. It's confusing enough accepting that you're gay, but bisexuality is whole other level of confusion I wouldn't even be able to help you understand. If you're not ready for a youth group, then maybe you can talk to Liz. She's more familiar with the topic than I am."

I looked at Denise in surprise. "Liz is bisexual?"

"She went back and forth like you for a long time until we met. She says I pushed her over to the dark side, but I think she was just more attracted to women than men and I sort of convinced her which was the better species," Denise said, poking her chest out proudly.

I chuckled. "You think she would be willing to talk to me while you're here this week?"

"I don't see why not. I'll ask her. In the meantime, enjoy your big day without worrying about anything but having a good time."

"Thank you, Denise."

Denise pulled me into a hug. "Anytime, Ness."

"How'd it go?" Nikki accosted me as soon as I walked out the door.

"It went well. I'll tell you about it later."

"Okay, cool. Justin just got here."

I looked around and found him talking to Uncle Frank. "How's he acting?"

"Like his old self. I think he just needed some time to patch up his wounded pride."

"I wish there could have been a gentler way to deter him."

"Girl, you did that four years ago. It's not your fault he chose to ignore it. You never gave him any reason to think you had changed your mind, and one night of getting caught up in the moment isn't going to change that."

I pulled Nikki into a hug. "You are so good for my ego."

Nikki laughed. "What are best friends for. Now, I think we need to taste test the special birthday punch Liz and Denise made for us and hid in the fridge. I hear it's got a special kick to it. Maybe bring a glass to Justin as a peace offering."

I looped my arm through hers and walked back toward the house. "You don't have to ask me twice."

After the last guest left, my family insisted that I go and enjoy the rest of the evening. Nikki's moms stayed to help clean up, and Nikki and

I headed to her house. At some point during the party, we decided to change my meetup location with Maya to Eagle Rock Reservation, a large forest reserve and recreational park that bordered three towns. It had an awesome lookout point of the Manhattan skyline and was also where a lot of young folks liked to hang out after dark. There was a winding road that led up from one of the entrances nicknamed the Seven Bends. As you got toward the top of the bends, just before you reached the main park, there were points along the way where people wanting a little privacy would pull off the road to park and do whatever a couple needing privacy did late at night. I had never been one of those people. I was too paranoid about getting caught by the county police who patrolled the area, but I'd heard things.

I called Maya to let her know after we arrived at Nikki's.

"Yeah, you all hooked on that. All that smiling from one week of phone calls and a kiss?" Nikki said after I hung up.

"Shut up," I said, grinning. Her teasing didn't even dampen my mood.

"You sure you want me coming along? I could just drop you off and Maya could bring you home. I feel like I'm gonna be a third wheel."

"Yes, I'm positive. You'll keep me from doing something foolish like suggesting we pull into one of the little make-out holes up there and do something my heart is not ready to handle."

Nikki rolled her eyes. "So basically, I'm your human chastity belt."

"More like chaperone."

"Yeah, okay. Can I least call someone to meet me up there as well?"

I was surprised by that question. I had no idea Nikki was seeing anyone. "Sure. Something I need to know?"

To my disbelief, Nikki blushed. "I ran into Carrie the other day on my way to work, and she asked if I was free this weekend. I told her I'd let her know. Thinking this might be a good opportunity for us to hang. That way you and I can keep each other out of trouble."

It was difficult to keep what I really thought from my face. I didn't like Carrie, but if that's what Nikki wanted, who was I to tell her no. "Sure."

"Look, I know how you feel about her. That you think she's a stuck-up, bougie princess, but there's more to her than that." There she was, reading me like a book. "Besides, this way she'll have proof we're just friends because you'll be with Maya."

"Okay, okay, but it's my birthday. If she decides to start any shit with me, don't expect me to sit and be all nicey-nice."

Nikki chuckled. "If she starts any shit, I'll kick her to the curb myself."

"Cool. Let me just go freshen up, then we can head out."

We arrived right on time. Maya was already there looking a combination of cute and sexy as she leaned against her VW dressed in a denim miniskirt, jacket, and yellow tank top grinning just as broadly as I probably was. Nikki pulled into the spot next to hers and Maya opened the door for me.

"Hey, birthday girl." She leaned forward and pressed a soft kiss to my cheek, and it had the same effect as if she had kissed me on the lips.

"Hey there," I said.

We gazed at each other for what seemed like forever before Nikki clearing her throat interrupted us.

I felt my face heat with a blush. "Oh, uh, this is Nikki, but I'm sure you already know that since you've met before."

"Nice to meet you again, Nikki." Maya gave Nikki a friendly smile and offered her hand.

"You too, Maya."

Maya turned back toward me. "So, do you guys want to find a bench to sit on or go and enjoy the view?"

"Why don't we enjoy the view. We're waiting for one other person," I said.

"Your other friend Justin?" Maya asked.

"Uh, no. Nikki's date," I said, giving Nikki the side-eye.

Nikki rolled her eyes. "It's not a date. We're just hanging out. Like you guys."

Maya quirked a brow at me. "So, this is a date?"

My teasing Nikki seemed to backfire. "Uh…"

Maya gave me a playful shove. "I'm just teasing you. I would hope our first date would be the result of you officially asking me out on one."

I gave a nervous chuckle. "Oh, yeah, of course."

I glanced quickly over at Nikki and saw her trying to hold back a laugh. I gave her my silent "Shut up" look and she gave me her "What? I didn't say anything" look. The three of us leaned on the wall that bordered a sheer drop but gave a clear perfect night's view of Manhattan and the starry sky above.

Maya sighed. "I've only been up here once at night. I'd forgotten how pretty it was."

I looked at her profile and my heart skipped a beat. That's when I remembered I had brought my camera. I had been so distracted by Maya that I left it in the car. "Aw, man, I left my camera in the car. I'll be right back."

"No, stay here, I'll get it," Nikki said.

"Thanks."

"You were serious when you said you bring your camera pretty much everywhere," Maya said.

"Yeah, I never know what I might see that would make a great shot."

"I can't wait to see your portfolio."

"It's nothing fancy like you would see a professional photographer carry. More like a photo album than portfolio. I have to organize them better. Nikki's mom was helping me in the beginning, but it fell to the wayside with all the other activities I was doing."

"I guess so, cheerleader, school newspaper, yearbook committee, part-time job, taking care of your little brother. You sure you have time for a new friend?"

I turned to face Maya. "I'm sure I can fit one in."

She turned toward me. "Good, because I'd like to see you at least half as much as I talk to you on the phone."

Our hands were on the wall. Maya shifted hers so that our fingers touched. "I'd like that too."

"Hey, look who I ran into in the parking lot," Nikki said.

I had to tear my gaze from Maya's dreamy hazel eyes. Nikki and Carrie were walking toward us. "Hey, Carrie."

"Hello, Janesse. Happy birthday." Did I detect a genuine smile on Miss Stuck-up's face?

"Thanks. Carrie this is Maya, my…friend. Maya, this is—"

"Carrie Peterson, we've met," Maya said.

I turned to Maya and she didn't look too thrilled. I looked back at Carrie, and she was glancing down at her feet with an embarrassed look on her face, then I looked over at Nikki, who shrugged and looked as confused as I was.

"Maybe I should go. We can get together some other time," Carrie said to Nikki.

I looked over at Maya. "You two didn't…" I couldn't even finish the sentence.

Maya laughed out loud. "Hell no."

"Carrie?" Nikki gave her a questioning gaze.

Carrie looked guiltily at Nikki. "Maya and I met at a party once and didn't quite hit it off."

I snorted at that unsurprising revelation and everyone looked at me. "Sorry."

"Not quite the truth. You were trying to hook up with my date even though you knew she was with me," Maya said, sounding more annoyed than angry.

Nikki looked disappointed. "I'm sorry, Maya. I had no idea you two even knew each other when I invited her."

Maya shrugged. "It's all water under the bridge. Besides, she saved me some drama. The girl was all over the place and didn't know what she wanted."

I flinched. That hit a little too close to home.

"If it's worth anything, I apologize," Carrie said.

She looked and sounded genuinely sincere. Carrie Peterson contrite? I didn't think I'd ever see that day.

Maya looked between Nikki and Carrie. "Apology accepted. Besides, I don't want to ruin Janesse's birthday with old drama." She displayed those dimples and my heart fluttered.

Nikki looked relieved. "Here's your camera."

I gave her a nod of encouragement, although Carrie had just added one more item to the "Why I Don't Like Carrie Peterson" list.

"Wow, that's a nice camera. You don't play," Maya said.

"Yeah, Janesse is serious about her art. I can't wait till she hits the big time, and I can say I knew her when," Nikki said proudly.

I caught Carrie frowning. Oh Lord, here we go. When I turned back toward Maya, she was still looking impressed, Nikki's compliment of me not bothering her in the least. I took a few pictures of the skyline.

"I can imagine that's going to be a great shot. Like a postcard," Maya said.

"Would you like to take a few?" I asked.

I rarely let anyone touch my camera. Nikki had been the only one to ever do so, and even then, she was so afraid of breaking it she handed it back to me as if she'd catch fire from holding it. I stood behind Maya and held the camera up so she could grab hold of it.

"Now, look through the lens and tell me what you see?" I was in my element when it came to my camera, so I barely noticed the fact that

Maya's rounded behind was pressed up against me while I showed her how to use it.

"It looks like a bunch of blurry lights," Maya said.

"Okay, you need to adjust the focus so you can see it clearly, like this." I took her hand and placed her fingers around the lens to show her how to focus. "Now, turn it until you get a clear view."

Maya twisted the lens a few times. "Okay, it looks clear."

"Good." I shifted her finger to the button to take the picture. "Now just press this."

The camera clicked multiple times. "Oh, that took like three pictures. Did I do something wrong?" Maya asked nervously looking over her shoulder at me.

Our faces were mere inches apart from each other. I could lean forward just a little and brush my lips across hers. It was then I noticed how close we stood. How her curves fit so well with mine. When Maya licked her lips, I almost gave in.

"No, I have it set to take multiple pictures just in case anything comes into the frame as I'm taking my shot."

Maya turned and looked through the lens again, her hair brushing along my face and sending shivers of pleasure down my body.

"I don't know. I still think yours will be better."

Maya's voice was low, husky, and did things to my body that left me wondering if her voice affected me this way, what would her hands do? I cleared my throat and hesitantly put a respectable distance between us. She turned and handed me the camera. I stepped over to stand beside her and noticed Nikki and Carrie trying to look in every direction except at me and Maya. I clicked a picture of their profiles not because it was picturesque but as a distraction from the heat running through my body from Maya's closeness. I then turned and looked at Maya through my lens. Now that was picture worthy as she gave me a sexy smile. I took the picture and knew that it would always be the moment I fell hard for her.

The four of us spent the next hour taking pictures, being silly, and just talking. To my astonishment, Carrie was nice and proved she did have other things on her mind besides money, clothes, and looking good. She and Maya seemed to have silently squashed whatever beef lay between them, and we all got along like it really was a double date. I guess, technically, it was, but I wasn't ready to put a label on it yet and just enjoyed the moment.

I stifled a yawn, but Maya caught me.

"I guess since we all have school tomorrow, we should head home," she said.

"Yeah, I guess so," I agreed.

"I'm going to walk Carrie to her car. She's parked a little farther down," Nikki said.

I quirked a brow in her direction. She gave me the "Shut up" look and I gave her the "What? I didn't say anything" look.

"Okay, I'll meet you at the car."

"Cool." She handed me her keys and the four us made the short walk together to the parking lot.

"Thanks for letting me hang with you guys to finish out your birthday," Carrie said to me without her usual condescending tone.

"It was fun. Maybe we can do it again sometime." I genuinely meant it.

"I'd like that. Good night," Carrie said.

"Good night," Maya and I answered in unison.

Maya and I walked toward her and Nikki's cars as Nikki and Carrie walked to the other end of the parking lot.

"I'll wait with you," Maya said.

I leaned against Nikki's passenger door, and Maya stood across from me leaning against her car.

"This was fun," she said.

"Yeah, it was. Thanks for hanging with us."

"I wish I could have been at your party, but I understand why you didn't feel comfortable inviting me."

My face heated in embarrassment. "I'm sorry."

"There's no need to apologize. Like I said, I don't want to push you into something you're not ready for."

"Thanks."

"Nikki and Carrie are an interesting pair."

"Yeah, it seems Carrie knew what she wanted long before Nikki did."

"You don't like Carrie, do you?"

"Before tonight, I would've said no. We haven't gotten along since the first day we met. She's been nasty toward me ever since. I guess seeing you and me together has finally convinced her that Nikki and I really are just friends. She no longer sees me as a threat."

"I see," Maya said. "From what I saw with how you two act

with each other and how much you talk about her over the phone, it's obvious you and Nikki are close."

"Does that bother you?"

"No. I think it's cool to have a friend who cares about you and has your back like that. I would never try and come between that."

I didn't realize I was holding my breath waiting for her answer until it came out in a sigh of relief. "Cool."

I stood quietly debating with myself what to say or do next. Just do it, Janesse, I told myself. "So, would you like to go on a real date with me?"

She gave me that beautiful, dimpled smile. "Just you and me?"

I gave her a goofy grin in return. "Yes."

"Then yes."

"Okay. How about a movie next weekend?"

"Sounds good to me."

"Then it's a date."

"Yes, it is."

"I'll call you tomorrow with movie times."

I worked at the theater and normally could spout all the movies currently playing, ones that were coming soon and times, but for the life of me, at that moment, I couldn't remember any of that. I spotted Nikki walking toward us with a peppier step than usual.

"You ready to go?" she asked.

I smirked at her knowingly. "Yep." I looked back at Maya.

"Good night, birthday girl," she said.

"Good night." It took everything I had not to pull her into my arms and kiss her. I settled for the gentle squeeze of her hand and the air kiss she blew me.

We climbed into our respective cars, and Nikki waited for Maya to pull out of her spot before she backed out.

"I take it you had a good night with Maya," Nikki said.

"Yes. I take it Carrie got to her car all right," I teased her back.

"Shut up," she said, the two of us grinning happily.

CHAPTER EIGHT

As I stood outside the theater waiting for Maya, I fidgeted with my sweater, running my fingers along the collar because I felt as if I were being strangled.

"Hey."

Maya had come up from behind, scaring the crap out of me. "H-Hey."

She looked at me from head to toe and chuckled. "I guess we had the same look in mind."

I looked her over to find we were dressed similarly. As if we had called each other to plan our outfits, except her sweater was pink and mine was white.

The humor of it eased my nervousness a bit. "I guess so."

"Do we need to get tickets?" Maya asked.

"Nope. I know somebody who works here." I gave her a wink and opened the door for her. "After you," I said with a slight bow. My heart skipped a beat as she flashed me with her dimples.

We decided to see *Sixteen Candles*, which turned out to be the perfect first official date night movie. Not only did we develop a mutual crush on Molly Ringwald, but I got to hold Maya's hand the entire time once the lights went down. After the movie we walked up to Church Street, stopped to grab a couple of slices at a pizzeria, and found a bench outside to eat and talk.

"Are you looking forward to graduation?" Maya asked.

"Yes and no. I'm looking forward to finally getting out of high school but nervous about the next step. I've never really been on my own so far from home."

"I think my parents are more nervous about it than I am. They're flying down with me even though I told them there was no reason to do so since we have family down there that can help me get settled."

Would Mom and Dad want to fly down to Spelman with me as well? We hadn't really talked about it since I told them I had decided to accept the scholarship. "I guess it'll be nice for you to have family there."

Maya shrugged. "As long as they let me live my life and don't feel the need to check up on me to report back to my parents, I hope so."

"Do they know you're gay?"

"Yes. The whole family doesn't know, but enough family gossiping has been done that most do."

I looked down and fidgeted with the greasy napkin in my hand. "I wish I had your and Nikki's confidence."

Maya took the paper plate and napkin from my hands and tossed them in the trash can nearby with hers then sat back down next to me. She turned to face me, propping a leg up on the bench and resting her arm along the back of it.

"I told you before, it wasn't easy for me to come out to my family. It took me a year after I could no longer deny it to myself to get up the courage to do it. My mother grew up in a conservative Christian home, so it was not easy for her to accept. She still has moments when she hopes it's just a phase and that I'll change. It's not all roses and flowers for me. I imagine it may be a little easier for Nikki considering her mothers are gay. You'll know when it's time. Don't force yourself to do it before you're ready."

"You wouldn't mind dating someone in the closet?" I asked.

She gave me that heart stealing smile. "I'm here, aren't I."

I turned and mirrored the way she was sitting, placing my hand on the back of the bench close enough to hers to let our fingertips touch. "Yes, you are, and I'm glad."

A few weeks later, I stood in my cap and gown with a cheesy grin as the Montclair High School Class of 1984 graduation ceremony ended. When Nikki, Justin, and I finally worked our way through our fellow classmates to find each other we wrapped our arms around each other for a group hug, laughing, crying, and whooping with joy.

"I can't believe this is it," Justin said, not even trying to hide his tears.

I wiped my nose with the tissue I had stowed in my dress pocket. "Me either."

Nikki sniffled. "Our childhood has officially come to an end."

We looked at each other wistfully as the reality of this new chapter in our lives hit us.

"I know none of us are leaving until August, but let's promise to stay in touch as much as possible when we do. Even if it's just sending one of those corny greeting cards that says 'Thinking of You' every now and then." I was trying not to bawl like a baby.

Nikki put her pinkie out. "I promise."

Justin wrapped his pinkie around hers. "I promise."

I wrapped my pinkie around theirs. "I promise."

"Aww…isn't this sweet," Jackie teased us. "Your parents are growing impatient to shower you with praise and affection."

Justin swaggered up to Jackie with one of his cocky grins and his arms spread. "What's wrong, Jackie, you needing a hug 'cause you're going to miss me too?"

Jackie snorted. "Boy, please. You wouldn't know what to do with all this woman."

Justin didn't give up. "Guess there's only one way to find out."

I swatted Justin upside the head, knocking his cap off. "Give it up, Justin." I looped my arm through Jackie's.

"Can't blame a man for trying."

We all laughed and made our way up and out of the amphitheater to where our parents were gathered. Mom was talking to Justin's parents as Dad was talking to Nikki's. Since Nikki, Justin, and I had to come to the school early, I'd left with them. Dad offered to drive everyone else, so I was worried about him and Mom being together for the first time since their divorce.

"How've they been?" I whispered to Jackie as we walked toward the group.

"So far they've at least been courteous toward each other. I don't know how well that will last once we get to Uncle Frank's for dinner with Tanya there." Jackie sounded as worried as I was.

After kicking the young homewrecker to the curb not long after J.J. and I visited Dad that first summer, he hung solo for a while. Then two years ago he met age-appropriate Tanya at a travel conference and had been genuinely happy ever since. They were both executives in the same industry, had been married previously, and had grown kids. Well, Tanya had grown kids. Dad still had J.J. as his youngest, who Tanya adored. Mom had gotten jealous after hearing J.J. talk about how great Dad's girlfriend was after our visit last summer. Before the decision had been made to have J.J. live with him, she'd threatened not to let

J.J. visit this summer claiming she didn't know who Dad was bringing around her son. Mom had started going to therapy since then, and she and Dad had a long phone call one night with her apologizing for the threat and, upon her therapist's suggestion, she even spoke with Tanya since she and Dad were now living together. Her therapist thought it would help Mom feel some comfort in knowing Tanya would be good to J.J since he was going to be living with them. I still worried, though. They were all friendly now, but this would be the first time Mom and Tanya would meet in person and there was no telling what direction that would go. Mom wouldn't make a public scene since other people would be there, but she could change her mind really quick about letting J.J. go back with Dad as planned in a couple of weeks.

"There they are. Our esteemed graduates." Dad was beaming happily.

I rushed into his open arms. "Hey, Dad." He and Tanya had arrived late last night, so this was the first I'd gotten to see him.

"Hey, Nessy. I'm so proud of you." He squeezed me tight.

I officially introduced him to Nikki and Justin, still finding it strange that this would be their first time meeting him. After hugs all around, we headed to Uncle Frank's for dinner. The introduction between Mom and Tanya was like watching two female lions approaching each other warily with Dad in the middle. They were courteous toward each other, but there was no lengthy conversation. They went about their way with no issues or evil eyes, and we all seemed to breathe a collective sigh of relief.

Dad walked over and wrapped an arm around my shoulders. "How are you feeling? Turned eighteen last month, graduated high school today, heading off to college in a couple of months."

I blew out a breath. "A little overwhelmed but happy. Happier than I've been in an awfully long time."

"I'm so glad to hear that. How've things been with your mom?"

"Good. I think the therapy is helping. Hopefully, she'll keep it up after we're all gone. This will be her first time alone and I'm nervous for her."

"Uncle Frank and I had a long talk about that last night. He'll do his best to keep her on track. When are you guys leaving for your graduation getaway?"

"In the morning. The drive is only a little over an hour, but we want to get there as early as possible to get as much time to chill as we can."

"You have enough money to cover everything Nikki's moms aren't covering?"

"Yes, Justin, Nikki, and I have been saving up for this for months. We just have to cover food, incidentals, and entertainment."

"All right. You be safe. As you know, Tanya and I will be staying in the city for a week for some sightseeing, but don't hesitate to let me know if you have any problems and I'll drive down."

I wrapped my arm around Dad's waist and gave him a squeeze. "We'll be fine, Dad. No need to worry."

"You're my baby girl, I'll always worry."

After dinner, Nikki, Justin, and I decided to head to the basement for a game of pool.

"How did Carrie take the news that we weren't inviting anyone else on our vacation?" I asked Nikki.

"She whined about me caring more about my friends than her and told me maybe some time away from each other would be good."

"Wow. Are you okay?" I asked.

Nikki nodded. "I'm actually relieved. Here I was, all these years, intimidated by her confidence and she's even more insecure than I am, which makes her really needy."

Justin smirked. "Why do you think she always had her crew with her? They hyped her up."

"Yeah, I'm seeing that. Especially now that they aren't around as much since we started seeing each other," Nikki said.

"Hey, whatever works for you." I was only glad I no longer had to worry about Carrie breaking Nikki's heart.

Nikki stood to take her shot that had been delayed by our conversation. "Besides, we both decided once we go off to school it's over. Neither of us is into trying to do a long-distance thing our first year of college."

"What about you and Maya. You going to try and keep seeing each other since you'll both be in Atlanta?" Justin asked me as he took his shot.

"We haven't talked about it. When we first met, we talked about how cool it was that our schools will be so close, but not since then." Honestly, I hadn't even thought about it. Did I want to be trying to maintain a relationship during my freshman year and first time away from home on my own?

"See, that's why I chose not to be saddled with a girlfriend this past year. Too much work," Justin said.

Nikki gave him the side-eye. "You chose or did all the girls at school figure out your game and weren't interested in playing it?"

"What game? I'm honest with every chick I date. I'm just out for a good time, not to be tied down. It's too bad Carrie's into girls. We would've been perfect for each other," Justin said.

"Believe me when I tell you that she would have you pussy-whipped so bad, all your swag would be like smoke in the wind." She waved her hand in the air.

Justin shrugged. "Only one way to find out."

Nikki looked at him as if to say "Fool, please," then they burst out laughing.

I walked between them and wrapped an arm around both of their waists. "I'm so glad we're spending this week together. I'm definitely going to miss this."

Justin pulled Nikki and I into a hug. "One last hurrah for the Montclair Musketeers."

After our graduation dinner, Justin and I went home to grab our things for our week at the shore and met back at Nikki's house, where we decided to spend the night to save time when we left in the morning. After a trip to the grocery store to buy food and supplies, we watched a couple of movies then called it a night. It was funny how much had changed from the last time we had all slept over at Nikki's. The sight of Justin's sculpted naked torso and low-riding pajama pants still made me feel unexpected things, but I was better able to hide it, and morning didn't find me ogling him in his sleep like last time. With it being a weekday, we only had a little traffic and made it to Seaside Heights in record time.

"You know, this would be a great party house," Justin said as we put our groceries away.

Nikki gave Justin a look of warning. "This is not a frat house, Justin, it's a rental that my parents are paying for. Partying is not happening here."

"What? Just a few people, grill some burgers and dogs, get a few cases of beer, and chill. I'm not trying to turn this into Animal House," he said.

"Unless it's people we know that just happen to be down here, it's not happening," Nikki said with finality.

Justin poked his lips out. "Yes, Mom."

I bit back a laugh. Nikki gave me a frown. "You did sound like one of our mothers."

"Shut up," Nikki said.

"Once we're done with this, why don't we change and hit the beach and boardwalk. Maybe have lunch there," I suggested.

They agreed and we each went to our rooms to change. I took the time to call Maya.

"Hey, Maya."

"Hey." I heard the smile in her voice and could picture her dimpled cheeks. "How was your graduation?"

"Boring, but dinner was good. Mom and Tanya seem to be on friendly terms for now."

"That's good. I know you were worried. Are you at the beach house?"

"Yeah, we just got here about an hour ago. We're going to head down to the beach. I just wanted to give you a quick call."

"You miss me already?"

"Only if you miss me."

"I do."

I sat on the bed and twirled the phone cord around my fingers. "I miss you too. Maybe I can call you tonight, before I go to bed."

"I'd like that," Maya said, her voice sounding sexier than usual.

"Janesse, you ready?" Nikki yelled as she barreled into the bedroom, then stopped short and covered her mouth as she noticed me on the phone. "Sorry," she mouthed and tiptoed back out of the room.

"I guess you have to go," Maya said.

"Yeah. Talk to you tonight?"

"Yep. Have fun. Call me as late as you like."

"Okay, bye."

"Bye."

I hung up grinning and feeling like I was floating around the room as I dug through my luggage. I wore the bathing suit Maya had picked out for me with a pair of cutoff denim shorts, flip-flop shoes, a floppy beach hat, and sunglasses. I grabbed my beach bag then made my way downstairs.

"Well, excuse me, did we pick up a celebrity on the way here?" Nikki said as I came down the stairs.

I did a little spin. "You like?"

"Was that all picked out from your future celebrity stylist girlfriend?" Justin asked.

"Everything but the shorts. Jackie left these behind, so I sort of claimed them."

"Well, you fill them out quite nicely." Justin stared and grinned for a little too long then turned away holding his backpack in front of him. "I left my hat in the kitchen. I'll be back."

We watched his retreating figure. "I think somebody has been a little too long without some loving."

I wrinkled my nose in disgust. "Eww."

"I don't blame him." She looked me up and down approvingly. "Maya did a great job with that bathing suit. You look hot."

I blushed a little. "Thank you."

Justin came back, baseball cap low over his eyes, keeping them averted from me. "Y'all ready?"

Nikki and I both did our best to hold back our amusement, but a few snickers escaped. He ignored us and headed out the door.

By the time we hit the boardwalk Justin slowed down enough for us to catch up and seemed to be over his annoyance with us. Moments later, Nikki and I were relaxing on our beach blankets as Justin ventured out into the surf, hopping the waves or riding them in on his belly. Once it started getting crowded, he made his way back up to us. We sunbathed and chatted before Nikki decided to head to the shoreline to hang out, leaving Justin and me alone.

"So, things between you and Maya seem to be getting pretty serious," Justin said.

"I don't know if it's getting serious, but we are getting close."

"You seem different when it comes to her than you did with Dante. Is it because she's a girl?"

"No…maybe…I'm not sure. I just feel like I can be myself around her."

"And you can't do that around Nikki…or me?"

"Of course, I can but it's different. You and Nikki are my friends. Maya is something more."

"Do you think you could ever find that something more with a guy?"

I turned to face Justin. "I honestly don't know. When I was with Dante it was nice, but I felt like there was something missing. With Maya, it feels easy and natural. I don't have that feeling of something missing."

Justin looked back toward the shoreline then back at me. "The night of prom. When we slow-danced, I know you felt something.

Then, later, at Nikki's, there was something then as well, or was I just imagining it?"

I hesitated in answering. I cared too much about Justin to lie to him, but I also didn't want to hurt him. "You weren't imagining it." When a cocky grin began to appear, I raised my hand to cut off any thoughts he was having. "But it was only physical attraction, Justin. I value our friendship too much to act on something that isn't going to go anywhere."

"So, you are attracted to me," he said, undeterred.

I threw my hands up in frustration. "Did you not hear the rest of what I said?"

He took my hand. "I heard you and I also value our friendship, but why can't that attraction and friendship turn into something more? My grandparents started out as friends. My grandpa said he knew the moment he saw my grandma that she was going to be his wife, but it took her a couple of years to figure it out. He said because they were friends first it bonded them in a way that jumping right into romance wouldn't have. They've been married for seventy-five years," he said proudly.

I looked at Justin, thought about our friendship, and tried to imagine being married to him for that long, and the thought scared the hell out of me. Not because of him personally, he really was a sweet, easy-going, caring guy under all that cockiness, and I loved him, but the problem lay with him being a HIM. I mean, right now, I couldn't see myself married at all, let alone seventy-five years, but whenever Nikki and I imagined what celebrity we would like to marry, it was always a woman for me. While most girls my age were dreaming of one day meeting Michael Jackson and falling in love, I dreamed of his sister Janet. I slid my hand from Justin's.

"Justin, I don't see us that way."

Justin looked down at his empty hand and back at me with disappointment. "So that's it. You meet Maya and you no longer like guys?"

"I didn't say that." How could I explain it to him when I didn't understand it myself?

"So, it's just this guy."

"I didn't say that either."

Justin shook his head. "You're not saying much of anything, Ness." He got up and walked down to where Nikki stood in hip deep waves.

I watched her greet him by shoving him in the water then he stood back up and they started talking. I self-consciously wondered if I was the topic of their conversation. If Justin poured his heart out to Nikki the way I did. Nikki had brought our little trio together and seemed to be the glue keeping us from unraveling, but would it be enough if I kept hurting Justin's feelings? Why couldn't I bring myself to tell him I didn't want us to be more than just friends? Nikki leaned in and whispered something to Justin. They turned and slowly made their way up to the shoreline and stopped. They faced each other and Justin smiled at something over Nikki's shoulder. I turned to see that he was looking at a woman standing nearby, who looked to be a little older than us. The woman boldly smiled back at him, and Justin winked at her. He said something to Nikki then made his way over to the other woman while Nikki walked back up toward me. I looked back toward Justin, watching him and the woman talk. I recognized Justin's playa face and saw the woman giving it right back to him and turned away to find Nikki watching me curiously.

"What?" I asked in annoyance.

Nikki shook her head and sat beside me. "Nothing. Justin and I were talking about grabbing something to eat. You ready to go?"

"Yeah. Is he? Seems a little busy." It took everything I had to focus my attention on looking through my bag for my shorts and not at Justin.

I ignored the sting of hurt to my pride as I wondered how he could be asking me about being more than friends one minute and pushing up on some chick the next.

"Look, Janesse, I saw you two talking a few minutes ago and have a fairly good idea what you were talking about. It's probably not my place to say this, especially since both of you are my friends, but until you tell Justin outright that you are not attracted to him or want to be more than friends, you're going to keep hurting him. That," she said, indicating Justin flirting with the other woman, "is his way of dealing with it."

"I told him I value our friendship and that just because we have a physical attraction for each other doesn't mean we have to act on it."

Nikki frowned at me. "That was a cowardly explanation, especially since you know his feelings are more than physical."

I looked down at my lap in shame. "I know, but I can't explain it to him the way I need to. Everything I say will either be weak or a lie."

"Then lie to him. Take him out of his misery. Unless you do have feelings for him."

I threw my head back. "I don't know," I groaned out.

Nikki chuckled. "Do you like the boy or not?"

"Of course, I like him, he's my friend, but I also think he's hot and it's weird to think a friend is hot."

Nikki quirked a brow. "You used to think I was hot."

I threw my shorts at her. "I got over it though."

"Damn, that hurt," she said playfully.

"Seriously, Nikki, what am I going to do? I really do like Maya and want to keep seeing her, but it seems like every time I get around a half-dressed Justin, my body has a mind of its own. If it's just a physical thing, why hasn't it completely passed since I started seeing Maya?"

"With Maya, is it more emotional attraction or physical?" Nikki asked.

I thought about how comfortable and free I felt around Maya. I also thought about how just kissing her was never enough for me. How the anticipation of going all the way with her was killing me. "Both."

"Have you guys had sex yet?"

"You know I would have told you if we had."

Nikki shrugged. "Hey, I don't expect you to tell me every time you get your freak on with someone."

"You can at least expect to hear about the major ones." I frowned. "Maya said we should wait until I'm sure. I keep telling her I am, but I don't think she means when I'm sure I want to have sex."

"Probably not. She wants to be sure you're not one of those chicks that bounces back and forth because they're too scared to come out or simply curious."

"I'm not curious, I really do like girls."

"Yeah, but you also have no problem liking guys either. Some lesbians may be fine with dating a bisexual chick, but most prefer not to be a pastime until the right guy comes along."

"It's not like that with me."

"You sure about that? You fooled around with a couple of chicks from your squad until Dante came along, then you pretty much kicked them to the curb. You got tired of Dante, ended up with Maya, and now you're faced with feelings you've had for Justin but won't admit to. You're my girl, and I love you, but I gotta be honest. I think you're too confused about your sexuality to be trying to get serious with someone like Maya. It's obvious she's not into playing games and trying to be in this with you on a serious level. She's out, she's hot, and she's got her head on straight. She could have any chick she wants, and she chose you, Janesse. You better be damn sure you want to choose her."

I looked over toward Justin. He and the woman were still talking. She reached up, slid a hand down his bicep, and licked her lips seductively. I quickly turned away.

"I was checking her out earlier and noticed her watching Justin while he was out in the water. He looked upset when he came back out with me so I pointed her out thinking it might cheer him up," Nikki explained. "I thought it might also help keep him distracted with someone other than you. Give you some space."

There was that glue, trying to keep the trio from falling to pieces. "Thanks."

A moment later, Justin jogged over and squat down before us. "Ready for some food? I'm starving."

"When are you not starving?" Nikki said.

Justin grinned. "I've got a date tonight. I need sustenance to keep my strength up."

"Tonight? You just met the girl." I hoped that didn't sound as petty as it felt saying it.

Justin narrowed his gaze at me. "You almost sound jealous, which couldn't be the case since we're…just friends."

I sat up and shoved him so that he fell on his ass with a "oof" then shoved my stuff into my bag. "I'm going to rinse my feet off. I'll meet you guys up there."

"You can be such an asshole," I heard Nikki say as I stomped away.

CHAPTER NINE

After lunch we headed back to the house. Since Justin had plans of his own, Nikki and I decided to go back to the boardwalk after we showered and dressed. Justin stayed behind to, in his words, rest up for what would probably be a long night. Nikki and I spent the rest of the afternoon and evening at the arcade and then drinking and dancing at a nearby bar. When we got back to the house the lights were on, but Justin wasn't there. He left us a note telling us what hotel and room number he was going to be in case of an emergency. It was probably the effects of the alcohol, but I had an insistent urge to march over to the hotel, bust into this chick's room, and beat the shit out of Justin. I'm sure most girls would beat the shit out of the other girl, but it wasn't her fault Justin was acting like a complete ass. Then again, if anyone were to blame, it was me, but I couldn't very well beat the shit out of myself. At least not physically, but I sure did it mentally before I decided to call Maya at one in the morning.

"Hello," Maya answered sleepily.

"Hey, Maya," I slurred drunkenly. "Did I wake you?"

"Hey, yes, but that's okay." I heard her shuffling on the other end. She must have been sitting up in bed. "You must be having a good time."

"Yeah, Nikki and I went dancing and drinking."

Maya chuckled. "Are you drunk calling me?"

I grinned stupidly. "Maybe. I miss you."

"I miss you too."

"You should come down here. You could stay in the room with me or if you're not comfortable with that there's another bedroom. It has two sets of bunk beds, but they look comfortable and you can sleep in a different bed every night you're here." I knew I was drunken rambling, but I couldn't get my thoughts straight to talk coherently.

"Janesse, maybe you should get some sleep."

"But I don't want to sleep, I want to talk to you. I want you here with me so that I can touch you and kiss you and do all the things I dream of doing to you."

Maya sighed. "You're drunk, and I would rather not have this conversation while you're like this. Sleep it off and we can talk tomorrow. Okay?"

"Fiiiine. G'night."

"Good night."

I did something I never do when Maya and I talked on the phone. I hung up first. Annoyed that she had blown me off. Yeah, I was drunk, but that didn't mean we couldn't talk. I flopped back on the bed in frustration. What was wrong with me? Was I one of those girls who had to have her cake and eat it too without any regard to others' feelings but my own? I wanted Maya. REALLY wanted Maya. I also wanted Justin but not like I did Maya. Maya was like a delicious full entrée that you know will appease your hunger and leave you satisfied. Justin was like the tempting dessert you sometimes crave having before the entrée. You know that you're going to be too full to really appreciate it once you finish the first two courses, so you decide to appease yourself by sneaking a taste of the dessert and then end up eating it all, spoiling your dinner. I yawned, too drunk and too tired to continue with such a complicated line of thinking. I kicked off my shoes, not even bothering to take my clothes off, curled up on top of the covers, and fell asleep.

The next morning, while Nikki and I made breakfast, Justin strolled in looking like he hadn't slept all night. His shirt was barely buttoned, the high top of his fade was misshapen, and his eyes were barely open.

"Coffee?" Nikki asked.

"Bed," Justin croaked as he trudged his way up the stairs.

"Well, guess it's just the two of us today. Another beach day?" I asked Nikki.

"We are at the beach. Maybe come back and throw some burgers and dogs on the grill for lunch?"

I shrugged. "Works for me."

"Are you okay?" Nikki asked as we sat down to eat.

"I'm fine," I lied.

"Mm-hmm." Nikki looked at me skeptically.

"Shut up," I said half-heartedly.

Justin joined us when we came back for lunch then hung out on the boardwalk with us until dinner. Nikki and I threw together some stir-fry and sat and watched TV for the rest of the night while Justin changed into a less casual outfit and left to meet up with his college girl. This was the routine for the next few days. Justin would stumble in around seven in the morning, sleep until noon, spend the afternoon with Nikki and me, and then bounce back out around eight at night. He and I were back on friendly terms but not enough for me to ask about what he was doing every night. I knew he wasn't drinking because he never came in smelling of alcohol. He did come in smelling of perfume and sex, which I unsuccessfully tried to ignore until I fell asleep at night and had several vivid dreams of him and Miss College having wild sex all night long. Like she was a succubus draining Justin of all his energy as she got sexier and more beautiful. In one dream I even joined her, literally sucking Justin dry and laughing with her as he withered away into a hollow husk of himself. That scared the hell out of me, and I woke up sweating and crying.

Then, one night, Justin didn't rush upstairs to change his clothes. He squeezed between Nikki and me on the sofa with a bag of chips and watched TV with us.

"Staying in tonight?" Nikki asked, reaching into his bag of chips.

"Yeah," Justin said, not taking is eyes off the TV screen.

"What happened to your friend?" Yeah, I had to be the one to go there because I was obviously a glutton for punishment. I could see Justin looking at me from the corner of my eye, but I looked down at my bowl of ice cream as if it were the most interesting thing in the world.

"It was fun for a few nights but got old really quick," he said.

"Well, welcome back," I said.

We watched TV until late into the night then headed to bed. As tired as I was from spending another day on the beach and boardwalk, I tossed and turned for an hour. I had called Maya earlier in the evening and didn't want to wake her so I decided a cup of tea might help. As I made my way downstairs, I noticed a light was on and heard someone in the kitchen. Justin was raiding the cookies Nikki had made for dessert dressed in those damn low-riding pajama pants and no shirt. I started to go back up but figured I couldn't run forever. If things were going to get back to normal, me avoiding being alone with Justin wouldn't help.

"Mind if I join you?" I asked.

"Were they calling you in your sleep too?" He waved a cookie in front of me.

"No, I was just coming down for some tea, but what's tea without cookies?"

"Yeah, especially Nikki's famous chocolate chunk peanut butter cookies."

I nodded and put the kettle on the stove for some tea as Justin poured himself a glass of milk and added about four tablespoons of chocolate syrup.

I wrinkled my nose in disgust. "How can you eat so much sweet on top of sweet?"

"It's my one vice," he said.

I snorted. "Oh, you think you only have one?"

Justin's eyes widened in mock innocence. "What other vices could I possibly have?"

Just as I started to speak, the kettle went off and Justin cracked up at my open mouth combined with the whistling sound of the tea kettle. I shook my head and quickly removed the kettle from the burner so it wouldn't wake Nikki.

"Wanna sit out back?" Justin asked as I topped my tea off with some milk and honey.

"Okay."

"I'll bring the cookies."

He got a small plate and stacked about four cookies on it. They had to be stacked because Nikki didn't know how to make small cookies. They were always as big as a saucer.

"As big as those things are, I'm probably going to just eat one of them," I said.

"Oh, I know. The rest are for me." He held the plate close to his chest.

"I should've known."

We headed out the back door to the yard and sat together in one of the double wide lounge chairs. Justin passed me a cookie and we quietly munched on our late-night treat as we gazed up at the clear night sky.

"Hey, I'm sorry about the other day," Justin said.

"No need to apologize. You had every right to ask about my feelings for you. I wasn't as clear as I would've liked to be in explaining things to you."

"You don't owe me any explanations, Ness. You made it clear years ago that we're just friends. I've just been too hardheaded to believe it. Guess I'm not used to anyone resisting all this charm and good looks."

"Boy, you are so full of yourself."

Justin was quiet for a moment. "I'm really not. People expect me to be because I'm the light-skinned pretty boy athlete all the girls want, so that's what I give them. But you and Nikki are different. You guys see past all that and accept me in all my geekiness. Nikki's my boy. I know that's strange saying that about a girl, but you understand what I mean. But you, Ness." He faced me. "You're something different. You're fun, honest, and real. I watch you with your brother and how you've stepped up over the years dealing with your mom and her issues, and I see such a strong chick. I tried to get over you. Tried seeing you as just a friend, even when you were dating Dante, I tried to keep my distance, but it was killing me the whole time. Every girl I date I end up comparing to you, which is why I don't stay with them for long because there is no comparison. What I feel for you is real, not some schoolboy crush."

I started to speak, but Justin shook his head.

"Let me finish. What I feel is real, but I also understand you don't, and may never feel the same way. I know you're trying to figure stuff out about your sexuality so I'm not going to make things even more confusing by coming at you like I did the other day. I won't lie to you about how I feel. I care about you, Ness, and I'll be here for you no matter where your life goes. If Maya is what you want, I accept that. If it's guys, but not this guy, I'll accept that too. But I want you to know that if, by some chance, you have more than friendly feelings for me I'm open to accepting you as you are, bisexual or straight, as long as I'm a part of your life."

I looked at Justin in disbelief. "You would be willing to be in a relationship with someone who's attracted to women?"

"Not just someone, you."

"And what if I decide I love you but want to be with a woman too?" I wanted to make sure I understood what Justin was saying.

"If we dated, I wouldn't mind if you wanted to date women as well."

I shook my head. "Justin, I'm not into any kind of freaky threesomes or anything like that."

"As hot as I think that could be, that's not what I'm saying. I'll take what I can get from you to be able to have you in my life. If that means I have to share you with another woman, I'll do it. That's something I can't compete with, so I'll just accept it because it's who you are."

I couldn't believe what I was hearing. "You're saying you'd be fine with having an open relationship with me so that I could date women when I want?"

"Yes." There wasn't a shred of doubt in his eyes.

My mind was blown. It was like a perfect and tempting solution to my problem being laid before me, but was it what I wanted? Could I do that? Would he honestly not get jealous of me spending time with someone else, even if it were another woman? I thought of Maya and knew, just from the short time we'd known each other that she wouldn't be okay with that. If I wanted Maya, Justin and I would have to remain just friends and I would have to figure out how to deal with my attraction for him without hurting anyone. If I wanted Justin, which, in the back of my mind, I knew I did, then I would have to stop seeing Maya. Then I thought about both and realized, no matter who I chose, it would not be a casual relationship. I was already beginning to care about Maya more than I did Dante, and I knew that since I already cared deeply about Justin, if we took our relationship to the next level, it would become serious very quickly. I covered my face and groaned in frustration. Justin took my hands and removed them.

"Ness, I'm not forcing you to make a decision. I'm just letting you know how I feel. Be with Maya, figure out what you want and who you are. I'm here for you as a friend or more, whatever you want. Just don't shut me out of your life."

I looked into Justin's eyes and saw my best friend of four years and saw what I always knew was there and tried to ignore. I found, tonight, I couldn't ignore it. I leaned forward and pressed my lips to his. Justin hesitated in responding for just a moment, then tentatively began kissing me back. It was soft and sweet at first then heated up into a passionate play of lips and tongues exploring and delving. Before I knew it, Justin was lying back on the lounger, I was straddling his lap as we kissed, and I smoothed my hands over his muscled torso while his slid up the back of my pajama shirt and massaged and kneaded my back and shoulders. I shifted and felt the hard bulge beneath his pants and a little voice in my head told me to stop. This wasn't going to help my situation in the least. For once, I listened to that little voice.

I pushed up and away from him. "I can't do this. I want to, but I can't."

I climbed off Justin's lap, sat back down beside him, covered my face, and cried pitifully.

Justin pulled me into his arms and held me. "I'm sorry."

I shook my head. "It's not your fault. You didn't do anything. I initiated it."

I moved from the circle of his arms and put some space between us. "I know I've been all over the place with my attraction toward you, but the one thing I know for sure is that I don't want you to think I don't care about you. Yes, I'm sexually attracted to you, but I don't want to be anything more than friends. I'm beginning to really care about Maya. I don't want to mess that up just as we're getting started or ruin our friendship by doing something we can't take back."

"I understand." He touched my cheek and placed a kiss on my forehead. "I'm going to head back to bed."

He looked so sad it made my heart ache.

"Good night," I said.

Justin nodded then grabbed our dirty dishes and left me alone out in the yard. I waited until I thought he might have gone upstairs, let out a shuddering breath, and cried. I was overwhelmed with so many feelings. Confusion about what I wanted, doubt that I would ever be able to make myself, let alone, anyone else happy, and anger at myself for almost giving in to something that would have only led to more heartbreak.

A couple of days later, Nikki pulled up in front of Justin's house and we all sat silently in the car for a moment as if we were hesitant for our time together to end.

Justin leaned forward to stick his head between the front seats. "Well, folks, it was a blast, but like all good times, it must come to an end."

Nikki and I both turned to him and laughed.

"Boy, you're stupid," Nikki said.

I didn't say anything. It was like everything changed but somehow still managed to stay the same. I still adored him as one of my best friends, but I honestly wouldn't change a thing that happened the past week. I was sure if I had let things go too far then I would probably feel differently.

I placed a hand on Justin's cheek. "Thank you for understanding me."

Justin nodded and gave me a quick peck before turning to get out of the car. Nikki gave me a nod and joined Justin at the back of the car to get his things out of the trunk. I watched as they chatted briefly before he headed up his walkway. I turned and gazed out the front window, trying to hold back tears as Nikki got back in the car. She reached over and placed her hand over mine.

"You okay?" she asked.

The lump in my throat kept me from speaking, so all I could do was shake my head.

"You need some time before you go home?"

Home, where my family waited for me because Jackie, J.J., and I were going out to dinner with Dad and Tanya.

I swallowed the lump down and forced the tears back. "No. We can go."

Nikki nodded and gave my hand a gentle squeeze. Then pulled away from Justin's house. I chanced a look in the side mirror and saw him standing on the porch watching the car drive away.

After our little family dinner, I sat alone on our porch debating with myself whether I should call Maya. I had planned to call her as soon as we got back, but I chickened out. I had no idea what to say to her. Did I just act like what happened with Justin and I didn't happen, or did I tell her? Not telling her would be just as bad as lying, and I didn't want to start us off by lying. Especially since I knew I was falling in love with her. I needed to figure this situation out because if I didn't, I was going to push myself into an emotional breakdown like my mother had. I just needed some time to myself. Time to figure out what it was I really wanted. I went in the house then realized there was no place quiet to go. Mom and J.J. were watching TV and Jackie was in our bedroom since she was home for the summer. I backed out of the room with a sigh.

"What's wrong? Your sister back to hogging the phone again?" Mom asked.

"Yeah. I'm running over to Nikki's. I was just going to call her, but since Jackie's using the phone, it'll probably be easier just to go over there."

Mom gave me a half-hearted smile. "You guys didn't get enough of seeing each other during the week? You could always use the phone in the kitchen."

I tried not to roll my eyes in frustration. "I think I left something in her car."

I was getting so tired of still having to lie to her about half the stuff I was doing because it was usually either with Nikki or Maya. She must not discuss her homophobia in therapy because she still just tolerated my friendship with Nikki and barely spoke to her mothers. With Maya I still didn't even feel comfortable bringing her over because there was no way Mom wouldn't be able to see we were more than just friends.

"Okay," she said, looking annoyed, and turned back toward the TV.

I rolled my eyes and left the house. Fortunately, Nikki answered the door.

"Hey, didn't expect to see you again so soon."

"Sorry, if this is a bad time—" I started to turn to leave.

"Girl, please. When have I ever turned you away? C'mon in."

"Thanks."

She frowned and looked at me curiously. "What's wrong?"

"I need some time in The Room," I said wearily.

Nikki nodded in understanding. "That bad?"

I just nodded and tried to hold back the tears that were burning my eyes waiting to fall. "Where are your moms?"

"Date night, so you'll have The Room all to yourself. I'll be in my room, so just come get me when you're ready."

We walked up the stairs, and when Nikki split off to go to her room, I continued up toward their attic, which had been transformed into a meditation room. Nikki and I had named it The Room because we didn't know if it was due to all the crystals or spiritual cleansings her mothers did, but it had led to quite a few lengthy and enlightening meditation sessions when we'd used it. I was hoping the same would happen again now because I truly needed some enlightenment on my situation. I removed my shoes and left them sitting outside the door. When I walked in and hit the light switch, the room filled with colors from the light bouncing off the various large crystals hanging along the ceiling. Each crystal represented the seven Chakras.

I reached up to gently run my hand across all seven hoping to get a little extra mojo from them, then pushed "play" on the stereo to start the soothing new age music that played throughout the room via speakers placed in each corner. I sat on the large floor cushion in the center of the room, lit some nag champa incense to help with clearing my mind a little better, and picked up the crystal lotus blossom carved from selenite that Nikki's moms gifted me when I began taking my meditation seriously. Sitting cross-legged, I laid my hands in my lap, gently holding the lotus so that it sat right at the center of my core. The incense filled the room, I closed my eyes, and took several deep breaths to clear my mind as best as I could. Carol told me that some people never completely cleared their mind, so it was best just to try to clear the loudest noises until there were only dull murmurs left. Being the overachiever, I sometimes tried to see if I could clear everything out, but it never worked. I would just end up frustrated with a headache, which defeated the purpose of meditation.

Once I felt my body relax and my mind clear of all but the dull murmurs, I gave myself over to the lightness I always felt as the combination of the incense, music, and colorful light reflections across my eyelids took me to a place of peace. I floated in that peace for a few minutes before quietly asking myself what I wanted. I didn't let thoughts of Maya or Justin enter my mental space. Just the question of what I wanted for myself. My first thoughts were love and acceptance. Well, that wasn't helpful. Wasn't that what everyone wanted, to be loved and accepted? I hadn't expected some great epiphany, but I had hoped whatever spiritual energy that floated through this room would be a little more detailed. I took another deep breath to release the oncoming frustration I sometimes got when I felt answers weren't coming quickly enough.

"Patience, girl," I whispered to myself with my last deep breath.

Once again, love and acceptance whispered through my mind.

"Love and acceptance from who?" I mentally whispered back.

I sat quietly for a moment just letting the music and the incense wash over me. My body grew warm and relaxed. My palms grew even warmer where I held the selenite lotus. The colorful lights from the crystals moved and shifted behind my eyelids until they became a blurred circle of soft white light. The light became a mirror in which I saw myself reflected. It was such a brief glimpse that I thought maybe I imagined it as the mirror became that blur of soft white light, then the crystal colors again. With a sigh of frustration, I slowly blinked my eyes open and sat for another moment just to allow the frustration to dim a bit before I got up. I gently set my crystal lotus on the table and slowly stood, as the incense tended to make me light-headed. I turned off the music and light, grabbed my shoes, and made my way down to Nikki's room. I heard voices and realized Carol and Frieda had come home some time during my meditation. I looked down at my watch, surprised to find I had been up there for almost a half hour and had no enlightenment to show for it.

Nikki's door was open, so I just walked in and flopped into a huge, plush wingback chair.

Nikki was sitting up in bed reading. "Want to talk about it?" she asked.

"Nope." I curled my feet up under me and laid my head on the arm of the chair.

"Are you staying over?"

"Yep."

Nikki nodded and went back to reading as I thought about my situation. Even though Nikki's house was full of as many people as mine, they knew when I needed space and kindly gave it to me. This home had become my sanctuary over the years. I was completely accepted here, flaws, goofiness, confusion, and all. There were no expectations to fit anyone's mold but my own. I was lovingly teased, respectfully advised, and encouraged to question. Such a big difference from home where everyone tiptoed around in fear of setting Mom off. None of us wanted to be the reason she was pushed over the edge. It had come pretty close the night after I told her about Spelman and J.J. announced he wanted to live with Dad. I had almost told her about the confusion with my sexuality, but we were lucky Uncle Frank had been there to calm her down just from her reaction to those announcements. I couldn't imagine how bad it would have gotten if I had told her I might be gay, or at least bisexual, which would have been a whole other conversation. Love and acceptance with my mother came with stipulations.

Love and acceptance. Those two words kept coming into my thoughts during my meditation. Was that what I needed to help me figure out what, and who, I wanted? But whose love and acceptance? I couldn't really say if Maya loved me, not this soon, but I knew she accepted me. Was it love and acceptance from my family that I needed? I believe I already had that from most of them. Jackie and Denise were the only ones who knew the whole truth about me and still accepted me. I had no doubt Uncle Frank and J.J. would as well. Dad sort of knew from my admission that first summer visit and he was fine with it, but we hadn't talked about it since then.

Mom, on the other hand, didn't have a clue, and even when she assumed after I became friends with Nikki, she was not the least bit accepting or loving about it. Just her reaction tonight when I told her

I was coming over to Nikki's showed she was still not happy with our friendship. I could only imagine her reaction if I told her that I was dating another girl. Was that what was holding me back from deciding about being out in the open with Maya? Fear of upsetting and disappointing my mother? Was her love and acceptance of me needed to live the way I wanted? I groaned miserably and beat my forehead against the winged arm of the chair.

"Oh, hey, you two. It was so quiet we didn't realize you were here," Carol said.

"Hey," Nikki and I said in unison, but mine sounded pitiful.

I turned my head to look in her direction. She and Frieda leaned against the doorway smiling cheerfully at us.

"You look like you had a good night out," Nikki said.

"We saw *Torch Song Trilogy*, the new Harvey Fierstein play. It was great. We'll have to take you guys before you leave for school. Janesse, I think you'll really connect with some of the storyline," Frieda said.

"I'll have to check it out," I said noncommittally.

Carol looked at me worriedly. "Everything okay?"

All eyes turned to me, and I wished I could curl up in a ball and disappear. I simply shrugged in response.

"Must be serious. I smell nag champa," Frieda said.

"I'm having an identity crisis," I said.

"Ah, I see. If you need to talk, we're here for you," Frieda said.

I smiled for the first time all evening. "Thank you."

Carol walked into the room toward me and opened her arms. Without hesitation, I stood up and stepped into her embrace. As she squeezed me tightly, rubbing her hands up and down my back, I had to swallow the lump forming in my throat and closed my eyes to stop the tears threatening to fall. We stood that way for a moment, then she pulled away and took my face in her hands.

She looked at me the way I always hoped my mother would. "Janesse, you're a beautiful, intelligent, gifted, and loving young woman. If there's someone who can't see that and chooses to judge you for who you love rather than the person you are, then it's their loss. The key to solving an identity crisis is learning to not to depend on someone else's love and acceptance of you but learning to love and accept yourself. Nikki, what does our teachings from Buddha tell us?"

"Peace comes from within. Do not seek it without," Nikki quoted.

"Exactly." Carol placed her hand over my heart. "Find your peace and you'll find yourself. Understand?" She smiled broadly.

I smiled in return. "Yes."

"Good."

She gave me one more quick embrace then walked back toward Frieda, who watched her with such deep love I almost looked away because it felt like I was intruding on an intimate moment.

Frieda took Carol's hand. "Good night, ladies." She wrapped an arm around Carol's waist and walked her out of the room.

"Good night," Nikki and I said.

Nikki climbed off her bed and walked over to me. "I'm going to grab a couple of cookies we had left over from the beach. You want to join me?"

I nodded. Baked goods, especially Nikki's, always made me feel better.

Later that night I lay in Nikki's other bed thinking about what Carol said and how it was as if she had seen what I'd experienced during my meditation. It was then that I remembered seeing my reflection in the mirror and connected love and acceptance with it. My mom wasn't the only one I needed to worry about not accepting my sexuality. It wasn't that I was ashamed of my attraction to women, I was just afraid of the fact that I was also attracted to men. I was afraid that at the rate I was going, I would never be able to settle down and have a life like Denise and Liz or Carol and Frieda. That if I settled down with a man, I would always feel like there was something missing, like I was living a lie. If I wanted to settle down with a woman, would I have to narrow my options to another bisexual woman? If she was lesbian, would she constantly worry that I would leave her for a man? There were so many ifs and doubts that it just caused me more confusion and frustration. I knew that my attraction to women was much stronger than my attraction to men. With Dante, I could do with or without him. Breaking up was no big loss. With Justin, I think the intensity of my feelings for him had more to do with our strong friendship. I couldn't even imagine that with any other man.

But Maya, she was everything I could want in a girlfriend. She was sweet, funny, romantic, smart, and confident. So confident it scared me sometimes because I felt like she could do so much better than me. When we were together, she made me feel like the most special person in the room. We'd only been seeing each other for a month, but I felt like it had been forever. Like Nikki, she seemed to understand me, sometimes better than I understood myself. Unlike Nikki, every time I was alone with her it took every ounce of my willpower to respect her wanting to wait before we had sex. Just thinking about her sexy, gap-toothed, dimpled smile gave me tingles. I still hadn't called her, and I'm sure she knew I was home by now.

I looked over at Nikki snoring lightly, then glanced over at the clock on the nightstand between the beds. It was just after midnight. I got out of bed and quietly walked over to her phone sitting on a table next to the chair I was sitting in earlier. The cord was long enough for me to take it into the bathroom. I closed the door behind me, sat on the floor, and dialed Maya's number.

"Hello." She didn't sound like she was asleep.

"Hey, it's Janesse. Did I wake you?"

"No, I couldn't sleep. Was wondering if you were going to call me. You sounded weird last time we talked."

The last time Maya and I spoke was our last night at the beach house. I called her right before we had gone out to the bar since I knew we'd be home late. It was a short, casual call because guilt over kissing Justin had been killing me.

"Yeah, it had been a weird day. How are you?"

"I'm fine. The question is, how are you?"

I hesitated. Did she know? "Uh, I'm fine. Why do you ask that?"

"Janesse, look, if you're losing interest in me just tell me and I'll leave you alone. First the drunk call, then the weird call, now not even calling me until after midnight when you said you'd call once you got home. It's like you're avoiding me. I already told you, I'm willing to be patient until you figure out what you want. You like me or you don't, but don't play games with me."

Shit, I was messing this all up. "Maya, I like you. I really do. I've just been going through some stuff and haven't been the best girlfriend. I'm sorry about that."

"Girlfriend. Do you really feel that way?"

I hadn't even realized I'd said it, but now that I had, I liked the thought of Maya as my girlfriend. "Yes, if you feel the same way."

"I've felt that way for a while now. I was just waiting for you to catch up." I heard the smile in her voice.

"Maya, why me? I'm all mixed up and I'm sure there's some out and proud chick out there you would have an easier time with."

"If I wanted easy, I wouldn't have approached you in that dressing room. You don't know this, but ever since the first time I saw you cheering I've wanted to ask you out. I even went to a few Montclair home games just to watch you cheer. There was something that kept drawing me to you. Then I saw you with Nikki a couple of times after the games and thought maybe you two were dating so I stopped going unless Montclair played West Orange."

I was flattered at the idea of Maya checking me out all that time. "You were stalking me?"

Maya chuckled. "I guess if you want to call it that."

"I wish I would've known."

"And what would you have done if I'd approached you then?"

I stopped smiling. What would I have done if Maya approached me after a game and asked me out? I was dating Dante at the time. That thought brought me back to my current dilemma.

"Janesse, you still there?" Maya asked.

"Yes. Are you free tomorrow?" I avoided answering her question.

"Yes. After church. You want to meet somewhere or come over here?"

I had been to Maya's house on several occasions. Even met her parents, but she still had not been to my house other than dropping me off. "Can you pick me up and we can go up to Eagle Rock?"

Maya was quiet for a moment. "Yeah. Are you sure?"

I had always met her places to avoid her having to ring my bell and chance meeting Mom. "Positive."

"Okay. I'll see you tomorrow."

We said our good nights and I sat there listening to the dial tone, wondering what the hell I was thinking inviting her over. I knew what statement that action would make, but was I really ready for it?

CHAPTER TEN

Mom wasn't too pleased with me when I walked through the door the next morning. I hadn't even bothered to call and tell her I was spending the night at Nikki's.

"So, what, you think because you're eighteen and about to go to college you're too grown to let your mother know where you're spending the night?"

I sighed. I hadn't gotten much sleep after talking to Maya. "Mom, I told you I was going over to Nikki's. Where else would I have spent the night?"

Mom narrowed her eyes at me. "You better watch that tone. For all I know you two could've gone out and spent the night God knows where, as lenient as those women are."

Here we go. "Four years, Mom. Four years we've been doing this, and you still can't even acknowledge them by name or give them the same respect they give you. Nikki is my best FRIEND, and if I choose to spend my free time hanging out with her, I don't understand what the problem is. Her and her mothers are not going to try and recruit me, turn me, or have me out at some wild lesbian orgies all night long. If you took the time to talk to them, you'd know how nice they are and that they're just two mothers trying to do best for their child."

I didn't even wait for a response. I went to my bedroom and slammed the door behind me.

"Well, okay then," Jackie said from her bed, startling me.

I held my hand over my racing heart. "Geez, I forgot you were here."

Jackie smirked. "I see. You okay?"

I threw myself facedown onto my bed. "She's never going to change," I said into my pillow.

I felt my bed sink as Jackie sat down and began rubbing my back the way Carol had done last night. "Probably not if she doesn't have anything to change for. When it comes to Nikki and her mothers, she doesn't see any reason to change. To accept them. If it was someone that she was close to, she may not have a choice."

I lifted my head out of the pillow, folded my arms, and rested my cheek on them. "She still hasn't for Denise."

"Denise is not her daughter and lives on the other side of the country."

"You actually believe she'll be more accepting because it's me?" My sister had far more faith in our mother than I did.

"Only one way to find out."

"I'm not even sure which side of the line I'm on. How am I supposed to come out to her?"

"Ness, you don't have to know exactly what's going on to tell someone how you feel or even what you've been going through. Maybe, if she hears how much you've been struggling, she'll be more willing to listen."

Jackie had become a glass half full kind of person since she escaped this house of madness while at school, and I seemed to have taken on her pessimistic attitude having been stuck here full-time.

"I'm not sure she would even be willing to listen after that rant I just gave."

"The lesbian orgy comment might've been a tad much."

"You think?"

"Look, she's been great this past week. Spending time with J.J., home every night to cook dinner, and genuinely happier than I've seen her in a while. She even talked to Dad for a good half hour when he came by to pick up J.J. to go to spend time with him the other day. The therapy is helping, Ness. Just give her a little more time."

"Well, Maya is coming over to pick me up to hang out this afternoon. I thought it might be time for Mom to meet her since we'll probably be seeing a lot of each other before we both leave for school."

"Oh, well, when I suggested more time I was thinking like a month, not a few hours," Jackie said worriedly. "Just so you know, Dad's coming by to pick me up. I promised to show him the campus and some of the places I hang out."

I buried my face back in the pillow with a groan. "I wasn't expecting to make it a family affair. Mom's been asking about this new friend I've been hanging out with, and I figured I'd introduce her."

"So, you want me to just go and meet him at Uncle Frank's?"

"No, makes more sense for him to come here and pick you up. Is Tanya going to be with him?"

"No, she's not feeling well so she's staying in for the day."

"Well, I guess I might as well get it over with. Dad sort of knows."

Jackie didn't know about me talking to Dad during that first summer, so I told her about it. I also told her about my talk with Denise at my birthday party.

"Well then, you've pretty much got everyone covered. You already know Uncle Frank will be cool, and J.J. adores you so I don't see him having an issue with it since he's already been around Nikki's family."

"Yeah, well, I had to be the one to explain that one to him when he started going to Nikki's house with me because he asked Mom why Nikki had two moms and he only had one. She told him because she was a Christian and they weren't."

Jackie frowned. "Geez, I had no idea."

"When I asked him if he wanted to go over there with me to play with Nikki's racetrack one day, he said no because they weren't Christians. I asked him how he knew that, and he told me what Mom said. I was mad, but instead of bad-mouthing Mom I explained to him that Nikki had two moms because they loved each other and wanted to share that love with a baby of their own. Fortunately, he didn't ask about the details of how they got Nikki. It wasn't my place to go into the sex talk with him. I just told Dad what happened, and he had the talk with him when we went out to Indy that summer."

Jackie's eyes widened. "So, Dad told him how they had Nikki?"

"I don't know exactly what he told him, but J.J. was cool about going over there after that."

"Does Mom know Dad did that?"

"I doubt it. She didn't even have the sex talk with me. When I started my period, she just handed me a pad and told me to stay away from boys and make sure I keep clean."

Jackie laughed out loud. "She told me the same thing!"

It was both sad and funny how badly our mother chose to avoid all uncomfortable conversations. Even to the detriment of her own children's well-being.

As the time approached when I figured Maya would be arriving, I was nervous as hell. I had changed my outfit twice and paced back and forth in my room. When the doorbell rang, I yelped like a scared puppy. Then I heard Justin shout "Dad!"

I took a few deep breaths and gave my lotus pendant a touch for additional courage, then headed out. Mom was in the kitchen on the phone and looked briefly up at me, frowned, then went back to her phone call. That couldn't be good. It meant she was still mad at me about my rant this morning. I hadn't spoken to her since then. When we got outside, Dad was talking to Carol over the bushes that separated our yards. She gave me a wave and Dad turned around.

"Hey, Nessy, I didn't expect you to be here as well. What a pleasant surprise."

"Hey, Dad."

He pulled me into a hug and placed a kiss on my forehead. "Carol here was telling me you guys got back yesterday. How was your week away from us grown-ups all up in your business?"

"It was great. We had a lot of fun. We're thinking it may be something we do every summer."

"That sounds like a good plan. I'm sure your mom told you, but we're planning to go down to Georgia with you to help you get settled in. I figured we could go down a week early, pick up everything you need down there instead of having to ship it down."

Well, that was a surprise to hear. "Uh, no, she hasn't told me."

"Oh, okay, well, maybe she hasn't gotten around to it. We talked about it last week." Dad looked annoyed.

Carol cleared her throat. "Well, I better go. It was nice catching up with you, Jacob. If I don't see you before you leave, have a safe trip home. Tell Tanya I hope she feels better soon."

"Same here, Carol. Thanks."

Carol gave me a smile and a wink before walking off. I couldn't blame her for making a quick exit.

Dad took my hand and walked me over toward Jackie. "So, what are you up to today? Wanna head into the city with your sis and me? It's been a long time since I've hung out with just my girls." He took her hand and placed a kiss on both our cheeks.

Just then Maya's car pulled up on the other side of the street. I gave him a nervous smile. "I wish I could, Dad, but I made other plans."

I watched Maya as she got out of the car and walked toward the gate, then looked back at Dad, who had been watching me.

He quirked a brow. "Ah, I see."

I turned bashfully away and met Maya as she came up the walkway. "Hey."

She looked just as nervous as I felt. "Hey."

"You want to meet my family, or would you prefer to just go?" I asked.

She glanced quickly over my shoulder then back at me. "What do you want?"

I looked into her beautiful hazel eyes, at her breathtaking smile, and decided I was tired of the secrets. "You…to meet my family."

Her smile broadened. "Okay."

I took her hand and led her back to where Dad, Jackie, and J.J. stood watching us curiously. Mom took that moment to walk out of the house, and I almost chickened out, but a quick squeeze from Maya's hand gave me the courage I needed.

"Dad, Jackie, J.J., this is my friend Maya."

Maya shook each of their hands. "It's such a pleasure to finally meet you guys. Janesse talks about you all so much I feel like I already know you."

"Same here," Jackie said with a grin.

"It's nice to meet you as well, Maya," Dad said.

"She's pretty, Ness," J.J. said, blushing.

"Thank you." Maya gave J.J. a wink, which darkened his blush further and made him look away bashfully.

I understood that feeling because I had it whenever she flashed me with her smile. I turned toward Mom, who stood on the porch looking back and forth from our held hands to my face as we walked toward her.

"Mom, this is Maya. The new friend I've been spending time with."

Maya smiled up at Mom and offered her other hand in greeting. "Mrs. Phillips, it's so nice to finally meet you."

Mom looked at Maya's hand as if it were a snake about to bite her, but Maya didn't cower. She continued cheerfully smiling and holding her hand up to my mother looking down on us from the top step.

"Mom." I tried not to sound annoyed.

Her eyes snapped toward mine, and I knew right then that everything Jackie said about it maybe being different if her own child were gay was wishful thinking. Mom pasted on her best Realtor smile and reached out to shake Maya's hand, but she only took her fingers as if she would catch something from grasping her whole hand. I felt Maya tense beside me, but her smile stayed in place.

Mom looked at me with a frown. "Are you going out again today?"

"Yes. I'll only be out for a few hours."

Mom looked at Maya, our hands, and back at me before turning and going back into the house without another word. I was pissed. I let go of Maya's hand and was about to go after her when she grabbed my hand again. I turned to her and she shook her head.

"Let's just go." She gave me a soft smile.

"She had no right to be so rude." I felt like I wanted to cry.

Dad came over and placed a hand on my shoulder. "You and Maya go enjoy yourselves."

I shook my head. "Dad, I don't want to put you in the middle of this."

Dad gave me a smile and placed kiss on my forehead. "I'm your father. I'm already in the middle. Go."

I looked at him then at Jackie and J.J., who were gazing at me with sympathy.

I looked toward the doorway again then nodded. "Okay."

I let Maya lead me down the walk and to her car, never once releasing my hand. It was as if she knew I needed that one act of defiant courage to keep me going. As soon as I sat in the car I sighed.

"You okay?" Maya asked.

"No, but I'm getting used to it. Can we just go?" I said wearily.

Maya started the car and we didn't speak again until we were parked at Eagle Rock.

"You mind if we just sit here for a while?" I asked.

"Sure, but you might want to roll down the window. It can get pretty hot in here."

We both cranked the handles to roll down our windows, and Maya turned in her seat to face me. "That was pretty brave. In front of your whole family like that."

I faced her as well. "I guess. To be fair, Dad already had a clue and Jackie knows all about you. The only ones I hadn't talked to were J.J. and Mom."

"Well, I still think you may need to talk to J.J., but your mom seemed to get the point," Maya said.

"I'm sorry about that. Unfortunately, it's about what I would've expected. Jackie had me convinced that maybe she would be disappointed but would find a way to accept it. What I saw in her eyes was not someone willing to take time to accept anything."

Maya reached over and took my hand. "Well, you did kind of bum-rush her in front of the whole family and me. I don't think she appreciated that too much."

"You don't understand. I've tried so many times to talk to her about dating, sex, my feelings, and she always says, 'not now, Ness, I'm tired' or 'Ness, this isn't a good time, I'm having one of my headaches.' Maya, I'm so tired of always trying to fit my feelings and who I am into her comfortable little box of expectations. She doesn't want any drama or trouble from anyone in her life, which is so unrealistic."

"You do realize when you get home you may have a fight on your hands."

"Maybe. That's another thing my mother is good at. Avoiding confrontations. It's funny how I never noticed that growing up. It wasn't until my parents started having problems that I noticed my mom didn't handle arguments well."

There were times when my parents were arguing, and when it started getting really heated, I would hear Mom say, "I can't deal with this right now," and Dad would storm out of the house looking so tired and frustrated. I now knew how that felt and understood why he left. To have to live with someone who didn't want to take the time to talk and listen, no matter how much they didn't like what was said, could wear on a person's patience and understanding. I was amazed Dad lasted as long as he did. I had gotten so used to having Dad to run to about problems because that's who Mom would always send me to when I tried talking to her. It made it difficult these past four years knowing I had to lean more on her.

Maya pulled me from my thoughts. "Why did you do this now?"

"Because I thought it was time for you to meet my family."

Maya looked at me suspiciously. "And there's no other reason?"

I'd hoped that answer would satisfy her, but I'd forgotten, like Nikki, Maya could read me like a book.

I fiddled with our entwined fingers, hesitant to say more. Maya touched my face with her other hand to coax me to look at her.

"You know you can tell me anything. What's the worst that could happen?"

I bit my lip. "You could not want to see me anymore?"

Maya smiled. "What are you always saying? Like a bandage, just rip it off and get it over with."

With a shuddering sigh, I grabbed the edge of my mental bandage and started ripping. "During our week at the beach something happened that made me realize that I'm tired of the secrets and want to be with you openly."

"What happened?" Maya asked.

She looked at me with such warmth and understanding that I hated the possibility of seeing it turn to hurt, but I was determined to start this relationship without any lies, of omission or otherwise.

"I kissed Justin but stopped it before it went any further," I shamefully admitted.

Maya's lips turned down into a frown, and the warmth and understanding in her eyes turned to hurt. She released my hand and moved away from me in her seat. "I thought you and Justin were just friends."

"We are, at least I thought we were until this week when he admitted he's felt more than friendship for me. I knew he had a crush on me back when we first met, but I thought it had passed."

"And you've had no idea, in the last four years, that he felt more for you?" Maya said accusingly.

I hesitated in answering. *No lies, remember?* "I had a feeling during prom night, but that was before you and I met, and I didn't encourage it."

Sighing in frustration, Maya ran her hand over her hair, partially dislodging the scrunchy that held her ponytail in place. "So, you want me to believe that Justin has had feelings for you for four years, but you didn't realize it until a month ago and didn't encourage him in any way. Yet, somehow, YOU ended up kissing HIM. Then to top it off, you tell me almost screwing him made you realize you want to be with me when I foolishly thought you were already with me for the past month."

Hearing it from someone else in a tone of pure doubt made me realize how stupid my explanation was.

"Do you have feelings for him?" she asked.

"Not like that. I love Justin as a friend. I'll admit that after prom night I started to feel a physical attraction for him, then I met you and things changed." I could see by the look on Maya's face that I had screwed this up so bad.

I reached for her hand and she snatched it back. "Maya, please, believe me, what happened was just as much of a surprise to me as it is to you." I quickly explained what happened on the beach between Justin and me and everything that followed.

Maya looked so sad that it was breaking my heart. "Janesse, do you remember the girl I mentioned that Carrie hit on?"

"Yes, you said Carrie did you a favor because she was all over the place and didn't know what she wanted." I realized Maya was comparing me to her, and she had every right to after what I just told her.

"It was more than that. I knew she was probably using me to appease her curiosity, but I fell for her anyway. After two months together, she had me convinced that it was more than that. That she was really starting to like me to. Then, one night she talked me into going to some frat party at Rutgers. At some point during the night, she left me to go to the bathroom. When I noticed she had been gone too long I went looking for her. Someone had seen her go upstairs, and I got worried that she was sick, or some guy had cornered her. When I got upstairs, I heard her voice. I walked into the room it was coming from and found her bent over a desk being screwed by some guy I had seen her talking to earlier that night. She was so into it she didn't even notice me, but he did. He grinned and winked at me like I had been the one who sent her up there just for him."

Tears fell from Maya's eyes. I reached up to wipe them away with the pad of my thumb, relieved when she didn't pull away from my touch.

With a sniffle, she continued. "I left without even saying good-bye. She called me about an hour later. It took her an hour to even notice I left." Maya took a deep breath. "Anyway, she called me crying, apologizing, and saying he was an ex of hers, she'd had too much to drink, and didn't mean to bail on me like that. Told me she really did care about me and that she had gotten men out of her system and my stupid behind fell for the tears and begging. A month later, she broke up with me and got back together with that same guy. I found out she had started seeing him again after the party while she was playing me for a fool."

I felt like crap after Maya finished. "I'm so sorry, Maya."

She gave me a sad smile. "I thought you would be different. There was something about you, about how easily we connected that made me think taking a chance with another closeted girl would be different this time."

I grabbed Maya's hands. "I am different. I'm not like that girl. I know I was confused, but I'm not anymore. I want you." I realized I probably sounded just like her ex. "I'm not her," I cried. Desperately wanting her to believe me.

Maya slid her hands from mine and turned to look straight out the front window. "How do I know that? You and Justin have a history. You and I just met a month ago." She looked back at me with tears in her eyes again. "How do I compete with that? With a guy?"

"Give me a chance to prove to you that it's you I want," I begged.

Maya reached over and gently stroked my cheek, then turned back to face forward again. "I need to think about it."

"Okay," I said dejectedly.

She started the car and I felt like my heart was shattering into a thousand pieces.

It was a sad, quiet ride back to my house. We hadn't been gone that long, but I was surprised to see Dad's car still there.

"I'm sorry, Maya," I said before turning to get out of the car.

Maya grabbed my hand before I opened the door. I turned to face her.

"Janesse, I really care about you and feel our connection is something that's hard to find. I believe that you believe you know what you want, but I need to be with someone who has accepted themselves and their sexuality without question. I can't bear to go through what I did with my ex again."

"Maya, please, give me a chance. I've never felt with anyone like I do with you." I was surprised I could speak past the lump in my throat and the pain in my chest. I felt the tears running down my face and didn't even bother to wipe them away.

"I'm sorry. As much as I want to, I just can't." She leaned forward and pressed her lips to mine for a soft final kiss, then pulled away.

We were both crying at this point, and I was close to getting on my hands and knees to beg Maya not to leave, but she was right. I was all screwed up and she didn't need someone like me breaking her heart all over again. I got out of the car before I could say anything else that would only prolong the inevitable and slowly walked up to the house trying to pull myself together before going into whatever drama awaited me. Within an hour, I had pretty much come out to my family, broken my girlfriend's heart, and been deservedly kicked to the curb. Not one of my best days.

Before climbing the steps. I heard Maya start her car and turned around just as she was pulling away. I covered my mouth to stop the whimper about to escape and took a deep, shuddering breath. I wiped my face as best as I could and entered our apartment to find Dad looking out the window, which meant he must have witnessed that whole thing. He gave me a sad smile and held his arms open to me, and I didn't hesitate to run into his comforting embrace. I let the pain of my heartbreak run through me and cried in my father's arms like I hadn't done since I was six and had been sent home from school for fighting some girl who kept picking on me. As my tears subsided, he walked me over to the sofa. At that point, Mom and Uncle Frank came out of the kitchen and Jackie out of J.J.'s room. The sound of my misery must have drawn them all out. Jackie sat next to me so that I was sandwiched between her and Dad. Uncle Frank sat in one of the other chairs and Mom stayed out of my line of sight.

Jackie took my hand. "What happened?"

"Maya doesn't think we should keep seeing each other."

"Did we make that bad of an impression?" Dad tried to joke.

I gave him a sad smile. "No. It was all completely on me. I did something stupid that hurt her. I don't want to go into it."

"Well then, it obviously wasn't meant to be, and you can stop all this foolish behavior. I knew spending time with those people would bring you nothing but trouble," Mom said from behind me.

"Janet!" Uncle Frank said angrily.

Dad sighed and shook his head and Jackie gave my hand a squeeze. I turned around to find Mom standing in the kitchen doorway with her arms crossed, giving me an angry glare. I was sitting there with my heart broken and she had the nerve to be mad at me. I stood up and Jackie continued to hold my hand to keep me there, but I was tired of this. I looked down at her and she must have seen the determination in my eyes because she let go. I walked over to Mom and stood directly in front of here so she had to look me in my face as I said what I needed to say to her.

"Mom, whatever I am or however I act has nothing to do with Nikki's family. I've tried so many times to talk to you. To tell you what I was going through, but you chose to keep putting it off and ignoring the problem. Do you have any idea what it's like to be going through an identity crisis and you can't talk to your own mother? To know that there's something about who you're becoming that your mother despises? You can barely look at Denise, let alone speak to Nikki and her mothers. You act like who they are is something you can ignore and if you do, it doesn't exist. Well, Mom, I'm right here, I like girls and you can try and ignore it, but it's not going to make it go away."

Mom looked at me as if she had no idea who I was. She shook her head and moved around me. "I won't listen to this nonsense. You're just going through some rebellious phase."

"Mom! Please don't walk away from me!" I cried.

Dad got up and blocked her way. "Janet, why are you doing this? Can't you see our daughter needs you?"

"How dare you walk up in this house and act like you care. If you cared, then you wouldn't have walked out on us!"

"Dammit, Janet! I didn't walk out on them, I left because of this!" He waved his hands around in frustration. "Life isn't always going to be the way you want it. You can't keep running away from the things you don't want to see and hear, especially when it comes to your children."

"Get out!" Mom shouted at Dad.

"What?" he said.

"Get…out! I don't want to see you anywhere near here until the day you pick that boy up!" she shouted even louder, drawing J.J. from his room.

"Mom!" Jackie said angrily. She walked over to stand beside Dad.

Mom frowned at her. "What? You don't like it, then you can leave too. As a matter of fact, why don't you all leave. It would make my life a whole helluva lot easier." She pushed past Dad and Jackie, went to her room, and slammed the door, leaving all of us in stunned silence.

"Did she mean that?" J.J. asked, tears in his eyes.

I walked over to him and wrapped my arms around him. "She's just upset, buddy."

"Because you have a girlfriend instead of a boyfriend?" he asked.

I looked down at him and didn't see anything but curiosity in his gaze. "That's part of it."

Frank stood up. "Look, why don't you all come to my house. Give her some time to stew in her mess. I'll call her therapist to let her know what's going on."

"I'm staying. I'll come by later," I said.

"Nessy, I don't think that's a good idea," Dad said.

"Dad, I'm not going to be like her and run from this. She's going to hear me out one way or the other." They all looked at me as if I were making the biggest mistake of my life and I probably was, but even if I had to talk to Mom through the closed door, I was finishing what I had to say.

Uncle Frank walked over to me and placed a kiss on my forehead. "I always knew you were the brave one. Since I walked over, I'll just ride over to the house with you guys, Jacob," he said.

Dad gave me a hug. "If you're not at the house within the next hour I'm coming back for you."

I smiled. "I'll be fine, Dad."

Jackie and J.J. were next. They both gave me a hug and a kiss on each cheek.

"Good luck," Jackie said.

"Ness, I don't care who you like, I love you no matter what," J.J. said, making my heart swell with love.

"Thanks, buddy. I love you too," I said, ruffling his hair.

They all left me standing in the middle of the living room staring at Mom's closed door. I took a couple of seconds to gather my thoughts, then walked right into her room without bothering to knock. Mom was sitting on her bed with her head in her hands and looked up in surprise, which quickly turned to anger.

"I thought you left with the rest of them."

I leaned against the doorway, crossing my arms, trying to look a lot cooler and calmer than I felt. "Nope. We're not finished talking."

"Janesse, I told you—"

"I know what you told me," I interrupted her, letting my hurt and anger guide me. "You're always the one doing the telling and the talking and never letting anyone say what they have to say because it doesn't fit into your idea of what they should be. I'm leaving for college in less than two months, and I refuse to go without having closed this chapter of my life."

Mom started to speak, and I held up my hand. She cut off whatever she was about to say. "I have tried to be everything you've wanted me to be, the straight A student, the social butterfly, the sugar and spice and everything nice girly-girl. I stopped being ME to keep from stressing you out, afraid if I said or did the wrong thing it would push you over the edge the way Dad leaving did. We've all tiptoed around this house for the past four years to protect you. Well, now it's time for me to do something for myself. This is me, Mom." I poked my own chest. "You can accept me for who I am, every part of me, whether you like it or not, or you can lose me. I won't continue trying to live up to your expectations only to have my friendship with Nikki, my relationship with her family, or who I choose to date being thrown up in my face like nothing else I do matters."

"I just don't understand why you prefer being over there instead with your own family?" Mom said, looking confused and hurt.

"You seriously don't see what you do?" Could she really be that clueless about her own behavior?

"What? Provide a roof over your heads, nice clothes on your backs, food in your mouths? What else could you possibly need?" Mom said.

I shook my head in disbelief. "How about love, Mom? How about acceptance? How about interest and concern in our lives?"

"You and Jackie are practically grown. You don't need my acceptance for anything, and J.J. is so much like his father nothing I could do would satisfy him."

"Wow, do you honestly believe that? You think because Jackie and I are grown we no longer need our mother to be a shoulder to lean on when we're going through something difficult? Is that what Grandma Elaine did to you? Is this how she treated you?"

Mom glared angrily and pointed a finger at me. "Don't you talk about your grandmother like that. My mother was a strong Christian woman who would give the clothes off her back for anyone in need. Her faith carried her through an abusive husband who left her in the backwoods of Alabama with two babies to take care of alone. That's why she moved us to Brooklyn, to be near her family. It's what I did for you guys when your father walked out for that piece of trash he was going around with. She didn't coddle me. She made sure I knew how to take care of myself and deal with my own problems without depending on some man to solve them for me. You all think I'm supposed to spend the rest of my life drying your tears, bandaging your scrapes, and cooing poor baby every time you're hurt, then I obviously didn't raise you right."

I didn't recognize the cold, bitter woman standing before me. Memories came to me of times when Jackie or I came home scraped or crying to her over something and how she would tell us to go straighten and clean our faces then come back to her. Once we did that, she would ask us what happened and what we learned from it. If we couldn't think of a lesson learned, she wouldn't even tend to our wounds until she went through a whole lecture of what she thought we should take away from what happened. I think I was about five when I stopped going to her and would take care of my own scrapes and scratches and cry to

Dad if he was home. Jackie was pretty much the same. She would take care of herself and go on about her day. I realized my mother had never truly been a mother once we stopped being cute and dependent babies. It was the same thing she did to J.J. Once he started showing who he was becoming, coming into his own little personality, she stopped caring. The fact that he also was the spitting image of Dad, constantly reminding her of him, probably didn't help.

I knew then, I could talk until I was blue in the face, but I would never be able to lean on my mother for support or have her acceptance. She was so busy trying to be the strong woman that she'd sacrificed being a good mother. She didn't have it in her to be both. I felt a heavy sadness not only for her but for what I would be missing as a woman coming into herself. I wouldn't have my mother to go to for advice or share special moments with because unless they fit into her little picture of how things were supposed to be, she wouldn't care. I ached so badly for my mother's acceptance, and I was angry at myself for doing so. My vision clouded with tears.

"You want to know why I spend so much time next door? Because not only do I feel more at home there than I do here, but I feel like, for a little while, I have a mother who cares about me, my feelings, and what I want. I get the support, love, and acceptance that I don't get from you." I tried to explain it to her without sounding bitter and angry.

"Acceptance? Of course they accept you because they're not your mother. They expose you to their disgusting lifestyle, make you all confused, then send you back here defiant and ungrateful. Is that what you want for your life? To live like them, never being accepted in society, never able to marry and give your kids a normal life?"

"Normal? Is this what you call normal? Your husband and kids are afraid of talking to you. Your daughter feels so alone she has to get acceptance from strangers rather than you. Your son questions if you love him or not. If that's what you consider normal, then yes, I'll take the life Nikki's moms have over a normal one any day." Now that came out bitter and I didn't care.

My mother looked at me in shock. "You really mean that, don't you?"

I nodded. "I love you, Mom, I truly do, but I can't do this anymore. I'm tired of either keeping quiet or fighting, which seems to be the only two choices with you. I had my heart broken today, and I can't even talk to you about it. I'm leaving for school in less than two months, and I'm trying to figure out who I am and what I want, and I can't even lean on my own mother for advice or support, and that breaks my heart even more."

I turned to leave, hoping she'd stop me and tell me I was wrong about everything. That she accepted me no matter what and that she was there for me. But hoping for that was like hoping every day would be sunshine. I made it to my room without being stopped, packed about a week's worth of clothes, including my work uniform, in a duffel bag, and left to go over to Uncle Frank's without Mom even coming out of her room to say bye. As I passed Nikki's house, I considered asking if I could stay there instead, but then decided I didn't want to get them any more involved in this mess than they already were.

I called and left Nikki a message since I knew she was at work to let her know where I would be. It took everything I had not to call Maya. I doubted she would change her mind and call me, so it didn't make any sense to let her know where to reach me. All I could think about was that maybe I shouldn't have told her about Justin. Or, even better, I shouldn't have given in in the first place. I felt like crap mentally and physically and touched my lotus pendant for comfort. Was this the swampy muck I had to get through to bloom? I hoped so because I couldn't imagine feeling any more mired down by the mess that I'd created than I already did.

Chapter Eleven

I kept myself busy prepping for Spelman, working, and avoiding confrontations with my mother. I also went back home after Dad, Tanya, and J.J. left for Indianapolis. It was hard to say good-bye to my little sidekick, but I knew he would be much happier and feel more secure about himself being with Dad and Tanya. Dad's recent promotion required much less travel, so he would be home with J.J. more often, and Tanya was able to provide that mother figure he needed so much in his life. Dad and I had a long talk about the plans he and Mom had made to go down to Georgia with me. He was still determined to do it, whether she went or not, and made me promise to leave the discussion for him to have with her so there would be no reason for us to get into another battle. Since Jackie, who decided to stay at a friend's place in the city for the summer, and J.J. were gone, it was like two ghosts haunting the apartment. We barely spoke to each other unless we had to. I spent as much time as possible away from home, and when I was home, I stayed in my room.

It went on that way until two weeks before I was scheduled to leave for Georgia. Dad told me the previous night that he'd spoken to Mom about the trip, but she still hadn't confirmed if she was going. I was in my room trying to organize what I was taking with me and what could be shipped later when Mom knocked on my door.

"Yes." I didn't even bother looking up from what I was doing.

"I've decided not to go to Georgia with you and your father."

It took me a moment to respond because even though I had been expecting her to tell me that, it still hurt. How was it possible for me to keep allowing her to hurt and disappoint me? My eyes burned as I tried to hold back tears that I refused to continue to shed because of her.

"Okay." I could see out of the corner of my eye that she stood there a moment longer before she sighed and walked away.

I finished what I was doing, showered, changed my clothes, and headed next door. Nikki and I were going to a club in the city later, but I didn't want to stay in the house any longer than I had to. If I did, I would've been too tempted to ask Mom why. If she had a good excuse as to why she wouldn't see her own daughter off to college, her alma mater, then she would've told me. I was done. I'd be gone in two weeks, leaving her to wallow in her "poor me" pity party alone. I knew that seemed cold, but I refused to let her continue pulling me down into the pit with her.

"You look like you really need this night out," Nikki said.

"I do, and I plan on drinking heavily so I may need to stay here for the night. Drunk me would not be good having to deal with my mother."

Tipsy Janesse was just silly and all about a good time. Drunk Janesse had no filter. I said what was on my mind without hesitation or regard for anyone's feelings. I needed Drunk Janesse tonight because I was needing to release some serious stress. We took the train into the city. Since I had gotten to her house earlier than planned, Nikki decided we could do dinner and pre-cocktails at Bonnie's Restaurant, which was above Bonnie & Clyde's, the nightclub Nikki had been wanting to take me to all summer, but I'd been too cowardly to go. Since I was leaving in two weeks and this was going to be our own private farewell celebration, I figured what the heck. Nikki was also making dinner for Justin and me for our musketeer farewell next weekend.

"Just a couple more weeks and you'll be heading South," Nikki said.

I picked at my salad. "Yeah, I guess."

Nikki frowned. "You don't sound particularly thrilled about it."

I laid my fork down, not feeling very hungry. "I am. Mom told me she wasn't flying down with me and Dad."

"What? Why?"

"She didn't volunteer the information and I didn't bother asking. I'm tired of fighting."

Nikki nodded in understanding. "Yeah, I guess I would be too if I were in your situation. I wish there were something we could do for you."

"You can help me enjoy tonight. No more talk about any of my issues. So, what's going on with you and Carrie? I noticed she hasn't been around lately."

Nikki shrugged. "It's over. I think we got all that we could out of it."

"Do you regret it? Do you think you should've just left it as one of those things you would always wonder what would've been?"

"Not at all. I'm glad we got together. I think it helped me figure out what kind of relationship I want when that time comes and helped Carrie do the same. She's definitely not a monogamous type of woman and I respect that. It's just not the lifestyle for me."

"So, you don't think she'll ever meet that one person who could make her want to be in a monogamous relationship?"

"I obviously wasn't that person, but I honestly can't imagine her changing that much. She's pretty set and confident in who she is and what she wants. She said if she ever did settle down it would probably have to be part of a polyamorous relationship."

I looked at Nikki in confusion. "A what?"

Nikki chuckled. "You really need to read more about sexuality and the different relationships. It may help you figure out your own confusion. A polyamorous relationship is one with more than one person at a time. It could be two guys and a girl, two girls and a guy, or all three could be the same sex. They could be gay, straight, or bisexual. It all depends on what the people in the relationship are looking for. Although Carrie is more into women, she's into dudes sometimes also. She says she doesn't believe in limiting her pleasure and experiences to one or the other."

"Was she seeing other people while she was with you?"

"Not that I'm aware of, but she's pretty straightforward so I think she would have told me if she was. Especially if it was a dude because she knows I don't play that way."

The waiter brought our main entrees.

"You think that's something I would be happy doing? Being in an open relationship like Justin suggested?"

Nikki raised an eyebrow. "I thought we weren't supposed to be talking about your issues."

I grinned. "We're not exactly talking about an issue so much as a solution to an issue."

"Okay." Nikki looked doubtful. "Truth telling?"

"Truth telling." If I could count on anyone to cut the bull and give me their honest opinion it was Nikki.

"No, I don't. I think a polyamorous relationship would just cause you more problems. You'd end up spreading yourself too thin and driving yourself crazy trying to please two different people and not even think about what makes you happy, which is what you need to figure out before trying to be in a relationship with anyone. You need to take your time doing that. Just be by yourself for a while. When you get horny, find a friend or two with benefits to help you out. Someone you know you won't have any emotional connection with but know they could hit it right when you need it."

I stared wide-eyed at Nikki. "I can't believe you just suggested that."

A flash of humor crossed her face. "Just because I don't do it doesn't mean it might not work for someone else, and college is the perfect time to explore and figure out what you want for yourself and your life. Personally, after my summer with Carrie, I'm cool with not dating or sleeping with anyone for long while. You, on the other hand, need to take some time to explore your options."

I took a moment to think about what Nikki was saying. Maybe it was good that Maya and I wouldn't be together right now. I did need some time to just be by myself and get to know me. Figure out who Janesse was and what she wanted.

I nodded. "I think you're right."

Nikki gave me a smile of encouragement. "You got this. You know you can always call me if you need a pep talk."

I reached across the table and took Nikki's hand. "Thank you. You know I truly love and appreciate you, right?"

"Of course I do. The feeling is mutual."

After dinner we made our way downstairs to the nightclub. It was still a bit early, but there were a good number of women already there, and they were mostly Black women. It was sort of surprising to me. Obviously, I knew several Black lesbians, but I had been around the same women for so long that seeing so many I didn't know was a shock to the system.

"You're looking real fish out of water right now," Nikki said, grinning as we walked toward the bar.

I shut my mouth, which I hadn't even realized was slightly agape, and moved my wide-eyed stare in her direction. "There are so many of us."

I knew I sounded stupid, but I couldn't help it. My introduction to gay women had been my cousin, Nikki's mothers, Nikki, and Maya. Other than Nikki, everyone else pretty much represented the feminine lesbian. As I looked around the room, there were femmes, butches, and some that I would have sworn were men if it weren't for the swell of breasts underneath their shirts.

I glanced over at one woman standing along the wall nearby who grinned and winked at me. I quickly looked away and leaned toward Nikki. "Nikki! How does the chick behind me have boobs and a bulge?" I whispered.

Nikki subtly glanced over my shoulder and grinned back at me. "Some studs like to pack their pants with a dildo to impress the chicks who may be into that."

I looked at her wide-eyed. "Oh."

"Janesse, just relax. There are women in here who can smell a virgin a mile away, especially if you sit here looking around like you've never been out of the house before."

I looked at her in confusion. "I'm not a virgin."

Nikki quirked a brow. "So, you've had sex with a woman?"

"Oh, that kind of virgin."

Nikki didn't bother hiding her amusement. "Yes, that kind of virgin. I'm sure there are plenty of women here who would be happy to relieve you of that burden."

Nikki ordered my usual vodka and OJ, and I sipped at it as I tried to discreetly peruse the room while bopping on the barstool to the music.

Nikki sipped on her drink as she did the same. "In about an hour the crowds will start arriving and by eleven it'll be packed. There's a pool table and some quiet space upstairs if the music or crowd starts to get too much for you. If it becomes too overwhelming, just let me know and we'll leave. Do you want me to stay with you or wander off at some point, so it doesn't look like we're here together?"

"But we are here together." Once again, my naivete showed.

Nikki outright laughed. "Janesse, you're killing me."

That's when I understood what she meant, and my face heated in a flush of embarrassment. "Geez, I should've stayed home."

Nikki shook her head. "No, I was just as bad as you the first time I came out to one of these bars. How about we do this. If there's someone you see that catches your eye, I'll take a quick stroll upstairs so you can do your thing."

"What thing? I don't even have a THING to do."

Yeah, I definitely should've stayed home, I thought as I gulped down the rest of my drink. It was a good thing we had eaten before coming down here because as fast as I drank that, it would've gone straight to my head. I turned back toward the bartender for another when she set a full glass in front of me before I had a chance to ask. I looked at Nikki and she shrugged. I looked back at the bartender, who pointed to the end of the bar where a gorgeous woman who looked to be about Jackie's age smiled and saluted me with her glass. I gave her a tentative smile, lifted my glass to her, and looked down at it like it was the most interesting thing in the world.

Nikki chuckled. "Damn, we're here fifteen minutes and you're already pulling them in."

My face heated once again. "Shut up."

"Face it, Janesse, you're hot. I've always told you that. Especially in that dress."

I had chosen something tight, short, and sexy because I knew it would be something Mom would not have been too happy to see me in. Fortunately, she was in her room when I left. The sleeveless black dress had a low-cut neckline in the front and back.

"Thanks."

"No need to thank me for the truth."

Within a half hour, I had two more drinks bought for me even though I had barely finished the second one. Well, at least Nikki and I wouldn't have to spend too much money on drinks for my plan to get drunk. The other two drinks came from two other women who were more of the soft butch type and were also a little older. The music picked up and I glanced over at the first woman who bought me a drink, and she gave me a sexy smile as she stood and made her way over toward us. Her walk was slow, confident, and sexy as hell. She was dressed in a low-cut sleeveless gold top that might have been a bodysuit the way it fit her like a second skin emphasizing nicely shaped breasts, flat abs, and muscular arms, a pair of ivory wide-leg slacks that couldn't hide her generous behind, and gold platform heels. With the heels, she looked to be a few inches taller than me which meant she might be my height without either of us wearing heels. Her hair lay in soft curls, smoothed, and held up on one side of her head with hairclips and lying past her shoulders on the other side. My fingers itched with my sudden need to find out if it was as soft as it looked or if my fingers would come away covered in hairspray.

"Stop staring so hard," Nikki whispered.

I blinked several times and quickly looked past the woman to the people on the dance floor.

She stood directly in front of me, changing my view of the dance floor to her cleavage. "Hello."

I opened my mouth to speak but nothing came out, so I tried clearing my throat. "Hello," I managed to croak.

"If your friend doesn't mind, I'd like to ask you to dance." She looked over at Nikki.

"That is completely up to my FRIEND," Nikki said. I could hear the amusement in her voice as she emphasized that.

The woman looked back at me. "Would you like to dance?"

I took a long sip of my drink and handed the glass to Nikki. "Yes, thank you."

She offered her hand and I let her lead me onto the dance floor. I quickly glanced back at Nikki, who was giving me a thumb-up like she used to when I hit the sidelines to lead a cheer routine. I lost sight of her as we entered the mass of bodies on the floor. I turned back toward my dance partner just as she found a spot for us to get our groove on. It was tight but it was enough room for me to do my thing. The only activity I loved doing almost as much as photography was dancing.

As I let the bass from the house music run through me and watched the sexy moves of my partner, I danced away all my doubts, worries, and fears. I set my mind free and gave my body control. I could spend hours on the dance floor just letting the rhythm guide me along until I was drenched in sweat but content. Dancing and photography were the only things in my life I had no doubts about. How I felt on the dance floor and looking through the lens of my camera were things I knew no one could take away or make me feel ashamed of. As I watched the woman across from me move with the same freedom and abandon, I wanted her with such an intense physical need that my lower body clenched with desire. She looked at me in that moment, and I knew she saw what I was feeling in the way I looked at her. She smirked and pulled me close so that we were moving as one with the beat.

Despite the gyrating and heat of the bodies around us, all I could see was the intensity of her dark eyes and feel her body moving so naturally with mine I shivered at the sensation of her hand sliding from my waist, down my hips, and cupping my behind. I placed my hand on her hips and loved the feel of her curves. I loved watching a trickle of sweat run down her neck, over the curve of her breasts and then get lost in her cleavage. I inhaled the exotic scent of the perfume she wore mixed with her own musk rising the longer we danced. I lost track of time as her soft curves bumped with mine.

She leaned in toward me and her lips brushed along my ear. "You're so fucking sexy."

I grinned and brushed my lips along her jawline. "So are you."

She moved back just enough to look me up and down, bit her lip, and shook her head. I licked my lips and smiled. The alcohol and music made me bold and let loose some wild, uninhibited part of me I had no idea was there. She pointed toward the stairs, which I took to mean she wanted to go up to the lounge area. I nodded and she took my hand once again to lead me off the dance floor. As we walked up the stairs, I glanced toward the bar. Nikki's seat was occupied by someone else. I knew she wouldn't leave me, so I assumed she was probably dancing.

"Would you like a drink?" my mystery woman asked.

"Yes, vodka—"

"And OJ," she finished with a teasing grin. "There's a table over in the corner. Why don't you grab it for us?"

She was bossy. I sort of liked it. "Okay."

I strolled over to a nearby seating area. On the other side was a pool table where several women were chatting and playing a game. Besides the bartender, we and the pool players were the only occupants of the lounge. The bass of the music thumped beneath us. I sat on the sofa trying to calm the sudden nervousness that overcame me the moment we left the dance floor. It had been my security blanket and now I was on my own.

Mystery lady walked over with our drinks, handed me mine, and sat facing me. "Here's to making new acquaintances."

She raised her glass, I tapped mine against it, then took a large gulp of my drink for courage. It burned its way down my chest. My eyes watered a bit, but I managed not to cough and choke. The upstairs bartender was a lot more generous with the vodka than the one downstairs.

The mystery woman chuckled. "My name is Keisha."

I realized with embarrassment that we had practically made out on the dance floor and were just now introducing ourselves. "Nice to officially meet you. I'm Janesse."

"What a pretty name. Is this your first time at this club?" Keisha asked.

"Yes." I was sure she already knew it was, so there was no sense in lying. "Do you come here often?" Geez, if that didn't sound like a corny movie pickup line.

"I come here frequently. I've seen your friend, but I haven't seen you before. She is just your friend, right? I'm not stepping on any toes talking to you?"

"No, you're not. Nikki and I are more like sisters."

Keisha scooted closer to me. "Good. So, Janesse, are you here out of curiosity?"

I took another sip of my drink. "I'm here just enjoying a night out with my best friend," I said noncommittally.

Keisha looked me up and down. "I'm going to be honest with you. I'm out here looking for a good time as well, but I'm not sure it's the same good time you're out for. The moment you walked into the club I wanted you, but I'm not here to waste my time with little girl games."

Keisha leaned in toward me and placed her lips on mine. They were so warm and soft and tasted sweet, which must have been from the martini she was drinking. She ran the tip of her tongue along the outline of my lips, and I almost dropped my drink. She pulled away with a chuckle and placed both our glasses on the table, then moved so close that the only thing separating us was a thin strip of air. She began kissing me again and I finally joined in. The intense need that ran through me on the dance floor hit me again. It was purely physical, like a hunger that needed to be fed. I don't know how long it lasted, but the sound of snickering brought me back to the reality that we were sitting in a nightclub not a bedroom.

The look Keisha gave me seemed to say she wished we were in a bedroom. "Well, you definitely know how to kiss a girl."

My face heated with a blush. That was about all I knew how to do with a girl, but I wasn't going to tell her that.

She looked at me curiously. "How old are you?"

"How old do you think I am?" Nervousness had me leaning on sarcasm.

She quirked a brow. "I told you I'm not into games."

"Eighteen."

"Have you ever had sex with a woman?"

"Does it matter?"

Keisha leaned forward, picked up her drink, and stood. "It was nice meeting you, Janesse. Thanks for the dance."

Dammit, what was wrong with me? I had a hot older woman trying to seduce me and I was blowing it. "No, I haven't," I blurted.

Keisha sat back down. "So, you and that good-looking friend of yours have never explored anything more than friendship?"

"No. Like I said, she's like a sister to me."

"Would you like to be with a woman?"

Boy, was that a loaded question. Until now, there had been only one woman I had wanted to finally take that step with, but I had blown that one. Now my body was still on fire from Keisha's kiss, and I felt like if I didn't take advantage of what she was so openly offering me I would never understand what was holding me back from finally opening to my sexuality. I leaned forward and pressed my lips against Keisha's. We had another passionate kiss before she smiled against my lips.

"I guess that's a yes."

"Yes, it is. Since you asked me, do you mind telling me how old you are?"

"Does it matter?" She gave me a wink.

I liked how she turned that back on me. "No."

"I'm twenty-five."

That made her older than Jackie but not as old as I would have thought from the way she carried herself. She also seemed a lot more experienced than any of the high school girls I'd been fooling around with.

"Dance with me some more," Keisha said.

I nodded and we headed back downstairs, passing a dancing Nikki on our way. She gave me a "So, what's up?" look and I gave her an "I think I'm in over my head" look but also a discreet thumb-up so she'd know I didn't need rescuing yet. She nodded. Like twins, we had our own silent language. We danced until Nikki squeezed through the people around us and pointed to her watch. I had lost track of time and we had to catch the last train back to Jersey. I nodded and looked at Keisha.

"I'll walk out with you!" she yelled over the music.

The three of us made our way through the crowded room toward the exit. As soon as we walked out the door, my ears began ringing slightly from the sudden silence. I awkwardly stood between Nikki and Keisha, who both looked at me expectantly. Not knowing what else to do, I introduced them. They greeted each other and then Nikki told us she'd go hail us a taxi.

"I'd like to see you again," Keisha said.

Even with the alcohol still coursing through me, I suddenly felt shy. "I'd like to see you also."

"Good."

She reached into the back pocket of her pants, pulled out a small silver case, took out a business card, and handed it to me. "That has my business and personal number. Give me a call this weekend."

"Okay. I will."

Keisha took my face in her hands and gave me a slow, soft kiss good-bye. "I'll be looking forward to hearing from you," she said in a sexy voice.

I opened my mouth to speak, but nothing came out, so I turned around and walked toward Nikki and our waiting taxi. We climbed in. Nikki gave our driver our destination, then turned and looked at me.

"You okay?" she asked in amusement.

"She gave me her business card and told me to call her." I showed Nikki the card.

"You gonna call her?"

"I don't know. I feel like she's way out of my league."

"She doesn't think you are."

"Do you think I should call her?"

Nikki snorted. "If I were you, I would. You're leaving in two weeks, and I can't imagine that she's looking for something serious. I've seen her at the club often. She seems to have quite a fan club who weren't too happy seeing you with her most of the night."

"While we were talking up in the lounge, she told me what she was looking for. She was straightforward about it."

"Well, you gotta admire a woman who knows what she wants. So?"

I gazed back down at Keisha's business card. "She's only looking for a good time, she's sexy as hell, and obviously has plenty of experience. I'm lonely, horny, and really want to have sex with her."

Nikki chuckled. "You're calling her."

I smiled. "I'm calling her."

I thought I was nervous getting ready for my first date with Maya, but that was nothing compared to the anxiety I felt on my way to Keisha's. The cab pulled up in front of a row of brownstone buildings in Greenwich Village. I paid the driver, got out, and slowly walked up the stairs to Keisha's building. I rang the doorbell with "DOUGLAS" prominently displayed for the second-floor apartment.

"Is that you, Janesse?" Keisha asked over the intercom.

"Yes."

"C'mon on up."

A loud buzzer sounded followed by a click, and I went through the heavy ornate door. For a moment I stared up the staircase debating if I was really ready for this, then I took a deep breath and marched my way upstairs as if I were going into battle. I'd barely lifted my hand to knock when the door suddenly opened. Keisha stood in the doorway dressed in a black satiny looking lounge set.

"You get lost coming up the stairs?" she asked.

It took me a few seconds to tear my eyes away from her large nipples outlined by the thin material. "Uh, no, sorry."

Keisha stepped aside and directed me to come in. "Can I get you something to drink? You look like you could use a little something to relax."

I gave her at tentative smile. "Yes, thank you. Vod—"

"Nope," Keisha cut me off, wagging a finger at me. "Let me surprise you with something different. Less boring. After all, I'm hoping this will be a night full of new experiences for you." She placed the finger she wagged at me under my chin, leaned forward, and pressed a warm, soft kiss on my lips.

"Have a seat, get comfortable. I'll be right back," she said.

As she walked away, I found my feet seemed to be rooted to the spot as I watched the sway of her hips and noticed how smooth the satin material was over her rounded behind. She either had to be wearing a G-string or nothing at all under there. She went around a corner, taking the tempting sight out of my line of vision and finally giving me the ability to move. With a shuddering breath, I walked farther into the apartment. The furniture looked comfortable but expensive, so I was afraid to sit on it. I didn't come dressed like a bum, but I also felt a little underdressed in my black slacks, pearl button-down blouse, and black ballet flats for such a classy lady's home.

Keisha returned with two filled martini glasses and handed one to me. The drink looked just as fancy as everything else in the place. I sipped, expecting not to like it, and was pleasantly surprised.

"You like it?" Keisha said.

I nodded. "It's good."

"Better than a boring old vodka and orange juice."

I smiled. "Yes."

"It's called Between the Sheets."

I choked a little on the sip I had just taken. Keisha winked and sat down on the sofa, tucking her leg up under her and patting the pillow beside her. After clearing my throat, I perched on the edge of the sofa as if I were ready to make a run for it if needed.

"You know, I honestly didn't expect you to call."

I looked over at her in confusion. "You didn't want me to call you?"

"I didn't say that. I wanted you to call, but I thought you might not be ready."

I knew what she meant. She thought I would chicken out because I had never been with a woman before. I took a long drink of my cocktail and set my glass on her coffee table.

"I guess I'm ready." I sat back on the sofa trying not to look like I wasn't.

"You guess?"

This time I looked Keisha directly in the eyes. "I am."

"Good. Then there's no need for the pretenses."

Looking at me seductively, Keisha set her glass next to mine, took my hand, and stood. I followed her down a hallway to a softly lit bedroom. She left me standing by the bed as she walked over to a stereo system and turned on some soft jazz. It reminded me of the music they played during sex scenes in movies.

As she came back toward me, shedding what little clothing she wore with each step, I felt like I was in one of those movies. I was playing the part of the nervous but eager young high school virgin about to be seduced by the sexy older woman. I was right. She had been naked under her loungewear and was completely bare of any hair except for what was on her head, which framed her face like a soft curly halo. Her nipples stood proudly erect and the dark brown of her areolas looked like tempting chocolate treats against her tawny brown complexion. Her breasts were full and beautiful, her small waist merged into generously curved hips and behind. Other than the *Playboy* magazine collection hidden in a crate in the back of Nikki's closet, I had never seen a naked woman who looked like Keisha. She could have walked right off one of those centerfold pages.

Keisha stood before me with a sexy smile. "You like what you see?"

I nodded. "I wish I had my camera." It was the only thing I could think of when I saw something beautiful, and she was, without a doubt, beautiful.

She looked amused. "I'm assuming that's a compliment."

My face heated with a blush. "Yes, I'm a photographer, well, I want to be one."

"Really? Next time you'll have to bring your camera and show me what you got."

I gulped. "Next time?"

"Depends on how tonight goes." Keisha reached up and began unbuttoning my blouse. I tried helping her by pulling it out of the waistband of my pants, but she shook her head.

"Tonight is about your pleasure. If that next time happens, then you can call the shots."

I was once again speechless. I simply stood there as Keisha undressed me, but it wasn't a simple removal of clothing. With each bit of skin revealed, she laid a soft kiss, spending a little extra time at each of my nipples, driving me to the point of whimpers, then kneeling before me as she worked on my pants and underwear. I was so glad I had worn my black lacy matching bra and panty set instead of my usual cotton Fruit of the Looms. She stopped and, with disappointment, I thought the teasing kisses were done, but she waited until I had stepped out of my shoes and the pile of clothes at my feet to return to her task. As she kissed an outline around the patch of hair at the juncture of my thighs, I had to grab one of the bedposts to keep my knees from buckling. I also thought about shaving that area as soon as I got home. Then her hands began smoothing up along my legs, hips, and kneading my behind. I began trembling.

"Lie down," Keisha said.

Somehow her firm, sexy voice breached the fog of desire clouding my mind, and I did as I was told. The way I was feeling I would have done anything she asked me. She joined me on the bed, hovering above me, and began her soft rain of kisses. This time she added the tip of her tongue and fingers to the party. I was practically writhing off the bed and making noises I had never heard myself make before. After each intimate kiss was laid upon me, her fingers would follow with soft caresses that grew firmer the farther down my body they traveled. She stopped at my navel and stroked it with her tongue as she plucked at my nipples. I gasped when each pluck and gentle pinch triggered a growing throb within my clit and inner walls. I could feel moisture gathering in the curls surrounding my vagina.

I moaned loudly, reached down, and tangled my hands in Keisha's hair, then changed my mind, grabbing the bedding instead to keep from yanking her hair out. Suddenly, her lips and hands were gone. I opened my eyes wide to find her kneeling at my feet looking at me with eyes grown so dark with desire they were practically black. Once again, I wished I had my camera because this woman was ten times sexier than any of those *Playboy* chicks.

"Prop yourself up a little on the pillows and spread your legs for me, Janesse."

I did as she asked without question, then watched her slowly lower herself between my legs, holding my gaze the whole time. She ran her fingers along my vaginal lips, met my clit, and her eyes widened. This was it, I thought, my abnormally huge clit was going to turn her off. She gazed down between my legs then back up at me, but I didn't see disgust; she was looking at me in anticipation.

"What do we have here?"

She took her fingers, wet with my moisture, gently grasped my clit, and slowly stroked it. I tried to watch, tried to keep eye contact with her because I had never seen anyone look so turned on by my clit. Not that I had a lot of people to compare it to, but it was the sexiest thing ever and it was making my orgasm come a lot quicker than usual. My inner walls clenched, my clit strained against her touch, and colorful lights, like the ones in Nikki's meditation room, flashed behind my eyelids.

"Ohgawdohgawdoh…gaawwd."

"Yes, baby, come for me."

Well, since I had been doing so well following her instructions so far, I thought I might as well keep going. My orgasm seemed to go on forever, and I thought it was over until I felt her lips around my clit. Keisha sucked and flicked the tip of her tongue over it and somehow held on as my hips rose off the bed, and I shouted so loud I was convinced that whoever lived upstairs would not be happy with the noise I was making. When the explosion below my waist ended and the lights behind my eyelids dissipated, I lay there unable to lift a finger. I hadn't even realized Keisha was no longer between my legs until I opened my eyes and saw her lying beside me, her head propped up on her hand, licking her lips and grinning like she'd just had the most satisfying meal ever.

She reached over and softly ran her fingers along my breasts. "You are quite the pleasant surprise."

My face heated in a blush. "I assume that's good."

Keisha looked very happy. "Oh yes, incredibly good. I think we're going to have lots of fun together."

Seeing the desire in Keisha's eyes and seeing her sensual body lying naked beside me caused the blood that seemed to have left my limbs after my orgasm to flood back in a wave of desire that had me wanting to make Keisha feel just as good as she made me.

"Would you like to touch me?" she asked knowingly.

"Yes." I fought the shyness that came over me.

Keisha lay on her back, arms above her head, her legs slightly spread with one knee up, and gave me a look that sent a jolt through my body. "Touch me wherever you like."

I sat up, looked over at Keisha, posed and offering herself up to me like some concubine in a romantic novel, and I was at a loss as to what to do next. *"Just do what she did to you,"* the little voice in my head said, which made perfect sense. If I want to make her feel the same way she made me then I should do what she did to me. I hesitantly leaned in to kiss her and, just as she had done to me, I explored her body with my lips, tongue, and hands. When I reached her breasts my mouth practically watered. I took one of her aroused nipples into my mouth and moaned in pleasure. There were two things about a woman's body that instantly turned me on, nipples and butts. I don't know why just the nipples and not the whole breast. It could be that when I saw an erect nipple it was like looking at a tempting piece of candy for me to suck and savor. That was how I treated Keisha's chocolate-colored nipples. I suckled and savored them until I heard Keisha moaning and felt her writhing beneath me.

Knowing what I was doing was pleasing her gave me the confidence to go from there. I continued my descent, inhaling her clean, musky scent, loving the feel of smooth, soft feminine skin and curves beneath my hands and lips instead of the hard angles and planes of the one guy I'd been with. When I reached the juncture of Keisha's thighs, she spread her legs wider for me. I gazed up at her to find that she was watching me with passion-filled drowsy eyes, lips slightly parted and breathing heavily. It was a boost to my inexperienced ego to know that I had made her look that way. I settled myself between her legs and became fascinated with the treasure that lay there. This was my first time giving pleasure to another woman, and I felt very self-conscious about my lack of experience. I closed my eyes and took a moment to remember what had given me pleasure during oral sex prior to tonight as well as what Keisha had done to me. When I opened my eyes, they met Keisha's patient and expectant gaze.

I lowered my head and did my best to please Keisha, not realizing how much pleasure I would get from giving oral to another woman. It was so much less invasive than with a man for the obvious reason that needed no explanation. I enjoyed her slowly, exploring every fold of her womanly lips, savoring the taste of her, inhaling the scent of her arousal, feasting on her like she was my last meal. Keisha's hips rose off the bed, her hands tangled in my hair, and her pants of pleasure combined with my own rising arousal and brought on a chorus of moans and cries from both of us. Keisha's body tensed and she called out my name just before she drenched me with the liquid warmth of her orgasm, which sent my own orgasm firing through my body. Afterward, as she lay slack beneath me, I laid my head on her thigh just enjoying being anywhere near her pretty sex.

"I think someone has undersold their experience," Keisha said.

I placed a light kiss on her smooth mound and pulled myself up to lay beside her. "That really was my first time doing that. I started off just doing what I liked to have done to me, then you tasted so good I did what would give me even more of you."

Having never really talked so openly about sex with someone I barely knew, I felt my face heat in embarrassment.

Keisha turned onto her side to face me and must have seen my blush. She stroked my cheek. "Well, I think you're a natural." She gave me a teasing wink and kissed me. "Do you have to be home tonight?"

The look of eagerness on Keisha's face gave me pause.

"Uh, no," I answered.

"Good."

I wasn't given the opportunity to sleep until the wee hours of the morning. When I woke up around ten, the sun was shining brightly through the curtains and Keisha was gone. My clothes were folded neatly in a nearby chair, and a note lay on top of them from Keisha explaining she had a job today, told me I was welcome to shower and grab something to eat, and that the door would lock automatically when I left. She also told me to call her if I was interested in seeing her again later this week. My body still tingled from our sex-filled night, and the thought of doing it again left no doubt in my mind that I would be calling her. I had no qualms about what this was between us. She had made it clear last night that this was strictly for pleasure, nothing more. I was fine with that. I could use a fun and drama-free distraction in my life right now.

CHAPTER TWELVE

The next night, I would've sworn I was dreaming if my body wasn't tingling from the past hour of sex with Keisha as I stood over her while she posed seductively on the bed while I snapped pictures. When she told me to bring my camera, I didn't really think she would offer to pose nude for me, but as I looked through my lens at the vision of her still glowing from sex, hair sexily mussed, and a satiated expression on her beautiful face, I was glad she did. I even got adventurous and took a few of what I called artistic shots of just her body, with a few focused on a particularly just licked and glistening area. I don't know what made me take those pictures, but her sex was so beautiful to me.

"I'm assuming you aren't taking these to a regular film developer," Keisha said after one of my more intimate shots.

"No, I set up a darkroom in my basement."

Keisha looked impressed. "You really are serious about this?"

I sat on the edge of the bed to reload more film. I was finished, but just in case she wanted to do more I would be ready. "Yes. It's going to be my major with writing as my minor."

Keisha propped her head on her hands and watched me. "What school?"

"Spelman."

Keisha sat up. "No kidding! That's my alma mater. Got my business degree from there three years ago."

I looked at her in surprise. "I had no idea?"

"Why would you? We haven't talked much." She gave me a wink.

I blushed. "Yeah, I guess we haven't. How did you like it?"

"I loved it. I was a legacy. My grandmother and mother graduated from there."

"I'm a legacy too. My mother."

Keisha nodded. "Small world. If you really are serious about your photography, I can introduce you to some people. As a matter of fact, I'm doing hair and makeup for a fashion shoot on Friday. Why don't you tag along? Afterward, we can come back here, order some dinner," she leaned forward and took one of my nipples into her mouth, "and enjoy each other for dessert."

My breath caught and I barely got out an "Okay," in response.

"Good, we'll talk during breakfast in the morning. Right now, I'm going to continue enjoying what's on tonight's menu."

I arrived home feeling satiated, a little sore, and content. Keisha and I didn't pull an all-nighter like we had during our first time together because she had an early client, but we filled the time we did have constructively. As well as when she joined me in the shower that morning. The image of her sitting on the shower bench with my leg over her shoulder as she did things with her tongue that had me almost pulling the bar off the wall would be burned in my mind for quite some time. Not even seeing Mom's car still in the driveway could put a damper on my mood. I had a sexy, fun, uncomplicated lover, who also happened to work on photo shoots with many well-known fashion houses and publications. She was scheduled to work a shoot for Harlem fashion designer Dapper Dan, and I would be tagging along. I was on cloud nine and nothing was bringing me down.

"Where the hell have you been!" I had barely walked into the apartment and Mom was marching toward me looking angry as heck. I could practically see the steam coming from her ears.

I gave her a smile. "Good morning to you too." I was refusing to let her get to me. "I told you I was staying at a friend's overnight."

"No, you didn't!"

She was practically in my face now, giving me little room between her and the door. I kept my expression as pleasant as possible.

"Yes, I did. I told you two days ago, and I reminded you before you left for work yesterday." I squeezed by her and headed toward my room.

Mom followed and I had to repeat a mantra of *"not today, Janet"* in my head to prepare me for the craziness she was more than likely about to rain down on me.

"This is the second night you stayed out with God knows who doing God knows what, and I don't like it."

I went through my closet and dresser to find clothes to change into. "Sorry to hear that because it's happening again on Friday."

"Look at me when I'm talking to you," Mom said.

I took a deep breath and turned to her. "If all you're going to do is yell at me then there's nothing to talk about. The first time I called to let you know, and the second time I gave you advance notice, so what's the problem?"

"The problem is I don't like this sudden change in you. You're never home anymore, you're out all hours of the night and barely say two words to me." She looked genuinely hurt by it all.

My cloud nine was beginning to drift away. "You do remember I'm leaving for school in a little over a week. There are a lot of things I need to do before I go."

"I guess spending time with your mother isn't one of those things," she said accusingly.

Here came storm clouds darkening my mood. Why did I let her do this to me? I ran my hand through my hair in frustration.

"Mom, a couple of months ago you pretty much kicked everybody out the house, have barely spoken to me since, and you recently told me you weren't going down to Spelman with me and Dad without giving any explanation as to why. Do you really expect me to want to spend any more time in this apartment than I have to?"

"I expect you to act like the respectable young lady I raised you to be. Not the one spending the night with people I don't know and coming home in the same clothes you left the house in like someone with loose morals." The look of disgust she gave me hurt.

"I'm not doing this. I'm done fighting and I'm done with you trying to make me feel bad for being who I am. Can you please leave my room? I need to get dressed."

Mom stood there, looking as if she were daring me to make her leave. I shook my head, went around her, and went to the bathroom to get dressed, making sure to lock the door behind me in case she decided she needed to finish bashing me. I sat on the edge of the tub trying to take slow, calming breaths to keep the tears at bay, but it didn't help. I tried to find the feeling I had when I first got home, but it had gone the way of my self-confidence whenever these battles happened with my mother. I started to feel a little ashamed of what I'd been doing with Keisha. Sex-filled nights with a woman I barely knew anything about. A strong, independent, confident, sexy woman who, in just two nights made me feel almost as independent, confident, and sexy as she seemed. Although our nights were filled with passion, there were moments in between when we chatted. Not about anything major until the night when we discussed school and my career choice, but enough that I was starting to feel good about my body, my sexuality, and my choice to just do me for a while. Now, in a matter of minutes my mother had put a dent in my confidence armor. I stood up and looked at myself in the mirror.

"No, I'm not letting her do this to me. I can't," I said to myself.

I touched my lotus pendant. "You're blooming. Don't let her throw mud back over you and bury what progress you made so far."

I was enjoying myself, I wasn't hurting anyone, had been offered the opportunity to network with a professional photographer to help guide my career, and would soon be leaving my mother's bitterness behind. I wiped away my tears and got myself mentally and physically together. Nikki, Justin, and I were meeting for a day at the mall and lunch, and I was not going to spend our last days together before we separated wallowing in the residual of Mom's mess.

I stood naked gazing unseeing out Keisha's bedroom window. It had been an unbelievable day. Not only did I get to meet Dapper Dan himself, but the photographer let me shadow him for the day as well as take a few test shots. Fortunately, at Keisha's suggestion, I had brought my portfolio with me, and during the lunch break he looked it over, gave me some tips, and told me to reach out to him if I needed a job next summer. It was so awesome to be in the midst of it all that I knew I had chosen the right path for my career. He didn't mince words. He told me it wouldn't be easy, that I'd probably spend my first several years as an assistant or overpaid gofer, but I didn't care. If it eventually led to me doing what I loved, it would be worth it. My excitement from the day spilled over into the bedroom after Keisha and I had dinner. Feeling confident and respected not just by my interaction with the photographer but how Keisha treated me as her equal when she could easily use me and set me aside had me feeling pretty bold that night. Thinking about our passionate night helped to dispel the melancholy my mom had brought on.

"What has you staring contemplatively out the window at this hour?" Keisha asked as she wrapped her arms around my waist and kissed the nape of my neck.

"Guess I'm just still excited about the day we had." I turned and wrapped my arms around her waist. “Thank you again for letting me hang with you today. I learned so much and it helped cement what I want to do with my photography.”

Keisha gave me a soft kiss. “You’re very welcome. Mack really liked you. It was a nice touch to have done your research on him. To drop those compliments about his style from particular shoots was a good idea.”

“I couldn’t walk up into a Mack Taylor shoot not being able to ask him about his work. That would just be sacrilegious.”

Keisha chuckled. “Janesse Phillips, you are so much more than what I expected the night we met.”

I smoothed my hand over her behind and cupped one of her cheeks. “Is that good or bad?”

Keisha moved a knee between my legs and pressed her thigh to my now waxed sex. The lack of hair made me more sensitive than I could’ve imagined, and I loved it. I moaned as my clit swelled and came into contact with her thigh.

“Come back to bed,” she said seductively.

I gladly followed and was rewarded pleasurably.

We fell back to sleep tangled in each other’s limbs. The next morning, I woke up to find Keisha already up, dressed, and in the kitchen drinking a cup of coffee.

“Why didn’t you wake me?” I asked, placing a kiss on her cheek and pouring myself a cup. I rarely drank coffee, but Keisha had all these flavored creamers, so I was able to tolerate it if I drowned it with one of them.

“I figured since you didn’t sleep too well, I’d let you sleep in a little.”

I leaned against the counter next to her. “Thanks. Full schedule today?”

Keisha nodded. “It’s also going to be our last morning together. I have to travel for a job next week. I had planned to tell you last night, but we barely finished dinner before you ravished me.” She grinned as she sipped her coffee.

I could feel a blush coming on and willed it away. Whenever she caught me blushing or embarrassed by being overzealous when it came to sex, Keisha would tell me to never be ashamed of my passion. It was a lesson I was slowly learning.

“So, I guess this is it,” I said.

“Don’t make it sound so final. I hope, despite how we started, we at least became friends this week and that you'll stay in touch with me. Maybe call me when you're home on break."

"I'd like that."

"Good, I have to get downstairs to the shop, but I left you a parting gift in the foyer. Don't open it until you get home."

"You didn't have to get me a gift."

"I know, but I wanted to, so I did. Come here." She held her arms open to me.

I set my coffee down and walked into her embrace. I felt a little sad but also good about our parting. I had learned so much about myself this week with Keisha.

"You take care of yourself, Janesse, and don't take yourself so seriously. I hope you enjoy your college experience as much as I did." We had one final, passionate kiss before she left me standing alone in her kitchen.

I finished my coffee, placed our mugs in the dishwasher, then showered and dressed. This time I brought a change of clothes instead of wearing the same ones from yesterday home. After making sure I wasn't leaving anything behind, I walked out to the foyer to find a camera bag with a bow on it sitting by the door. It wasn't just any bag. It was an expensive one that I had been looking at for some time but couldn't imagine spending the money for. I wondered why Keisha said not to open my gift until I got home when it wasn't even wrapped, then I picked the bag up and realized it was full. I was so tempted to open it and see what was inside, but I would do as she asked and wait until I got home. I left the apartment, and when I got outside, I saw that her shop, located just outside the apartment building, was already busy. I tapped on the glass of the door to get Keisha's attention, not realizing that everyone else would look up as well. I focused on her hoping my face hadn't turned too red, gave her a wave, and mouthed "Thank you," pointing to the bag. She signaled, opening it, and I shook my head. She gave me a thumb-up, then blew me a kiss. If my face wasn't already a mottled blush color, then that would do it as I quickly blew her a kiss and rushed away.

Mom wasn't home when I got there. She left a note on my bed letting me know she had an open house today and tomorrow. I was relieved. We hadn't spoken since the other morning and I didn't mind at all. I know it probably should have bothered me, especially with me leaving at the end of the week, but I really couldn't handle dealing with her anymore. I went to my bedroom, cleaned out my overnight bag, then sat down to see what was in the camera bag from Keisha. My jaw almost hit the floor when I opened the bag. It was a Canon T70 35mm single-lens reflex camera with the full system, components, and accessories. I'd have to work for months just to save up for the bag alone, but the camera and components cost a fortune. It would take me years to save up enough to buy the whole kit sitting before me. I picked up my phone and called Keisha's shop.

"Keisha, this is too much. I can't accept it," I said when she came to the phone.

"You can and you will. Consider it me investing in your future. I could be working for you some day, and I'll be happy to do it knowing I had a hand in your success. If you want to be the best, you need to have the best equipment. Now, say thank you." I could hear the amusement in her tone. It made me smile.

"Thank you."

"You're welcome. I've gotta go. Take care, Janesse."

"You too, Keisha."

After we hung up, I sat there staring at the camera bag until my vision clouded with tears. Even now, when I should be feeling like I was on top of the world, I couldn't help to think that a woman I had only met a week ago believed in me more than my own mother.

I stood in the middle of Nikki's living room surrounded by what had become my second family, Nikki, Frieda, and Carol. Nikki and I were trying to hold back tears while her mothers let them flow freely as I said good-bye to them.

"You sure you don't want me to come to the airport with you?" Nikki asked.

"Positive. What kind of friend would I be to subject you to the awkward car ride home with my mother?"

"I'd suffer through it for you."

"I know you would." I pulled her into a tight hug. "What am I going to do without you?"

Nikki sniffled. "You're going to make it through because you're stronger than you think." She separated us, gently grasped my shoulders, and looked intently into my eyes. "You have to believe in yourself just as much as all of us believe in you. You're a smart, loving, and beautiful person who I'm honored to call sister-friend these past years as well as many more years to come. Don't let anyone, that includes your mother, have you believing otherwise."

Aw, man, that did it. I felt the warmth of tears sliding down my face. Carol and Frieda wrapped both Nikki and me in a group hug and planted a kiss on each of my cheeks.

"I couldn't have said it better," Frieda said.

"I'd like to add one more thing." Carol stepped away to grab a box nearby and hand it to me. "So you'll not only have a little piece of us with you but also to keep you focused on your spiritual self just as much as your physical self."

I opened the box to find my crystal lotus cushioned on a bed of tissue paper. "Thank you." I was full-on crying now. Runny nose and all.

We had one more group hug before Nikki walked me out.

"You're gonna kill it at the Culinary Institute," I told her, trying to take the focus off me.

"I hope so. I guess we'll call each other in a couple of weeks to check in on how we're doing."

"Definitely. I love you, Nikki."

"I love you too, Janesse."

We embraced once more, and I hurried away before it got even harder to leave.

About an hour later, Mom and I were pulling up at Newark Airport. Dad's flight from Indianapolis was arriving soon and we planned to meet at the gate for our flight to Atlanta. We got out of the car, and Mom helped me grab my suitcase, duffel bag, and the camera case from Keisha. Mom had asked about the case when I loaded the car, and I told her I had saved up for it. She had no idea how much it was, just that it was new. I was sure if she had gotten a look at the equipment inside, she would know it wasn't something I could afford on my own. We checked the suitcase and duffel bag, and I kept the camera case and a backpack with essentials with me.

"Would you like me to wait with you until your father's flight arrives?" Mom asked.

It was the first time she had spoken since we left the house.

"No. I'll just wait for him at the gate. I want to grab some snacks on the way for the plane."

"Do you need any money?" Mom started to reach into her purse.

"No. I got it."

We stood in awkward silence for a moment.

"Mom."

"Ness."

We spoke at the same time then smiled. "You first," I said.

Mom nodded. "I know the past weeks haven't been easy. We've both been out of sorts, but I hope you know that no matter what, I love you."

Out of sorts? I tried not to snicker aloud at that description of what it had been like with her. She looked like she genuinely meant what she said, so I couldn't fault her for at least trying.

"I know you do. I love you too."

She looked relieved. To my surprise, she pulled me into an embrace. I tentatively wrapped my arms around her, and we held each other for a long moment. It had been so long since I felt my mother's arms around me, I almost cried, but I held it together. Showing signs of weakness around my mother did nothing but cause her to go on the defense. I didn't want to leave with us in a bad place.

"Have a safe trip and let me know when you arrive. I-I'm sorry I can't go with you, but I've got several showings this week that can't be rescheduled." The look on her face said she believed that as much as I did, but I let it go.

I gave her a slight smile. "It's okay, Mom. I better go."

She nodded and released me. I adjusted my backpack, grabbed my camera bag, and turned to leave but stopped. "Mom, I hope you'll take this time to find what makes you happy," I said, walking away before she could respond.

Move-in day at my dorm was hectic, exciting, and daunting. Mom's alumni pull got me into the Howard-Harreld Hall, the largest of the freshman dorms. Dad and I had spent the week shopping for bedding, bath linen, and decor for my side of the double dorm room. The room was open but separated by wardrobes, so it gave a nice bit of privacy and the opportunity to fix up my space without worrying about clashing with my roommate. When Dad and I arrived, my roommate was already there and putting the finishing touches on the left side of the dorm room which I had hoped I could get because it was away from the door and the side of the room I had at home. She obviously had been smart enough to get here a day early and stake her claim, so I couldn't fault her for that. After all the shopping, Dad and I had decided to take a day to do some sightseeing, which was why I would be living on the right side of the dorm for the next ten months.

"Hi, you must be Janesse," she greeted me with a broad, cheerful smile and offered her hand. "I'm Connie Baldwin."

"Nice to meet you, Connie. This is my father."

"Nice to meet you, Mr. Phillips." Connie shook Dad's hand then smiled back at me. "I hope you don't mind that I got here early and staked my claim. I shared a room with my sister and always slept on the left side."

"No worries," I said.

"Great! I'm just going to finish up and head to the dining hall for lunch. Maybe I'll see you there?" Connie said.

"Maybe I'll make it there by dinner," I said, indicating the cart full of bags and luggage my dad had pulled into my side of the room.

"Okay, well, have fun getting settled." Connie left the room with a wave in parting.

"She seems nice," Dad said.

"Yeah, and she definitely likes pink."

Dad looked over my shoulder at Connie's side of the room, which was covered with frilly pink bedding, pillows, curtains, and other pink accessories. There was a bit of green thrown in here and there, but it looked like a cotton candy factory had blown up on her side of the room.

"Looks like she brought every stuffed animal she owned from home," Dad said in amusement.

"As long as she keeps to her pink paradise over there then I'll be fine." I began unpacking my warm, soothing, earth tone color palette decor, and got to work making the currently stale space my own cozy peaceful home away from home. The one good thing was that Connie and I were both used to sharing a room so I didn't foresee any issues, but you never knew. Even Jackie and I got on each other's nerves sometimes, but we didn't have anything dividing our space like the dorm did. With Dad's help, we were finished within a couple of hours, including unpacking my clothes.

"Well, kiddo, that's it. It looks good," Dad said, surveying our work.

"Yeah, it does."

It wasn't home but it was all me and that's what mattered when it came to me adjusting to living away from home. I had even managed to set up the lower shelf in the wardrobe for my meditation items.

The only thing missing was the incense since I didn't know how my roommate would have felt about it, or if I could even burn it in the dorm. I would have to settle for taking a good inhale from the bottle of nag champa oil I brought.

"Well, I guess I better get going. My flight is in a few hours," Dad said.

I had managed to keep it together all morning, but Dad leaving me here alone made this moment that I had kept placed in the back of my mind rush front and center. So did the tears.

"Aw, Nessy, you're going to be fine," Dad said, wiping a tear off my cheek. I could see he was fighting to hold his own back. It made my heart swell knowing he felt just as emotional about this as I did.

"Thank you for being here, Dad. It meant a lot."

He pulled me into his arms. "I couldn't let you tackle such a momentous occasion in your life alone." He took my face in his hands. "The rest is up to you. Focus on you and your goals. Let everything and everyone outside of that handle their own stuff. This is your time, Nessy. Embrace and enjoy it for the wonderful experience it'll be. I love you, baby girl."

The tears really came now. This was what I needed, a parent's love and encouragement, and I knew I could always depend on Dad for it. "I love you too."

We embraced once more before Dad placed a kiss on my forehead and left. I took a deep breath and released it slowly. This was it. I was on my own for the next ten months. I went to the window between my bed and wardrobe and gazed down at the courtyard of students and parents just arriving or saying good-bye. It was comforting to know that I wasn't alone in this journey. That we would all be sharing the same experience but in our own way. This was the start of a new and exciting path, and I planned to embrace everything that came with it, the good and the bad, with my arms and eyes wide open.

I watched Dad walk down the path toward the parking lot and, for just a moment, I wanted to open the window and yell for him to come back and take me home, but the feeling passed just as quickly as it had come. There was nothing at home but frustration and heartache. This was where I needed to be to move in a more positive direction in my life.

❖

I made my way to the dining hall and spotted Connie at a table with four other girls as she talked very animatedly. I was just about to leave when we made eye contact.

"Janesse!" she shouted my name across the room, excitedly waving me over to her table.

"So, you're all settled in?" Connie asked.

"Yeah, pretty much. I just came looking for something to eat."

"Oh, there's still another hour before they close the kitchen, so you made it in time."

Connie introduced me to the other girls at the table. They gave me a friendly greeting, but one named Andra kept squinting at me curiously.

"I know you from somewhere," she said.

Andra had a practically shaved head, big, hammered copper earrings, and wore an Afrocentric jumper dress with a black short sleeved mock turtleneck. She had a deep mahogany complexion, dark brown eyes, a straight nose, and full lips. As far as I could tell, unlike the other girls at the table, her only makeup was a wine-colored lipstick. She didn't need makeup to enhance her natural beauty.

I definitely would have remembered meeting her before. "Where are you from?"

"New Jersey. You?"

"Me too. Montclair."

Andra nodded. "You're friends with Nikki Carter. My last name is Peterson. I'm Carrie Peterson's cousin."

"Oh." I tried to keep a pleasant smile on my face, but I don't think I fooled Andra because she chuckled.

"Yeah, I'm related to her and I'm not a fan. You probably don't remember meeting me at her sweet sixteen party. I'm one of her Newark relatives, so she doesn't deem to talk to me too much."

I couldn't help but grin. Carrie and I might have gotten along a little better when she and Nikki started dating, but she was still bougie.

"What a small world," Connie said cheerfully.

Her face held the same exact expression it had when we first met. I'd never met anyone so happy before, and I wasn't sure how that was going to work with us rooming together. Especially when I got into one of my moods where I had little patience for all that grinning.

"I haven't eaten yet either. I'll go with you to find out what's good here," Andra said.

There was a station for freshly made sandwiches, a hot food and grill station, a salad bar, and refrigeration units with drinks and desserts. Since my academics were taken care of with the scholarship, Dad decided to foot the bill for housing with a meal plan so I could focus on my studies and not worry about how I was going to eat from one day to the next. The food looked pretty good so I couldn't see myself starving. I still had money stashed away from working at the theater if I decided to splurge and get something from off campus.

"My cousin wasn't too crazy about you, which leads me to believe that we'll get along great," Andra said in amusement as we waited for our burgers and fries.

I grinned. "That's good to hear. Wouldn't want to make enemies on my first day here. Did you know Connie before?"

"No, me and the others were debating whether we could still get lunch when she volunteered to walk with us over here. She seems to know everything there is to know about campus. Gave us a mini tour as we walked."

"She must have gotten here early this week because her side of our room was all set up when I arrived this morning."

"Yeah, Connie was telling us that she's a fifth-generation legacy student and has an aunt who's an English professor. She practically grew up here. Her father is a Morehouse man. If she had been a boy, she would have been a third-generation legacy there."

"Wow, I'm surprised she doesn't have a dorm room all to herself."

"She said she told her mother she didn't want any special treatment. She wanted to experience everything just like a regular student here for the first time."

I snorted. "I jumped at the chance to take advantage of being a legacy. That's how I ended up in a double rather than the quad I was originally assigned."

Andra wrinkled her nose. "Yeah, I wish I could've done that. I'm not a legacy. I'm the first in my immediate family to go to college, so I got stuck with the quad. I've only been here a day, and I already know I'll probably be spending a lot of time studying in the library or lounge. All my roommates have talked about since they arrived is what party over at the Clark campus they were going to hit up first and which sorority they were pledging."

The mention of Clark brought on memories of Maya that I had thought were locked away. I hadn't forgotten she was just a short distance away at Clark University, I just chose not to think about it. I wondered how she was doing. If she was settled into her dorm and making friends. If she would meet someone who gave her more than I could. If she still smelled like citrus and sunshine.

"Hey, Earth to Janesse, you still with us?" Andra was snapping her fingers in front of me. I hadn't realized I'd drifted.

"Sorry, got a little distracted in thought."

"Yeah, I guess you did. He wants to know if you want pickles on your burger."

I looked from her to the cook with an embarrassed smile. "Oh, no, thank you."

We grabbed our food and headed back to the table.

"You looked a little sad while you were off in your thoughts back there," Andra said.

"Yeah, sorry about that. Was thinking about someone." I tucked thoughts of Maya into the back of my mind. "So, what are you majoring in?"

Andra took the hint and we chatted about our majors as we got to the table, which had collected a couple more girls who were pulled into our conversation when they realized what we were discussing. It was nice to be around such a diverse group of Black girls who all know what they wanted for their education and life and weren't hesitating in getting it. For the first time in my life, I felt I was where I belonged.

CHAPTER THIRTEEN

I had just put the finishing touches on my new dorm room when the door banged open and Andra stumbled in with two large suitcases.

"Hey, roomie!" she said cheerfully.

I ran to hold the door open for her. "Hey. You need me to grab something for you?"

She pushed her suitcases into the space just inside the door and turned to go back out. "Nah, I got it. If you could just hold the door, I'll be good."

It was the start of our second year at Spelman and we had requested to be roommates in our new hall. Fortunately, I managed to get another double for the year, so it was just Andra and me. We were both thrilled. I was because as sweet as Connie had been, I didn't think I could take another semester of sharing a room with her overly bright disposition. I needed someone down-to-earth and real who wouldn't hesitate to tell you the truth, even if it might hurt your feelings. That was Andra. She was like the straight version of Nikki. Andra was just thrilled not to have to share an overcrowded room with three other girls who were more into partying than their education. She walked back in with another huge suitcase then flopped back on her bare mattress.

"Whew! I am beat," Andra said.

I closed the door and sat at her desk. "What in the world did you bring with you? You plan on going home at all?"

"My mother got a new job over the summer making more money and insisted I needed all new bed and bath linen. That last suitcase is enough to last me a few weeks without having to repeat a set."

I grinned in amusement. "I'm assuming the other two are clothes?"

Andra looked embarrassed. "Yeah, she decided to take me shopping for a new wardrobe as well. One suitcase is what she bought.

The other is what I'll actually be wearing. She thinks I need to dress less Bohemian and more fashionable." Andra pushed herself up and sat crossed-legged. "Enough about my ridiculous luggage, tell me how your summer break went? It's crazy how we were just a couple towns over and still didn't get to see each other with my summer camp gig and then having to stay in Philly for a month to help my grandmother."

"Yeah. I was also busy with my summer job. The hours were crazy. Up at the crack of dawn and working until late into the night sometimes."

"You have to tell me all about it. Did you meet any big-time models or designers?"

I smiled. After a busy but exciting first year at Spelman, I had reached out to the photographer Keisha had introduced me to and got hired for a gofer's job with him for the summer. As soon as anyone heard I was working for a major fashion photographer they assumed I was working in the limelight with celebrities in the fashion industry, but I had spent more time running errands than I did at the actual shoots. I didn't mind because I got paid, and it might have been from way in the background, but I had still learned more about the industry than I would have working at Wellmont Theater for another summer. My boss had taken time with me in between shoots to teach me the craft of fashion photography. It was an awesome experience that I wouldn't have traded for the world. I told Andra all of this.

"Well, it still sounds glamorous to me. Especially since I spent my summer babysitting a bunch of hormonal preteens then helping my mom care for my grandma."

"I was sorry to hear about her stroke. How's she doing?"

"She's doing well. We had to sell her house and move her into a senior village. She seems to like it."

"That's good to here. Well, I'll let you get unpacked. We can finish catching up later. I have a couple of calls to make."

"Okay, cool. Tell Nikki I said hi."

"Will do." My phone wouldn't be hooked up until after the weekend, so I went out to one of the phone cubbies down the hall. Nikki wouldn't be going back to school until the following weekend.

"Talk to me," Nikki said when she answered the phone.

I chuckled. "You're so silly."

"Hey, you."

"Hey. I just wanted to let you know I'm all settled in."

"Cool. You and Justin must be on the same wavelength. I just hung up with him. He's already talking about heading out to some welcome party at one of the frat houses."

"Why am I not surprised. I don't know how he manages to party so hard and keep his grades up. I need like a week to recover from some of these college parties before going to another."

"Hey, at least you guys have parties to go to. As you know, I'm out in the boonies, there's no partying or clubbing for me unless I go into the city, which wouldn't be worth it."

"Well, you know I've never been a party girl unless there was dancing. There seems to be more drinking than that going on, so I rarely venture out to them."

"From what he told us over the summer, it sounds like Justin is doing enough partying for the three of us."

Over the summer, the three of us all worked and rarely got together. My gig kept me busy, Justin had gotten more responsibilities at his uncle's construction company, and Nikki got a baker's assistant job that had her working overnight some days. The most time we spent together was our pre-planned week at the shore, kicking off our annual event. We had seen each other briefly during the holidays, but it was the first time just chilling together, and it was better than the previous year. Justin and I were cool. Any drama that had been between us had been put behind us, and it had made the week so much more relaxing and fun.

"Yeah, but as long as he's happy, that's all that matters. Are you ready to head back to school?" I asked.

Nikki sighed. "Yeah, but I'm wishing I would've applied to the Institute of Culinary Education in Manhattan to be closer to home. It wouldn't be so bad if we weren't out in the boonies and people didn't look at me like I'm some sorta freak when I leave the campus. I'm thinking of just finishing out this semester and seeing if I can transfer to ICE."

"Wow, I didn't know it was so bad. You never say anything when we talk."

"I know. You've got enough on your plate and it's not like you can do anything about it. I've been dealing with it, but just thinking about another semester there makes me dread going back."

I hated hearing the sadness in Nikki's voice. It wasn't fair how she was judged and treated by her masculine appearance without people even taking the time to get to know her. "You tell your moms about it?"

"They agree with looking into transferring. I'm going to ICE this week to see what I need to do to apply."

"If you got into Culinary Institute, I can't imagine you not getting into ICE. I'll send some positive vibes your way."

"Thanks. So, did you see Keisha before you left?"

Memories of my last night before leaving for Georgia flooded my body with heat. "Yeah, we had an early dinner and spent the rest of the night saying good-bye."

"Aw, suki suki now. You got your own little sugar mama," Nikki teased.

"Shut up. She's not old enough to be a sugar mama. She's sort of like a mentor."

Nikki laughed. "A sexual mentor. Maybe I'll find one of those once I transfer."

I smirked in amusement. "It's more than sex. We're friends with benefits. I told you last semester she would call me every now and then to check on me. It was the only reason I was able to get the gofer job. She put in a good word for me and had my interview all set up by the time I got home. She also took me to a few parties over the summer and introduced me to some more photographers and videographers in the fashion and music industry."

"Sounds to me like you're getting all the benefits. You get hot sex and get to be arm candy for a fine ass woman as she introduces you to important people to help get you established. Sounds like the typical sugar mama and girl toy relationship to me."

I knew Nikki, and probably the few others that knew about Keisha, saw us that way but I didn't. It made what Keisha and I had cheap, which was far from it. We were genuinely friends. Yes, the sex was hot and would sometimes go for most of the night, but there were times when we would lie in bed and just talk afterward until the early morning. And not just silly stuff, but deep philosophical talks about life. What had started out as a brief encounter turned into something far more than either of us expected. We weren't in love or anything like that, but we did have something that couldn't be considered a casual fling. If it hadn't been for her, I probably would've stayed at Uncle Frank's instead of with Mom when I came home for summer break.

Mom and I had another falling-out when I decided to go to Indianapolis for spring break instead of home. After spending Christmas break trying to avoid her as she questioned why my wardrobe was so risqué now, why I still insisted on spending so much time at Nikki's, and why I barely called her while I was away, just the thought of a week going through that again gave me anxiety. Finding out I was going to Indy sent Mom into one of her woe-is-me episodes, and I went off on her. I don't even remember exactly what I said, but I know "self-absorbed" and "miserable old woman" were used. She eventually hung up on me and we didn't speak again until she called me for my birthday acting as if nothing ever happened. At that point I had planned to call Uncle Frank and ask to stay with him for the summer, but a couple of weeks later, our elderly landlady passed away, and Mom bought the house from her son with the intention of moving upstairs to the bigger apartment and renting out what had been our home. Keisha suggested I offer to pay Mom rent for the summer to stay in our old apartment. That way she wouldn't feel I had completely abandoned her again and I would still have my own space. To my surprise, Mom agreed to the idea. By the time I got home for summer break she was happily ensconced upstairs and left most of our furniture downstairs. It worked out great for us. I would go up occasionally to have dinner with her, talk about anything that didn't set her off, and then go back to my own space to chill. Keisha's suggestion had been a lifesaver and our friendship would be one I knew would last for a long time.

"Keisha suggested I do a summer in Europe. Expand my portfolio internationally," I said.

"That sounds cool and expensive."

"Not if I go with her," I said hesitantly.

There was a moment of silence on the other end. "Wow, she wants to take you to Europe with her?"

"Yeah, it wouldn't be until after I graduate but it's something she's wanted to do and has been saving up for so she could go without worrying about money. She thinks it'll not only be nice to have someone come along but for that person to be able to grow from the experience. I haven't given her an answer yet. Told her I needed to think about it."

"You sure she's not getting more serious about your relationship than you are?"

"Positive. She said she sees a lot of herself in me and just wants to help me enjoy and experience life the way she has."

"Then you should go. I wish someone would offer to take me to Europe for a summer. Could you imagine what I could learn from European pastry chefs? That would take my skills to another level."

"You don't think that would be weird? Planning to traipse off across the world in two years for a whole summer with a woman I occasionally have sex with and hooks me up with jobs?"

"Yeah, but it also sounds freaking awesome. Besides, who knows what will happen between now and then. Say yes for now with the agreement that if anything changes between you guys, she won't hold you to it. It would be pretty awkward taking a trip like that with someone you no longer speak to."

"Good idea. Maybe, by then, you could come with us."

Nikki snorted. "Yeah, I'm sure Keisha wouldn't be too thrilled with the idea of you inviting a friend along."

"You never know. Maybe I'll suggest it as an opportunity to help you build your experience also."

"Good luck with that. Hey, I gotta go, we're going into the city for dinner. I'll call you later in the week to let you know what happens with ICE."

"Please do. Good luck and give your moms a hug from me."

"Thanks. Will do."

As I walked back to my room, I thought about how much had changed in a year. I had gained so many new acquaintances and friends, found my independence, and sort of found myself. That still needed work. I was no longer self-conscious about my appearance, I had learned to embrace my curves, even wearing more form-fitting clothing. The issue still lay with my sexuality. Anybody who thinks being a woman attracted to women going to an all-women's college would be a dream come true has another think coming. I thoroughly enjoyed the strong feminine energy and the feminine companionships I had experienced my first year because it gave me such a wonderful sense of community. It also made accepting my sexuality more difficult, especially when I found myself attracted to someone. I knew there were gay women on campus, but I didn't feel confident enough to approach anyone who was open about their sexuality, for friendship or otherwise.

I was afraid of repeating the debacle that happened with Maya. Especially when the guys from Morehouse came on campus for joint events with Spelman and I found myself attracted to any of them. It didn't happen often, but it was enough to keep my doubts and confusion in the forefront of my mind. I had been asked out by both sexes and managed to turn them down without hurt feelings by letting them know as flattered as I was, I needed to focus on school. That was partially true. The workload for college courses was ten times heavier than high school, but I had been able to keep my grades up with a little extra effort, so I don't think they would have suffered by dating anyone, but the people asking didn't know that. The best thing for my sanity and my heart was to just keep focusing on school and leave my urges locked down until my breaks when I could go home and take them out on Keisha.

One late afternoon while Andra and I made our way across campus, I had the shock of my life seeing Maya walking toward me. I stopped abruptly, my mind and body frozen. As if they no longer knew what to do. She was busy talking to another girl and hadn't spotted me yet. Andra had been talking to me and must have reached a point in our conversation where I was supposed to respond because she stopped a few steps ahead of me and looked back at me in confusion. I felt my eyes grow wide in panic as I looked from her to Maya and back again. I had to get away before Maya noticed, I looked around frantically trying to find an escape, but we had reached an open area with nothing but open grass and low shrubs. I was considering throwing myself into the shrubs when I heard something that weakened my knees.

"Janesse?"

My name on Maya's lips was like a siren's call. I slowly turned toward her and was greeted by wide eyes and that beautiful gap-toothed, dimpled smile.

"H-Hi, Maya."

"I can't believe this is the first time we've managed to run into each other," she said.

She walked toward me with her arms open and I felt an all-new sense of panic set in. I just knew that if she touched me, I was going to fall to my knees, begging her to forgive me and give me another chance, but I couldn't move. Her arms came around me, the smell of citrus and sunshine, enveloped me, and everything I felt for her that I had shoved away into the back of my mind burst forth. I wrapped my arms around her and closed my eyes with a shuddered sigh. We stood that way for probably a moment too long because someone nearby loudly cleared their throat. Maya and I slowly separated, but she continued holding my hands and smiling happily at me.

"You look good," she said.

"You do too." She was casually but fashionably dressed as usual, and her hair lay in loose, natural curls along her shoulders. "Your hair is so long now. It looks pretty."

She looked down shyly. "Thank you."

"Yo, Maya, we gotta get going."

I glanced over Maya's shoulder to the two girls she had been walking with. One gave me a knowing smile, the other gave me such a hard stare I thought the ground was going to open up and swallow me whole. I was used to those looks from the days before Carrie and Nikki dated, so I simply gave her a nod of acknowledgment and focused back on Maya.

"She's right, I have to go. We're going to a lecture in your Black literature department and I don't want to be late. What dorm are you staying in? I'd really like to talk," Maya said.

I told her what building and room number. "We should be back about six. If that's too late, we could meet up this weekend." I was not blowing a second chance with Maya. I didn't care how wishy-washy my sexuality was. The fact that she seemed happy to see me and wanted to make plans to talk gave me hope that I hadn't totally effed everything up between us.

"No, six is fine. There's a mixer afterward that I wasn't sure I was going to stay for, but now I will. I'll see you then. It really is good to see you, Janesse." She gave my hands a quick squeeze before releasing them and continued walking.

Her friend gave me what I guess was her best look of warning to back off then followed behind Maya and the other girl like a lovesick puppy dog.

"Wow, what was that all about?" Andra said.

"What?"

She pursed her lips. "Don't give me that innocent look. There was so much heat coming off you two I thought it was going to melt the rest of us."

My face heated in a blush. "She's an old friend." I had told Andra I was bisexual and briefly about Keisha, but I hadn't told her about Maya at all.

She looked at me skeptically. "Old friend, my ass."

"Long story short, we dated for a bit and I screwed up."

"Must not have been too bad. She greeted you like she wanted to reignite whatever you guys had. Although, I don't think her friend would be too happy about that."

I thought about the way Maya's friend looked at me. That look was filled with pure jealousy, but if there was more than friendship between her and Maya, I didn't think Maya was aware of it. She hadn't even bothered introducing the chick.

I shrugged. "I'm not even going to try to guess what's on Maya's mind or her intentions. I'll find out when she comes by to see me later."

"I'll be sure to make myself scarce when she does," Andra offered.

"You don't have to do that. We could sit in the lounge or something."

"No, you should have some privacy. Besides, I have to go to the library to do some research anyway."

"Okay, but don't feel obligated to leave if you change your mind."

I would have preferred having Andra there as a buffer. I had a feeling that whatever Maya wanted to talk about was going to be a major game changer in how easy and uncomplicated my life was right now.

A little after six, the lobby called to tell me I had a visitor. I had meditated for a few minutes after Andra and I got back to calm my nerves, but they were once again fraught with anxiety. When I arrived at the lobby to meet Maya I was once again mush at the sight of her smile.

"Hi," she said.

"Hi."

"Is now still a good time?"

"Yes. My roommate is out for a while so we can go to my room, or if you prefer, we can sit in the lounge."

"Your room is fine."

"Great, it's just down the hall here."

We walked quietly side by side. At one point someone was coming from the other way, and Maya placed her hand on the small of my back as she moved to walk behind me. It was a brief touch, but it was enough to send a flame of desire surging through me. My face felt hot and I fumbled with the keys trying to open the door.

"Here we are. My space is on the left." I directed Maya to my side of the room. Fortunately, I didn't have to haggle with Andra to get the left side of the room because she preferred being near the door. She said it was an easier escape if anything happened.

"I see you're keeping up with your meditation." Maya cocked her head at the little nook I had created in a corner near the end of my bed.

It was just enough space for a small cushion and my altar, which held my crystal lotus, electric oil heater, and mala beads.

"Not as frequently as I'd like, but I get at least ten minutes in first thing in the morning. My roommate meditates as well. It makes it a lot easier when someone understands and isn't slamming stuff around or talking on the phone during sessions."

Maya sat on my bed. "Was that your roommate you were with earlier?"

For a moment, I was conflicted about sitting on the bed beside her or sitting in my desk chair. I chose the bed so that she wouldn't think I was trying to avoid being near her.

"Yeah, that was Andra. Funny coincidence, she's Carrie Peterson's cousin."

Maya's eyes widened. "Really? And you get along?"

I nodded. "She's NOTHING like Carrie, which is why we get along so well."

There was a momentary lull in our conversation. I looked over at Maya, who was chewing on her bottom lip. She looked nervous. I was the one that caused our breakup. What would she have to be nervous about?

"Maya, why did you want to talk?"

She sighed and turned toward me. "I owe you an apology. One that should've been given over a year ago."

"I don't understand. What could you possibly owe me an apology for?"

"The day we broke up, you were trying to be honest with me and I treated you so wrong."

Maya looked as if she were about to cry, which gave me a tightness in my throat and made my eyes prick with unshed tears.

"You don't owe me an apology. I messed up and I wouldn't have expected you to do anything less than to kick me to the curb."

"No, you didn't deserve that. You had gone through something confusing that ultimately made you realize what you wanted, which was me, and all I could see was the hurt my ex had caused. You aren't her. You didn't do anything half as bad as she did, and I should've been more understanding. I should've talked to you about it instead of running away. I'm sorry." The tears finally fell, and she looked so sad that it broke my heart.

"It's okay." I wiped the tears from her cheeks with my thumbs. "I understand and I accept your apology even if it isn't necessary."

"You do?"

I nodded, grabbed a box of tissues off my desk, and handed it to her. "Maya, you were right. I wasn't ready for a relationship with anyone, whether they were a male or a female. I had a lot to figure out about myself in addition to adjusting to being on my own away from home for the first time in my life. It wouldn't have been fair to either one of us to also try to be in a serious relationship."

Maya blew her nose and nodded. "I guess that's true, but that doesn't make how I treated you right. There were so many times I had almost come over here and wandered the campus looking for you freshman year but chickened out because I thought you wouldn't want to see me."

"We must have been on the same wavelength because I almost did the same thing."

A sad smile touched her lips. "It's too bad we didn't do it. We could've said all of this so much sooner."

I gave her an encouraging smile. "Better late than never."

Maya cocked her head and gazed at me curiously. "How've you managed to stay so easygoing?"

I shrugged. "I've tried to keep the mindset that there are some battles not worth expending energy over. A negative mindset just brings negativity."

"You're going to have to teach me how to do that," Maya said, then looked down at her hands. "That's if you'd like to hang out or something some time."

"What, as friends?"

She looked warily back up at me. "Yes, if you'd like."

I reached over and smoothed a curl from her face. "Is that what you want? Friendship."

Maya licked her lips and sighed deeply. "After all this time, I still want you, but I'm not going to assume you feel the same way. A lot could've happened in a year. You could be seeing someone."

I quirked an eyebrow at her. "You could be also. The chick who was with you earlier in the denim dress looked mighty jealous while we were talking."

Maya looked confused for a moment. "Lena? We've been roommates since freshman year. I don't see her that way."

"Well, she definitely sees you that way."

"You think so? I never gave her any reason to think I was attracted to her."

"Maybe she's been crushing on you from afar. Either way, if looks could kill she would've skewered me earlier."

Maya grasped my hand. "Well, just for the record, I'm not seeing anyone."

I managed to keep my cool despite wanting to pull her in my arms and kiss her silly. "Neither am I."

Maya grinned. "Let's do this properly. Janesse Phillips, would you like to go out with me?"

I looked up as if I were seriously considering my answer. "I don't know. This all seems so fast. After all, we just re-met."

Maya's brows furrowed in thought. "You're right. I should just take back my question."

I smiled at her calling my bluff. "No, don't! Yes, I'd like to go out with you," I hurriedly said.

"Are you free tomorrow night?"

"Yes. Any time after four. That's when my last class ends."

"Okay, how about six? I'll meet you here and we can get a taxi into town. Have you been to Pittypat's Porch?"

"No, but I've heard about it all last semester and had planned on going this year."

"Good. Let me be the one to introduce you to it," Maya said excitedly.

"Okay." Her infectious smile made me smile also.

"Well, I've gotta get back. I have a paper due in a couple of days and I'm not even half finished."

"I'll walk you out." I tried not to sound disappointed since I would be seeing her in pretty much twenty-four hours.

We headed toward the door when Maya stopped me and pulled me toward her. Our lips met and it felt like a jolt of electricity ran from our lips and zipped throughout my body. We kissed as if we had been starving for it. Our bodies meshed, and we clung desperately to each other. When I thought about Maya over the past year and how we were together I thought I had exaggerated the sense of home I felt in her arms, but as that feeling overwhelmed me while we kissed, I knew it was very real. It wasn't a matter of whether I should be with a man or woman, it was that I needed to be with Maya.

A few minutes later, we came up for air, breathing heavily as we grinned at each other.

"I've been wanting to do that since we walked in here," Maya said.

"Me too."

We continued just gazing at each other, then, with a sigh, Maya stepped out of our embrace.

"You've gotta go," I said.

"Yeah."

I walked her out of the dorm, we had a more sedate good-bye hug, and I watched her until she disappeared around the corner of the building. As I turned to go back in Andra came from the other direction and looked at me knowingly.

"Judging by how you look like you're glowing and the smile practically splitting your face, you had a good get-together with Miss Maya."

"It was okay," I said, unconvincingly trying to be nonchalant.

Andra chuckled. "Yeah, okay."

I looked back toward the direction Maya had gone and realized that all my plans to stay out of any kind of romantic involvements flew right out the window and I didn't mind in the least.

I had been a nervous wreck when Maya and I started our date, but within moments it was as if a year, and heartbreak, hadn't come and gone. We got caught up on what had been going on in our lives over that time and got to know the people we had become since then. I hesitantly even told her about Keisha, wanting to start things off with full disclosure. As it turned out, she knew of Keisha. Fashion, hair, and makeup stylists worked closely together in the industry, and Keisha was one of the stylists Maya had hoped to work with one day. I wasn't sure how I felt about that but set that concern aside and focused on enjoying our date. It was so good it led to many more. By Thanksgiving break, we were officially dating but we weren't open about it except within our circle of family and friends. For me, on the Spelman campus, that consisted of Andra and Connie. Outside of Spelman, pretty much everyone important in my life knew. Nikki and Justin, everyone in my immediate family, except for Mom. Knowing how she felt about that part of me, we stayed away from the topic of my love life. I also told Keisha, who was disappointed our affair was over but happy for me and insisted on meeting Maya when we came home. It felt weird thinking about introducing them considering the extent of both relationships, but Keisha could help Maya make some good connections for her career and I wouldn't want to get in the way of that.

Fortunately, I had plenty of time to get used to that idea since we wouldn't be going home for Thanksgiving. Maya's parents and brothers were flying to Atlanta to spend the holiday with their family here, so she asked if I wanted to stay also and spend it with her family. I had already met her parents and brothers when we dated previously but meeting the entire family on a major holiday was serious.

"If you're not ready to take that step, I understand," Maya said after asking me.

I thought I was ready. I mean, we had only been dating for a couple of months, but I couldn't imagine us not going for the long haul. The next step would be meeting the family.

"I'm ready. I just wasn't sure if you thought we had reached that point in our relationship already."

We sat studying together in the lounge of her dorm hall. She reached under the table and gave my leg a squeeze. "I reached that point weeks ago."

Out of habit, I gazed around to see if anyone saw the discreet show of affection then looked back at Maya just in time to catch her bright smile dim a little. Public displays of affection were the only thing I found difficult. Behind closed doors, I couldn't keep my hands off Maya, and we still hadn't had sex yet, but out in public, I was paranoid. We were never obnoxious about our affection in public, maybe a hand-hold, a quick kiss in parting, or subtle touch while we talked, all of which I had been fine with until a week ago when an incident occurred while we were sitting in one of the dining halls at Spelman. Maya had placed her arm along the back of my chair while she was talking to Andra and absently started running her fingers along my shoulder. I barely paid it any mind as I talked to Connie until someone at a nearby table tossed a balled-up napkin at us and told us to take our nasty lesbian asses someplace else. We all turned toward where the napkin had come from to find a table full of girls, a few of which I took classes with, looking at us in disgust.

While Andra jumped to our defense, exchanging a few ugly words with the group, Connie turned a shade of red and tried pulling Andra back while Maya and I just looked at each other. The look of resignation on her face made me realize she had grown used to such cruel comments, but this was my first experience of homophobia directed at me from someone other than my mother, and it bothered me. It brought back the shame I had thought I'd gotten past since leaving home. Since that incident, I had pretty much stopped showing public affection toward

Maya. Knowing how much it affected me, she tried to keep her shows of affection discreet. I felt like I was responsible for shutting down such a vital part of who she was.

Despite my paranoia, I reached under the table, grasped her hand, and tried to give her a reassuring smile. "I'd be happy to spend Thanksgiving with you and your family."

Maya looked relieved. "You're going to love it. I figured we could get away from campus and stay at a bed and breakfast near my aunt's house. Of course, you can have your own room."

I quirked my brow teasingly. "Sounds to me like there may be another option to choose from."

Maya blushed and looked away bashfully. She was always the bolder of the two of us. "If you'd like, we could share a room."

It had finally come. The chance to spend the night with Maya. I wasn't going to get too hopeful and assume there would be more than sleeping going on. After all, she could mean getting a room with two beds, but I'd take what I could get at this point. "I'd like that."

She looked back up at me and gave me a smile that sent my heart racing. "Great. I'll make the arrangements."

Chapter Fourteen

The day before Thanksgiving, we went straight to Maya's aunt's house to help some of her family prep for the next day. It was so much fun and reminded me of Thanksgiving at home when we would all gather at Uncle Frank's the morning of with the Brooklyn aunts and cousins to prepare the day's meal. It was the only time Mom was agreeable to be around for a whole day. Maya and I peeled, sliced, and smashed enough apples and sweet potatoes to make at least a dozen pies. By the time we finished and her aunt ordered Chinese food for dinner, which Maya informed me was their traditional pre-Thanksgiving meal, I didn't want to see another apple or potato. This small contingent of Maya's family, which was her mom's siblings, were just as nice and welcoming as her parents. The rest of her cousins and father's side of the family would be joining us the next day. Maya told me her father's side of the family were the ones not as accepting of her sexuality, but they were never offensive about it. It still worried me meeting them, especially since I was the first serious girlfriend she ever had.

"You sure me being here isn't going to cause trouble?" I asked Maya after we had bid everyone good night and checked into the bed and breakfast.

Maya gave me an encouraging look. "I'm positive. Whoever can't deal with it can go kick rocks. They've known who I was for years now. It shouldn't be such a big surprise when I finally bring a girlfriend home for everyone to meet."

"Do your parents' families always get together like this?"

"Practically every Thanksgiving since they were kids. My parents grew up together and have pretty much been in love with each other from the beginning."

I sat down to take off my shoes. "Wow, that's cool. To know from that early on that you want to spend the rest of your life with someone."

When I looked back up Maya stood by the bed watching me with an intensity I had never seen in her eyes before.

"What?" I asked nervously.

"I knew the moment I saw you that I wanted you. Sometimes you can just feel when a person is right for you. When they're the one you can't imagine your life without. You know?"

I nodded. It was as if she were saying what had been in my heart since the day we met. She offered me her hand. I stood, walked over to her, and took it. This was it. The moment had come, and I was more nervous than I had been my first time with Keisha. I'd wanted this—Maya—for so long that I was afraid I'd built the experience up to an unreachable level. Especially since I had hoped she would've been my first. With Maya, it would be making love. I didn't know if I was capable of such a thing after what Keisha and I had been doing, which was pure, carnal sex. No serious emotional attachment, just physical pleasure. During my time with Keisha, I was happy with the idea of having had her experience and patience for my first encounter with a woman, but now, standing here before Maya, I felt unsure.

Maya smoothed a finger across my furrowed brow. "What's going on in that head of yours? Do you not want to do this?"

"Oh, no, that's not it. I…" I struggled to find the words.

"Janesse, talk to me."

I blew out a slow breath. "I've never made love to anyone. Obviously, as you know, I've had sex, but I've never felt for them the way I feel for you, and I don't want to disappoint you." There, I'd said it, and she didn't laugh in my face. Although I didn't expect the combination of amusement and relief.

"Ever since you told me about Keisha, I've been nervous that I might disappoint you."

"What? Why?"

"C'mon, do you really have to ask? Keisha is fine and sexy as hell. She looks like she'd be unbelievable in bed."

I started to speak, but Maya raised her hand to stop me. "I don't need to know if she is or not, I'm nervous enough as it is, I just want this to be good for us and what we share."

"I wasn't going to tell you what she was like. I was just going to say that you could never disappoint me." I grasped Maya's face and kissed her with everything I felt for her.

Her arms wrapped around me and I buried my hands into her hair as if I were trying to mind meld with her to show her how much better this was than with anyone I'd ever kissed before. We separated and quickly started undressing each other. I don't know how we accomplished it without our hands and arms getting tangled, but we stood completely bare before each other, and I suddenly felt self-conscious about the ten pounds of the freshman fifteen I still had left distributed between the slight bulge in my belly and extra width in my hips. Maya looked just as perfect now as the day we met wearing that swimsuit. Not Playboy model perfect but perfect for me. I brushed my fingertips along the curve of her full breasts, along her narrow waist, and over her softly rounded hips.

I pulled her hips toward mine and met her heated gaze. "You're so beautiful."

Maya's face darkened with a blush and she gave me a shy smile. "So are you." She wrapped her arms around my waist and brushed her lips across mine. "I've been dreaming about this moment since the day we met up in your dorm."

Her hands were so warm as they trailed up and down my back, setting me on fire with the simple caress. "Me too," I said as she cupped my behind.

"Did I ever tell you I'm an ass girl? Yours has been the focus of many sexy dreams. Especially when I saw it falling out of that bathing suit."

I never knew my butt could be so sensitive until Maya's firm hands massaged my cheeks. I moaned and arched my back like a cat forcing someone to pet them.

"Can we get in the bed? I don't know if my legs are going to hold out much longer," I said.

Maya nodded. I almost whimpered when her warm hands left my body. I hurriedly hopped on the step stool for the high bed and Maya was right behind me.

"Lie on your stomach," she said.

I did as she asked and felt the bed shift as she straddled my back.

"Just relax," she said as she began to massage and stroke my neck and shoulders.

I moaned in relief as I felt her warm hands manipulate and loosen tight muscles that I didn't know I had. I grew more relaxed and aroused as she worked her way down my back, her hands growing warmer as she went along. Then she shifted to straddle my behind and I sucked in a breath as I felt the heat and moisture from her sex. I arched upward and Maya whimpered in response to the contact. She ground her sex on my behind and I rotated my hips until we had a steady rhythm going. Maya's moans and whimpers were like an aphrodisiac, I grew more aroused with each sound. After several minutes, she grasped my hips to still my movement.

"I don't want to come yet," she said breathlessly. "I just want to touch you right now."

"Okay," I said, just as breathless.

She continued her massage and stroking. I tried lying still, but when she reached my butt, massaged a cheek with one hand, and dipped the other between my thighs I almost bucked her off the bed, which probably would have broken a bone or something considering how high off the floor it was. I guess Maya liked my reaction because she dipped her fingers farther and stroked me until I felt my own juices dripping onto my clit, which was throbbing with arousal.

"Janesse, lift your hips and spread your legs for me."

My inner walls clenched at hearing Maya say my name followed by her sexy instructions. Once I was in the position, I looked over my shoulder to see her lying on her back between my legs. She slowly slid her tongue up along my entire sex, then wrapped her lips around my clit and sucked gently. I grabbed a pillow and buried my face to stifle what would have been a very loud and prolonged annunciation of the F-bomb. I don't know who was in the rooms around us, but that was not something I wanted anyone I might have to face during our stay to hear. Several other obscene words were buried into the pillow as Maya showed some serious multitasking skills by giving my swollen clit a tongue lashing while delving her long fingers into my now dripping sex and doing her best to knead my butt cheek into human bread dough. It didn't take long for my orgasm to rage through me like an inferno. I felt as if I was spontaneously combusting as my inner walls clenched then let loose a torrent of liquid pouring out of my vagina. I called out Maya's name as she moaned and lapped it up hungrily.

Normally, after such an intense orgasm I was a boneless puddle in need of a few moments of recovery, but I found myself feeling energized and ready to return the pleasure. Maya moved to lie beside me, and I was on her before she could even get comfortable, taking my time to explore her from head to toe with kisses, nibbles, licks, and caresses, intentionally bypassing the treasure at the juncture of her thighs. I don't know what made me do it, but when I reached her feet, I lifted one and put a painted big toe in my mouth and sucked. It was something Keisha had done to me and was surprisingly stimulating, but she had been too ticklish for me to return the favor. Maya moaned so I knew I was doing something right. I did the same to her other toes and foot, and by the time I began moving back up her inner leg toward her sex, she was squirming and panting beneath me. I reached up and grabbed one of the pillows on the bed and urged her to lift her hips. I placed the pillow beneath them and settled down between her legs and inhaled the musky scent of her arousal.

I enjoyed the scent of women's natural fragrance. It was intoxicating to me, and I became intensely aroused when I was immersed in their scent and taste. Mind you, I had only been with one woman before Maya, but each time with Keisha, my enjoyment of her smell and taste had gotten more intense. With Maya, I felt drugged and my mouth was salivating just thinking about dipping my tongue in her honey pot. As I lowered my head, I noticed her clit peeking through her soft curls, and I was pleasantly surprised to find she was just as endowed as I was. It explained why she hadn't seemed surprised by mine. My own clit jumped in excitement. I decided to save that little treat for last as I delved my tongue into her glistening lips and feasted as if she were my last meal, relishing the flavor on my tongue. I didn't know if it was the anticipation of this moment happening or how I felt about Maya, but I found I didn't want this moment to end. That I could lie between her thighs all night savoring her. Maya moaned, whimpered, and buried her hands in my hair as I made love to her with my tongue and lips. I don't know how long I was down there, but by the time Maya came she was convulsing and screaming into a pillow as she bathed my face with her orgasm.

I laid my head on Maya's thigh as she shuddered with little aftershocks.

"Janesse, hold me," she said.

I moved up beside her and pulled her into my arms. She cuddled up next to me, wrapping her arms around my waist, tangling her legs with mine, and laying her head on my chest. We were both breathing heavily as I stroked her hair.

"I love you, Maya," I said breathlessly.

Maya squeezed me tighter. "I love you too, Janesse."

I fell asleep happier than I'd ever felt in my entire life.

Thanksgiving weekend with Maya and her family was one to remember and not just because we ended every night making the most wonderful love, but because her family was far more entertaining than mine. They sang, danced, argued, laughed, and played some almost violent games of spades and dominoes. There was a full house of people every day, and everything they did was with a joy and passion for life that I could only dream of having. I already thought Maya was beautiful but seeing her basking in the love of her family, even the ones who didn't agree with her lifestyle, she practically glowed. I think I fell deeper in love with her, and with her family, that weekend.

As we spent an hour saying good-bye after spending that Sunday morning in church and then eating a brunch of reinvented leftovers, Maya and I headed back to campus.

"I hope that wasn't too overwhelming for you. Especially church since I know you usually don't go," Maya said.

"Not at all. Your family is a blast, and the pastor is pretty young and hip, so I didn't feel preached at. It was a fun weekend."

Maya looked relieved. "I'm so glad you enjoyed it. My family can be a lot for one day, I wasn't sure how you'd handle a long weekend with them."

"I loved watching you with them. It was like watching the sun rise every day. You're so bright, happy, and beautiful surrounded by all that love."

Maya blushed. "Thank you. Just so you know, they all loved you."

It was my turn to blush. "That's nice to hear. The feeling is mutual."

We were now what I would call officially serious, which meant I couldn't hide the truth much longer from Mom. Especially if we went home for the holidays. Jackie was now renting and living full-time in our old apartment since she finished school and couldn't afford anything in the City while she worked at Hahnes and went on auditions, so I wouldn't have the place to myself again. She did offer to let me stay there to help keep the peace between me and Mom, but I didn't even think that would help once she found out about Maya. With a sigh, I decided I would deal with that road once we hit it. For now, I had to find a way to get over my fear of public affection while Maya and I were anywhere outside a bedroom. I tried to do better this weekend, and by Saturday I was comfortable enough to at least hold her hand around her family, but I still hesitated before accepting her touch. I could see that it bothered Maya, but she never said anything. I don't think I was ashamed of us. I think I was just afraid of being treated differently. Like what we shared was wrong or disgusting. I knew I shouldn't care what a bunch of strangers thought of me, but I did.

That night Maya spent the night in my dorm as Andra wouldn't be returning until the next day. As we lay in bed, I glanced over at her. Her lips were slightly parted revealing her adorable gap, her chest rose and fell steadily, then a snore escaped, and I grinned. Maya vehemently swore that she didn't snore when I told her she did. She said her roommate never complained about it. I told her that since her roommate was secretly crushing on her she probably thought it was just as cute as I did. God, I loved that girl and at the same time was paranoid as hell that I would screw up somehow and lose her again.

Christmas break came, and Maya and I flew home together on Christmas Eve. Her father picked us up from the airport and dropped me off at home. Fortunately, Mom was working so I had time to get my thoughts straight before broaching the subject of Maya. Our plan was to spend Christmas morning with our individual families, and then Maya was joining me at Uncle Frank's for dinner. The only person who would be missing was J.J., but he knew all about Maya, had even spoken to her a couple of times, since I told him and Dad about us dating.

Jackie walked out onto the porch as I grabbed my luggage from the trunk of the car. Maya walked to the house with me and was greeted with a hug by Jackie, then she turned to me, and I was at a complete loss as to what to do. I gave her an awkward hug and a kiss on the cheek and was met with a strained smile.

"I'll call you later?" I said.

Maya sighed and nodded. "Nice to see you again, Jackie."

"You too," Jackie said.

I watched Maya get in the car and gave a wave as they backed out of the driveway but didn't get one in return. She wasn't happy with me again.

"How long have you two been dating again?" Jackie asked, giving me a look of disapproval.

"Three months, why?"

Jackie just shook her head and turned to walk back into the house. I knew why she was asking, and I felt like crap for what just happened. I had gotten a little better since Thanksgiving but somehow, being home got me all messed up again. I followed Jackie into the apartment and was shocked to see it looking so different from when I had spent the summer there. Then, it was our same old apartment with just a few items missing. Now, Jackie had made it her own. The living room was completely reconfigured, refurnished, and repainted.

"Wow," I said.

"You like it?" Jackie asked.

"Yeah, it's cool."

"Believe it or not, Nikki's mom Frieda helped me. We ran into each other at the Montclair bookstore and she noticed the interior design magazines I was buying. We started talking about the apartment, and it turned out architecture wasn't her first career choice. She loved interior design as well, but I guess you already knew that."

"Yeah. I bet Mom loved that."

Jackie frowned. "Yeah, she wasn't too happy to come home and find Frieda and me here choosing paint colors, but, of course, she was polite and didn't say anything until after Frieda left."

"Was it bad?"

"I think it had more to do with Mom being upset that I had accepted Frieda's help and not asked for hers."

"Well, you guys did an awesome job. I don't even recognize the place."

Jackie grinned happily. "Wait until you see what I did with J.J.'s room. It's now my dance studio."

After a quick tour, I settled in what would be my room, ironically, my mother's old room. Jackie had been kind enough to put in a wall of built-in shelves that displayed my Converse collection. Yes, I still had them and would probably keep them for as long as I could. I planned on being an eighty-year-old lady pushing my walker down the street proudly wearing my Converse instead of some old funky pair of orthopedic shoes. It seemed Nikki had also been by to add her touch to the room by setting up a beautiful meditation space that took up a whole corner of the room. I ran my hand over the golden Buddha sitting happily on the low table and blinked back tears. I didn't know how I had gotten so fortunate to have such wonderful and caring family and friends, but I deeply appreciated it.

I took a quick shower, changed my clothes, and headed next door. Since Nikki would be spending Christmas in Brooklyn with Frieda's family, we decided to spend Christmas Eve together. Her mothers were going to a holiday party, so I was going to help her with all the baking she was doing for the next day and then we were going to chill with some holiday music and alcohol. I knew I probably should've waited until Mom got home to at least say hi before I ran next door, but I thought the longer I avoided her, the more time I'd have to figure out how to tell her about Maya.

"There's our girl!" Carol said as I walked into the house.

"I'd hug you, but…" She hefted a box she was carrying farther up into her arms.

"Let me help you." I rushed over and grabbed the box from her.

"Thank you, sweetie." She kissed me on the cheek. "We're just going in the living room."

Frieda grinned happily at me as she hung an ornament on the tree. "Merry Christmas, Janesse."

As it always was this time of year, their house was decked out with holiday decor. Nikki and her mothers spent the entire day on Christmas Eve searching for the perfect tree then decorating their house to look like something out of one of those holiday editions home and garden magazines. I loved being a part of their traditions. My family's celebration had changed drastically since the divorce. We used to be just like Nikki's family except ours would start the day after Thanksgiving and took up until Christmas Eve to complete when Dad would turn into a madman putting up a light display outside that had made the newspaper one year and brought folks from all over Indianapolis to see it. That first Christmas after we moved to New Jersey paled in comparison. Mom bought a fake tree that we used every year since. We decorated it, hung stockings over the fireplace, and that was it. She had lost all motivation and joy for the holiday.

I set the box near the tree and walked into her open arms. "Merry Christmas."

"Let me get some of that love." Carol wrapped her arms around me as well.

"Oh, oh, me too!" I heard Nikki say and felt another set of arms encircle us.

I lapped up all the love and attention from my second family and laughed as my face was peppered with kisses.

"We've missed you so much," Carol said as we stepped out of our group hug.

"I've missed you all also."

"We were sad to hear you were staying in Georgia for Thanksgiving. I hope you didn't spend it alone in your dorm room," Frieda said.

I glanced over at Nikki, who knew where I had spent the holiday, but I guess hadn't told her mothers. "No, I spent it with a friend and her family."

Frieda looked at me knowingly. "A friend, huh?"

My face grew hot and I couldn't control the huge smile on my face. "My girlfriend, Maya."

"Is that the young lady you were seeing that one summer?" Carol asked, grinning.

"Yes, she attends Clark University, which is pretty much next door to Spelman. We ran into each other a few months ago and got reacquainted."

"Well, I don't need to ask how things are going. Judging by your expression, you're happy."

I nodded.

"She's in looove," Nikki said with a dreamy expression and sigh.

I gave her a playful shove.

"Well, I'm happy for you," Frieda said. "Hopefully, we'll get to meet her before you guys head back to school."

"We're all going out for New Year's Eve, so I'll bring her by then."

"Excellent, we'll have a toast before you guys head out," Carol said.

"Well, for now, I'm stealing Janesse as she promised to be my baking assistant," Nikki said, grabbing my arm and pulling me toward the kitchen.

I looked around the kitchen in bewilderment. All the fruit that needed peeling and chopping was done, the cakes were baked, and I could smell cookies baking in the oven. "Looks to me like you've done all the prep work already, which is usually my job."

"Yeah, sorry, my baking class has taught me how to be more efficient and productive in the kitchen, so I actually started prepping yesterday," Nikki said guiltily.

I shook my head. "You could've told me you didn't need my help."

"I could still use your help. The cakes need frosting, which you were always so good at, and the pies need to be constructed."

I looked at her skeptically. "Yeah, okay."

Nikki chuckled. "Besides, by the time we're done with all this, Justin will be here."

"Justin's coming over?" I said happily. I hadn't seen and had barely talked to him since the summer. "The more the merrier."

Nikki divided our workspace up with me on one end of the kitchen island with vanilla, chocolate, and carrot cakes to frost, and her with the makings of sweet potato, apple, and pumpkin pies. I tasted a teaspoonful of each frosting she had made from scratch and sighed with delight.

"I'm in so much trouble when you finally open your bakery. My fat rolls will end up putting the Michelin Man to shame."

Nikki chuckled. "Well, you have at least two to three years before that happens."

"I take it the meeting with Keisha's restaurant contact went well."

"It was great. We met the other day after my classes. He was cool and gave me an honest look at what I have to expect if I decide to open my own place sooner rather than later. I told Keisha I owed her drinks for the hookup, that is, if you don't mind." Nikki gave me the side-eye.

I smiled and shook my head. "Keisha is a grown woman. I had no say in who she chose to spend her time with before Maya, so I definitely don't have one now."

"I know you two still talk. It's just drinks, but I still wanted to make sure I wasn't crossing any boundaries."

"We've spoken maybe three times since I've been back to school."

"And Maya doesn't mind?"

"Funny enough, not at all. She was a big admirer of Keisha's work way before I had a thing with either one of them. She's spoken to Keisha a couple of times."

Nikki chuckled. "Is she planning on introducing Maya to some people too?"

"Actually, yes. They have a meeting scheduled the day after Christmas."

Nikki quirked a brow. "And you're cool with that?"

I plopped the frosting spatula back in the bowl with a sigh. "I'm not sure how I feel about it. On the one hand, I think Keisha could get Maya even better connections than she did me since they pretty much work in the same field. But on the other hand, it feels weird knowing my girlfriend is going to be hanging out with, and possibly working with, my ex-lover. I trust them both because I know Keisha is big on helping young Black women, especially gay women, get their foot in the door of whatever career they're going for, whether it's in her field or not."

"That's pretty cool."

"Yeah, it is. Since she helped me and now you, who am I to tell her not to help Maya? That would be pretty selfish of me."

Nikki nodded. "Yes, it would."

We continued our work, and as Nikki said, were finished before Justin came by an hour later bearing gifts. We placed them under the tree and then jumped in to help Nikki's moms with putting up the last of the ornaments. Once we were finished, I took some pictures and then Carol and Frieda left us alone to get ready for their party. Nikki ordered pizzas, mixed a batch of eggnog, and the three of us lounged on pillows around the fireplace laughing and joking as if we hadn't been apart the past four months.

It was after midnight when I tried entering the apartment as quietly as possible. Forgetting the new furniture arrangement, I almost tripped over a footstool on my way to my room. I managed to steady myself and gave Jackie's door a worried glance. When I didn't hear any noise from her room, I circumvented the stool and made it to my room without incident. Too tired and drunk to bother undressing, I just lay down in the bed and started drifting off to sleep until I heard footsteps above my head.

"Shit!" I said as I realized I hadn't come home in time to talk to Mom about Maya.

She knew when I was arriving and I was sure Jackie probably told her where I was, which probably annoyed her and would also not make the Maya conversation any easier. She was obviously up and about judging by the creaking of the floorboards above me, but I was too drunk to have any type of coherent conversation with anyone right now, let alone Mom, so I closed my eyes and decided tomorrow morning—after a strong cup of coffee—would be a better time to broach the topic before we headed over to Uncle Frank's.

I woke up to knocking on my bedroom door and groaned because it sounded more like a sledgehammer than someone's knuckles.

"Whaaat?" I moaned, placing my pillow over my head to dull the banging.

The door opened. "Wake up, sleepyhead. It's Christmas!" Jackie said cheerfully.

I peeked out from under the pillow to find her grinning at me like a Cheshire cat. "What time is it?"

"A little after nine. We're supposed to be upstairs for breakfast with Mom in like thirty minutes. I've got a pot of coffee and some toast waiting for you. We're supposed to be at Uncle Frank's around noon to start cooking, which gives you a few hours to tell Mom about Maya, so up and at 'em."

I threw my pillow at Jackie, who squealed. "You missed!" I heard her say as she walked out of the room.

I slowly sat up, holding my head as if it were about to fall off, and took a few deep breaths to help quiet the banging now going on in there.

"Nothing a hot shower and a hot cup of coffee won't solve, or at least make bearable," I said to myself.

A half hour later, Jackie and I were heading upstairs to Mom's apartment.

"Are you sure you're ready to do this?" Jackie said. "Dealing with Mom sober is hard enough, I can't imagine you doing it with a hangover."

"I'm not going to make the same mistake I did when I first introduced her to Maya by springing it on her with no warning. That's not fair to her or Maya. I'm also not going to keep hiding the truth from her. That's not fair to me."

"I agree and I'm right here with you." Jackie gave me a smile of encouragement and a half hug before opening Mom's apartment door. I took another deep, cleansing breath, pasted a cheerful smile on my face, and followed her in.

"There you are. I thought maybe you forgot. Merry Christmas," Mom said.

I sighed inwardly. We were only five minutes late. "Merry Christmas, Mom." I accepted her tentative hug.

"Merry Christmas, Mom," Jackie said, receiving a much more genuine hug from her.

I tamped down the twinge of jealousy that arose. If I let her start getting to me already, I'd be a mess by the time I told her about Maya.

"Presents first." Mom walked toward the tree framed by her front window.

"Is that a real tree?" I asked in surprise.

Mom grinned happily. "Yes. My friend Alex brought it over yesterday afternoon. I wanted you girls to come up and decorate it with me, but neither of you were home, so he stayed and helped me." Alex was her new boyfriend.

She cocked her head to the side. "I was just going to put up our regular tree, but he insisted a real one would look perfect in front of the window and I think he's right. What do you guys think?"

"It looks great," I said, wondering who this happy woman was and what she did with my mother? I definitely had to meet this Alex because he might be even better for Mom than the therapy she was still going to.

We exchanged gifts, which had me thinking I must have woken up in a parallel universe when Mom presented me with the very thoughtful gift of a pair of Converse sneakers with the Spelman logo. We chatted as we ate breakfast and Mom gave me the perfect leeway to bring up Maya when she mentioned Alex would be joining us for Christmas dinner.

"That's great," I said. "I'm having a friend join us as well."

"Oh, really? Do I know them?"

"Yes, you met her two summers ago. Her name is Maya." I tried to act as nonchalant as possible, focusing on making sure jelly covered every inch of my toast as I waited for the explosion. It came a lot quieter than I expected as I heard Mom's utensils quietly clink onto her plate.

"Is this the girl you brought over here the day you decided you were gay?" Mom said calmly.

That calmness frightened me a little. I knew from talking to Jackie that she was probably trying to practice the restraint she had been learning while in therapy to keep from going off the deep end like she normally did when confronted with what could be an uncomfortable conversation. I looked up and met her angry, narrowed gaze. Well, there went the Christmas cheer.

"Yes, and that wasn't the day I decided I was gay. It was the day I decided to stop fighting my attraction to women."

Mom pursed her lips as if trying to keep herself from speaking. She took a deep breath then shook her head. "No."

"No?" I asked in confusion.

"I will not allow you to ruin Christmas by bringing that into our celebration." She went back to eating her breakfast.

I looked at Jackie, who looked at Mom with disappointment.

I looked back at Mom. "What do you mean by THAT?"

Mom sighed and put her utensils carefully back down on her plate before looking at me as if I were an annoying fly that she'd prefer to swat than sit across from. "You know exactly what I mean. It's bad enough I have to put up with Frank allowing Denise to flaunt her disgusting lifestyle in our face. I will not allow you to do the same."

I shook my head in disbelief. "All that therapy and you still haven't worked through your prejudice?"

Mom looked offended. "I'm not prejudiced. I just choose not to condone a lifestyle that is sinful and disgusting. What you choose to do behind closed doors is your business, but I will not be forced to witness it."

"Then I guess you won't be going to Uncle Frank's. I'm not uninviting Maya. She and I have been dating for a few months now, and Uncle Frank says she's more than welcome to come to dinner, so you either deal with it or spend Christmas here alone," I said angrily and walked out before she could respond.

By the time I got downstairs I was in tears. Tears of anger, disappointment, and, unfortunately, shame. I knew I had nothing to be ashamed of, but my mother somehow always managed to bring it out in me. Had me second-guessing myself and my decisions. I had to call Maya. I needed to hear her voice because doubt was beginning to eat away at the happiness that I had gathered with her over the past few months.

"Merry Christmas!" Maya answered cheerfully.

"Merry Christmas. It's Janesse."

"Hey! I wanted to call you when I got up, but I forgot to get your sister's phone number when we dropped you off."

"Oh yeah, let me give it to you now." I gave her Jackie's phone number, trying to keep my voice cheerful so she wouldn't know how upset I was.

"How's your Christmas morning going?" Maya asked.

"A little hungover from too much eggnog and cookies at Nikki's last night, but it's good."

"You don't sound like it's good. Everything okay?" She knew me too well.

"I told Mom about you joining us for Christmas dinner and about us in general."

"Oh." It was quiet on the other end of the line for a moment. "Do you still want me to come?"

I hated that it took me even just a few seconds to answer her. "Yeah, yeah, of course."

I heard Maya sigh. "Janesse, I need you to be sure about this."

"I'm sure. I want you there. I just let Mom get in my head as usual," I said guiltily.

"Okay. I'll see you around one."

"Okay, and Maya…"

"Yeah."

"I love you."

"I love you too."

I hung up feeling like if I didn't get things right with Maya this time around, I would spend my life alone and depressed.

❖

Christmas at Uncle Frank's wasn't any less subdued but was a less crowded affair than Thanksgiving, which had family from all over gathered in his house. Christmas was just our immediate family with the addition of each of our own guests. Mom invited her new man, Alex, who seemed a little too full of himself for my liking, but he made Mom happy. Uncle Frank's longtime girlfriend, of course Denise and Liz, Jackie had invited her best friend, and I anxiously awaited Maya's arrival.

"You know, watching the clock isn't going to make it go any faster," Denise teased.

"Will it slow it down?" I asked.

As if on cue, the doorbell rang. Since Maya was the last guest still not there it had to be her.

"I'll get it!" I shouted as I ran from the kitchen, which made no sense since Uncle Frank would probably get to the door first since he was in the living room and closer to the front door.

I practically slid to a stop in the foyer as he grinned knowingly at me and opened the door. There Maya was. Looking festive and downright adorable in green jeans, red Converse, a red sweater with a Black smiling Santa, and wearing a Santa hat of her own. Yeah, Maya absolutely loved Christmas and I absolutely loved her for not being the least bit afraid to show it. She gave me a little wave as Uncle Frank took her coat and I joined them.

"It was a pleasure to finally meet you, Maya. I'll leave you in Ness's capable hands now," Uncle Frank said, giving me a wink.

Maya did a little spin. "Too much?"

I gently grasped her face and kissed her. "Perfect, just like you."

"Thanks." Maya blushed but also looked relieved, and I had a feeling it had nothing to do with my approval of her outfit but how I greeted her.

She walked back toward the door and picked up a dish and a bag from a credenza there. "I've come bearing gifts." She handed me the dish. "Pecan pie." Then held up the bag. "Sparkling cider for the nondrinkers and sparkling wine for the drinkers."

"You didn't have to bring anything."

She shook her head with an exasperated look. "I'm from the South. What would I look like coming to dinner emptyhanded?"

"Apologies. Thank you. Everyone is pretty much in the kitchen."

"Lead the way."

I hesitated and Maya gave my arm a squeeze.

"It'll be okay. The worst is over," she said, giving me a warm smile.

I nodded even though, knowing my mother, the worst was yet to come. I took a deep breath and led Maya to the kitchen. As soon as we walked in all eyes landed on us followed by smiles from everyone except Mom, who turned her back and continued stirring something in a pot on the stove.

"Everyone, this is Maya." I then went about introducing her to those she didn't know, and Jackie greeted her with a hug.

I was happy to see Maya greeted warmly, complimented on her festive attire, have her pie drooled over by Liz because of their shared Southern background, and treated like she was already a part of the family. Even Uncle Frank's girlfriend thanked her for the sparkling cider since she wasn't a drinker. Mom was the only one who completely ignored her presence. Maya, my brave, proud girlfriend, didn't let that stop her from walking over to Mom to speak to her.

"Merry Christmas, Ms. Phillips. It's a pleasure to see you again." Maya didn't back down at the haughty gaze Mom gave her. She seemed to stand even taller in the face of it, causing Mom to look a little unsure of herself.

"Merry Christmas to you as well," Mom said politely then looked back down into the pot.

Maya turned to find all of us watching the standoff expectantly. "What can I do to help?" she said with a smile.

I had never felt prouder of being her girlfriend than at that moment. "You can help me set the table," I said.

Dinner went without an issue. There were furtive glances and frowns from Mom, and sometimes Alex, if Maya and I or Denise and Liz showed the slightest bit of affection to our partners, but I did my best to ignore it. It wasn't until we all gathered in the living room for dessert around the tree and Denise announced she and Liz were having a baby that things took a turn.

"What do you mean you're having a baby?" Uncle Frank asked excitedly.

Denise took Liz's hand and smiled. "We both were inseminated and mine took first. Your first grandchild will be here in six months."

Uncle Frank whooped loudly, pulled Denise up into a hug, then released her, pulled Liz into one, and took both their hands in his. "Are you sure you're ready for this?"

Both Denise and Liz nodded. "We've wanted this for a long time and decided to stop being afraid and just do it."

"We're planning for two. Next year I'll do the next rounds from the same donor," Liz said.

Tears of joy streamed down Uncle Frank's cheeks. "I'm going to be a grandpa."

Denise nodded, reaching up to wipe away his tears. "The coolest grandpa on the planet."

Denise was treated to a round of hugs from everyone except Mom, of course, who didn't bother hiding the look of disgust on her face. Then she opened her mouth, and the ugliness came out.

"So, you shot some stranger's semen up in you to impregnate you? You couldn't even go about that in a respectable way?" Mom said.

The room was suddenly quiet as we all looked at her in shock.

"How dare you!" Uncle Frank said. "What you do and say outside of here is your own business, but I will NOT allow you to come into my home and insult my child."

"Frank, you can't be serious. It's one thing to accept her lifestyle, it's another to accept her bringing children into that lifestyle. You're honestly fine with your grandchild never knowing who their father is? Being raised by homosexual mothers? A child should have a mother and a father."

Uncle Frank shook his head. "A year's worth of therapy and you're still the self-righteous, unforgiving woman you've been since Mom died. It's like she somehow possessed you and turned you into her. Denise is my child, and any child she brings into this world, no matter how it came about, will be loved just as much as she is. Look to your own home before you start criticizing mine."

"What's that supposed to mean?" Mom said indignantly.

"You know damn well what I'm talking about," Uncle Frank said, glancing in my direction.

The last thing I wanted at that moment was Mom's attention on me. She waved her hand dismissively in my direction. "Janesse is just going through a phase. She was perfectly fine until she started spending time with those people next door. I had hoped while she was away at school and no longer under their influence that she would get over it, but it seems she needs more time. Until then, I don't care what she does, as long as she doesn't bring it into my house."

Maya shifted closer to me and took my hand. I knew it was her way of showing me support, which, judging by the glare she gave me, made Mom angrier.

"Then I guess it's a good thing I'm staying with Jackie."

Mom suddenly looked amused. "You do realize that is still my house. Jackie may be paying rent, but I'm paying the mortgage."

"Mom!" Jackie said.

"Janet!" Uncle Frank said.

They spoke in unison with various gasps of disbelief from the others around me. Alex was the only one not looking the least bit shocked by anything that was happening. As a matter of fact, he looked almost smug as he shifted closer and took Mom's hand just as Maya had done to me.

"Why do you hate me?" I asked as my chest grew tight from fighting back the tears of anger and frustration that threatened to overwhelm me.

"I don't hate you, Janesse, I just don't respect the choices you're making with your life. I'm doing this because I love you and know that you're better than these base needs you let take over your life."

"Aunt Janet, being gay is not a choice or as simple as a base need. It's who we are. As hurtful as they are, I ignore your disapproving glances and snide comments, but I cannot sit back and watch you hurt your own daughter this way. You don't have to agree with how she lives, but you could at least show some compassion for who she is," Denise said.

As much as I appreciated Denise coming to my defense, I was realizing that the more people defended me, the worse it made things with Mom.

"Janesse knows how I've felt for some time now. She thinks she's grown enough to make her choice, then she's grown enough to deal with the consequences of it."

"How could you be so cruel to your own child?" Maya said angrily.

I squeezed her hand. "Maya, don't."

"I'm sorry, I can't just sit here and watch her hurt you with each cruel word she spits out." She turned to face my mother. "Ms. Phillips, do you even know how wonderful, kind, and loving your daughter is? That she worries so much about what you think of her that just the thought of coming back here gives her full-blown anxiety attacks? That she doesn't even trust the genuineness of her own feelings because you've beat so much doubt in her? Like Denise said, you should be showing your daughter some compassion instead of cruelty," Maya said, tears streaming down her face as she gripped my hand so tight it was almost painful.

Mom looked at Maya as if she wanted to slap her. "Who do you think you are to tell me how to treat my daughter? What does your mother have to say about this? Have you even introduced Janesse to her?"

"As a matter of fact, my mother doesn't agree with my lifestyle, but she loves me enough to accept that I'm happy and that's all that matters. My parents and the rest of my family have met and adore Janesse," Maya said.

It wasn't said smugly. She was simply answering Mom's questions, but I could tell by the look on Mom's face that she didn't like the answer. She looked around the room.

"I see, so I'm wrong for wanting my child to have a normal life. For wanting to see her married and have children of her own. For not wanting to parade my gay daughter around like she's a badge of honor. What has this world come to that so many people condone this." She looked at me. "This isn't how I raised you. You dated that boy Dante for almost a year, which tells me you at least had some sense in you then. I'm sure once the excitement and novelty of this," she waved her hand between me and Maya, "wears off, you'll come back to your senses once again. Until then, don't expect me to happily sit by and watch you ruin your life. Alex, I want to go home." She stood and Alex quickly followed her out of the room without so much as a good-bye.

"I'm sorry," Maya said.

I shook my head. "You don't have anything to apologize for. I should be apologizing to you for bringing you into the middle of all this."

"Janesse, you did nothing wrong. Your mother obviously has far deeper issues than I imagined and she's either not discussing them in therapy or resisting whatever help she's getting. I think I speak for everyone else in saying we're glad you and Maya chose to spend the holiday with us and that you are brave enough to walk in your truth," Uncle Frank said, pulling me into a hug that brought forth the tears I had managed to hold back.

Maya and I left shortly after that. I didn't want to go straight home, so we went up to our spot at Eagle Rock, choosing to sit in the car instead of standing out in the cold to enjoy the view.

"Why didn't you tell me how bad it was with your mother?" Maya asked.

"Because I didn't want to scare you away."

"Your hesitancy to be affectionate in public, the way it seems like you're holding a part of you back, the anxiety attacks about coming home, it makes so much sense now."

"Here's your chance to walk away," I said only partially joking.

Maya placed a palm on my cheek. "Look at me, Janesse."

I did as she asked and was met with the sweetest smile. "I'm not that easily scared away. I'm not going anywhere."

"But wouldn't you rather be with someone without all this drama and baggage?"

"No, because she wouldn't be you. I love you, no matter how much baggage you've got stored away. I think I'm strong enough to help you carry some of it."

I wanted to believe Maya, but that little niggling voice of doubt kept whispering in the back of my head that this was too good to be true and that I was going to screw it up, sooner or later.

CHAPTER FIFTEEN

1988

I stood outside Maya's dorm room laden with balloons and flowers. It was her birthday, and I had made arrangements with her roommate to surprise Maya by filling her room with them. Fortunately, she had a different roommate than her first couple of years. The previous one had been crushing on Maya and moved out shortly after Maya and I started dating. Erica opened the door and hurriedly ushered me into the room.

"You're late. I'm supposed to be meeting my boyfriend in like ten minutes," Erica said.

"Sorry, do you know how hard it is trying to be discreet walking across two campuses with a bouquet of balloons and flowers? I was playing hide-and-seek with anyone who even resembled Maya."

Erica laughed. "You do look like some manic delivery person all wide-eyed with sweat pouring down your face. Good luck, and you guys have the room all to yourselves tonight."

"Thanks, Erica. I owe you," I said.

"No problem," Erica said before leaving me alone in their suite.

It had a communal living area and two bedrooms on opposite sides of the living area. I went right to Maya's room. She thought I had a meeting with my photography group, so we were planning to meet for dinner later. There was a meeting, but I skipped it to surprise her. I tied a cluster of balloons to each corner of her bed, broke off petals from a few of the flowers to sprinkle on her bed, and then set the rest in a vase I found in their kitchenette on her dresser. She would be coming home from her last class any minute now so I lounged on her bed in what I thought might be a sexy pose, holding a single rose, and waited for her. I must have been more tired than I thought and drifted off. A door closing woke me up. I looked at my watch. An hour had passed since I first arrived. Maya should've been back at least forty-five minutes ago. She must have stayed late after class.

I stood up, straightened up the bed and my clothes, picked up the rose, and walked toward the door ready to step out and surprise her. I reached for the doorknob but was stopped by the sound of laughter. Maya wasn't alone. Had Erica come back early? It didn't sound like Erica's voice or loud boisterous laugh. Common sense said to just walk out and greet her as planned. Curiosity had me opening the door just a crack to be able to hear what was going on.

"Nice room. You have a roommate?" a deeper, feminine voice asked.

"Yes, she's probably out with her boyfriend. She spends the weekend at his apartment off campus. I still can't believe you're here. Can I get you something to drink?" Maya sounded happy and surprised by whoever this visitor was.

"Your aunt told me you were here, so I thought that since it's your birthday and I'm in the area I would surprise you."

"Well, you certainly did that. Thank you for the flowers, they're lovely. So, what have you been doing with yourself? Last I heard you were traveling abroad with some volunteer organization," Maya said.

"Well, you know since we were kids that college just wasn't for me. My high school guidance counselor suggested Habitat for Humanity International, so that's what I've been doing for the past four years," the other woman said.

"Wow, so you've been traveling around the world building housing for people?" Maya said in awe.

"The first two years I traveled to different countries, but Africa was where I felt the most connected, so I stayed there for the last couple of years. I just got back a week ago, ran into your aunt, and charmed her into telling me about you."

Maya chuckled. "I'm sure that wasn't too hard to do. She adored you when were kids."

"I was happy and disappointed to hear you have a girlfriend," the woman said.

I anxiously waited for Maya's reply, which, fortunately there was no hesitation in receiving.

"Yes. We've been dating for a couple of years now. I think you'd like her," Maya said.

"Are you happy?" the woman asked.

I smiled cockily to myself until I realized it took Maya a moment longer to answer that question than the first one.

"Yes."

"You don't sound too sure of that," the woman said.

"Yeah," I said to myself.

"I love Janesse. She's a sweet, wonderful, beautiful, and talented woman, but she's got a lot of baggage. It's been more difficult handling it than I thought. She's out to her family who mostly are very accepting of her and our relationship. The problem is her mother's intense bias toward gays seems to be making it difficult for her to really accept her own sexuality."

Maya sounded sad. Then the realization of what she was saying hit me. She wasn't happy. We'd been together for two years. Two years of pretty much acting more like best friends than a couple because of my hesitancy to be completely open in public. Maya had seemed fine with that. Told me she knew I needed time considering what I was dealing with at home. I knew it bothered her that whenever we were both back home at the same time, we had to be even more guarded to avoid me having to deal with Mom while I was living under her roof, but, once again, she seemed to understand.

"You and I have both known since we were in grade school that we were different. We've also never tried to hide it, so I can't imagine you being with someone still in the closet."

"It's not something I wanted either, but I love her."

"You love her enough to spend another two, maybe more, years in a closeted relationship?"

I knew I should've walked out of the bedroom right then, but something held me back. I needed to hear Maya's answer. What I hadn't expected was the silence that followed. It spoke louder than any words could.

"I didn't think so," the woman said a little too smugly for my liking. "Maya, you're a beautiful, independent, and strong woman. You always have been. I'm sure this Janesse is great, especially if she's got your love, but you deserve to be with someone who can return it in the same open way you are."

It was too quiet for a moment, and a disconcerting image ran through my mind as to what could be going on in the silence. An image of whoever this woman was comforting and kissing Maya. I was just about to barge into the room when Maya spoke.

"I have to get ready. Janesse is taking me to dinner for my birthday."

"Let me guess, Pittypat's Porch?"

"How'd you guess?" Maya said.

"Because it's your favorite place. You didn't think I'd forget even after all this time. Our families went there regularly, remember?"

Something inside me cracked hearing the softness in the woman's voice at their shared memory. I heard their footsteps as they walked to the door.

"I'd love to take you to lunch or something for your birthday while I'm in town. I'm staying at the Howard Johnson, room 105. If you have some time this weekend, give me a call."

"Maybe. I have to see what Janesse has planned," Maya said.

"You're welcome to bring her along. I'd love to meet the woman who captured the heart of my childhood crush."

"Yeah, right," Maya said. I could picture her rolling her eyes.

"Seriously, you were. When your family moved to Jersey it broke my heart. I was just about to admit my feelings for you but chickened out." The woman's voice sounded wistful.

"Chris, we can't have this conversation," Maya said, her tone sad but serious.

"I know. I really would like to take you to lunch and meet Janesse. She must be pretty special," the woman said.

"She is," Maya said.

It was quiet for a moment. They said good-bye once more, and I heard the door close. I slowly opened Maya's bedroom door to find her leaning with her back against the door to the dorm room and her eyes closed as if she were trying to hold back tears.

"Maya?" I tried to say as gently as possible so as not to scare her too much.

Her eyes flew open and she squealed in fright and took a defensive stance. When she saw it was me, she closed her eyes and tried to calm herself, then looked at me in confusion. "Janesse? What are you doing here? How did you get in?"

"Erica let me in. I was trying to surprise you for your birthday." I held the rose I had out toward her.

Maya walked toward me and hesitantly took it. "Why didn't you come out sooner and let me know you were here?"

"I-I didn't want to interrupt."

That was so obviously a lie, and judging by the look Maya gave me, she knew it and, thankfully, didn't call me out on it. She peeked past me into her bedroom and her eyes widened.

"You did all of this?" she asked.

"Yeah. I ditched the meeting tonight so that I could be here when you got back from your last class of the day. I must have fallen asleep because I didn't realize you weren't here until I heard you guys come in."

"That was so sweet. Thank you."

Maya gave me a chaste kiss on the lips, which worried me because our kisses, at least in private, were rarely chaste, even if we were saying thank you.

"So, uh, who was that?" I asked, hoping I didn't sound as jealous as I was.

"Why don't we sit down?" Maya said, her expression a little too serious for me.

I figured we would go into her room, but she walked toward the sofa and sat down looking at me expectantly. I sat down beside her not liking the ominous feeling I was getting.

"That was Christina, an old friend of mine when I used to live here. We haven't really spoken since I moved away. I was surprised to see her sitting in the lobby downstairs when I got back from class. Since I assumed you were at your meeting, I stayed after to talk to my professor. That's why I was late. If I had known you were here, I would've come straight back."

"Well, then it wouldn't have been a surprise." I grinned, trying to lighten the serious mood that permeated the room.

"I really wish you had come out and said something. Did you hear our conversation?"

I lowered my head guiltily. "Yeah. I wasn't trying to eavesdrop or anything. It just felt awkward to jump out yelling surprise once you guys started talking about us."

Maya sighed. "So, you heard all of that?"

I nodded.

"I wish you hadn't."

I looked back up at her and she met my gaze with a sad smile. "Why didn't you tell me you felt that way?" I asked.

"I didn't know how without sounding like I was unhappy."

"Are you unhappy? I heard your friend ask you that and you never responded."

"I love you, Janesse, with all my heart, I really do..."

"But you're not happy with me," I said quietly.

"I'm not happy with having to be with you in the closet. I thought I could handle it but having to hold myself back from simply holding your hand as we walk or innocently place my hand on your arm or leg as we talk around other people is hard. I'm not the least bit ashamed of our love, and holding back like that makes me feel like I am. Like you may be."

I vigorously shook my head. "I'm not ashamed of our love. Sometimes I feel as if I don't deserve it, but I'm not ashamed of it."

"See, that's part of it. How could you possibly feel as if you aren't deserving of love?"

I was afraid to answer. As if speaking my fears aloud would make them come true.

"Janesse, talk to me."

"Sometimes I feel like you could do better than me. Be with someone more confident and surer of herself and her sexuality. Someone not afraid of what people will think of her when she holds your hand. Someone not so afraid of screwing things up that she doubts her own feelings."

"What do you mean you doubt your own feelings? Do you not really love me?" Maya asked worriedly.

I grabbed her face and pressed a soft kiss on her lips. "No, that's not it. I KNOW I love you, but I don't know if loving you is enough because I don't know if I even love myself." I dropped my hands in my lap and gazed down at them. "Sometimes I look in the mirror and I hear my mother's voice telling me this is just a phase. You'll come to your senses sooner or later. And then I think about how I still find guys attractive. I don't want to sleep with them or anything, but I do find myself checking them out occasionally and I start worrying that maybe she's right." When I looked back up at Maya she looked as if she were about to cry.

"I'm not saying I want to leave you for some guy, but I don't think it's right that I still have that attraction for them. It feels like there's something wrong with me and that keeps me from fully opening up to you that way," I quickly explained.

Maya looked relieved and nodded in understanding. "You're afraid of your own sexuality, of being bisexual."

"I hadn't thought of it that way, but I guess that's it."

Maya was quiet for a moment then nodded as if she had come to some conclusion. "Janesse, I've tried to be patient. Tried understanding what you're going through, which is no fault of your own, but it's been two years. I had hoped that us being together, that the acceptance of most of your family as well as my own would be enough to help you accept who you are, but obviously that's not the case. For us to be together, I need you to be all-in. I need you to be able to trust and believe in yourself or you will never be able to trust and believe in us."

"I know, I've been trying."

Maya looked doubtful. "Have you really? You keep making excuses not to attend the LGBTQ peer group I told you about or go see the campus counselor for private sessions. It's like you don't want to help yourself. Like you just want to wallow in doubt and confusion, so you'll have an excuse not to fully commit to us."

"What? How could you say that? I've been with you for two years now. That doesn't show I'm committed to us?" Her words hurt, but I wasn't sure if it was because she doubted my feelings for her or because they were possibly true.

"I'm your girlfriend, Janesse, and you're afraid of holding my hand in public. You've even just admitted that you've been holding a part of you back, what does that say to you?"

"It just says, unlike you, that I don't need to flaunt the fact that I'm a lesbian for the whole world to see," I said angrily, reverting to my old ways of lashing out when I was hurt.

Maya flinched. "That's what you think of me? That I flaunt being lesbian?"

I ran my hand through my hair in frustration. "No, I'm sorry, I didn't mean that."

"I don't hide the fact that I'm gay, but I also don't tell everyone I meet. That still doesn't make it any easier for me, especially on a college campus, which can be just as bad as being in high school. There are homophobes everywhere, Janesse. You just have to learn when to tune them out and live your life the best way you know how."

We sat quietly for a moment. I was at a loss as to what to say. I had concluded that my self-acceptance would always be an issue between us if we kept going this way and loving each other wasn't enough to overcome it.

"I think we should skip dinner tonight. I'm not feeling very celebratory," Maya said.

Great, I had managed to screw up her birthday. "Okay. Tomorrow night? We don't have to go out. We could order in and watch a movie."

Maya gazed down at her lap then back up at me with the saddest expression. "Maybe we could just chill on our own this weekend. Give you some time to think about what we talked about."

"Oh, okay, if that's what you want." My chest felt tight and a lump began to form in my throat. "I'll go." I stood and walked toward the door.

"Janesse," Maya said.

Maybe she changed her mind. I turned back but she still held that sad expression. "Yeah."

"I love you. I know you love me. I want this to work out between us, but I can't wait around forever for you to figure out who you are and what you really want."

"I understand."

I swallowed the ever-growing lump in my throat. I walked out of Maya's room, shut the door, and practically ran out the building and across Clark's campus toward Spelman trying to hold back a fountain of tears that threatened to escape and hold together my breaking heart.

After spending most of the night crying on Andra's shoulder, then a fitful night of sleep, I spent the entire next day in the photography lab's darkroom working on my final assignment to keep me distracted, but as I developed the roll of film with the pictures I needed, there were about a dozen of Maya I had taken when we went to Key West Valentine's Weekend. I hadn't noticed it at the time, but her smile dimmed the further along the pictures went. By the last day, she no longer held that happy smile I had fallen in love with. I thought back on the day it was taken and remembered an argument that we had.

We were staying at a bed and breakfast for lesbian clientele and Maya had gotten frisky while we were in the pool. She had backed me up against the wall and tried to kiss me. I had given her a quick peck and nervously looked around at several other women who were lounging in and out of the pool as well. She had called me a prude when we got back to the room and I accused her of trying too hard to prove how gay she was. Just because we were around other gay women didn't mean that my public display of affection inhibitions had changed. Yes, I had felt more comfortable holding her hand or giving each other a quick kiss here or there, but I didn't think we needed to shove our tongues down each other's throats to prove anything to anyone there. She had stormed out of the room and came back a half hour later slightly drunk and apologizing. I had let it go, but I hadn't realized she had possibly held on to what happened until I looked at the pictures.

I had been clueless as to how unhappy she was, and she hadn't said a word about it. I wondered if it would have made much difference if she had instead of me having to overhear it in her conversation with her friend. I knew she wasn't trying to force me into public make-out sessions. She just didn't want me to reject her. Maya was a very affectionate person. I was forcing her to curb that part of her to appease my insecurities. It wasn't fair and it was selfish of me to do that to her.

I felt guilty about being such a sucky girlfriend. She had been so accommodating to my needs the past two years, and I hadn't given her anything but more of my issues to bear in return. I hung the pictures of Maya up to dry then sat down staring at them and crying miserably.

I woke up late the following morning with a resolve to fix things with Maya. I found out when the next LGBTQ peer group meeting was and made sure to clear my schedule to attend. Then I left a message with the campus counselor to schedule a one-on-one session. I knew I wouldn't hear back from her until Monday, but I didn't want to wait until then to call her and come up with some excuse as to why I wouldn't be able to do it. Finally, after a pep talk from Nikki and despite Maya suggesting we not see each other this weekend, I went over to her campus's chapel to catch her as she was leaving church and beg, if I had to, to talk to her.

I arrived about a half hour before services usually ended and sat on the bench where I usually met her every Sunday going over in my head what I wanted to say. Obviously, an apology was the first thing in order. Then I would tell her about my efforts to help work through my issues so that I could fully commit to her without any doubts or hesitations. The chapel doors opened, and as everyone filed out, I searched the crowd for Maya but didn't see her. She was usually in the first wave of people that exited. I stayed until the last person walked out and the doors were closed. Maybe she went to the earlier service and was already back at her room.

I walked over to Maya's dorm and was waved past by the girl at the desk, who was used to seeing me there. As I approached her room the door was slightly ajar. A young Michael Jackson crooning the "ABC" song and the sound of laughter drifted out into the hall. Erica must have come back. I tentatively opened the door to find Maya wasn't with Erica but someone I didn't recognize. The woman and Maya were doing a dance routine with their backs to me before they did a spin. The joyous expression on Maya's face was one I rarely saw these days. That beautiful, gap-toothed, dimpled smile I had fallen in love with was shining brightly and her laughter was genuinely happy. Her brightness dimmed when she spotted me in the doorway.

"Janesse," she said, breathless from her dancing.

"I'm sorry to show up unannounced again. I waited for you at the chapel, but when you didn't come out, I figured you must have gone to the early service, so I came here."

"I didn't go to service today. Chris and I went to breakfast. I thought we weren't seeing each other this weekend."

Was that a look of annoyance? "Yeah, I know you suggested that, but I did a lot of thinking since we last saw each other and I wanted to talk to you."

"You've figured everything out in a day?" Maya said skeptically.

"Well, no, but I know what I need to do to figure it out. Can we talk?"

"Why don't I go down to the lobby and give you guys some privacy," Chris said.

I gave Chris a cursory glance, annoyed that not only had she taken my girlfriend out to breakfast but that she had brought Maya's smile back.

"No, you can stay. We can talk in my room. By the way, Janesse, this is my friend Chris. Chris, this is my girlfriend, Janesse." Well at least she was still calling me her girlfriend, I thought with relief.

Chris walked over, smiled charmingly, and held out her hand. "Nice to meet you, Janesse."

I didn't want to be rude and make things worse, so I accepted Chris's hand. It was warm and calloused. "Nice to meet you also."

She was an attractive woman. About my height, with a smooth dark brown complexion, bright friendly eyes, and an equally bright white, perfectly straight-toothed smile. Her hair was styled in dred locs that framed her face and went down to her mid back. She wore a pocketed red button-down shirt, tan cargo pants, and brown moccasin shoes. She seemed almost genderless. The best way I could describe her was androgynous.

Maya barely waited for us to finish our handshake before she turned and headed to her bedroom. "Let's go talk."

"Good luck," Chris said with a look of understanding.

I was a little annoyed that I'd just met her, and she probably knew my whole story. "Uh, thanks."

Maya was sitting on her bed when I walked in and closed the door behind me. "So, you weren't in the mood to go to dinner with me the other night, but you skipped church to go to breakfast with Chris?" Yep, that was pure, unadulterated jealousy in my tone and I instantly regretted it.

"No, you are not making that"—Maya pointed toward the other room—"an issue where there isn't one. You and I had a very revealing discussion for which I asked you to take the entire weekend to think about and had hoped you would take it seriously enough to do so."

I sat down beside her and took her hands. "I did take it seriously. I know what my issues are, and I'm ready to try and fix them. I just need you to hold on for a little while longer."

"We've been through this before, Janesse. It was the reason I suggested the peer group."

"I know, but it's different this time, I'm—"

"Different how?" Maya interrupted. "Why did it have to take you overhearing me talking to someone else then telling you I can't keep doing this for you to want to change? Would we even have had that conversation the other night if you hadn't overheard me talking to Chris about us?"

"I guess not, but you've never told me you weren't happy."

"That's true and I'll take responsibility for that. I assumed, as well as we've been able to read each other since we first met, that you would know. But we've had similar conversations before about your constant fear of being outed and your serious issues with insecurities and shame in yourself. I'm not saying you need to shout to the rafters that you're gay, bisexual, or however you identify, I just want you to at least be able to admit it to yourself without looking as if it was the worst thing in the world to be. I want, and need, you to have pride and acceptance in who you are. I have never seen that in you, and I think it's going to take a long time and a lot of therapy to get there. Time, I don't know if I can continue giving."

I swear my heart stopped beating in my chest for a moment before stuttering back up again. "What are you saying?"

Maya released my hands and walked a few feet away before turning back to me, her eyes shining with moisture. "I spent the past day thinking as well. I love you, Janesse, but it's not enough if you don't love yourself. I can't be the only one in this relationship giving it my all. It's going to take the both of us, and I don't think you're even close to being ready for that."

She was breaking up with me, I realized in disbelief, then went straight to defense mode to avoid the heartbreak hurtling toward me. "Is Chris ready for that," I said snidely.

Maya just looked sad and the tears she held back began to fall. "I'm going to let that slide because I know you're just lashing out. This is strictly between me and you. I have loved you since our first summer together. I haven't looked at or been interested in anyone but you since we reunited so please don't insult me, or what we've shared, that way. I wish, with all my heart, that my love could miraculously cure you of all that you're going through, but it can't. I can't. You're the only one who can do that. It's a horrible thing to say, but your mother is never going to change and you're going to have to find a way to accept that and move on with your life or you will never be happy with anyone, female or male."

I touched my chest above my heart to make sure it wasn't literally falling apart like I felt it was. I couldn't even argue with her because I knew Maya was right. She didn't tell me anything different than what everybody who cared about me had been telling me. I simply nodded, got up, and walked out of the bedroom. I saw Chris stand from the corner of my eye, but I didn't even acknowledge her. If I did, I would probably curse her out because, in a way, I felt like her visit triggered all of this. If she hadn't come here Maya wouldn't have talked to her about us, we would have celebrated her birthday, and everything would be fine. But would it? I had to ask myself. I had no one to blame for this but myself. Chris was just the catalyst that brought the truth to light.

I don't even remember the walk back to my dorm, but I do remember calling Nikki and bawling so hard I could barely get the words out to tell her what happened. Although I knew she had told me this could happen many times if I continued the way I was, she thankfully didn't say I told you so. She listened to me blubbering nonsensically and sympathized with me when I needed it until I was emotionally drained and wanting to just curl up in bed and sleep until the pain went away. After my call with Nikki, I changed into some sweats and crawled under the covers. I barely acknowledged Andra when she came into our darkened room and caught me in one of my crying jags that had been going off and on all afternoon. She tried talking to me to find out what was going on, but every time I tried to tell her what happened the words got stuck in my throat. I finally managed to get out Maya broke up and that was it before I started crying tears I didn't know I still had. I was going to be a dehydrated, snotty-nosed, red-eyed mess within a few hours. Andra kindly placed a box of tissues, a pitcher of water, and a cup on my nightstand before she headed out to the dining hall. Then she brought back a cup of chicken noodle soup, but I could barely keep it down. Andra left me to my misery until morning when she tried to get me out of bed to go to class, but I refused to budge. What was the point? My life was over. I had lost the best thing in it just as I knew I would eventually.

I stayed that way for a week, only getting out of bed to drag myself to the bathroom and back. Andra continued to supply me with water before she left in the morning and soup when she got back. It only took a day for my body to decide it wasn't into starvation no matter how bad my heart was broken. The smell of the soup and the continuous ache and growling in my stomach won out over my personal drama. A call from my photography professor reminding me that I only had a week left before spring break to turn in my final project finally got me out of bed. I went through the motions of getting up each morning, throwing on whatever was easiest to wear, grab a pastry from the dorm lounge, and go to my classes. I may have been heartbroken, but I wasn't stupid enough to throw away four years of hard work and not graduate on time.

Going to class was the easy part. Dealing with spring break was another. Maya and I were supposed to be going to Miami. Obviously, that wasn't happening now. I couldn't bear to stay on campus. Dad and Tanya were taking J.J. to Disney World that same week, so going to Indy wasn't an option. The only other place to go would be home. I dreaded that almost as much as having to spend the week alone on campus. Andra and most of our friends would be gone, leaving me to sit and wallow in my feelings for another week. I exchanged the Miami ticket for one to New Jersey and tried not to think about having to deal with Mom while I was an emotional wreck.

To my embarrassment, I ended up spending most of the flight crying because the inflight movie was *Sixteen Candles,* the movie Maya and I saw on our first date. There was only one other person in my row, and he slept the whole flight, so I don't even think he noticed the weeping woman next to him. Uncle Frank picked me up from the airport and didn't hide the shock on his face when he saw me. I had stopped at the bathroom after deboarding and saw what I looked like. My face was bloated and blotchy, my eyes were streaked with red, my hair was sitting atop my head in a messy bun, and my clothes were loose and baggy. I guess a daily diet of water, a pastry, and soup worked wonders for the figure. I had lost a good ten pounds in the two weeks since Maya broke up with me. Uncle Frank held his arms open for me and I shook my head.

"If you hug me, I'll just start crying again," I said.

"Okay, how about a half hug." He wrapped one arm around my shoulder and gave me a brief squeeze before stepping away.

It almost brought on the waterworks, yet it was comforting at the same time. "Thanks."

He grabbed my bag and we headed out of the airport.

"You sure you don't want to stay in your own room at Jackie's instead of my place?" he asked.

"Positive. I am not in the right frame of mind to deal with Mom's foolishness."

Uncle Frank nodded. "I understand. Jackie brought some of your things over she thought you might like to have with you. I haven't told your mom you're coming home, but I can't stop the possibility of her seeing you while she's at the office. She tends to use the bathroom in the house rather than the one in the office like everyone else."

That's Mom, always having to go the extra mile to be difficult. "That's fine. If she sees me, she sees me."

"I'm sorry about you and Maya."

"Thanks." I had told Uncle Frank about the breakup when I called to ask if I could stay with him while I was home.

The first couple of days I slept in, spent time at Nikki's before she left for New Orleans for the week with a few of her cooking school classmates for a restaurant tour, and managed to avoid Mom because she had an open house and wasn't in the office or home. The third day, I forgot about Mom using the downstairs bathroom instead of the office one and ran into her as I was heading to the kitchen for a snack. We both stopped and stared at each other as if we were seeing a ghost.

"Hey, Mom."

"Ness, what are you doing here? I thought you weren't coming home for spring break."

"My plans changed."

"Why are you here instead of at the house?"

I hesitated, wondering how I answered that question without

causing a confrontation I wasn't equipped mentally to handle now. "I needed some time to myself."

"And you couldn't get that at home?"

I sighed in resignation. I should've known she wouldn't let it go so easily. "Not really. I was just going to grab something to eat. I don't want to keep you from work."

"I don't have any appointments until this afternoon. What's going on, Ness?"

"Look, Mom, it's been a rough couple of weeks at school with final projects and exams coming up. I just needed some time to myself to get my head straight, that's all."

"Okay. I'm just surprised. Last I heard you were going to Florida with your…friend."

"Like I said, plans changed." I turned my back and headed toward the kitchen before the prickling behind my eyes became too much to bear.

I was surprised to hear the clicking of heels behind me.

"Ness, I know we don't always agree, but I would hope you would feel comfortable enough to come home when you're struggling with something."

I kept my back to her as I made a cup of tea. "Mom, it's nothing. I just needed some space."

"From Jackie? From me?"

Why did she insist on pushing? I just wanted some time to wallow in my self-pity and go back to school to finish out with a clear mind. I turned to her.

"Mom, please. I can't deal with this right now." I couldn't control the catch in my voice, but I managed to keep my tears at bay.

Mom looked concerned now. "Janesse, what's going on? Why is this the way I'm even finding out your home?"

The pain in my chest that had become a dull ache this past week throbbed once again, and the tears fell. "Maya and I broke up," I said quietly.

"I can see that you're hurting and I'm sorry it had to happen this way, but maybe it's for the best," Mom said, a genuine look of sympathy on her face that did nothing to take away the sting of her words.

It was like I was five years old again coming home cut and bleeding after falling from the monkey bars at the playground crying for comfort from Mom but only getting reprimanded for being so careless in return.

"This is why I didn't come home," I said, walking out of the kitchen without food or my tea.

I went up to the guest room, changed into some jeans and a sweatshirt, and left. I didn't have a destination, I just walked and ended up at the high school. I sat on a bench near the freshman building watching kids rushing from one building to the next or gathering in the amphitheater and wishing I could go back to that time when I dramatically thought that being in high school was the toughest thing in life. How naive and wrong I was. I felt the tears beginning again, reached up to grasp my lotus pendant that I never took off, took several deep shaky breaths, and tried to calm the emotional breakdown I felt coming on. After a few moments, the urge to cry went away but the ache in my chest throbbed again. I had to leave before I lost it, and somebody called the police on the crazy lady crying uncontrollably in front of the high school.

I headed back the way I came and remembered Justin saying he would be home for spring break. I stopped by his house but hesitated at ringing the doorbell. When we spoke a few weeks ago Justin was happily in love and thinking of proposing to his girlfriend. I wasn't sure if I wanted to bring my misery to his doorstep and turned to leave when the door opened.

"Ness?"

I slowly turned back around. "Hey, Justin."

"Hey, did you ring the bell? Why were you leaving?"

I noticed he looked tired and his eyes were red and puffy. I knew that look well but had never seen it on Justin. He'd been crying.

"Uh, no, I didn't ring the bell. I was thinking I should've called first, so I was leaving."

"Well, you're here now, so you might as well come on in." Justin stepped aside to let me into the house. We settled on the sofa in the living room.

"Weren't you just leaving? I don't want to hold you."

"No, I just needed some fresh air. I've been cooped up in the house all weekend. Hey, I'm sorry to hear about you and Maya."

"I guess Nikki told you."

Justin nodded. "I called her last night, wanting to catch her before she left for her trip. She told me about you guys after I told her about Sheila and I breaking up." Justin's voice caught.

"Oh, Justin, I'm sorry. Just a few weeks ago you were talking marriage, what happened?"

Justin shrugged. “She’s been talking to her ex on the side for the past six months. They hooked up last month and realized they still loved each other. He proposed to her and she said yes. Ironically, this all happened the weekend I was talking to you about proposing to her.”

“Aw, man. I’m so sorry to hear that.”

“I probably should’ve known something was up when she started avoiding us spending the night together.”

“Is he someone on campus?”

“No, but he lives and works in DC, so she was spending her nights with him and would be back on campus in the morning. He’s older.”

“Oh, wow.”

“What about you? Nikki didn’t give me any details. She just said I should probably call you. That it might help both of us to commiserate together.” Justin gave me a sad smile. “I called but your sister said you weren’t there.”

“Yeah, I’m staying at my uncle’s. I didn’t want to have to deal with Mom on top of this.”

“I understand. Do you want to talk about it?”

“Basically, I screwed up like I always thought I would.” I told him everything that happened without breaking down completely. I guess knowing he was pretty much going through the same thing made it easier to talk about.

He reached up and wiped a tear from my cheek. “What a fine pair we make,” he said, a tear escaping the corner of his eye.

I wiped his tear away, and the look he gave me was filled with so much pain and sadness it was like looking in the mirror.

“I feel like it’s never going to stop hurting,” he said.

“Me too.”

I pulled him into an embrace and we quietly cried in each other’s arms. It felt so good to share the pain with and to be held by someone. I couldn’t tell you who made the first move or if it was a mutual action, but one minute, we were holding each other and the next our lips met in a kiss filled with desperate need. It didn’t feel like a sexual need. More like a need to ease the pain we were feeling and comfort each other in some way that would distract us from it all. I straddled Justin’s lap needing full contact as we practically devoured each other’s mouths. There were no words spoken as he clasped his hands under my thighs, stood, and as I clung to him, carried me to a guest bedroom they had downstairs. I was relieved we didn’t have to go up to his room because

I don't think we would've made up the stairs. The moment my feet hit the floor clothes were flying everywhere.

My head barely hit the pillow before Justin was easing himself inside me. I didn't think about the fact that because I had been dating Maya, I had stopped taking the pill years ago, or that I hadn't asked Justin to put on a condom. I just needed to feel something other than pain and heartbreak and I think Justin felt the same way. The sex started out with us clinging desperately to each other, frantically thrusting, and clutching at one another as if we were trying to fuck the pain away. Then I started crying. I don't know why, but it felt like a dam was breaking with each thrust and it finally reached its limit ending in a moan and gut-wrenching sobs. Justin eased out of me and shifted us so that he could hold me. I buried my face in his chest.

Justin held me tight, rubbing my back as I cried.

"I'm…sorry…" I hiccupped after I was able to calm myself down.

"You have nothing to apologize for. We could just lie here if you want."

"No, I need to feel something good right now."

I pulled Justin back on top of me. This time our kiss, and everything that followed was slow and gentle. For a little while, I got out of my head, ignored the ache in my chest, and allowed myself to feel nothing but the physical pleasure Justin and I gave one another. The two of us trying to fill a hole heartbreak had punched through our hearts. Afterward, Justin drove me back to Uncle Frank's. I didn't see Mom's or Uncle Frank's cars outside the home office, so I assumed they had gone on a call, which was fine with me. I was not in a conversational mood and just wanted to go back to my self-imposed isolation.

"Are you all right?" Justin asked.

"Yeah. Are you going to be okay?"

"I'm sure eventually I will be. Right now, I just need to wallow in it a little bit."

I nodded in agreement. "I know the feeling."

"Ness, what happened today…" Justin paused and looked up as if he were trying to search for the right words. With a shrug he looked back at me. "I think we both needed comfort and I don't regret what happened, but I hope this won't affect our friendship."

I stroked Justin's cheek and tried to give him an encouraging smile. "We're good."

His shoulders dropped in relief and he returned the smile. "Call me if you need to talk, a shoulder to cry on, or just someone to sit with. I'm here for you."

"The same goes for you."

Justin nodded and pulled me into a hug. This time there were no tears and my chest only ached dully. We said good-bye once more before I climbed out of the car. I didn't allow myself to feel guilty over what happened with Justin. Besides both of us recently becoming single, I agreed with him saying that we both needed it. Yes, it was dipping a toe outside the friend zone, but I truly didn't think, with how the both of us were feeling about our recent heartbreaks, that it would affect our friendship.

By the end of my break, when I headed back to school, I was in much better shape than I was when I arrived home. Or at least I was until I arrived back at my dorm to find a letter from Maya under the door telling me she was sorry the way things ended, she would always love me and wished me nothing but happiness, and that she was going to California after graduation for a job offer. The waterworks were kept at bay, but the vise around my heart tightened so painfully I thought it would collapse in on itself. Well, if there had been a smidgen of a chance for us to work things out, it was gone now. I was either going to have to force myself to move on or drown in self-pity. Moving on would be the grown-up thing to do, and I planned on doing that but not before letting my world crash in on me for a few more days.

Moving on meant going through the motions of preparing for graduation. A little over a month had passed since my world was turned upside down and I had managed to at least get it back to teetering on its side where the slightest breeze of drama or heartbreak could send it reeling back off its axis. My family would all be here for the ceremony, and I dreaded the thought of dealing with Mom with my emotions still a bit fragile. Like I had done with everything else in my life after the breakup, I put it in the back of my mind and dealt with things one day at a time. The only thing I thought ahead about was my plans after graduation.

Keisha and I had remained friends and kept in touch regularly throughout the past four years, so when she found out about Maya, she told me the offer to go to Europe with her for the summer was still on the table. With Maya moving to California, no job prospects in sight, and the likelihood of having to move back under my mother's roof until

I found a job and got a place of my own, I jumped at the offer. With the condition that our relationship stay strictly platonic.

When I called to congratulate Justin and Nikki on their graduations and told them about the trip, they both agreed it was a great idea. They said they would miss our annual getaway to the Jersey shore, but they probably wouldn't have been able to make time for it anyway. Justin was starting right up with his uncle's construction business to learn the ropes before officially becoming a partner, and Nikki had snagged a job as sous chef for a high-end restaurant in New York City, thanks to the connections she made through Keisha. Justin and I had bonded more since our heartbroken sex episode, as we called it, and talked almost every day. It had been good for both of us to have someone to talk to and a relief to me that we were able to maintain our friendship. I think it was because we were both still hurting too much to even think about being in another relationship so soon.

After the graduation ceremony, Dad announced he made reservations for us at Pittypat's Porch, and I felt the axis wobbling under my world before I excused myself to go to the ladies' room to wedge it back in place. I locked myself in a stall, gripped my lotus pendant as if it were an anchor keeping me from floating off, and did a few tear-filled breathing exercises.

"Are you all right?" Jackie asked when I joined them again.

"No, but I'll be fine."

"You sure you don't want to ask Dad to go someplace else?" Jackie knew about Maya's love of Pittypat because we had taken her there when she came down for a visit once.

"No, with so many of us on a graduation day it'll be hard to get into any place else."

"Okay," Jackie said, rubbing my back in comfort.

Fortunately, I knew there was no chance of running into Maya and her family there because I knew from when we were still dating, that they were having a big family celebration at one of her uncle's houses not too far from the campuses. The plan was for me to bring my family, as it was supposed to be a chance for our families to meet, which, in hindsight, would've been extremely awkward with Mom considering how she felt about our relationship.

I managed to keep my composure through dinner as Uncle Frank kept us laughing through most of it. I decided to announce my summer plans during dessert.

"Can I have everyone's attention?" Once talking stopped and all eyes were on me, I continued. "First, thank you all for coming down for the graduation and for all your support these past four years." To avoid causing a scene, I nodded at Mom as well when I acknowledged everyone even though she had caused me nothing but headaches.

"You know we've always got your back, Ness," Uncle Frank said, raising his glass to me.

"Yeah, we love you, Ness," J.J. said, raising his glass of soda as well.

Everyone else followed suit. I felt a lump in my throat and quickly swallowed it down. I knew that if I started crying, I wouldn't stop.

"Thank you," I whispered then cleared my throat.

"I wanted to let you all know I'm going to take a little break before jumping into the job market. I've been offered the opportunity to spend the summer in Europe with a friend and I accepted. It will give me some time to figure out my next step and broaden my portfolio with some new perspectives."

"That sounds like a great idea. Do we know this friend?" Dad asked.

I smiled because I knew he was asking as the overprotective dad not to be nosy. "You know of her. Keisha Douglas. She's the one who connected me with the photographer I worked with over the past few summers."

Except for Mom, everyone else expressed praises and well-wishes with the announcement. She sat there with her lips pursed looking at me disapprovingly. I chose to ignore her, not just to avoid causing a scene but for my own emotional well-being, but that didn't seem to stop her.

"How are you paying for this trip?" Mom asked.

"I still have money saved from my summer jobs, and Keisha will be covering the major expenses."

Mom quirked a brow. "You mean to tell me that some woman, whom I've never met, and is, if I remember correctly, ten years older than you, has asked you to spend three months in Europe with her, all expenses paid, and is asking for nothing in return," she said skeptically.

"Mom, you promised you wouldn't do this," Jackie reprimanded her.

Mom looked at her in annoyance. "I can't ask my own daughter about a situation I don't feel comfortable with?"

"As long as I feel comfortable with the situation, that's all that matters. Keisha and I are FRIENDS, that's it, if that's what you're concerned about. If we weren't it wouldn't be any of your business anyway." I didn't bother to keep the attitude from my tone and looked away from her before she could say anything else.

"Dad, it's been a long day and I still have some things to do before my flight in the morning. Do you mind if I head back? I'll take a cab so you guys can stay and finish."

Dad signaled for the server. "No, kiddo, we can take you back."

"Thanks."

Mom said nothing further. As we left the restaurant, she announced she'd wait by the car for Uncle Frank and Jackie and walked away without even a glance in my direction.

"I'm sorry, Ness. Uncle Frank and I had a talk with her before we even left for the airport where she promised she would keep things civil."

I shrugged. "She did for the most part, so I'm grateful for that. I'll see you guys at the airport in the morning."

"You made sure to book your seat next to me?" Jackie asked.

"Yep."

"Good. We'll be two rows behind her and Uncle Frank, so you'll have nothing to worry about."

"I'll take your word for it."

I said good-bye to Jackie and Uncle Frank, then followed Dad, Tanya, and J.J. to their rental car.

During the car ride back to campus, I talked to J.J. about what was going on with him. He was thirteen years old now and almost taller than me. He had stopped his summer visits to New Jersey the first summer after he moved to Indy with Dad because Mom worked all day, leaving him home with me, once again, and barely spent time with him when she was home. He didn't ask to visit the following summer and Mom didn't seem to mind, so I only saw him when I went to Indianapolis or he came to New Jersey for a special occasion, which were few and far between. He had bloomed living with Dad. Was playing soccer, had a crew of friends he regularly hung out with, and attending serious art classes. He was a genuinely happy kid who had successfully done what I had been failing at for these past four years, escaped Mom's ridicule and misery. I was proud of the way he spoke up all those years ago and that Dad had been there to support him.

We arrived at the campus and everybody filed out of the car for our good-byes. I probably wouldn't be seeing them until possibly the holidays.

"I'm so proud of you, Nessy," Dad said as he pulled me into a hug.

I held tight, needing the comfort of feeling like that little girl in her daddy's arms once again, even just for a moment. "I know you've been through an emotional wringer this past month, but don't let that keep you from enjoying your time in Europe. If any of us deserves such an awesome break, it's you. Don't stress about what's going on with your mother or what your next step is. Just take it day by day, take lots of pictures, send us a postcard every now and then, and soak up everything you can from the experience."

"Thanks, Dad. I'll try."

Dad smiled in understanding. "That's better than not trying."

"Your dad and I have a graduation gift for you, which you can probably use for your trip," Tanya said, handing me an envelope.

Inside was a Congratulations Graduate card and a check for a thousand dollars. "This is too much, especially since Dad paid for my room and board and incidentals for school."

With an affectionate smile, Tanya placed a hand on my cheek. "Consider it an investment in your future. You can pay us back by being happy and continuing to reach for your dreams so your father can brag about his famous photographer daughter." She pulled me into a tight embrace and gave me a kiss on the cheek.

"Thank you," I said, trying to hold back tears of happiness instead of despair in what felt like forever.

"My turn!" J.J. said. "Can I walk with Ness to her dorm?" he asked Dad.

"Of course," Dad said.

I threw my arms around Dad's neck once more and placed a kiss on his cheek. "I love you."

"I love you too, baby girl."

J.J. and I walked from the parking lot toward my dorm. I smiled when his long fingers grasped mine as we strolled along. J.J. had always been an affectionate kid, and I was glad that hadn't changed about him.

"I've never thanked you for everything you did for me, especially when you stood up to Mom for me," J.J. said.

"There's no need to thank me for anything. You're my little brother and, don't tell Dad or Uncle Frank, but my favorite fella." I bumped him playfully with my hip.

J.J. grinned. "Don't tell Jackie, but you're my favorite sister."

"I better be."

We both chuckled. We had reached the dorm. Graduates and their families were milling about or going in and out of the building. Most, like me, would be leaving the campus for the last time in the next few days. I would miss what had become my home away from home and somewhat a sanctuary from the drama there. In some ways, I had come into my own at Spelman. I found a new, diverse group of friends, discovered a confidence in myself as a woman I never knew I had, and I had confirmed what I wanted to do with my career. Growing my knowledge and skills in the field of photography to better suit what I wanted to do. Unfortunately, I hadn't gained any confidence in myself when it came to love, relationships, and my sexuality. I still had a long way to go for that.

"I have a gift for you also. I guess it's kind of a graduation and birthday gift since your birthday is next week," J.J. said, pulling me from my overcrowded headspace. He handed me a flat, gift wrapped item he had been carrying with him.

"You didn't have to get me anything."

J.J. grinned. "I know, but I wanted to."

I removed the wrapping to find an 8½ x11-inch canvas of a white lotus flower floating on a lake. The painting could almost pass for a picture, especially with the reflection of the lotus on the water. "You did this?" I asked in awe.

"Yeah. I've been playing with oils for a little bit now, and I saw a photograph that looked like this and it made me think of you, so I painted it. Sort of in honor of all the photos you took for me to practice my sketching and because I know how much you love the lotus flower. Do you like it? I tried to make it small enough for you to be able to pack in your luggage. If you wrap a T-shirt or something soft around it and cushion it between your clothes in your suitcase or put in your backpack, like I did, it should travel fine."

"I love it," I pulled him into a hug. "Thank you."

We held each other for a long moment before we separated, and I placed a kiss on his cheek. He gave me a shy smile in return.

"This is going to be the backdrop for my Buddha in my meditation corner at home."

"Cool," he said proudly. Then his expression turned serious. "Ness, don't let Mom get to you. Don't let her turn you into her, okay?"

I placed a hand on his cheek. He was always such an observant and empathetic kid. It was a good thing he had gotten out of Mom's clutches because she would've surely broken him even worse than she'd broken me. "I won't. I love you, buddy."

"I love you too." We hugged once more, and I watched as he walked back to Dad and Tanya. I gave them a final wave and headed into the dorm to pack up what I hadn't shipped home already and prepare to move on to the next stage of my roller coaster of a life.

Chapter Sixteen

Three days after I flew home from Spelman, I was back on a flight with Keisha heading to London, the first leg of our trip. Keisha kept us busy enough with touristy stuff and hanging with friends she had there for me to not to even have time to think about Maya, home, or what my next step in life was. After two weeks in London, we spent a month in Paris, where I had more time by myself since Keisha was attending workshops. I visited museums, took a tour of the village of Montmartre, which had once been known as the Harlem of the City of Lights, and tried not to think about how much Maya would have loved being there.

Halfway through our time in Paris, I woke up feeling a bit queasy. I figured it was probably because I hadn't eaten much the night before, so I dug into the basket of pastries and baked goods that the landlord had left for us. I had quickly finished off two croissants with a cup of tea before I felt it all coming back up. The sound of me retching must have woken Keisha up because as my head was in the toilet, I heard water running then felt something cool and wet on the back of my neck.

"Are you all right?" Keisha asked.

"I think I just tried to eat too much too fast after not eating most of the day yesterday."

"Janesse, you really need to snap out of this funk. You barely eat, those bags under your eyes are going to require a claim ticket soon, and you haven't been the fun, entertaining travel companion I had hoped for."

I sat on the floor, took the wet cloth Keisha had placed on my neck, and put it over my eyes with a sigh. "I'm sorry. I wouldn't blame you if you sent me back home."

"Nope. You're not getting out of this trip that easily. You need this trip. Clean up, I'll make you a cup of tea."

The queasiness continued and after almost a week of not being able to keep anything down in the morning except tea and dry toast, Keisha kept giving me these curious looks and insisted I go to the clinic, skipping one of her workshops to go with me. When the doctor asked if I could be pregnant, I laughed until I remembered that afternoon, two months ago, with Justin. We had stupidly not used protection. I had worried a bit after until I got my period as usual. Sitting in front of the doctor I felt like an idiot realizing I hadn't gotten it since then. It usually came like clockwork around the same time each month. I had never missed one before. The morning queasiness, not being able to keep anything in my stomach, a sudden craving for ice, and the recent bloating I chalked up to, ironically, PMS and stress, it couldn't have been more obvious.

Still in denial, I took the pregnancy test, believing it would come back negative and that everything was from the stress of the breakup, graduating, and worrying about what I was going to do with myself after Keisha and I got back home. Not too surprising to find out that stress wasn't the cause because that's just the way my life was. A series of stupid actions that led to life-changing consequences. The doctor said the ice craving was due to me being anemic from not eating correctly. He gave me a prescription for prenatal vitamins as well as some samples and warned that if I didn't take better care of myself, I could lose the baby. I was in shock as we made our way back to our cottage. Keisha led me to the sofa.

"Sit. I'll make you a cup of tea," she said gently.

I nodded, staring unseeing out the window. People strode by outside, laughing and chatting, as if my whole world weren't collapsing around me…again. First Maya, now this. I faintly heard the squeal of the kettle and realized it wasn't the kettle. I clapped my hand over my mouth, but the sound kept coming. I started rocking back and forth trying to stop the scream from escaping and arms wrapped around me.

"Go ahead, let it out," Keisha said.

I frantically shook my head and kept my mouth covered.

"Janesse, you can't keep holding stuff in like this. It's going to drive you crazy if you do." She shifted us apart and pulled my hand away from my mouth. "Scream, yell, curse, do whatever you need to do because you have some serious decisions to make."

The wall I had so carefully erected and kept every bit of heartbreak, frustration, and anger shoved behind cracked and it all spilled forth in one word.

"Fuck...Fuck...FUCK...FUUUUUCK!" I stood up and began pacing. "How could I be so stupid? What the hell is wrong with me that I keep fucking up my life this way?"

Keisha just watched as I continued to berate myself for my carelessness and idiocy. When I was finished and just continued pacing senselessly, she stood, blocked my path, and grasped my shoulders firmly to keep me still.

"Enough! Stop bashing yourself for being a human who makes mistakes like everyone else. It's not going to solve anything. You need to stop looking at what led you here and start looking at how you plan to handle it," Keisha said sternly.

I knew she was right, but it didn't stop the little voice in my head from continuing to tell me how stupid I was. I sat back down, picked up the tea she had brought me, and inhaled the herbal scent while letting the steam bathe my face. I felt a bit calmer, so I took a sip and sat back grasping the cup to warm my chilled hands.

"Do you know whose it is?" Keisha asked.

"Justin's," I said quietly. I hadn't told anyone about that day. I gave Keisha a condensed version of what happened.

"Okay, so this was just a one-off. You two haven't discussed it since then?"

"No. I mean I worried about the chance of being pregnant but then my period came like it normally did. Until we just saw the doctor, I didn't even think about the fact that it wasn't as heavy as usual."

"Stupid...stupid," the voice said again. I shook my head to shut it up so I could think straight.

"Here's what I suggest. Take some time to think about what you want to do. Whether you want to keep it and, if so, how to tell Justin about it. In the meantime, I'll make arrangements to get you a flight home—"

"NO!" I shouted. "I'm not ready to go home. It's still early, I have plenty of time to figure out what to do. Please, Keisha, I need to be here. Going home will only make it more difficult to figure out what I want without being bombarded with what everyone else thinks I should do."

Keisha gave my knee a squeeze. "Okay, whatever you want. You just have to promise me you'll take better care of yourself while we're here. Take the prenatal vitamins, start eating full meals instead of foraging like some squirrel, and don't beat yourself up like I know you will."

I gave her a slight smile. "Yes, ma'am."

Keisha frowned. "Ugh, and definitely don't call me that."

"Thank you, Keisha, seriously. You've really been a big help in keeping me from jumping off the deep end emotionally."

"You're welcome. Believe it or not, having you here has made what would've been a lonely trip very enjoyable." She kissed me on the forehead. "I'm going to make us something for lunch. Why don't you go lie down and I'll let you know when it's ready?"

I nodded and took my tea into the bedroom with me. I sat on the bed staring down into the cooling cup, then set it down and walked over to the corner where I had set up my meditation area. I knelt on a throw pillow from the bed and looked at everything I had collected that I thought would help bring peace and serenity into my life. The jade Buddha Maya had bought for me when we visited a holistic shop in New Orleans, J.J.'s lotus oil painting as his backdrop, the crystal lotus from Nikki, Carol, and Frieda, and the nag champa incense that I had bought in bulk before our trip. Meditation had been my coping mechanism, but despite making sure I had a corner set up wherever I went, I had been slacking since Maya and I split. I could count on one hand the number of times I had done it since we'd left for Europe. Meditation meant I had to sit and either clear my mind or let it go in whatever direction it chose to lead me to whatever epiphany I needed to find peace.

I laid my hand over my belly, splaying my fingers where my child, who, according to the doctor, was the size of raspberry right now, would be growing. I might not have been sure about much in my life, but one thing I knew was that I wanted children. To shower a child with all the love and affection a mother could give and which I had none of. To have someone love me without having to know what my sexuality was or why I couldn't figure out what made me happy if I loved them back. But did I want it this way? If I knew Justin as well as I think I did, as soon as I told him he would be planning our wedding because it would be the right thing to do, something I had no desire to do. I would raise this child alone if I had to, but I refused to marry someone because it was the right thing to do.

I lit incense, picked up my crystal lotus, held it close to my belly, closed my eyes, and let the scented smoke wash over me. The first thought that came to mind was finding out if inhaling this stuff would affect the baby. After that I took several deep breaths and tried to let my mind go. It had been some time since I truly meditated so it took a little longer to reach the relaxed state that I needed to clear away most of the noise. I avoided doing what I normally did, asking a question to try to lead to whatever answer I was seeking. I just let it all go and felt a sense of calm come over me. I continued holding the lotus in one hand as I splayed my fingers over my belly with the other. I knew then that I could never take his or her life. It wasn't their fault how they were conceived. They might not have been conceived of the romantic love you would hope your child was created from, but it was still a love between two people who cared deeply for each other in every other way. Whatever decision Justin made about being a part of our child's life wouldn't affect how I would love and care for them. I would do whatever it took to give them a good life filled with love and security.

Keisha and I completed the remainder of our trip with time in Spain, Italy, and Greece. I had decided not to tell Justin about the baby until after we returned home. I needed this time away to not have any other drama in my life for the time being. Like a light switch, all my self-pity about the breakup, the lack of accepting my own sexuality, and the insecurities and doubt my mother constantly fed within me, flipped to making sure I did whatever I had to, to keep myself and the raspberry that grew within in me healthy and safe.

"I don't know how I'll ever be able to thank you for this trip," I said to Keisha as we enjoyed dinner on our last night in Greece.

"No need to thank me. If anything, I should thank you." For the first time since I'd known her, Keisha looked unsure of herself as she fidgeted with her wine glass. "I had never really had a close, platonic girlfriend before you. Although our friendship didn't start out the most conventional way, I feel like you've shown me that I don't need to use sex to keep people in my life. I've treasured spending this time with you these past few months. If you, or the baby, need anything, don't hesitate to call me."

"Thank you for the offer, for all the connections for me and my friends, for this, and most of all for allowing our friendship to happen when you could've just kicked me to the curb after that first summer. I love you, Keisha."

Keisha looked surprised for a moment then smiled broadly and squeezed my hand. "I love you too. You're like the little sister I never had. I hope that isn't too weird to say considering how we met."

I grinned. "Not weird at all."

It was the perfect end to our trip.

Keisha and I parted at the airport. As I got closer to home, I began to feel the anxiety that had become a regular fixture of my makeup. I placed one hand on my lotus pendant and the other over my belly, breathing softly to find that sense of calm I had found in Paris. There it was, deep within me. I liked to think it was my baby sending me the peace I needed, starting out as a kernel of thought and slowly spreading throughout me. By the time we pulled up into the driveway the anxiety was all but gone. I knew there would still be some residual considering the announcement I was going to be making, but it wasn't overwhelming me.

It was late at night. I had called Jackie from the airport to let her know I had arrived and was on my way home. She, and to my happiness, Nikki hurried out to greet me. I ended up smothered in a group hug with Jackie and I laughing and crying and Nikki planting lip-smacking kisses on my cheek.

"You would've thought I was gone for years," I said as I swatted both away and wiped my eyes.

"You might as well have been considering we got more postcards than phone calls from you," Nikki complained with a frown.

"Sorry, it's hard to link up the time zones to figure out the best time to call."

Jackie waved her hand dismissively. "Whatever, I'm just glad you're safe and home. Let's get your luggage so we can see what you brought us."

We grabbed the luggage the driver unloaded, Nikki tipped him for me, and we headed into the apartment.

"Mom is out tonight," Jackie said when she noticed my glance up the stairs to Mom's apartment.

I shrugged. "That's fine. I didn't expect her to be here to greet me with open arms." There was none of the old hurt or bitterness in my tone, which I think Jackie and Nikki noticed, judging by the curious looks they gave me.

"You are fine, aren't you?" Jackie said.

"Yep."

"I knew it would be good for you to go on that trip," Nikki said.

"It really was. Now, Jackie, the suitcase you have is where all the goodies are."

I presented Jackie with a print of Josephine Baker when she performed at the Moulin Rouge and Nikki with a cookbook from Le Cordon Bleu Paris. Both were thrilled with their gifts and I ended back up in a group hug.

"Okay, enough, I need something to eat." I hadn't eaten anything since our lunch on the flight. I had slept through dinner service and my little peanut was not letting me forget it.

"I just went grocery shopping, but I don't have anything prepared for a full meal," Jackie said.

Rubbing her hands together and grinning like a mad scientist, Nikki headed to the kitchen. "Not a problem. I'm sure I can whip something up."

After Nikki pulled together a pasta salad and grilled chicken, we sat around the table as I told them about my travels. I left out the discovery that I was pregnant. That information was something I had chosen to share with Justin first. It was only fair since he was the father. We talked for a good two hours before I started yawning.

"Jet lag hitting you?" Nikki asked.

"Yeah." It was more the baby letting me know that late nights were a thing of the past, but I wasn't saying that.

"Well, you go rest. Nikki and I will clean up."

"Thanks, guys." I wished them a good night and dragged myself to bed. I needed all the rest I could get before talking to Justin tomorrow.

I called Justin first thing in the morning to ask to see him. He suggested meeting at his place after work. He had just moved into his own apartment, conveniently located a couple of blocks from our house.

"Hey, stranger!" Justin said as he greeted me at the door with a hug.

"Hey. I guess working with your uncle is paying off. Got your own place already."

He shrugged. "It's the same pay as his other construction managers. I have to spend a few years as a manager before he'll move me up to the position of partner."

"Making you work for that title, huh?" I teased him.

"Yeah, which is cool with me. Working for him throughout high school as a laborer, then spending the past four summers learning each role as a carpenter, electrician, and equipment operator was the best learning experience I could've had. I've got more experience under my belt at twenty-two than most guys just starting out at my age."

I couldn't help but smile at the pride in his face and demeanor. "It's so good to see you taking pride in doing something you love. You're all grown up now." I faked a sniffle and wiped away an imaginary tear.

Justin laughed. "Whatever. Can I get you something to drink? I've got some wine coolers in the fridge."

"No. I'm off the alcohol for now. A glass of water is fine."

"Too much fancy European wines while you were away?" he teased me.

"Not at all."

He gave me a skeptical look. "Yeah, okay. Have a seat."

His apartment was a nice size. It had an open concept with the living room, what I assumed was the dining room but looked to be set up more like an office, and the kitchen all separated by an open doorway. There was a hallway off the kitchen that must have led to a bedroom and bathroom.

"Nice place," I said as he handed me a glass of water.

"Thanks. It's bigger than I originally wanted, but it was the only corner apartment they had available." He flopped down on the sofa next to me and placed his socked feet onto the coffee table.

"Why was a corner apartment so important?" I knew I was stalling, but I was nervous.

"Lighting." He pointed toward his office. "You see how bright it is? The corner apartment has more windows. Better for working on my plans."

Justin hadn't gotten into construction just because he liked to work with his hands but to be able to design and construct new homes. His office had a drafting table and tall chair directly in front of a wall of windows. There was also a rack that held stacks of architectural design drafts. Nikki's mom Frieda had tried to convince Justin to major in architecture after seeing his drawings, but he wasn't into the big skyscrapers and office buildings like her. He liked the idea of building something small and personal that would be filled with love and family. He was a sentimental mush beneath the devil-may-care attitude he showed to everyone. It was one of the very endearing qualities about him that would make any woman lucky to have him.

"Speaking of plans, I got you a little something." I handed him a cardboard cylinder.

Justin opened it and pulled out a poster-size architectural rendering of the Theatre of Marcellus in Rome by an Italian Renaissance architect named Pirro Ligorio. After I mentioned that Italy would be one of our stops, Justin had gone on a tangent about his favorite Renaissance architect and how he had changed the game with his understanding of what makes a good building, how he had chosen to use thicker walls and stone piers to give buildings endurance, and other things I couldn't even remember.

He looked at the poster, then at me in awe. "I can't believe you were actually listening to me drone on, let alone remembered."

"For you to talk about something other than sports and sex for longer than fifteen minutes obviously meant it was important to you," I said jokingly.

Justin gave me a playful shove then rolled the poster back into the cylinder. "I know just where I'll hang it after I get it framed. So, how was your trip, what exciting things did you do?"

I told him everything about the trip that I had told Jackie and Nikki, trying to ease into telling him the real reason I was here.

"It looks like it really did you some good. You look much better than you did when you left. Healthier and happier," Justin said.

"Well, it probably did have to do with the trip, but I think it's more from the news I got while I was there."

"What news was that?"

I picked at the hem of the loose blouse I was wearing to hide the fact that I could no longer button my shorts.

"Was it that bad?" Justin asked.

"I don't think it's bad, but I'm not sure if you will."

"Well, don't keep me in suspense, what is it?"

"I'm pregnant and it's yours because you're the only guy I've been with since Dante," I hurriedly blurted out.

Justin was quiet. I looked up to find him looking at me with his head cocked to the side in confusion.

"Say something," I said quietly.

"When did you find out?"

"A few weeks after we arrived in Paris."

"And you're just now telling me?" He sounded hurt.

"I needed time to think and decide what I wanted to do."

"What do you mean decide what you wanted to do? What decision needed to be made?"

"As screwed up as I am, as my life has been, I wasn't sure if I wanted to bring a baby into that mess."

Justin's confusion turned to an angry frown. "You weren't going to keep it? You were going to abort our baby without even telling me? Like I had no say in it?"

"First of all, I didn't say that I wasn't going to tell you. Second, it's my body to decide what I want to do with it," I said, annoyed at his anger.

"But it's OUR baby!"

"Are you serious right now, Justin? I never pegged you as one of those men who think they have a say over what a woman does with her own body. You won't be the one to carry it for nine months while your body changes in ways you never thought possible. You won't be the one in a hospital bed screaming and pushing that child out of your body. You won't be the one up at all hours of the night at the whim of that child, feeding them, soothing them, and changing their nasty diapers. That's all on the woman, yet men like you think because they stuck their penis up in you that they have a right to make decisions for you. Well, let me tell you something, buster." I jammed my finger in Justin's chest. "That shit doesn't fly with me. You should know me well enough to not even have said such an idiotic thing."

Justin ran his hand through his hair with a look of frustration. "Dammit, Janesse, why do you always have to take things from zero to sixty in a matter of seconds? That's not what I was saying. I just think it should have been a decision we made together. We created the child together, we should have made the decision together of what to do about it. If we decided not to keep it, I could have been there for you through the procedure. If we decided to keep it, then I would do whatever it took to make sure you and the baby would have whatever you needed. That's all."

I looked guiltily down at my lap. "Oh."

Justin took my hand. "Ness, look at me."

I looked up to meet his tender gaze. "Whatever you decide, I support you and I'm here for you."

"I-I decided to keep it. Since I made the decision, I don't expect anything from you. I'm not here to mess up your life like I have my own. I just thought you should know."

Justin shook his head. "There you go, zero to sixty."

"Sorry."

"I said I would support whatever decision you made. I'm glad it was that one because I think we would have an awesome kid together." Justin grinned.

"You really think so?"

"My beauty and your brains, where could we go wrong?"

"You're so silly," I said, laughing.

"In all seriousness, whatever you guys need, I'm here."

"Thanks." I pulled him into a hug.

"Ness, if you want to get married—"

"Don't even finish that sentence! You know neither of us is ready for a relationship with someone, let alone marriage."

I almost laughed out loud at the relief on his face. "Yeah, you're right. I just felt like it was the right thing to say."

"Justin, if and when you decide to get married, I would hope it would be more for than it being the right thing to do."

Justin nodded. "Like I said, my beauty and your brains."

I gave him another shove.

"I would like to make one other suggestion. Move in with me." He quickly held up his hands to stop my protest. "Just as roommates. No strings attached. I have two bedrooms, the second of which is just being used for storage right now until I finish unpacking. You and the baby could stay there, then I could help so you won't have to deal with your mother living right upstairs from you. The stress she causes you wouldn't be good for you or the baby."

It was actually a good idea. We could take care of the baby together and I would be free to live my life without Mom's interference. "Only if you allow me to contribute with the rent. I'm not living here for free. Next week I'm going to start looking for a job while I'm still barely showing that I can leave without worry when the baby comes."

"Okay, I have a counter request. You allow me to add you to my health insurance unless you plan on paying for your medical expenses yourself."

"I don't know, Justin. That's such a major thing to offer." That felt like such a "couple" thing to do.

"Ness, you're carrying my—*our*—child. You're going to need regular doctor visits, prenatal supplements, ultrasounds, the works. Do you really think you can cover all of that alone? This is no time to be stubborn."

Of course he was right. I knew, just from the amount of money I ended up spending in Europe for the two doctor visits I had and the cost of the prenatal vitamins, that having a baby wasn't going to be cheap. I didn't even want to think about the hospital costs for the delivery.

"Okay, I guess," I reluctantly agreed. "By the way, how do you know so much about having a baby?"

"Remember I was there for my second nephew's delivery a couple of years ago since my brother-in-law was shipped overseas and couldn't be home through most of Sam's pregnancy."

I couldn't help but smile remembering that summer. Justin had taken the role so seriously his sister, Samantha, was ready to kick him to the curb within a matter of weeks for all his nagging. In the end, when she ended up having some complications during delivery, she had been glad to have him there to keep her calm and be her advocate at the hospital. He was both uncle and godfather to his nephews. I remembered how good he was with J.J. through the years as well as his nephews, I knew that Justin would make a good father. I just never imagined it would be the father of my child.

"Can I touch your belly?" he asked sweetly.

I nodded and placed his hand over my rounded belly. "The doctor in France told me they're about the size of an apple right now."

Justin's eyes widened. "They?"

I chuckled. "I don't like calling the baby *it*, so I say *they*."

"Phew, okay, you had me scared for a minute. How about we come up with a nickname, like Munchkin, or something."

"Okay, Munchkin it is."

Justin slid off the sofa, sat on the floor beside my legs, and leaned his head toward by belly. "Hey, Munchkin, it's your daddy."

It was the sweetest thing I had ever seen. I decided, in that moment, that I couldn't imagine having a child with anyone else but my best friend.

The sweetness disappeared when it came time to tell my mother. I invited her and Uncle Frank over for dinner that night claiming I wanted to give them their gifts and show off the cooking skills I learned during some culinary classes Keisha and I, took in Paris and Rome. I kept it simple with a French quiche lorraine and pasta alla Genovese since those were the dishes I had done best during our classes. I also called Keisha for the best wine suggestions hoping a little alcohol would relax Mom. To my relief, Jackie volunteered to be there for extra support, and Nikki made chocolate mousse for me, Mom's favorite dessert. Was I trying to soften Mom up? Absolutely, but not to ease the blow for her as much as to keep things civil.

I used a real tablecloth, borrowed from Carol, as well as the good dishes Mom left for Jackie when she took over the apartment. Dinner went well. Uncle Frank kept the conversation going by asking me about my trip. I was so nervous I barely ate, claiming I had a big lunch. I knew I'd probably be fighting nausea later, but it was better than forcing myself to eat and getting sick during dinner.

I decided dessert would be the perfect time to present them their gifts and tell them about the baby. Mom had two glasses of wine by then, thanks to Jackie keeping her glass full, and she hadn't made any snide comments the entire time I talked about the trip or Keisha. Uncle Frank loved hats, so I got him a bowler hat from Laird Hatters in London, and Mom a silk scarf from the Chanel boutique in Paris. Mom seemed surprised that I had given her something so nice.

"This must have cost a fortune," she said.

"As long as you like it, it doesn't matter," I said, thrilled that I did something to put a genuine smile on her face.

She nodded. "It's beautiful. Thank you."

"Yes, thank you, Ness, this is awesome." He placed the hat on his head and struck a seated pose. "How do I look?"

"Very debonair," I said.

"Now I'll have to find an excuse to wear it."

I sent a glance Jackie's way and she nodded. "Who's ready for dessert?" She went to the refrigerator to retrieve the dishes of mousse and served them to everyone.

I took a moment to let them enjoy it before I possibly ruined their appetite. I cleared my throat nervously.

"So…um…I found out something interesting while I was away." I felt a little flip in my belly and splayed my fingers over it. It was probably the baby reacting to my sudden anxiety. No sense in beating around the bush and making it worse. I might as well just say it. "I'm pregnant. It happened before I left for Europe, but I didn't find out until I started getting sick while we were in Paris."

Mom's spoon was halfway to her open mouth and she froze as if someone had turned on the pause button.

"Well…okay then," Uncle Frank said, his face registering shock, then concern as he looked between me and Mom.

Him speaking must have snapped Mom out of her trance. Her

mouth snapped shut and she carefully placed the spoon back into her glass dish.

Her expression was unreadable. “So, you’re over that lesbian stuff?” she asked.

My belly fluttered again, as if to remind me not to let her get to me. “I didn’t say that.”

“Do you even know who the father is?” she asked.

I had to bite my tongue at the insult. “It’s Justin.”

Her eyes widened. “The boy you’ve been friends with all these years?”

“Yes. It was a one-time thing that happened during a difficult time for both of us. Despite that, he’s stepped up to offer to help take care of our child.”

“And what about doing the right thing by you?” Mom asked.

“Janet, this isn’t the fifties. Shotgun weddings aren’t a thing anymore,” Uncle Frank said.

“And what happens if he decides it’s too much and wants out? Janesse becomes another statistic of a single Black mother on welfare,” Mom said.

The ridiculousness and hypocrisy of what she was saying made me laugh out loud. “Zero to sixty. Now I see where I get it from.”

Everybody looked at me in confusion.

“Despite your obvious confidence in me,” I said sarcastically, “I won’t become a statistic, and Justin and I getting married won’t keep him from walking away if chooses to. We have a plan, but if he decides later that he can’t handle it, I’m not going to force him to stay involved. I’ll be fine.”

“What’s this plan?” Mom asked.

“Justin has his own place with an extra bedroom. I’m moving in with him, on a strictly platonic basis, so that we can take care of the baby together. I’m going to get a temporary job until the baby comes, then when I’m ready to go back to work I plan on pursuing my photography as I originally planned before all of this happened.”

Mom snorted in derision. “Do you seriously think it’ll stay platonic? He’s a man.”

I sighed in frustration. She was really testing my nerves. “A man I’ve known for eight years who has always been straightforward with me. Neither of us is ready to be in a relationship. Even if we were, he knows that I’m not interested in him that way.”

“And if he decides he wants to start dating again?”

"We'll deal with that road when we hit it. For now, our priority is our child."

"Well, you sound like you guys are handling this maturely. If there's anything you need, I'm here for you," Uncle Frank said, smiling in encouragement.

"The mature thing would've been to use protection," Mom said snidely.

"You don't ever stop, do you? This is why I chose to move in with Justin rather than stay here. It's not worth risking my emotional and physical health, or the physical health of my baby, to allow you to stress me out," I said angrily, then closed my eyes and took a deep breath to calm myself down.

"Mom, I love you, but I'm telling you right now, if you want to have a relationship with your grandchild then you're going to have to figure out what's more important. Trying to put me down every chance you get because I don't fit the mode you think I should or being a grandmother." I stood, picked up everyone's dishes, whether they were finished or not, and took them to the sink while trying to hold back tears.

The sound of a chair scraping, the click of heels, and the door slamming told me Mom had left. My body collapsed in on itself as if I had been holding it up for too long and a tear splashed into the remnants of mousse in a dish.

"Ness," Uncle Frank said from behind me.

I turned and threw myself into his big arms and cried.

"Hey, I think it went much better than we expected," Jackie said.

"Probably because of all the wine you were plying her with," Uncle Frank said, his voice laced with humor, replacing my sobs with laughter.

He took my face in his hands and smiled down at me. "I'm sure this isn't quite the time or way you expected to be making such an announcement, but it doesn't matter how that little miracle growing inside you came about, as long as you give her all the love she deserves, it will all be fine."

I quirked an eyebrow. "She?"

"My precious granddaughter needs a playmate."

"Thanks, Uncle Frank."

He kissed me on the forehead, then pulled a laughing Jackie into our hug.

CHAPTER SEVENTEEN

"How are you feeling?" Justin asked as I sat down with a groan.

"Like a beached whale," I said.

Justin chuckled. "Well, you're a beautiful beached whale."

He danced out of the way before I could punch him. "I'll get your egg roll. You want anything else?"

"Maybe some water. I didn't drink enough today."

"One shrimp egg roll and water coming up." He saluted and walked away.

This was my last week at work before going on maternity leave. I had managed to get a job at a Glamour Shots Photo Studio at the mall. Because I'm a thick girl already and wasn't really showing much, I was able to hide my pregnancy for the first couple of months on the job by wearing loose-fitting clothing. Then our lil' Munchkin decided to announce itself to the world by ballooning up to the point it was obvious I was pregnant, not just fat. Fortunately, the manager was a mom and understood, letting me stay on as a photographer practically up until my due date, which was a week from now. I'd been spending the past week training my replacement. Justin had insisted on picking me up after work this last week knowing how uncomfortable I was after spending most of my day on my feet.

I turned to look down into a shopping bag full of new baby clothes and pulled out a pair of baby Converse that I just had to buy when I heard someone call my name. I looked up to find Maya standing before me. I quickly shoved the shoes back in the bag.

"I thought that was you, but I almost didn't recognize you with short hair," Maya said with a smile.

I was too shocked to respond. We literally had not seen or spoken to each other since the day of the breakup. Since she moved across the country, I hadn't expected to ever see her again, so I never imagined what I would say to her if I did. I just sat there staring at her as if I had no voice. That bright, beautiful smile that still made my heart skip a beat slipped from her face and was replaced with a look of sadness.

"I understand if you don't want to talk to me. I'm sorry to bother you," Maya said before turning away.

That jolted me out my muteness. I stood as quickly as I could considering my bulk and reached out for her arm. "Maya, wait!" She turned back around with a look of relief. "Sorry, I was just surprised to see you, that's all."

"I'm just home for the holidays. Mom wanted to take advantage of some after-Christmas sales. I was just going to pull the car around while she's in the ladies' room and saw you sitting there. I can't believe you cut your hair, but it looks great on you. Draws more attention to your beautiful face," Maya said.

"Thanks." I felt my face heat with a blush and ran my hand over my short, cropped hair. It had become too much effort to keep it up while it was long, so I just had it chopped off into a soft fade, not caring how it looked as long as it was low maintenance.

"You look great. California must agree with you."

She didn't look great, she looked downright gorgeous. Her skin tone was a shade darker than the last time I saw her. Probably from the Southern California sun. She was dressed in a long red wool coat, a sexy red wrap dress, knee-high black leather boots, and fashionable gold chunky jewelry, and her sun-kissed light copper color hair lay in soft curls past her shoulders. I felt like such a frump wearing one of Justin's peacoats, a tan turtleneck, maternity jeans, and duck boots that I changed into after work. I realized that although the coat wasn't buttoned, it was big enough to hide my pregnancy belly.

"It's not as fast-paced as New York, but it's been good. I've been doing a lot of commercial and TV work dressing the models and actors, which is a lot different than photoshoots. How've you been?"

"I spent the summer traveling around Europe with Keisha, strictly platonic." I wanted to slap myself for saying that. I didn't owe her any explanations. She broke up with me. "I've been working at Glamour Shots here at the mall since then."

Maya looked confused. "Glamour Shots? With your portfolio and experience from your summer work you couldn't find anything?"

"I really haven't tried. After Europe I wasn't in a good position to start any long-term jobs." I spread my coat enough for her to see what lay beneath and placed my hand on my belly.

The look of shock on Maya's face was almost comical, but she recovered quickly. A tentative smile took its place, but it didn't hide the disappointment in her eyes. "Wow…okay…uh, congratulations. Looks like you're about to pop."

"Thanks. Yeah, next week." I could practically hear the calculator in her head trying to figure out the timing. "It happened after we broke up."

"You don't owe me any explanation."

"I know, but I want to give you one anyway. I was so hurt by you breaking it off like that. I spent a week in bed feeling as if I was dying, then another week walking around like a ghost until I decided to come home for spring break, you know, since I figured our Miami trip was a bust." I tried to joke and failed judging by the look of guilt on Maya's face. "Anyway, it turned out Justin and I had something in common, our girlfriends broke our hearts." Yeah, that was a dig, and I could tell by the subtle flinch Maya made that it hit home, but I continued. "We cried, we comforted each other, and this was the result of it." I gave my belly another rub. Lil' Munchkin shifted in response.

"So are you guys…" Maya couldn't even finish the sentence.

"No. We're living together so that he can help with the baby, especially when I start looking for more substantial work, but it's strictly platonic. Separate bedrooms and whatnot."

As if saying his name conjured him up, Justin walked over and set the tray with our dinner on the table.

"Hey, Maya," he said cheerily.

Maya greeted him with a tense smile. "Hey, Justin. Congratulations," she said, indicating my protruding belly.

"Thanks." He placed his hand over mine. "We're really excited."

I knew what he was doing, and I wanted to punch him. He was trying to add his own dig because she broke my heart. Once again, it landed home. If looks could kill, Justin's head would have been rolling across the floor of the food court. I slid my hand off my belly, taking Justin's with me to drop by our sides.

Maya looked back at me, and I felt a jab to my heart at the sadness in her eyes. "Well, I better go. I'm sure my mother is wondering where I am. It was good to see you again, Janesse. Take care."

"You too," I said.

Maya glanced back at my belly again, then walked away. I turned to Justin and punched him in the arm.

"What the hell was that?"

"What? I was just telling her how happy we were about our baby," he said unconvincingly.

I pursed my lips and rolled my eyes at him. "Yeah, right."

I flopped carefully back down in my seat, grabbed my egg roll, and bit angrily into it. Justin sat across from me, quietly eating his own.

"I'm sorry," he said a moment later. "I guess I got a little protective. I know how bad she hurt you, and I felt like I had to protect you from falling under her spell again."

"We were just talking. She lives across the country and I'm about to pop out a kid. There was no spell to fall under."

"I saw how you looked at her when she first approached you. I didn't want to interrupt at first, but when you showed her you were pregnant, I figured that was a good time to step in. You still love her."

"No," I said with a pout.

Justin quirked a brow in doubt.

"Maybe," I conceded.

"You should tell her before she goes back to California."

"Why? This," I pointed to my belly, "is proof that she was right about me. I was just as confused about my sexuality as she said."

Justin reached across the table to take my hand. "Janesse, getting pregnant doesn't prove anything except that we weren't thinking straight enough to be careful. Your sexuality has nothing to do with the love you obviously have for Maya, and from what I could see, she still loves you. You guys just need to figure out how to make it work."

"It doesn't matter," I said, placing my half-eaten egg roll back on the plate. "My focus is our baby and my career. Romance is the last thing I want or need in my life right now."

Three days into the new year, Sybil Jacqueline Crawford entered kicking and screaming into our lives at a whopping eight pounds, seven ounces. I thought I knew what love was until I looked down into her red, blotchy screaming face. She utterly stole my heart. I knew I would do anything and everything I had to do to make sure she was happy and loved.

"You will never know what it's like to not feel your mother's love. I will do whatever is in my power to make sure you know how much you are loved and how proud I am of you," I told her as she stopped crying, sucked vigorously on her tiny fist, and, even though I knew it wasn't possible, I swore she gazed at me as if she understood what I was saying.

"Isn't our daughter the most beautiful thing in the world?" I said to Justin, who had been by my side the whole delivery. Even when I started cursing him out for doing this to me.

"Just like her mother." He looked as heart struck with her as I was.

"Boy, love really is blind," I teased him.

Justin laughed and placed a kiss on my forehead then the top of our daughter's head. Saying "our daughter" made it more real than "our child" had. This beautiful, chubby, whimpering girl was our responsibility. That daunting fact hit me like a ton of bricks.

"What if I screw her up like my mother did me?"

"That won't happen because you aren't your mother and I know how much love you have in your heart. You're going to make a great mother," Justin said confidently.

I gazed back down at Sybil and knew in my heart that Justin was right. I would never want her feeling the way I did when my mother's venomous words struck home. I wouldn't wish that on my worst enemy.

"Is she still out in the waiting room?"

Mom and I had barely spoken since I announced my pregnancy except in passing when I went to use my dark room still set up in the basement of the house. She noticeably ignored me even during the holidays, although I would catch her surreptitiously glancing my way when someone would ask me if I had everything I needed or Justin's mother would be the doting grandmother-to-be, making sure I was okay or wanting to feel my belly if the baby was active. So, I was shocked when Justin told me she had shown up at the hospital with Jackie and Uncle Frank. Now that Sybil and I were both cleaned up and presentable and she was fed, I told Justin he could invite them in to meet her.

Uncle Frank and Jackie each took a turn holding her, and when she ended up back in my arms, I looked over at Mom, who stood just inside the door as if she were afraid to come all the way into the room. I had never seen her look so unsure, and it made me feel sorry for her.

"Would you like to meet your granddaughter?" I asked.

Mom hesitated for a moment before slowly walking toward me and holding out her arms.

"Mom, I'd like to introduce you to your first grandchild, Sybil Jacqueline Crawford."

She glanced curiously at Justin, who stood beside the bed. "You gave her your last name?"

Justin grinned. "Why wouldn't I? She's my daughter."

Mom nodded with a small smile and took Sybil from my arms. "I can tell already that she's going to have her mommy's height and build."

I made myself take the comment as just that, a general comment and not one of her usual verbal barbs. Sybil had been sleeping since I had fed her, but she opened her eyes and looked up at my mother. They both stared quietly at each other, and a miraculous thing happened. Mom smiled the most genuine and loving smile I had ever seen on her, then Sybil closed her eyes and went back to sleep as if they had come to some understanding.

"She's beautiful, Ness," Mom said as she carefully handed Sybil back to me.

"Thank you." I felt a lump of emotion in my throat at the tender look she gave me before she quickly turned away.

"I'm going to get some coffee. Anybody want any?" Mom said.

"I do. I'll go with you," Uncle Frank said, flashing me a wink and a smile on the way out.

After they left, I looked at Jackie. "Did that really just happen?"

Jackie chuckled. "Yeah." She sat beside me on the bed and looked down at Sybil. "I think we just discovered Mom's kryptonite."

Eight weeks later, with Keisha's help, I started interviewing for photography jobs. Justin's mom had recently retired and had volunteered to be our full-time sitter for free. Justin and I insisted she let us pay her a little something, and she soundly reprimanded us for thinking she would actually take money for babysitting her own grandchild. I found the differing styles of grandmothering from our mothers funny. Justin's mother had no issues with taking Sybil for a whole day, hearing her cry, having to change diapers, and dealing with the spitting up that occurred once we switched Sybil from breast milk to formula. Mom, on the other hand, was good with spending some time holding and talking to Sybil after she was fed and cleaned up, but once the crying or poop faces started, she handed her right back to us. If she had any snide remarks about the sloppy, tired mess I was the first five weeks when I was breastfeeding full-time, she thankfully kept them to herself. I guess she took my threat seriously about not seeing her grandchild if she couldn't be decent to me.

It took a month, but I found a job as an assistant for a commercial photographer in New York who did still lifes of products and people for marketing and advertising. The hours were a little long, but Justin was awesome when it came to stepping in where I couldn't. He would drop Sybil off at his parents' and pick her up and the end of the day. Have her fed and ready for me to bathe and read to at the end of the night. I made up for my absence on the weekends when Justin sometimes had to work. I would pick up the slack while Sybil and I had our mommy-daughter time. Justin and I made a great parenting team. Although we still slept in separate bedrooms, we shared all parenting, household, and financial responsibilities as if we were a couple. I think, in some way, what we had was safe. It was a loving partnership without the worry of someone's heart being broken. It had almost been a year since our individual breakups, but we were both still too afraid to put ourselves out there, so we looked toward each other for companionship.

Later that summer after Justin and I had spent the morning at a Gymboree class with Sybil and put her down for a nap, we lounged on opposite ends of the sofa reading. It was how we spent a typical Saturday if he didn't have to work. It was almost as peaceful as my meditations.

"Hey, Ness," Justin said.

"Hm," I said, not looking up from my book.

"I need to talk to you."

"Okay, give me a sec to finish this section." Once I finished, I placed my bookmark where I stopped, laid the book in my lap, and smiled up at him. "What's up?"

Justin nervously picked at a rip in the cover of his book. "I'm just going to come right out and say it. I met someone and I think I want to ask her out on a date."

I was momentarily stunned. I knew I shouldn't have been. After all, did I really think he would be happy living this way forever? Sure, it seemed like the perfect setup to me, but that didn't mean Justin wouldn't eventually want more.

"Uh, okay," was all I could lamely muster up in response.

"I know we've been living this idyllic little life, avoiding dating and any kind of intimate relationship for almost a year now, and I've been cool with it, but I also didn't expect to meet Beverly. She's the interior designer I told you about that I've been working on a job with for the past few months, so I've kept it mostly about business, but there are times when we just talk, you know, about our lives and stuff. She's really funny and smart—"

"Justin, you know you don't need my permission to start dating again, right?"

"I know, I just want to make sure you're cool with it. I mean, we are living and raising a child together."

He looked so much like that eager teenage boy I met back in the day. I gave him an encouraging smile. "I'm good. It sounds like you really like her, so go ahead and ask her out."

"You're sure you're good?" he asked skeptically.

I chuckled. "I'm fine. Did you expect me to dramatically declare my love for you and tell you not to ask her out?"

Justin snorted. "Yeah, right. Like that would happen."

I couldn't tell if he was joking or not, so I chose to take it as a joke. We had an understanding, and I didn't see any reason to assume he wanted anything more.

Several weeks later, I was feeling a bit neglected when Justin called to tell me he would be spending the night at Beverly's, which meant we would have to reschedule our brunch plans for the next morning at the restaurant where Nikki worked. Once a month, Justin and I tried to plan a grown-up activity to do to give us a break from all the kid-friendly activities we did for the rest of the month. I had spent plenty of days alone in the apartment without Justin, but not an entire night. I found myself waking up at the slightest noise and spent the night tossing and turning. I tried to keep busy the next morning by taking Sybil to the library to hang out in the children's section and then to the park.

I was so desperate to take my mind off where Justin had spent the night and all morning, I even dropped by Mom's only to find out she wasn't home. Jackie was working, so I just went back to the apartment to fix Sybil and I lunch and put her down for her nap. Afterward I sat flipping through the channels on the TV getting annoyed that Justin still wasn't home. When the intercom buzzed, I practically ran to the door hoping maybe it was Jackie or anybody that would keep me from obsessing like I was.

"Who is it?" I said into the intercom.

"Hey, chickie, I've got food!" Nikki announced.

"Thank God!" I said as she walked into the apartment a few minutes later.

Nikki laughed. "Have you not eaten today?"

"Oh, no, I had peanut butter and jelly and sliced apple with Sybil for lunch. I'm just glad you're here."

Nikki headed toward the kitchen. "Okay, what's up?"

"Why does there have to be something up? I can't be happy to see my best friend?"

Nikki gave me a skeptical look.

"Justin spent the night at Beverly's. This was the first night we've spent without him and it creeped me out."

"If that's the case, then why are you happy to see me now? You could've called me last night if you were that creeped out."

I helped her open the takeout containers she had brought. Brioche French toast with fresh berries, crab hash, smoked salmon, fat links of sausage, thick smoky strips of bacon, and home fries.

"Did you think you were feeding an army?" I asked.

"No, but you know how Justin eats. I didn't know he wasn't here. Speaking of which, you didn't answer my question." She leaned back against the counter and looked at me pointedly.

Sybil's whimpers through the baby monitor saved me from her godmother's probing.

Nikki smiled knowingly. "I'll get her."

A moment later, I heard Nikki cooing at Sybil. "Hey, sweet face, Auntie Nikki's here. Whew, girl, no wonder you were crying. I'd cry too if I had to sit in whatever I'm smelling."

Sybil giggled and chattered baby talk in response. She loved her auntie Nikki, and Nikki loved her goddaughter as if she were her own. Justin and I had asked Nikki to be Sybil's godmother before she was even born. We knew there was no one else we'd ask to care for our daughter if anything happened to us. After a conversation-filled diaper change, Nikki came back with Sybil bouncing happily in her arms.

"Hey, Munchkin, did you have a good nap?" I asked as I plopped a lip-smacking kiss on Sybil's cheek.

"Aaah," she said, pointing to the display of food on the counter.

"You're hungry already?" I said.

Nikki chuckled. "She obviously has her father's appetite." She put Sybil in her highchair at the table as I made her a plate of bite-sized French toast and sausage.

Nikki and I made our own plates and joined her.

"So, back to my question," Nikki said.

"Geez, you're like a dog with a bone."

"Yep, so you might as well answer it."

I sighed in resignation. "Okay. I've been perfectly fine with Justin going out with Beverly, but last night I got a little annoyed when he told me he would be spending the night and wouldn't be home in time for us to go to brunch."

"Maybe it's time for you to start dating again."

I rolled my eyes. "Please, I don't have the time or energy for dating."

"You would if you stopped playing house with Justin. You two are practically married without the fringe benefits."

"We're just trying to give Sybil a stable home life."

"What do you think, sweet face? You think it's time for Mommy to put herself out there?"

Sybil squealed and threw a piece of French toast across the table at me.

"See, she even agrees," Nikki said, laughing.

I picked at my food. "You don't think I've thought about it?"

"Then what's stopping you?"

"That I'll get my heart handed to me sliced into ribbons on a silver platter."

"Wow, okay, that's brutal. Look, you can either sit here mourning losing Maya and guarding your heart as the world passes you by or you can find some way to enjoy it. You don't have to go out looking for love. Just a little fun. After all, Justin obviously isn't letting his circumstances stop him."

I knew Nikki was right, but until Beverly came into the picture, I was content with what we had. Of course, I missed being intimate with someone, but that was curbed by some restrained but satisfactory late night "me" time while Sybil was sleeping soundly in her crib on the other side of the bedroom. For over a year I'd had Justin all to myself, never asking him for any more, or any less, than he voluntarily gave. I didn't mind sharing him with Sybil, family, or friends, but what was happening between him and Beverly was different. What if they got serious and he wanted her to move in with him? I was sure he wouldn't want me to stay. That would be awkward, his girlfriend and his baby's mother under one roof. If Sybil and I had to get our own place, then Justin and I would have to work out a visitation schedule that would confuse her even more than living apart from her father already would.

"Look, Sybil, Mommy's face is all scrunched up like it gets when she's overanalyzing something," Nikki said, grinning knowingly.

I rolled my eyes at her. "Shut up."

"Janesse, you sure you're not bothered by Justin's decision to start dating again because you've developed feelings for him? I mean, no one would blame you considering how close you two have become because of Sybil."

"No, of course not," I said, unconvincingly even to myself. "Justin and I had an agreement. We just failed to factor in something like this." I figured if I didn't admit to developing feelings beyond friendship with Justin then it wouldn't be true.

"If you say so. You want my honest opinion?" Nikki said.

I grinned. "Not really, but I'm sure you're going to giving it anyway."

"You two may have come up with your lovely plan for more than just Sybil. I think it was because misery loves company, and it was the safest way to be in a relationship that wouldn't lead to anything more than what you both provide for Sybil. What neither of you counted on was developing feelings for each other beyond parenthood."

"You're saying Justin has feelings for me? Well, dating another woman is a funny way of showing it."

"Do you remember our first summer at the shore when Justin spent half our vacation with that college chick?"

"Yeah." It was also what led to Maya breaking up with me the first time.

"Remember why I told you I thought he did it?"

"Because I couldn't give him a straight answer about my feelings for him. But that's not the case now."

"Isn't it? Except now it's both of you skating around the truth. Justin's afraid of telling you how he feels because he doesn't want to be rejected again, so he's trying to distract himself from the situation. You're afraid of admitting how you feel about him because it would mean that maybe you're still confused about your sexuality."

Nikki always managed to hit home when it came to her observations, and I hated it sometimes.

"Janesse, there are people who just love who they love. Sexuality goes beyond gender. It's about what's in here," Nikki said, tapping my chest. "It's possible you could marry and live your whole life with Justin, or you could meet a woman who makes you feel like she's the one and spend your whole life with her. It doesn't matter if you're happy, which you are with Justin. That doesn't diminish what you felt for Maya, and probably still feel for her. It just shows that your heart can't be contained by what society says it should be."

"When you open your bakery, be sure to put up another sign for therapist," I said, shaking my head in wonder at how intuitive she was.

Nikki chuckled. "No, maybe I'll be like those bartenders serving drinks and listening to people's woes except I'll serve baked goods instead of alcohol. You know I'm right, though."

"I didn't say that." I still fought admitting the truth to myself.

Nikki turned toward Sybil, whose face and hands were covered in berry remnants and sticky with syrup. "Looks like Mommy still hates to admit when Auntie Nikki is right. Why don't we go get you cleaned up to give her time to stew in denial?"

She removed Sybil from her highchair. I laughed out loud when Sybil grabbed Nikki's cheeks with her sticky fingers.

"You little rascal," Nikki said as Sybil laughed hysterically at the handprints she left behind.

"Serves you right," I said to her retreating figure.

We had a big celebration on Christmas Day for Sybil's upcoming first birthday so that we could have both of our families there. Dad, Tanya, and J.J. even flew out for it. We were all at Uncle Frank's house and I watched in amusement as Justin tentatively approached my father. Dad had not been happy when he found out about my pregnancy, accusing Justin of taking advantage of me at a vulnerable moment. He'd asked to speak to Justin and told him the same thing, despite me telling him it was mutual. Dad didn't insist on us getting married, but he had threatened that if Justin didn't step up and be a man to take care of his daughter and expected grandchild, he would be on the first flight out here to kick his ass. They had been on shaky ground with each other ever since. Dad and J.J. had come to visit shortly after Sybil was born and, despite seeing the effort Justin was making to take care of us, Dad refused to let him off the hook that easily, telling him that he was keeping an eye on him, so he better not mess up. Justin had been a nervous wreck since he'd found out Dad was coming for Christmas. I told him not to worry about it, that Dad was probably just messing with him because I was his baby girl, but judging by the sweat on Justin's upper lip, he didn't believe me.

Jackie walked up next to me. "What's that all about?" she asked as Dad and Justin left the room together.

I watched them curiously. "I have no idea. Maybe Dad wants to talk to him in private to intimidate him some more."

"Or he's asking Dad for permission to marry you."

We looked at each other for a moment then laughed out loud.

"Justin knows better than that," I said.

Whatever they had left the room to discuss in private must have been good because they came back smiling and laughing like old friends. Justin gave me a wink, making me wonder what he was up to, then went to talk to Nikki. I shrugged it off and continued enjoying the loud and boisterous blending of our families. The guest of honor was wobbling around the room dressed in a little elf dress and elf hat headband loving all the attention. Everywhere she stopped, she was picked up, kissed, hugged, and told how adorable she was. I certainly wouldn't have to worry about her having a complex. If anything, her head was going to be as big as a pumpkin with all the compliments she was being showered with.

I didn't think it was possible to love her any more than the day she was born, but my heart grew bigger with love for my sweet, rambunctious baby girl every day. She was my life, the human embodiment of a lotus blossom for me. She made me a better person because everything I did was to make her proud of me. Of course, at one year old she wasn't aware of pride, but when the day came that she was, I wanted her to be able to look at me and be proud that I'm her mother.

After serenading Sybil with the birthday song, watching her cover her face in frosting, and opening far too many presents to fit in our apartment, the craziness of the day began to hit me. After several yawns in the span of a couple of minutes while talking to Nikki, she shook her head.

"You look like you're ready to drop," she said.

"I am. Sybil may be too young to really understand what Christmas is, but she sure knew to wake up early for it. The sound of her chattering away across the room woke me up at six in the morning. At least an hour and a half before she usually wakes up if we let her sleep in. That was after we kept her up a little later so that she would sleep later," I complained, yawning again.

Nikki chuckled. "That's my godbaby, making her own rules."

"Yeah, well, with the missed nap and all the excitement she's had today, I'm hoping she conks out quickly so that I can get some rest before work tomorrow. I have to be at the studio by seven in the morning."

"Wow. Why don't I take her for the night? I'm off tomorrow, and my moms would probably love having a whole day to spoil her."

I felt guilty thinking how nice it would be to be able to just fall into bed as soon we got home. It didn't matter that it was only five o'clock in the evening. As tired as I was, I didn't think I'd have any trouble sleeping through the night. "Are you sure?"

"Of course. You know I bought a portable crib waiting for just such an occasion. Besides, with all the sugar she's had, I don't think she'll be crashing anytime soon." Nikki pointed toward where Sybil was gleefully trying to chase her cousin Chloe, Denise's daughter, who was two years older than her.

I shook my head. "She's like that without the sugar, you know that."

"Yeah, she's definitely a ball of energy."

"Okay, if you think you can handle that for a whole night and day, you are welcome to it. I'll just give you the diaper bag we brought since it has a change of clothes and plenty of diapers. Which reminds me, you may want to keep her in at least a onesie. If she's in anything that gives her access to her diaper, she will pull her clothes off and rip her diaper off to run around naked. She hasn't figured out the snaps on the onesies yet, so you should be fine. Fortunately, she only does it when her diaper is dry."

Nikki laughed. "Thanks for the warning."

"Let's go have Justin put the car seat in your car. I'm too tired to even fight with that thing."

After that task was done Justin looked at me and frowned. "You look like you're about to fall on your face. Let's say our good nights and go home so you can sleep."

I hated ditching out on everyone early, but Justin was right. I was practically sleepwalking. Besides, I would see most of them again tomorrow after work for dinner. We made our final rounds, I smothered Sybil with kisses, which she only took a few minutes of before she was wobbling off again. I didn't even think she'd notice we were gone with all the fun she was having. I was thankful we lived so close to Uncle Frank's because we were home within five minutes. As we were walking in the apartment, the telephone was ringing. Justin ran to answer it then handed it to me. It was my boss telling me the shoot we had in the morning was being rescheduled for after the New Year and to take the rest of the holiday off with pay as his Christmas gift to me. I could've kissed him over the phone. For the past month, we had pretty much been working six days a week on product shoots and projects that clients needed to have ready for the start of the year.

The spark of excitement from getting two weeks off wore off quickly when I hung up the phone. Then weariness set in with a vengeance and I dragged myself to my bedroom.

"You need any help?" Justin asked, standing in the doorway looking at me with amusement as I tried to muster the energy to take my boots off.

"Probably."

He not only took my boots off for me but pretty much undressed me down to my underwear and tucked me in as if I were Sybil.

"You're a good man, Justin. Beverly is lucky to have you," was the last thing I remembered saying before snuggling under the covers and letting sleep take over.

I woke up late the next morning feeling rested and reenergized. I gazed over at Sybil's crib and considered calling Nikki and letting her know I didn't have to work but then pushed the thought away. Sybil loved spending time with her godmother, and I could get some much-needed work done. I lounged in bed for a few more minutes and noticed how quiet it was. Justin must have gone out. I climbed out of bed and went to my meditation corner. I took advantage of the quiet by doing a deeper and longer session than I would normally have when Justin would kindly take charge of Sybil to give me a few minutes in the morning when he could.

I lit my scented candles, put on my Walkman headphones, grasped my crystal lotus, and lost myself in the chanting CD Nikki had given me for my birthday. It felt like being welcomed by an old friend's warm embrace. I didn't search for any answers or great enlightenment. I just let my body relax and mind wander in whatever direction it chose. The word *family* whispered through my mind with the memory of Justin holding Sybil as they watched the lights twinkling on our Christmas tree. It was such a heartwarming sight I had grabbed my camera to capture the moment. The memory faded and I could feel myself naturally coming out of the meditation. I didn't force anything, just let my body and mind guide me until I was slowly blinking my eyes open. I took a few deep cleansing breaths, then took my time resetting everything in its place before making my way to the bathroom. I heard noise in the kitchen.

"Justin?" I called out.

"Hey," he called back, peeking around the corner down the

hallway. "I smelled your candles burning so I didn't want to disturb you. I ran to the store to pick up a few things for breakfast."

"Oh, okay. Let me shower and I'll be out to help you."

"No, I got this. Enjoy being a lady of leisure for the day." He gave me a wink then disappeared back around the corner.

"Oookay." I shook my head and went about my way.

By the time I met him in the kitchen, he had a full spread laid out on the island. Pancakes with the butter still melting on top; cinnamon rolls with the icing oozing down the sides; spinach, tomato, and cheese omelet with steam still rising off it; and a platter of bacon and sausage looking as if there was still sizzle left to them.

"Wow, that's quite a spread. What's the occasion?" I asked.

"The occasion is you," Justin said, handing me an empty regular size plate and a smaller saucer. He knew I hated having my eggs and pancakes on the same plate.

"Me? How am I an occasion?" I followed him around the island as we filled our plates.

"You're not just an occasion, you're a phenomenon. You have completely awed me since the day you told me you were pregnant, and I wanted to celebrate you."

I could feel my face grow warm at the compliment. "Thanks."

"Any big plans for your unexpected vacation?" Justin asked as we sat down to eat.

"Maybe get some work done in my darkroom today and just spend some quality time with Sybil. How about you? Do you and Beverly have any plans?"

Justin didn't answer right away. "No, we stopped seeing each other a few weeks ago."

"I'm sorry, I didn't know."

"It's no big deal. She's looking for something more serious and we both decided I wasn't the guy for her."

Justin didn't look or sound the least bit upset by it. "Wait, a few weeks ago? I thought you'd been staying home on the weekends to help take care of Sybil because of my work schedule."

"I was going to do that whether I was seeing Beverly or not. It's one reason we stopped seeing each other. She didn't realize dating a guy with a kid would mean she played second fiddle to his responsibilities."

"Well, that was pretty naive of her not to think that a man with a child may actually want to be involved with the child and put them first."

"Yeah, that's also what I thought."

"What was the other reason?"

"Because I'm in love with someone else," Justin said matter-of-factly.

I almost choked on my orange juice. "You've been seeing someone else?"

"Yep. For over a year now."

He continued eating as if he hadn't dropped a bomb that blew my mind. I racked my brain trying to figure out when he would have had time to be seeing someone else practically the whole time we'd been living together. Before Beverly, he was either at work or home with Sybil and me. Also, if he had already been seeing someone else, why did he feel the need to check with me about dating Beverly? Then it hit me. His private conversation with Dad, Nikki volunteering to take Sybil for the night, and now this breakfast to, as he said, celebrate me.

"Justin—"

"Wait! Before you say anything, let me talk first."

"But—"

Justin grinned. "Janesse, for once, just shut up and listen before you put up an argument."

It was difficult, but I signaled locking my mouth and sat back in my chair with my arms crossed with my lips pursed shut.

"When I suggested we move in together it honestly was to benefit both of us being able to take care of Sybil. I had no other intentions but to support you in any way I could. Just like you, at the time I was still not over my breakup, and developing feelings for you wasn't even a thought in my mind. But over time, as I watched how beautifully you and your body changed with our child growing inside of you, how maturely you handled the situation, finding a job instead of taking up my offer to let me take care of you, having a front row seat to the wonderful mother you've become and sharing not only being a parent with you but also the quiet, silly, and fun moments with each other changed that." Justin reached across the table to offer me his hand. I tentatively took it.

"Janesse, believe me when I say I fought my growing feelings tooth and nail. It's why I started dating Beverly. I was hoping that the interest she piqued in me could become something more, but it only took the first couple of dates for her to know I was denying my feelings for you."

"Then why did you continue dating?"

"I did it hoping that in time I would develop feelings for her since

I knew you probably would never feel the same way about me. I can't even guess at the reason she continued with it, but when I told her we would have to take a bit of a break so that I could help with Sybil while you were working, she decided she was done. I'm embarrassed to say I was relieved. In the back of my mind, I knew it was over and that I could no longer deny my feelings for you, but I really did like Beverly and didn't know how to tell her without hurting her feelings."

I wanted so much to get up and run. To end this conversation, but something kept me seated and silent. The word *family* associated with the memory of Justin and Sybil that I had while I was meditating entered my thoughts.

Justin continued. "For the past few weeks, I went back and forth with myself over the reasons why I should and shouldn't do this, and there were more reasons why I should that I couldn't deny."

Justin stood, still holding my hand, and came around the table to kneel before me. I immediately started shaking my head.

"You promised you would listen before arguing," he said, giving me a teasing grin.

Technically, I wasn't arguing, I was outright saying no.

Justin nodded in satisfaction when I didn't bolt screaming from the room. "Janesse, I've loved you practically from the first day we met, and although you never felt the same way about me, I wouldn't trade the friendship we built over the years for anything in the world. You truly are my best friend, and despite knowing I play second fiddle to Nikki in that category for you, I know you've cared about me all these years. I also believe your feelings have grown even more since we started our adventure in parenting. I would even bet you've been denying it just as much as I have."

"Did Nikki tell you that?" I said angrily.

Justin grinned cockily. "No, but you just did."

I opened my mouth to deny it, but that would not have been fair considering what was happening right now.

"So, you do love me."

"Yes, but that doesn't mean you have to ask what you're about to ask."

"Yes, it does. I love you, you love me, we have a great relationship and a beautiful child together—if that isn't a good reason to get married, I don't know what is."

"How about the fact that I'm still attracted to women. Just because I haven't been dating doesn't mean that's stopped."

"I completely understand. You're bisexual, I'm fine with that. I told you once that I would be fine having an open relationship if it meant I would still have you. I'm still willing to do that."

"And I told you that I'm not into threesomes or any other freaky stuff like that."

Justin chuckled. "That's not what I mean. I'm talking about you being able to fulfill your sexual desires with women outside of our marriage, discreetly, of course. I'm not trying to change you or lock you into a relationship you don't want to be in. I just want to share my life with the only woman I have ever truly loved. If that means sharing a part of her that I can't satisfy with someone else, I'll do that."

I looked at Justin as if he lost his senses. "You would be willing to do that? To be okay with me cheating on you?"

"I wouldn't consider it cheating if it's an agreed upon arrangement. It would be different if it were other men. But obviously there is something you get from a woman that I can't, and won't even try, to provide you."

I couldn't believe what I was hearing. "And what about you? Will you be doing the same?"

"No, I honestly have no desire to. All I want is you. I've been doing a lot of reading and talked to Nikki. There's this type of relationship called polyamorous, and although most couples in these relationships are both looking for other partners outside of the relationship, there are some where only one partner is poly while the other is monogamous. We could do that," Justin said like an excited kid showing somebody how smart they are.

I tried to absorb everything he just said. Nikki and I had discussed such relationships before, and at the time she thought I would end up stretching myself thin trying to please everyone and not myself. That discussion seemed like so long ago, and I felt like such a different person now. I looked at Justin, who knelt patiently watching me figure this all out. It would be the perfect situation. I wasn't in love with Justin, but I loved him deeply. Sybil had strengthened the bond between us, and I couldn't imagine my life without him after sharing such an important part of it with him. Sybil would be raised in a home where she was loved and treasured as the gift that she was to Justin and me, and Justin and I would have the companionship and connection I craved without having to worry about my heart getting broken. I couldn't say whether I would look outside our marriage for a female partner because I honestly still hadn't gotten over Maya, but if Justin was serious about being in such a relationship, then it was something I could consider later when I stopped comparing every woman I'd met to Maya.

It wasn't the best reason to marry, but it also wasn't the worst. "Okay."

Justin looked shocked. "Seriously?"

I laughed. "Yes, seriously. You know when you feel confident enough to ask a woman to marry you, then you shouldn't be shocked when she says yes."

"I honestly hadn't expected a yes right away. I thought you would at least ask to think about it first," Justin said sheepishly.

"Is this what you were talking to my father about?"

"Yes, but I only asked for his permission, I didn't tell him about the rest." He smirked.

"What did he say?"

"He gave me his consent and told me I was either real brave or really stupid, either way, good luck."

I shook my head with a smile. "I would say you were both."

Justin laughed. "So, we're really going to do this?"

"It's not official until I get a ring," I said, wiggling my fingers in his face.

Justin slapped his head. "I'll be right back."

He ran to his bedroom and was back before I could even think about what I had just agreed to and was once again kneeling before me. Justin opened a ring box and presented it to me.

"I had it custom made for you."

Whatever second thoughts I suddenly had about my decision drifted away at the sight of the silver engagement ring with a single diamond set in the center of the petals of a lotus flower. To take the time to create something so personal showed how much he genuinely cared for me. My hand trembled as I held it out toward him to slide the ring on.

"Janesse, I know my feelings for you are probably much different than yours are for me, but I hope, in time, you could learn to love me the same way."

Justin took my face in his hands and kissed me so tenderly it brought tears to my eyes. I prayed to Buddha, Jesus, Allah, whoever was listening, to please not let me screw this up.

Chapter Eighteen

2018

"What do you think?" I stood in front of the dressing room mirror at Macy's trying on a swimsuit as Sybil came out of her dressing room wearing a sundress.

She cocked her head to the side in contemplation. "I like it. It's sexy. It doesn't hurt that you still have the body of a woman half your age."

I snorted. "Yeah, right."

"Mom, seriously, you're MILF material."

I looked at her in shock. "Okay, let's not go that far."

"She's right."

I looked up into the mirror and almost fell off the riser when I saw a mature and still gorgeous Maya, standing behind us. I had a flashback to the day we met in this very same dressing room over thirty years ago.

"See, Mom, told you," Sybil said, oblivious to the deluge of feelings overwhelming me. "What do you think of this dress?"

I tore my eyes from Maya's bright hazel gaze to look at Sybil. "Uh, it's nice."

She made a face. "Nice won't cut it. I'm going to try the red one you picked."

"Yes, do that," I said distractedly.

Sybil headed back to her dressing room as I stood there alone with Maya feeling utterly self-conscious.

"Hey, Janesse," Maya said with an easy smile.

"Hey."

"You really do look—"

I held up my hand at her, shaking my head. "Sybil, I'm going to change and see what else I can find. I'll meet you out there."

"Okay," she said.

I looked back toward Maya, and my legs felt like rubber. Afraid they would collapse beneath me, I tentatively stepped down from the riser, then walked past Maya to the dressing room. I collapsed onto the bench and stared at the door. Of all the Macy's in all the towns in all of New Jersey, she walked into mine. Seeing Maya after all this time was like going through a time machine. All the love and heartbreak I experienced thirty years ago came back as if it were only yesterday. How was that possible? Because she lived across the country, we hadn't seen each other since I was pregnant with Sybil. Our paths hadn't even crossed working in similar industries. I had followed her career and heard things from Keisha, so I knew she had made a name for herself as one of the top fashion stylists on the West Coast. I had avoided taking jobs that sent me anywhere near Los Angeles out of fear of running into her and this very thing happening. Okay, maybe it was just the shock of seeing her again. Maybe if I got dressed and went back out it wouldn't be as bad.

The speed at which I got that suit off and got dressed had to have been a record somewhere. I touched my lotus pendant, which was still a mainstay around my neck, and took a few breaths to clear my mind and calm my racing heart. Once I felt ready, I walked out of the dressing room to find Maya adjusting the dress Sybil was trying on. Seeing them together made my heart skip a beat. What would have happened if I hadn't been such a coward and loved Maya openly without fear? Would we have eventually had children of our own, like Denise and Liz? Would they be anything like my Sybil and Phillip?

"What do you think, Mom?" Sybil asked, jerking me free from my thoughts.

I smiled while I fought back a lump growing in my throat. "I like that much better than the other one."

"So do I. Thank you for your help," Sybil said pleasantly to Maya as she stepped down and walked toward me.

"This nice lady showed me how the dress would look if I got it adjusted in the waist a little more, and she's right," Sybil explained.

"That's not surprising. Ms. Lawson is a pretty famous fashion stylist," I told her.

Sybil's eyes widened. "Really?" She looked back at Maya.

Maya smiled at her. "I wouldn't say famous. Well-known sounds humbler."

There was that same heartbreaking dimpled smile. She had even kept the gap in her front teeth. Memories of running my tongue across that gap caused a shudder of desire to run through me. I was glad Maya was talking to Sybil so she wouldn't see that desire in my eyes.

"I'm surprised you and Mom haven't worked together before," I heard Sybil say as I slipped from my thoughts back to the conversation.

Maya cocked her head when she looked at me. "So am I. I've seen your mom's work through the years. She's one of the best in the business."

She'd been following my career. My body grew warm hearing that. "Thanks."

Sybil looked curiously between us. My daughter was very astute at reading situations, so I knew I had to shut this down before she read too much into this one.

"Sybil, you better get changed. If we want to get home and change before meeting Jackie in the city, then we need to get going soon."

"Okay. It was nice to meet you, Ms. Lawson," Sybil said, offering her hand to Maya.

Maya smiled and accepted it. "You too, Sybil."

"I'll wait for you outside," I told Sybil.

Maya walked out with me. "She's beautiful. She could be your twin instead of your daughter."

"Thank you." I hung the swimsuit I had tried on, on a rack just outside the dressing room.

"You're not going buy it?" Maya asked.

"I need another bathing suit like I need a hole in my head."

"Still just as sensible as ever, I see."

I shrugged. "Not much has changed about me."

Maya's smile softened. "That's not true. You're even more beautiful than I remember."

Our gazes held and I saw everything I was feeling reflected in her eyes. For a moment, I considered telling her I never stopped loving her. That she had been a ghost in my heart blocking anything but the love of my children from fully penetrating it. That I regretted walking away all those years ago without putting up a fight, allowing fear and shame to be my guide. Then I remembered all the lives that would be affected by that decision. Justin, our children, possibly Maya's long-time partner that I'd heard about. There would be no point in admitting to any of that. At fifty-two years old, our lives were set. It made no sense rocking the boat that way.

"You ready, Mom?" Sybil asked.

I tore my gaze from Maya's. "Uh, yeah."

"Thank you again, Ms. Lawson," Sybil said to Maya.

"You're welcome. It was nice to see you again, Janesse," Maya said before turning and walking away.

I almost took a step to go after her.

"Mom, are you okay?" Sybil asked.

"Yes, why wouldn't I be?"

"Because you're crying."

I looked at Sybil in confusion, then reached up to find a tear rolling down my cheek.

"Mom, what is it? Who is that woman?"

"I told you, a fashion stylist." I dashed away my traitorous tears. "We really should get going. Are you going to buy the dress?"

Sybil looked at me skeptically then sighed. "We'll talk in the car," she said rather bossily then walked to the cashier.

I shook my head. Sybil was all the things I wished I could be. Bold, brave, outspoken, and bossy. It was like nature took all the traits I lacked and put them in her. Where Sybil was like a wild wind just before a storm, her brother, Phillip, was like a calm breeze rippling across a lazy river. They were such complete opposites, yet they loved each other fiercely and devotedly. They were also my life, why I had chosen the life I had now, and found no reason to cause an upheaval in it.

"Okay, what was that little thing that happened between you and Ms. Lawson?" Sybil asked not even five minutes after getting in the car.

"It was nothing, Sybil," I said, turning to gaze out the window as she drove.

"You might as well tell me. You know I'll keep bugging you until you do."

I couldn't help but smile because it was true. Ever since she was little, when Sybil wanted to know something, she would drive us crazy until she got the answer. Especially if it was something that upset any of us. When her brother was being bullied in school, she harassed the poor boy to tears trying to find out who the kids were. Once she did, she methodically confronted and beat up each kid, getting herself suspended from school for a week. Justin and I had been equally angry and proud of her.

"Maya and I were friends a long time ago," I said, hoping that would appease her.

"Bullshit."

"Sybil!"

"Mom, I'm twenty-nine years old. I think I'm allowed at least one curse word a month around you," she said grinning. "The look you two were giving each other when I walked out of the dressing room was not the kind of thing you see between friends."

I guess she wasn't giving up. "Maya and I dated in college. It didn't work out."

Sybil didn't seem shocked by my admission, which surprised me. I hadn't told either of my kids about my dating a woman. Even when Phillip came out to us at sixteen, I never told him about the pain and confusion I had gone through with my sexuality. He had so much self-confidence and pride in himself that I thought he didn't need to hear any of that. Of course, because we all accepted him for who he was, he had such an easier time of it than I did. Even my mother's expected negative reaction didn't deter him. He told her that he loved her and that she didn't need to accept him, but he would cut her off without a second thought if she chose to continuously try to degrade him and his lifestyle. To everyone's surprise, that shut her up.

"You don't seem surprised."

"Don't get mad, but Gran said something once about it after Phillip came out."

"What did she say?"

"Something to the effect like mother, like son, then asked if I was going to be gay also."

"Damn that woman!" I couldn't believe Mom outed me to my kids.

"Mom, it's okay, really. We've always known Gran wasn't going to be the warm, kissy-face grandmother Grandma Sybil is. I can't imagine what your childhood was like or what it was like having to deal with the confusion of your sexuality with her as your mother. Just know that it doesn't change how we feel about you. We couldn't have asked for a better mother and I couldn't have had a better role model if we tried."

"Thank you," I said, tears of joy blurring my vision.

Sibyl reached across and gave my hand a squeeze. This was all I needed in my life. What all the sacrifices I had made regarding my own dreams and desires were for. To have my children feel the love and pride I had never felt with my own mother. For the first time in my adult life, I finally felt like I did something right.

Later that afternoon, I sat in my home office staring at old photographs of Maya I had taken and kept hidden in a drawer for years. Something I did at least once a year, usually on the anniversary of when Maya and I broke up. I didn't know if it was to torture myself or to remind myself of who I once was, but I never told anyone about it. I picked up one of my favorites. It was of a young Maya lounging nude in my bed at Spelman, the shape of her curves outlined by the sheet, her eyes reflecting the desire and passion we had just shared, her full lips curved in a sexy grin. I ran my fingers over her lips then touched them to my own, remember how soft and sweet they were. Why was life so cruel? Just when I thought I was finally content and where I needed to be in my life, Maya always seemed to show up. The day we first met I was in a good place in my life. Getting ready to graduate, looking forward to leaving home for Spelman, and no romantic drama. Then Maya was there looking sexy as hell in that bathing suit and stealing my heart on the spot. Then at Spelman when I had decided that focusing on my education was the priority and romantic entanglements weren't even a blip on my course at the time, she once again showed and turned my world upside down. Then the day we saw each other at the mall while I was pregnant with Sybil. I had accepted the fact she was gone, and my focus needed to be on my child. There she was, reminding me what I had foolishly let go.

Today, though, of all days for her to show up and to affect me so deeply. I had spent a half hour in the kitchen crying after Sybil dropped me off. Then I came down to my office off my darkroom to distract myself with work but had barely gotten anything done before I felt the urge to pull out these pictures of our time together that I kept hidden since we moved from the apartment to our forever home. The home Justin had designed and presented the plans for on our first wedding anniversary. In those plans had been a darkroom with an office and a meditation room designed just for me by Justin and Frieda. Two wonderful gifts that I suddenly felt like I hadn't deserved because of feelings I had carried for another that kept me from loving Justin the way he deserved.

"Ness! You home?" Justin called.

"Uh, yeah, in my office. I'll be out in a minute." I tucked Maya's photos back into a folder, wiped away my tears, and shook off the sadness that threatened to overwhelm me.

I found Justin in the living room. "Hey, babe," he said, pulling me into his arms. "Ready to celebrate?"

"I guess. Do we really need to go out? Can't we just have a quiet dinner at home?"

"What, like every dinner we have every other night? Nope, I want to wine and dine my wife on our wedding anniversary, and that's just what I'm going to do."

I gave him a tentative smile. "Okay."

Justin looked at me worriedly. "What's going on? You okay?"

"I'm fine."

"Then why do you look like you've been crying?"

I stepped out of Justin's embrace and sat on the sofa. Why couldn't this have happened on another day? A day where I would have been able to hide away in my dark room and work through the emotional wreck that I was with Justin none the wiser.

"I ran into Maya while Sybil and I were at the mall today."

Justin was quiet. When I looked up at him, he looked disappointed. "I hoped the feeling I've had the past few years was wrong. That maybe I was reading too much into your distance and waning affection, but I guess I wasn't."

I looked at Justin in confusion. "What are you talking about?"

"I'm talking about you never letting Maya go enough to let us work. Even after all these years she's still coming between us."

I shook my head. "Justin, I just ran into her today for the first time in thirty years."

"She doesn't have to physically be here to come between us, Janesse. The memory of her, the feelings you guard so ferociously for her, are enough."

I couldn't even deny what he was saying without calling myself a liar.

Justin sighed and sat beside me on the couch. "Why did you never take my suggestion of finding a female partner?"

I didn't know where he was going with the question or how it connected to Maya. "Because it didn't feel right. It felt like cheating. I made a commitment to you, and that's all I needed."

"You and I both know that's not really true. You don't think I notice how you look at women sometimes when we're out? How you've seemed less satisfied sexually as the years have gone on. Hell, I'm lucky if we have sex twice in a month."

"You know since my hysterectomy it hasn't been the same," I said, using the same lame excuse I had been using for the past four years.

"Janesse, no more excuses or lies. You and I have too much history to do that to each other."

I knew Justin deserved the truth. I was just too afraid to admit it myself. "I haven't sought another partner because I don't just want any woman. It's not about the sex but the connection. If I sought that from someone else, I couldn't stay married to you, and I honestly don't want that with any other woman."

"Unless it's Maya."

I nodded. "That's not an option."

"How do you know? Did you talk to her?"

"No, of course not. First, I'm married to you and she's been with someone for years."

Justin sagged back against the pillows and ran his hand down his face in what I knew was frustration. "I can't keep going on this way. I feel like we're right back where we started. Playing house with my best friend instead of enjoying my life with my wife."

"What are you saying?" I asked, even though I knew.

"I'm saying that I love you, and I always will, but it's not enough. I don't need a best friend. I need a life partner who loves me as deeply as I do her. Someone who isn't missing someone else when they're with me and devoting an entire day to mourn the anniversary of losing them every year."

My heart skipped a beat. "You know about that?" I said quietly.

"Love isn't as blind as you think. I've been fighting a losing battle trying to win your heart from someone who has had a death grip on it since day one."

I felt like shit. "I'm sorry."

Justin gave me a sad smile. "Ironically, I'm not. I wouldn't trade what we've had for anything. Our life together may not have been perfect, but it's been good. I know you've at least been content with it despite what you truly wanted, and we've raised two wonderful kids. I don't regret any of it."

I sat back against the pillows and took his hand, holding it between us. "I don't either. What I'm sorry about is not being able to be the woman you deserve."

"You were the woman I wanted. That's all that matters."

We sat that way together for a moment, both lost in our own thoughts, then Justin gave my hand a squeeze.

"I still think we should go out and celebrate," he said.

"Celebrate breaking up?"

Justin chuckled. "Well, we already know what it feels like to mourn breaking up, let's try something different."

I shook my head in wonder. "You're too good for me, you know that."

Justin grinned cockily. "I know."

A few weeks later, I was on a plane on the way to a fashion magazine shoot on the island of Anguilla. It was the reason I had been looking for a swimsuit the day I saw Maya at the mall. The day she, unwittingly, once again turned my world upside down. Justin and I made our mutually agreed upon split official with him moving into the guest house above the garage until he could get his own place. I had told him he didn't need to do that since we had plenty of guest rooms now that the kids were grown and had their own places, but he insisted. Told me it would be too difficult to be in the same house, even if our separation had originally been his idea. He said he built the house for me and the kids, so I should be the one to have it. I wasn't lying when I said he was too good for me.

His being so easygoing about the whole thing didn't mean he wasn't hurt. I knew from over thirty years of living together that the more agreeable Justin was, the more upset he was. He was just trying to hide it. When we told Sybil and Phillip, I think Sybil knew the real reason, but Phillip was young, only twenty-six, and a romantic at heart so he didn't understand how we could just grow apart after thirty years together. Justin and I decided the rest of the family didn't need to know right now. We wanted to do what we needed to do without outside interference. The only other person we told was Nikki, whose comment that she hadn't expected us to last past the first year pretty much summed up why we were all still friends.

During my taxi ride from the airport, gazing out at the clear blue waters and white sand beaches, I allowed myself to relax and not let what was going on at home distract me from the beautiful scenery I would get to enjoy while I worked. After arriving at the hotel, I decided to get an early start on scouting for the best locations for the shoot.

Anguilla wasn't your typical Caribbean vacation spot flooded with too many tourists. The lack of cruise ships, casinos, and high-rise hotels kept heavy tourism at bay on the small thirty-five-square-mile island north of St. Maarten. I spent about two hours walking along the beach, taking test shots, and getting to know the surrounding area. My assistant texted to let me know she had arrived at the hotel, so I headed back. When I walked into the lobby, I wondered what cruel joke fate was playing on me. Walking toward me, head down as she looked at her phone, was Maya. For just a second, I considered turning and running, but I was tired of running. Tired of hiding. Tired of denying myself what I really wanted.

"You know people have been known to step into manholes paying more attention to their phones than where they're headed," I said as she was about to pass me.

Maya gazed up and gifted me with that smile. She didn't seem surprised to see me. "Good thing there aren't any manholes around."

"If I didn't know any better, I would think you're following me." With the initial shock of seeing her again after so many years having happened already weeks ago, I felt more confident talking to her now.

Maya's brow quirked. "Would that be a bad thing?"

Thirty years, I had hoped for a moment like this. Where I was brave enough to shut off my mind and let my heart lead the way without guilt, fear, or obligations to anyone but myself. It didn't matter if Maya was with someone or not, I wouldn't let this chance pass me by without even trying.

"Not at all, especially if you were following me to the bar." I amazed myself with that bit of boldness.

Maya grinned. "Lead the way."

My heart raced as I walked toward a sign nearby that read Lounge. I hadn't really been heading to the bar. Hadn't even looked around the hotel earlier to note where the bar was, but I went with it since it seemed to get Maya to come with me. I probably should have thought the idea through, as the lounge was packed with late afternoon drinkers. We grabbed two seats directly at the bar and both ordered the resort's signature drink, a specialty rum punch with a lot of rum giving plenty of punch.

"Wow, I better take this slow. I haven't eaten since my flight this morning," I said, feeling the effects of the strong drink already.

"Why don't we order something to share. I'm starving." Maya picked up the small menu card, then ordered sliders and truffle fries.

"You know you're going to be the one to eat all the fries," I teased her. Fries were always her go-to snack when we went to clubs and bars with our friends. I would barely eat a handful before she had practically polished off the whole plate.

Maya grinned sheepishly. "Not anymore. It literally all goes straight to my hips now."

I cocked my head and looked her up and down. "Well, whatever you're doing looks good on you."

I hid my surprise at seeing her face darken with a blush. "Thanks."

"So, Maya Lawson, what brings you here and what's been going on with you for the past three decades?"

"I'm here for the same reason you are. I'm the stylist for the shoot. Amber requested me."

Amber Sims was a hot new pop star who was going to be modeling the fashions.

"Oh, there was another stylist listed on the itinerary that I received last week."

"Amber requested the change shortly after the itinerary went out. It seems she and the stylist they had chosen didn't work well together. I've been working with her whenever she's out in LA, so she requested me. You should've gotten an updated itinerary yesterday."

"I must have missed it."

I did recall receiving an email with the subject UPDATED ITINERARY, but I had asked my assistant to look it over and let me know of any changes. We were going to have to have a little chat later.

"I have a confession. You were sort of right about me following you. Our run-in at the mall was not really accidental. I was leaving when I saw you and your daughter walk into Macy's. I tried fighting the urge to go after you. I even stood outside pacing and talking to myself like some looney person trying to talk myself out of it. Obviously, it didn't work," she said, looking guilty. "Then, when I saw you in that swimsuit in the dressing room, it was like I was transported back to that day, seeing you for the first time. Still so sexy and beautiful. I haven't stopped thinking about you since then. As a matter of fact, I only took this job when I saw you were the photographer," Maya said, completely throwing me for a loop.

Fortunately, our food came, giving me time to absorb that bit of news.

Maya continued, not waiting for me to respond. "In answer to your other question, as you know, I went to California for an assistant stylist position. I stayed in that job for about five years while I went to cosmetology school to add on to my skill set. After that I took a job with one of the studios, stayed there for a while, then started getting requests to do side gigs for music videos and award ceremonies. Then I decided to go freelance, which was rough at first, but client referrals helped build my portfolio until I was getting so many, I had to turn jobs down. I was home to do a job with Keisha when we saw each other. Now, here I am."

She hadn't mentioned anything about a relationship with anyone, and I hated that the answer to that would determine if I could make it through the next two weeks working with her knowing I was free, but she wasn't.

"What about your personal life? I'd heard you've been in a serious relationship for some time."

Maya looked down at her drink.

"I'm sorry. I shouldn't have pried."

"No, that's not it." She sighed and gave me a sad smile. "We recently split up after ten years together."

"I'm sorry to hear that," I said sincerely. I had thought it would be something I wanted to hear, but I wasn't the type of person to feel joy in someone else's misery.

"I'm just sorry I let it go on as long as I did," Maya said, then waved her hand dismissively. "What's been going on with you besides raising that beautiful daughter of yours?"

I smiled with pride at the mention of Sybil. "I'm probably biased, but she is beautiful, isn't she?"

Maya nodded. "Just like her mother."

I blushed. "Thanks. Well, you already know what I did right after college," I said, not wanting to really rehash the memory of the first time we had seen each other since our breakup. "After Sybil was born, I got a job as a photographer's assistant for a commercial photography firm, worked my way up to a lead photographer position, and stayed with them for about ten years before going freelance. Like you, it was tough finding my footing the first five years, but business has been good since. I've got my own studio although most of my jobs are offsite."

"I've seen a lot of your work. The spread you did for *Maxim* magazine last month was beautiful. I could picture them all gracing some art gallery wall."

"You think so?" Next to my kids, my work was the other thing I took the most pride in.

"Yeah, I do. Hasn't anyone ever told you that?"

I shrugged. "Justin has, but I thought he was being biased."

Maya nodded. "I heard you two had married. Any more children besides Sybil?"

I couldn't tell if she was bothered by that information. "Yes, we had a son, Phillip."

"You gave him your last name as his first. I'm surprised he didn't become a Junior."

"Justin hated the thought of doing that to his son. He felt like it would be forcing him to live up to some standard because it would have made him the third generation of Justins. I jokingly suggested Phillip and he liked it, so we went with it. Sybil is named after his mother."

Maya reached over and tapped my wedding band. "And you guys are still married. It must be good."

I looked down at my hand. I kept meaning to take the ring off, but it seemed like such a final thing to do. Technically, until the divorce papers we filed last week came through, we were still married. I figured I'd just remove it then.

"Actually, we're getting divorced. I just haven't gotten around to taking the ring off."

"Oh, wow, I'm sorry. Are you okay?"

I smiled. "Yeah, I'm good. We're good. It was a mutual decision."

"I see."

The look Maya gave me made me feel as if she saw more than what I was saying. She started to speak when my phone started blasting Beyonce's "Freedom." Maya grinned.

"Sorry, it's my assistant." I answered the call. "Hey, Tracy, can I call you back?"

"Hey, Boss Lady, we've got an emergency. Lance just called. He has a family emergency and can't make it," Tracy said, sounding panicked.

I sighed. Lance was a freelance videographer I had recently brought on who seemed to be more trouble than he was worth. He was a prima donna who thought he could get away with being an ass because I was a woman. Always late, flirting with the models, arguing with me about shots. I'd only hired him because his work was great. That would teach me not to check references again.

"Okay, no worries. Do you think you can handle doing it? I brought my video camera just in case."

"Really? You think I'm ready?" Tracy asked.

I smiled. Tracy had been with me for two years now. She reminded me of myself when I'd first started. Just as eager to please and learn as I was. "Yes, I know you're ready. Why don't you meet me at my room in twenty minutes?"

"Okay, thanks, Boss Lady!" Tracy said.

"You've gotta go?" Maya said when I hung up with a sigh.

"Yes, sorry. Maybe we can meet for dinner or something before the shoot next week."

Maya gifted me with that smile I so loved. "I'd like that."

We exchanged room and phone numbers then I told the bartender to charge everything to my room and, holding back the urge to pull her into my arms, left Maya sitting alone at the bar.

After meeting with my assistant, I immediately called Nikki.

"Hey, how's paradise?" she asked.

"It's gorgeous. You and Chanel need to make this your next vacation spot."

"I'll definitely look into it. If it's so gorgeous why are you on the phone with me instead of putting in some beach time?"

"Because I'm freaking out right now. Maya is the stylist for the shoot."

"No way!"

"Yes way. We just sat in the bar catching up like we were old college buddies."

"And…"

I told Nikki about my conversation with Maya. "I have no idea what to do."

I heard Nikki chuckle. "Janesse, you and Justin are divorcing because you've held a torch for this woman for three decades. If you don't at least try and hit it while you're there, I'm flying out and kicking your ass."

I had to smile. "Wow, don't beat around the bush at all."

"Have you ever known me to? Isn't that why you call me?"

"Yes," I reluctantly admitted. "I don't know, though. She just got out of a relationship also. I'm ready to risk it all to finally be with her, but I don't want to be her rebound. I don't know if I could recover from another heartbreak with her."

"That's a fair point. You're both there for what, like two weeks, working closely together. Take the time to feel her out. Get reacquainted as friends, not the woman you've been in love with your entire adult life, to find out where she is mentally and emotionally. The worst that could happen is that you find out she's not ready to move on and you haven't laid a full platter of emotions out on the table only for her to lose her appetite and push it away."

I laughed. "How do you always manage to find a way to use a cooking analogy for everything?"

"I read an article once by a chef who compared life to a cooking recipe. Just like you control what and how much ingredients you put into a recipe, you also control what actions you take in life. Whether you want it bitter or sweet, it's up to you."

"Wow, that's deep."

"I know, right? Most people come to Sweet Therapy to pay for this philosophical gold. You get it for free because I love you."

Sweet Therapy was Nikki's bakery and bistro. The walls were covered in Buddhist and Hindu quotes about life. Twice a week, after hours, the bistro became a gathering place for LGBTQ youth where Nikki offered group therapy, cooking classes, and just a general place to feel safe, loved, and know that they're not alone. The kind of place I wish I would've gone to when I was younger.

"Don't ever think I don't appreciate it. I love you too."

We chatted for a few more minutes. I promised to send her lots of pics and keep her apprised of the Maya situation. Afterward, I sat down and racked my brain over what to do next. Nikki's suggestion was the best way to go about it. I knew where my head and heart were, but I had no clue what was going on with Maya. When she mentioned her relationship ending, she seemed to be more angry than sad, which didn't mean she wasn't heartbroken about it. I'd waited this long. What was a few more weeks of pining away for Maya from afar?

Chapter Nineteen

Later that night, sitting in bed enjoying a hot fudge sundae while watching TV, my phone buzzed on the nightstand. When I saw that it was Maya, I almost threw the bowl of ice cream across the bed to free my hands up to answer it.

"Hey," I said breathlessly.

"Hey," Maya answered back. "Did I wake you?"

"No. I'm just watching TV."

"Okay, I won't keep you. I was just wondering what you were doing tomorrow."

"My assistant and I are spending the day with a guide scouting for shoot locations."

"Oh, okay. Maybe we can meet for dinner when you get back."

"Yeah, that'll be cool. I'll hit you up when we do."

"Okay, well, I'll let you go since you probably have an early start. Good night."

"Good night."

I stared at the phone for a moment, then called her back.

"How'd you like to join us? If you don't already have any plans."

"I don't know, I made sooo many plans after we hung up just a minute ago. It'll be hard to cancel them all."

"Oh, you got jokes."

The sound of Maya's laughter was like music to my ears. "I'd be happy to tag along. Knowing the locations ahead of time will give me a head start on deciding what looks I want to put Amber in. What time?"

"We're meeting in the lobby at seven in the morning. We want to beat the tourists before they hit the major spots on the island. Be sure to wear comfortable clothes and shoes. We'll be doing a lot of walking in some areas."

"That's fine. I'll see you then."

This time when we said good night my face ached from my smile. "Calm down, girl. It's not like you're going on a date. She's just tagging along as you work," I told myself. My head agreed, but my heart, as usual, read too much into it.

"You all right, Boss Lady?" Tracy asked. "You get jumpy every time you hear the ding of the elevator."

Tracy and I had come down a little early to grab a quick bite. "Yeah, I'm good. Just expecting someone who'll be joining us. I want to make sure she gets here before the tour guide does."

Tracy looked at me curiously. "You usually don't have anyone scouting sites with us."

"It's the stylist. We talked last night, and she thought it might help her figure out looks for Amber."

Tracy nodded. "That makes sense."

A few minutes later, Maya walked toward us looking half her age with her hair pulled back into a ponytail, face clear of makeup, a pink T-shirt, denim Bermuda shorts, pink running shoes, and a small backpack. I fell in love with her all over again.

"Wow, she's hot," Tracy said.

I narrowed my eyes at her in warning. She held up her hands in surrender. "Hey, I'm not Lance. I know better than to mix business with pleasure."

"Good morning," Maya said cheerfully.

"Good morning. Maya, this is my assistant, Tracy. Tracy, this is Maya Lawson."

They shook hands. "You mind if I grab a coffee before we head out?" Maya asked.

"Sure, the guide isn't here yet and if they come, we'll wait for you."

"Thanks. Can I get either of you anything?"

"No, we're good. We had a quick breakfast a short time ago."

Maya nodded. "Okay, I'll be back in a flash."

I watched the sway of her full hips as she walked away, and memories of grasping those hips as I lay between her legs made my clit throb. It had been entirely too long since I had anything resembling sex. I had to force myself to look away and met Tracy's knowing grin.

"What?" I said in irritation.

She shook her head. "Nothing." Then squatted down to go through the video camera bag I had given her.

Maya and the guide arrived at the same time. After introductions, we headed out. There were so many beautiful locations in Anguilla, but it wasn't until our guide left us in the care of a well-known fisherman and tour guide, Nature Boy, that we discovered the prime location for us to shoot Amber's swimwear photos. Scrub Island, a deserted island off the coast of Anguilla. Pretty much untouched except for an abandoned airfield, crashed plane, and unfinished resort.

Maya squealed in delight when our guide took us to a natural shark nursery on the eastern end of the island. After confirming with Nature Boy that it was safe, Maya took off her shoes, waded into the clear blue pool of water, and stood knee deep as the sharks swam about completely ignoring her. Her skin already darkening from our day in the sun, her fresh face, and relaxed expression were simply breathtaking. I convinced her to let me use her for some test shots, but I think she knew I just wanted pictures of her. We left the island with plans to come back on our own time to go scuba diving and explore caves along the shore that our guide had pointed out during our ride there.

An hour later, Tracy, Maya, and I were back at the hotel excitedly talking about the results of our location scouting. Maya and I had never worked together before, but I found we had a similar creative thought process, especially when discussing which location to use for which shots.

"Okay so we've decided Scrub Island is our locale for swimsuit. What were you thinking for resort wear?" Tracy asked.

"The Valley," Maya and I said at the same time, turning and grinning at each other in amusement.

"All right, two out of three. Formal wear?" Tracy asked expectantly.

Maya quirked a brow in curiosity as she waited for me to answer.

"The hotel lounge," I said.

"I agree," Maya said.

Laughing, Maya and I looked at each other and something clicked into place inside me. Like a missing puzzle piece that was finally found. It was the same feeling I had when we first dated.

Tracy cleared her throat. "Okay, well, we got a lot more accomplished than I was expecting today so, Janesse, if you don't mind, I'm going to go get some gym time in."

I tore my gaze from Maya's and met Tracy's knowing grin. "Uh, yeah, that's fine. Thanks, Tracy. We can go over the test shots and video we took tomorrow morning, say around ten at my room?"

"Works for me, Boss Lady." Tracy turned to Maya with a smile. "I look forward to working with you, Maya," she said, then gave me a wink before leaving.

"I like her. She seems to be really eager to learn as much from you as she can," Maya said.

"Yeah, Tracy was an unexpected find. Nikki met her in an LGBTQ youth group she mentors with and sent Tracy my way when she found out she was into photography."

Maya smiled. "You've really done well for yourself. But then I wouldn't have expected any differently. You've always been serious about the direction you were going with your career."

I shrugged. "Yeah, I just wish I'd been that serious about the rest of my life."

"Well, from what I've seen, that hasn't been so bad. Your daughter obviously adores you, and I've seen some of her work as well in a *National Geographic* magazine I read at the doctor's office recently. I see she's followed in her mother's footsteps."

"No, Sybil is much more talented than I ever was. She's actually in Africa right now on a safari shoot."

"What about your son?"

I smiled proudly. "Phillip is definitely Justin's son. He started his foray into architecture and construction when he got his first set of Lego blocks. He just got his Master of Architecture degree this past spring and happily joined Crawford Construction."

"So, there are other parts of your life you were more serious about. You've raised two intelligent and talented children."

"I can't take full credit. Justin had a hand in it. He's a good man and an even better father."

"He must've been a good husband for you two to stay together for so long."

"He was. Probably too good for me. He deserved so much more than me for a wife," I said, feeling the guilt I'd been unable to fully shake, even after Justin told me he had been happy and wouldn't change a thing.

"I think you're selling yourself short. If he hadn't been happy, I doubt he would've stayed married to you as long as he did."

"That's what he said, but it doesn't change the fact that I didn't love him the way he deserved."

"But you did love him."

"Yes."

"Then that's all that should matter. It was obviously enough for him."

"You sound like you're talking from experience."

Maya frowned and I felt like I'd touched on something hurtful. "I'm sorry. Why don't we talk about something else?"

"No, I want to tell you." She sighed. "Ten years ago, I got involved with Gina, an artist, ten years younger than me. We met at one of her gallery showings. It started out purely physical, then it seemed we both got caught up in our feelings. Next thing I knew she was moving in with me talking about marriage and having a family. I'd had somewhat serious relationships up until that point, including Chris," she said, looking at me guiltily.

"Your friend who came to visit you that day?" Curiously, I felt none of the pain I used to at the memory of how that day ended.

Maya nodded. "It was about a year after that when she came home for good and we realized we were better off as friends. Anyway, until Gina I had focused so much on my career, I put relationships on the back burner. That's why they hadn't lasted. Gina seemed fine with that since she was the same way. Then, about five years in Gina would disappear at least once a month to her studio for days at a time. When she got home, she was distant and moody. I rarely visited her studio. She claimed she didn't like other people's energy messing up her vibe." Maya gave a bitter chuckle. "I should've known then something was wrong, but I knew artists could be sensitive about their work, so I chalked it up as an artistic eccentricity. Then I went to Vegas for two weeks to work a video shoot and Gina wasn't answering her phone the whole time. I called our friends and none of them had seen her. When I got home, I noticed our bed hadn't been slept in. At first, I thought she'd left me, but all her belongings were still there. I took a chance and went to her studio." Maya shook her head, a scowl marring her beautiful face.

"Maya—"

"No, it's okay. I haven't really talked to anybody about this because I was too embarrassed and angry."

"Okay." I reached across the table and took hold of her hands. She gripped my hands as if they were a lifeline and took a steadying breath.

"The studio reeked of unwashed bodies and rotting food. She and two other women were passed out naked on a bare mattress. Next to it was a glass pipe and a small bag of crystals. I screamed Gina's name and none of them even budged. It took me pouring a pitcher of cold water on them to get them to even stir. Gina saw me and started trying to explain but I didn't hear a word she said. I told her when she was done to come get her stuff and get out of my house, then I couldn't get out of there fast enough. She came home begging for me to listen. Told me she had stopped doing that shit when she met me. That being with me had made her realize she didn't need to get high to be happy. She didn't start back up until she lost her creativity. She couldn't paint without it. That's what she would be doing when she disappeared for days. This time around, a few hits hadn't worked so she'd gone out and gotten more. She didn't even remember bringing the women back to her studio."

I couldn't even imagine going through something like that. I wiped a tear from Maya's cheek.

"I don't know why I'm still crying. I think it's more from anger at myself than sadness. I stupidly let her back after she promised to go to rehab. She was there for three months and seemed to be good when she came home. I even had a studio added on to my house for her so she wouldn't have to go back to her old one and be reminded of what happened there. She started painting again, but no one was picking up her work. I guess the lack of drugs took away the edge to her work that was attracting galleries. She took a job as a graphic artist, but I could tell she wasn't happy. I told her to give it time, that maybe a break would be good for her. Then last year the mood swings started again, and I found an unlabeled bottle of pills in her studio. She claimed they were only to help her sleep, but I knew otherwise. I kicked her out that day. I didn't care where she went, I just needed her to go. I'd been in California long enough to see what happened when fleeting fame broke people's spirits. I refused to watch Gina kill herself."

"You tried to help her. You did everything you could." I said, hoping it would comfort her.

"I knew that. It's what my friends kept telling me when we heard she'd died of an overdose six months ago." Maya's voice broke.

I quickly scooted my seat closer to her and wrapped my arm around her shoulders. She laid her head on my shoulder and quietly cried as I held her. My heart broke for what she'd gone through. Jumping from one relationship to the next, then when she'd finally thought she'd found someone to share her life with it turned out so wrong. I realized something in that moment. If Maya was still hurting this much from that relationship, she was probably not even thinking about another one. There was no way I was going to tell her how I still felt about her. I didn't care what longing looks she gave me or even if she flirted. She probably just needed to feel something other than the misery still left from that painful time.

"I'm sorry, for this," she said, sniffling as she sat up and grabbed a napkin to wipe her face.

"There's no need to apologize. It's probably long overdue, especially if you haven't talked to anybody about it."

Maya nodded. "I guess so."

"You want a drink or something?" I asked as she composed herself.

"No, I think I should probably just go lie down. I'm suddenly really tired."

"Okay. I'll go up with you."

Our rooms were on the same floor but at opposite ends. We were both provided suites to accommodate any meetings we needed to have with our teams. I walked Maya to her room.

"Are you sure you're going to be okay?" I asked as she scanned her key card.

Maya gave me a sad smile but nodded. "I'll be fine. Thanks for letting me vent."

"Anytime. I'm just down the hall. Feel free to come knocking if you need to talk or just want some company."

Maya pulled me into her arms, embraced me tightly, then quickly went into her room, leaving me staring at her closed door. When I was able to convince my body to move, I went to my room to drown my confusion in a bottle of wine.

Maya joined Tracy and me to go through our test shots and videos to work out a storyboard for our shoot. With her help, by late afternoon, everything that would have usually taken Tracy and me a week to complete was done. Locations were scouted and confirmed, and our shot list was complete.

"What do we do now?" Tracy said.

"How about we just relax the next few days before the craziness begins," I said. "Take the rest of the week off and enjoy yourself. Not too much, though. I need you bright-eyed and bushy-tailed when Amber arrives this weekend."

Tracy grinned broadly. “Thanks, Boss Lady. Let me know if you guys decide to do the scuba trip at Scrub Island.”

“We will,” I promised.

Maya and I watched Tracy bounce happily out the room.

“She is a ball of energy,” Maya said.

“Yeah. So, do you have work to do or are you going to relax also?”

Maya gave me a sheepish grin. “I’m actually supposed to be relaxing now. I came down a week early for a pre-job break.”

“So why were you hanging out with us working?”

Maya shrugged. “I’m so used to working nonstop and haven’t taken a real vacation in so long that I’ve forgotten how to just relax.”

I shook my head. “Well, we’ll have to fix that, starting now. I’m assuming you brought a swimsuit?”

“Yes.”

“Good. Go change. We’re going to the beach.”

We spent the rest of the afternoon on the white sand beach lounging under an umbrella and swimming in clear blue water. Then we had dinner at a beachside restaurant, watching the sunset as we ate. I tried not to feed into the romantic undertone our day together brought, making sure to keep our interactions as platonic and casual as possible. It was difficult, but I was proud of myself for keeping my feelings in check. The next day was spent retracing our steps from our day with the tour guide, taking our time to explore some of the locations we visited in more detail. It reminded me of when Maya and I used to take little day or weekend trips together but without the pressure of worrying about what people thought of us together. Maya was still an affectionate woman, so when she grabbed my hand to pull me along to look at something, touched my leg to get my attention if we were sitting somewhere, and even looped her arm through mine and laid her head on my shoulder as we sat on the beach watching another sunset that night, I didn’t deter her like I used to. I just let it happen without worrying or reading too much into it.

Our last day before Amber and the representatives from the magazine arrived, Maya, Tracy, and I went back to Scrub Island to go scuba diving in the caves. I had bought an underwater camera during a family vacation to Hawaii a year ago and was glad I’d bought it on this trip because the shots I was able to get were going to be amazing. Particularly of Maya’s rounded behind as she swam ahead of me. That was going to be for my eyes only. At one point, Maya and I climbed out of the water in one of the caves to rest on the rocks while younger and more energetic Tracy continued ahead with our guide. Maya lay back, gazing up in wonder at the rock walls, while I gazed in wonder at her.

"You're even more beautiful than you were thirty years ago," I said without thinking, then wanted to quickly snatch the words back.

Maya turned her head toward me and smiled. "So are you."

I blushed. "You think so?" I ran my hand through my close-cut salt-and-pepper curls. "I think I look old. Nothing seems to work when I try to dye my hair."

Maya sat up, reached over, and ran her hand through my hair as well. "I like it. The cut really complements your face and I think the color is sexy." Her hand was warm as it rested on the back of my neck.

I grinned. "So, you're into gray-haired old ladies?"

Maya's expression softened as she looked over my face. "I'm into this gray-haired old lady."

When I felt the light pressure of her hand on the back of my neck bringing my face closer to hers, I didn't resist. When our lips met, the lush warmth of hers, the saltiness from the water, and the feelings I'd been holding back all week rushed forward. Our kiss went from a spark to an inferno in a matter of seconds. I guess Maya must have been holding back as well. The sound of voices echoing off the walls had us jumping apart like two teenagers caught by a parent. A moment later, light from our guide's headlamp reflected off the water, followed by him and Tracy swimming into view.

"Hey, are you ready to head back?" the guide asked.

I gave him a nervous smile. "Uh, yeah."

I slid off the rocks into the water and offered Maya a hand as she did the same. I knew she didn't need my help, but I needed the contact to let me know I hadn't dreamed what just happened. She smiled knowingly and took my hands as she slid into the water.

"Thank you," she said seductively.

I grinned. "You're welcome."

"Can we go before you two start setting this water to boiling?" Tracy said as she swam past us.

Maya and I chuckled and followed her out of the cave.

That kiss changed the platonic dynamic I tried so hard to maintain between me and Maya. On the boat ride back to Anguilla, Maya took my hand and didn't let go until we arrived at the harbor. During our taxi ride back to the hotel, Maya laid her head on my shoulder and rested our clasped hands on my thigh, and I didn't care that Tracy glanced at us with a grin or that the taxi driver peered disapprovingly at us in the rearview mirror. I felt free and wonderful. This was what I had been missing while I was holding myself back all those years ago. How stupid I had been. I turned my head and placed a kiss on top of Maya's damp hair, and she snuggled closer to me. When we arrived at the hotel, I reached forward to hand the driver his money. He snatched it out of my fingers and mumbled something about sinful Americans. I simply smiled, wished him a good day, then climbed out and took Maya's hand as we walked into the lobby and headed up to our rooms.

"It was a cool day. Thanks, Boss Lady," Tracy said.

"You're very welcome."

Tracy headed off, leaving Maya and me standing in the middle of the hallway.

"This was such a wonderful day. Thank you," Maya said.

"You're very welcome. Dinner tonight?" I asked.

"I'd love to. How about around six?"

I nodded. "Sounds good to me. I'll see if I can get reservations at that beachside restaurant we went to before."

"Okay."

We stood in the hallway holding hands and smiling at each other for another moment before Maya released my hand and began slowly backing away.

"See you at six."

I nodded and watched as she walked down the hall and disappeared around the corner to her room. I wanted so much to go after her, tell her everything I was feeling, then make slow sweet love to her but forced myself to tamp down those feelings. Telling myself it was too soon. That she was still raw from what she had gone through with her ex. That curbed any desire I was feeling as I made my way to my room to shower and get some work done before dinner. I was in the middle of editing some pictures from my last shoot when there was a knock on my door. Maya stood on the other side. Her hair was in damp curls framing her face and she was wearing slippers and one of the robes the hotel provided cinched tightly around her waist.

"Hey."

Maya gave me a nervous smile. "Hey. Can I come in?"

"Yeah, of course." I stepped aside.

"So, I've been thinking a lot about getting the opportunity to see you again, how well we still get along, that kiss in the cave, and how you no longer seem to have any fear of what people think about us being together in public. I feel like it's fate telling me we should be together. That we always should've been, but I was too selfish to really accept it." Maya gave me a tentative smile. "I think I've said this one too many times for you to believe it, but I'm so sorry for the way I pushed you away instead of giving you whatever time you needed to work through your issues. It's obvious I had some of my own that I let get in the way."

I was at a loss for words, but I knew that I couldn't just let her off the hook for what happened. Yes, I still loved her as deeply as I did then, but it was my turn to do what she had been doing then, guard my heart against whatever issues she currently had.

"Are you sure you want to talk about this now?" I asked.

"No, but I think we need to."

She was right. If there was the slightest chance of us getting back together after all these years, we needed to be truthful about what happened between us. I led her to the sofa.

"I've spent many therapy sessions and taken dozens of sabbaticals to see the truth about myself. I can honestly say that I was not ready for a relationship with myself, let alone you or anyone else around that time. You had every right to break up with me because there's no way I would've been able to give you what you needed. Having Sybil was a blessing in more ways than one but especially when seeing myself reflected in her eyes. I knew I couldn't be the best mother I needed to be if I continued making the same mistakes my mother did by letting insecurities and self-doubt turn me into a bitter woman who didn't know how to love her own children. The only way I could do that was to learn to love myself and accept who I was emotionally and sexually. I can't say that I was completely successful," I said with a sigh. "I still held some part of me back. Even when Phillip came out, I never told him what I'd gone through because he was so much more self-aware than I was."

Maya looked at me in surprise. "Your son is gay?"

"He came out ten years ago and told us in no uncertain term that we can accept him or not, either way, he was who he was." I smiled proudly at the memory.

"That just goes to show what great parents he had that he was so self-assured," Maya said.

"I hope so. We told him we were proud of him no matter what. To be able to give the acceptance to my child that I never received from my own mother was a gift to both of us. Although I never shared my experience with him, I learned to start accepting myself as well."

"They still don't know about your sexuality?"

"Yes, but only because my mother sort of outed me when she found out Phillip was gay. I had a long talk with them just before this trip. They've known all this time and it never changed how they felt about me. I told them everything, about my confusion, us, even the truth of how Justin and I ended up together. They accepted all of that, and me, without shame or anger. That was the final piece I needed to accept myself and finally focus on my own happiness."

"Is that why you and Justin are divorcing?"

"That's part of it." I hesitated to admit that running into her at the mall was the catalyst for Justin and me separating, but I knew there had to be nothing but open honesty between us if Maya and I were to move forward, either together or apart.

"The main reason for our divorce is because I never stopped loving you."

"What?" Maya whispered in shock.

"The day we ran into each other was my wedding anniversary. Seeing you threw me into a tailspin of emotion that I hadn't expected, so I wasn't in a good place to celebrate. Justin knew something was wrong, and when he asked me about it, I told him I'd seen you. Although he never said anything, Justin has known for years that I've never really gotten over you. That I loved him but have always been in love with you."

"Janesse—"

"Let me finish. I had hoped my feelings for you were more from the fantasy I built in my head about what could have been, but this week with you confirmed that it's far more than that. I still love you as much as I did then because you make me feel whole. Like there's been something missing in my life and every time you've come back into it, I've felt like I've found that missing piece. I'm not expecting you to feel the same way, especially with all the time that has passed and that you're probably still hurting from your last relationship, but I needed to tell you because I'm tired of shutting myself away and putting my own happiness aside."

There, I had said it. I'd poured my heart out, laid it all on the line, and no matter what the outcome was, I wouldn't regret it.

Maya sat silently looking at me. As if she were searching for the truth of my words in my eyes. "Do you know what I've realized this week with you? That the reason I've never really been able to stay in a relationship for long is because I was always searching for someone who would love me the way you did. I've also felt like a part of me has been missing since I let you walk out of my dorm that day. I'm so sorry you had to hear what you did while I was talking to Chris. I should've told you how I felt long before that. I should've been more encouraging and supportive in helping you work through your issues."

Maya stood up and walked over to the window, gazing out with her back to me. "When Gina and I met, she reminded me so much of you. Her talent and passion for her art, her personality, even her family's dynamic was so like yours. She was what I had wanted so much for you to be and it made me feel like I was kind of with you again but living openly like I'd always wanted us to do. I supported her through her time in rehab and after she came back home because I didn't want to abandon her. Like I was trying to make up for pushing you away when I should've been stronger. Well, we see how that turned out."

Hearing the heartbreak in her voice and how she was blaming herself for what Gina and I went through was breaking my heart as well. I walked over and turned her to face me.

"Maya, you shouldn't blame yourself for me or for what happened with Gina. We both had issues that we chose to ignore rather than look for help. Mine was using fear and shame to hide my insecurities, hers was much more serious by using drugs to hide hers. You couldn't have saved me any more than you could've saved Gina. The only people who could do that was us by admitting to and facing our problems. Unfortunately, Gina wasn't ready to do that and it killed her. I'm so sorry for your loss and I can't tell you how to cope with it, but blaming yourself will only drag you into a darkness you may not be able to pull yourself out of."

I wiped a tear that had begun to fall from the corner of her eye. When more began to fall, I pulled her into my arms and held her as she had done so many times for me after I'd spoken to Mom on the phone or visited home while we were dating. I rubbed her back and noticed that it was smooth beneath the robe.

"Are you dressed underneath this?" I asked.

Maya sniffled. "No. I planned to come here and seduce you and ended up in a therapy session."

I couldn't help but laugh as she pulled away and I saw the pout of disappointment on her face. "What, you planned to walk in, strip off your robe, and have me sweep you off your feet onto the bed?"

Maya smirked. "Something like that."

"I think you've been on one too many movie sets."

Maya laughed. "Yeah, probably."

I took Maya's face in my hands. "Maya, as much as I have wanted and still would love to sweep you off your feet and make love to you, I want it to be because you're sure. Not because you're trying to assuage pain and regret. I've been there before, and although it gave me my beautiful daughter, it led to more heartbreak and sadness for me for some time after. I can't do that to myself again."

Maya sighed. "I guess you're right."

I kissed her lips softly. "That doesn't mean that we can't continue to have fun and take things slowly. I've waited thirty years for you. I can wait a while longer."

Maya and I worked very well together over the next week of the shoot. We managed to keep it strictly business during the day and, other than a few nights when we had dinner with the magazine reps, crew, and Amber and her people, we got together for dinner or watched movies in our rooms until we fell asleep at night. There were so many times I would wake up with her in my arms and just stare at her in disbelief that we were together, even if there was nothing more than this. At that point I was happy with whatever we had if I got to hold or kiss her occasionally. We didn't even try to hide our growing affection for each other. There would be times I would reach for her hand or lay my arm across the back of her chair while we were at dinner or having drinks with other people and not even realize it. It was nice not to have to hide how I felt about her.

The final day of the shoot, Amber Sims invited everyone for a wrap celebration at a local reggae club, where we danced and drank the night away. Well, everyone else drank, I needed to keep my wits about me so that I didn't beg Maya not to leave me. We both had flights out later the next day and had avoided talking about what would happen between us after tonight. Being the elders amongst the group, a slightly tipsy Maya and I left Tracy with Amber and her crew a little after midnight to head back to the hotel. Without a thought, we both headed for my room. Maya lay on the sofa with a tired sigh as I sat in a nearby chair.

"I can't hang like I used to," she said.

I chuckled. "As you know, I've never really been able to hang."

Maya propped herself up on her elbows and looked at me with

amusement. "Remember when you sat on the sofa and fell asleep at that frat party at Morehouse?"

"Hey, that was your fault. You knew I couldn't eat a heavy dinner followed by alcohol and be able to stay up past midnight."

"It would've been fine if you hadn't started snoring," Maya said.

We both laughed.

"Well, for future reference, big meals and alcohol still have that effect, except I usually fall asleep an hour later now," I said.

"Is there a future?" Maya asked, suddenly serious.

"I'd like there to be. Are you ready for that?"

Maya walked over, knelt in front of me, and took my hands. "I'm ready."

"Then what? I love you, but I'm not interested in living in California, and I won't ask you to give up what you've built there to come back to New Jersey."

Maya was quiet for a moment and I could hear my heart hammering in my ears waiting for her response.

"Just before I accepted this job, I signed a one-year contract with a studio as a wardrobe stylist. I'm supposed to start as soon as I get back, but it's going to be my last job in California. I've been thinking of moving back home for a while. California was just supposed to be my jumping ground, I hadn't planned on staying as long as I did, but things took off and I just went with the flow."

"A year?" So much could happen in a year, I thought worriedly.

"Remember what you said last week? You've waited this long, what's a little longer?" Maya said with a tender smile. "I'll make it worth the wait."

She stood, pulling me up from the chair with her, and led me to the bedroom. Once there she began unbuttoning my blouse.

I laid my hand over hers. "You don't have to do this. I'll wait for you no matter what."

"I want to do this. I love you for wanting to protect me, but I've waited for you just as long as you have for me. This is long overdue."

I grasped her face and brought my lips down to meet hers. I wanted this moment to last for as long as possible, so I took my time rediscovering the joy of kissing and exploring her full, soft lips and the adorable gap in her teeth until she moaned deeply into my mouth just the way I remembered. I slid my hands from her face down to ease the straps of her sundress off her shoulders. I followed the same path with my lips as I pressed soft kisses along her jawline, to her ear where I nipped at her lobe, then made my way along her neck as I eased her dress down her arms to gather at her waist, leaving her bare from the waist up. She still smelled of citrus and sunshine.

"Not fair, I was supposed to be seducing you," Maya said breathlessly as I gently cupped her breast and lowered my head.

"Oh, I'm sorry." I flicked my tongue over her nipple. "Would you like me to stop?"

Maya sucked in a breath. "No, please don't."

I grinned. I had always liked it when she begged a little. I continued, taking her nipple between my lips, suckling, and rolling it in my mouth as if I were enjoying a piece of rock-hard candy. Maya whimpered and grasped my head to guide me to her other nipple. I lavished it with equal attention then lowered myself to my knees, eased her dress over hips and down her legs so that she could step out of it. I sat back on my knees and looked her up and down. She wore only a sexy pair of black lace underwear and red high-heeled sandals. Her body had gone through changes, as most women's bodies of our age had, but she was still the sexiest woman I had ever known.

"Is there something wrong?" Maya asked worriedly.

I grinned up at her. "Not at all. Just admiring how sexy you are."

"Even with my little pouch," Maya said, placing her hand over her barely discernable belly.

I almost laughed. She thought she had a belly, wait until she saw mine and the stretch marks framing it. "Yes, even that."

I moved her hand and replaced it with a kiss, then eased her underwear down her legs until she stepped out of them. I leaned forward to kiss a path from her navel to the juncture of her thighs. I grasped her hips, delved the tip of my tongue just at the top of her lips, slowly stroking in and out until she whimpered, and her lips grew wet with desire. I stood and led her to the bed. Maya bent to take her shoes off.

"No, leave them on and lie down," I said with a grin.

Maya quirked a brow but did as I asked, even striking a sexy pose and come-hither smile. It took everything I had not to rip my clothes off and jump on her, but I took my time undressing, enjoying the way she looked at me as I did. As I looked at her, I wondered how I possibly got through all these years without this woman? Without the intensity of her eyes, the brightness of her smile, the pure, unadulterated femininity she represented, and the depth of love she made me feel. Once I was undressed, I joined her in the bed, starting where I had left off, worshiping between her thighs, losing myself in her scent and taste.

When Maya shouted my name and her body tensed, then convulsed with her orgasm, I didn't stop. I gripped her hips, buried my tongue as deep as it would go within her, and continued until she was once again calling my name, gripping my head desperately, and flooding my mouth with the very essence of her. Maya was my addiction now, and I overdosed on her pleasure until I was just as weak as her from the effort. I rested my head on her thigh, once again inhaling her sweet exotic scent, and knew I had finally found home.

EPILOGUE

2019

"Janesse, seriously, if you don't stop fidgeting, I'm going to have J.J. come in here and hold you down," Jackie said with annoyance.

"I don't know why you insist on putting makeup on me for every special occasion," I complained.

Jackie grinned. "This isn't just any special occasion, and it's not that much. Some lipstick, blush, and eyeshadow to enhance your best features."

I sighed in resignation. Jackie loved this stuff and I loved her, so I let her do her thing. The door opened, and I could see Sybil's and Phillip's broad smiles reflected in the mirror.

"Hey, kiddos, I'd hug you but that would require your aunt letting me up for some air."

Jackie stuck her tongue out at me. "I'm finished anyway," she said, cocking her head for one last look.

I looked in the mirror and smiled. There was a touch of gold sparkling on my eyelids giving a shine to my eyes, my cheekbones looked more defined, and my lips looked fuller. "Flawless as usual, sis."

Jackie smiled proudly. "All I do is enhance your natural beauty."

I pulled her into a hug, and she squeezed me tightly. "Be happy, Ness."

"I am," I said.

"I'll see you out there."

I nodded, then watched her hug Sybil and Phillip as she left.

"Come here." I opened my arms and they walked into them.

"I'm so happy you're both here. I couldn't do this without you."

"We wouldn't miss it for the world," Phillip said.

"It was a tough choice, you or the Brazilian rainforest. Obviously, you won by a landslide," Sybil teased me with her father's cocky grin.

"Well, it's nice to know I rank so high." I gave them both a kiss on the cheek. "I better get dressed."

Phillip unzipped a garment bag hanging nearby that held a woman's white tuxedo and a blush pink silk blouse with a tie scarf neckline. He and Sybil helped me get dressed, and when they were done, they stood behind me in the mirror surveying their handiwork.

"It's just missing one thing," Sybil said, holding up a small velvet box. "From Phillip and me."

I turned toward them. "You all didn't have to get me anything."

"We know," Phillip said, taking the box from Sybil and opening it to reveal a rose gold and diamond lotus blossom lapel pin.

I gave them a teary-eyed smile. "It's beautiful."

"Just like you, Mom." Sybil took it from its velvet bed and placed it on my lapel.

They each took one of my hands.

"We just wanted you to know that we're so happy for you and that we couldn't be any prouder to have you for a mother," Phillip said.

"Or for a grandmother to your future grandchild," Sybil said, placing a hand on her rounded belly. "You've sacrificed so much of yourself to give us a good life, and we admire you being brave enough to finally claim your own happiness. I just hope I can be half the mom you are."

I wiped away a tear. "You two cannot have made me any prouder than I already am. I don't regret a thing, and I would do it all over again if it meant I was gifted with you."

Phillip gently wiped away another tear. "Aunt Jackie is going to kill us if we make you mess up your makeup."

"We should head out anyway. It's almost time. Love you, Mom," Sybil said.

"Love you," Phillip said.

"I love you too." I placed a kiss on both of their cheeks.

Once they were gone, I checked my makeup one last time, took a few cleansing breaths, and walked out to find Dad waiting for me in the hallway.

"I saw the kids leaving, so I thought I'd give you a minute. How're you doing?"

"I'm great," I said happily.

Dad smiled. "I'm so proud of you, Ness. It does my old heart proud to see you finally love and accept the wonderful woman we all knew you were."

"Thank you, Dad. For all your love and support."

Dad nodded, kissed me on the forehead, and headed outside. I heard the click of heels behind me and turned to find a vision walking toward me.

"You look stunning," I said as Maya stopped in front of me. Her hair was piled atop her head in an intricate chignon, her makeup was even more flawless than mine, and her blush pink strapless lace gown, which she designed, beautifully hugged her curves then flowed around her feet into a short train.

She smiled softly. "So do you. What a beautiful pin."

"It was from the kids. Wait here. I have something for you." I hurried into the kitchen and grabbed a box from the refrigerator.

"I know you said you didn't want to do a bouquet, but I think you deserve one, so here's my gift to you." I opened the box and handed her a bouquet of white lotus blossoms.

Maya looked at them in awe. "They're magnificent." She took the bouquet and held it to her face, inhaling the sweet scent of the blossoms. "I know how important the symbolism of the lotus is to you, and I'm honored you would share it with me. Thank you."

"You're welcome. Are you ready to do this?"

Maya smiled happily and nodded.

I offered her my arm as we walked out into Uncle Frank's backyard, now Denise and Liz's since Uncle Frank's passing a few years ago. A place that held so many memories and family celebrations in my life. This celebration was a bit different, but we were still surrounded by family and friends, except one. At almost eighty years old, Mom was still as stubborn as ever when it came to accepting Maya and me, so she wasn't there, but the ones who mattered were. As Maya and I walked down the aisle to a waiting Nikki, who would be officiating our wedding ceremony, I brushed my fingers over the pendant that Nikki had given me when we were so young, the pin my children had gifted me just moments ago, and then gazed over at Maya holding her bouquet and realized, like those flowers, I had finally blossomed.

I had spent most of my life mired down by the muck and swamp of self-doubt and fear, but no matter how stubbornly I hid just below the surface, refusing to break free, my family and friends continued nurturing me with their love and support, trying to coax my petals of self-love to unfold. Then came the sunshine of my children and Maya bathing me in their warmth, encouraging me to break through the surface and showing me how to love myself enough to blossom into something strong and beautiful. Now that I had bloomed, seen what had always been waiting for me, I refused to let anyone, including myself, drag me back under.

About the Author

Anne Shade loves writing stories about women who love women featuring strong, beautiful Black, Indigenous, and People of Color. Anne is the author of two novels with Bold Strokes Books—*Femme Tales*, released in March 2020 and short-listed for a 2021 Lambda Literary Award, and *Masquerade*, released in February 2021—and a collaboration with editor Victoria Villaseñor for the Bold Strokes Books anthology *In Our Words: Queer Stories from Black, Indigenous and People of Color*. Besides writing, Anne's other passions include planning dream weddings and envisioning her own dream of opening a beachside bed & breakfast on a beautiful Caribbean island.